The Possessor Wars

Book 2

I0621717

The Outcasts

Chad Spencer

This book is a work of fiction. Names, characters, places, and incidents used or described herein are either the product of the author's imagination or are used fictitiously. Any resemblance to actual events, locales, or persons, living or dead, is entirely coincidental.

No part of this book may be reproduced in any form without the permission of the publisher.

Editor: Keilani Conger
Illustrator: David Conger

Official Web Site: http://possessorwars.com/
Facebook: https://www.facebook.com/chad.spencer.165
Twitter: https://twitter.com/PossessorWars
To be notified of new releases, please sign up for the author's newsletter at:
http://possessorwars.com/subscribe.html

The Outcasts

Part 1
When Worlds Collide

"Every human being should strive to do better and to be better. If we don't have goals to achieve, what's the point of existing? Of course, achieving your goals always brings its own challenges. And sometimes ... sometimes it launches us into whole new worlds." *Thoughts on Life*, Hugh Benson, p. 300. © 2879 Megalon Interstellar Media, All rights reserved in this and all other universes, parallel or unparallel realities, unrealities, and planes of existence.

1

"Please try not to be so nervous, Harriet."

Harriet wasn't listening to her mother. She scanned the wide reception area, her bright green eyes searching apprehensively for Hugh. Nervously, she ran her hands over her waist-length, flaming red hair to make sure it was all in place. She noticed several boys looking at her and grew increasingly anxious.

'Did Hugh and I really make the right decision?' she wondered. 'This part of the arcology is so different from what we know.'

The arcology Harriet stood in was a tall building on the plains of the American Midwest with many other arcologies. It was 3000 stories high, cylindrical, and a mile wide. Each arcology housed millions of people, with apartments, schools, stores, recreation centers, and more.

Her father interrupted her thoughts. "Harriet, Earth to Harriet. Are you there, Harriet?" His green eyes flashed mischievously.

"What? Oh, sorry Daddy. I was trying to see if Hugh and his family are here yet," she explained.

"He'll be here," her father soothed as he gently placed a reassuring hand on her shoulder. "Don't worry."

A small, mostly spherical robot drifted toward her through the air, lowered itself to her eye level, pointed its bulging camera lens at her, and asked "Harriet Brightway? Are you Harriet Brightway?"

Harriet recoiled a bit; she wasn't expecting to be met by a robot. "Yes," she replied hesitantly. "I'm Harriet Brightway."

"I am here to escort you and your family to the Assembly Hall," the robot told her as it pointed one of its thin, three-fingered hands to the left. "Please follow me."

Harriet glanced upward at her father, who nodded. Taking that as its cue, the robot drifted toward a long corridor. Harriet and her family followed.

"Aren't you excited?" Harriet's older sister, Ruth Ann, asked as they wended their way through the crowd.

Harriet shrugged. "I guess. But I feel so out of place here."

Harriet's mother put her arm around Harriet's shoulders. "It's ok sweetheart. We'll help you get settled in. I'm sure you'll make lots of friends here."

"Look at how everyone's dressed," Harriet moaned, pointing at the elaborate clothes the other students wore. Looking woefully at her own plain outfit, she complained. "I stick out like a sore thumb."

"Don't worry, Harriet," her father broke in. "Once school starts you'll be wearing the same uniform as everyone else. It'll be ok. And if you need some fancy clothes for after school activities, we'll get you some." He smiled reassuringly.

Harriet hugged her father as they walked. "We can't afford that Daddy. Not after buying those expensive uniforms."

"You don't worry about that," her father instructed. "That's my job."

"Rick, you spoil these girls," Harriet's mother chided.

"That's what dads are for," he chuckled happily.

The robot guided the Brightway family into the Assembly Hall and indicated the front row of the ornate hall. Spotlights floated near the vaulted ceiling and shined down on the stage. The robot showed them to their seats and asked, "Will that be all?"

"Yes," Harriet's father responded.

"Good day to you then," the robot said. It drifted away through the Assembly Hall doors.

"Oh look," Harriet's mother called out, "here come the Bensons."

Gazing again toward the large double doors, Harriet saw Hugh Benson and his family coming through the crowd. A robot identical to the one that greeted them was guiding the Bensons to the front of the hall. Hugh trailed timidly after the mechanoid. He ran his hand through his close-cropped, sandy-colored hair. His parents walked right behind him.

When they arrived at the front, the robot escorted them to the seats next to Harriet and her family. Like their robot, it asked, "Will that be all?"

"Yes," Hugh's father responded.

"Good day to you then," the robot said. It drifted away through the Assembly Hall doors.

"Hi, Hugh," Harriet greeted as Hugh slid his slight frame into the seat next to hers. "Your robot said almost exactly what ours did."

"Same programming," Hugh mumbled back as he fidgeted nervously in his seat. "Gives them all the same behavior."

6

"What's the matter, Hugh? You look like you're expecting someone to start throwing grenades at you."

"I would like that a lot better," Hugh joked awkwardly. "I feel like I'm on another planet, not 2100 floors higher in the building I was born in. Do you see what they're wearing here? And why do all the guys have long hair? Their heads look like mushrooms. Don't they know that's not what guys are supposed to look like?"

Trying to hide her own uncertainties, Harriet scolded, "Hugh, don't be so fussy. Their hair isn't very long—just a little over their ears. Long hair was in down on our level back when my uncle was in high school. He had a pony tail down to the middle of his back. Styles change. You shouldn't get worked up just because the hairstyles up here are different."

"Everything's different here. I'm not sure coming up here was a good idea."

With bravado she didn't feel, Harriet scolded, "We worked too hard to get here to give up and go home now Hugh. Just think how much better our educations will be here than down in our old school."

"I suppose," Hugh agreed. He didn't sound convinced.

An attractive middle-aged woman approached them and asked, "Are you Harriet and Hugh?" They nodded. Extending her hand, she introduced herself. "I'm Beth Scrivener, your Supervising Instructor here at the Westfald Academy. You'll be in my homeroom for your Core Classes, Group Interaction, and Personal Study Sessions. Here are your student packets." She handed them each a box that was not much bigger than a loaf of bread.

The smiling Mamsen Scrivener informed them, "They'll be introducing you at the start of the orientation. It was Principal McBride's idea. She's so excited to have the two of you here. I'm afraid you're the biggest celebrities she's had as students."

Apprehensively, Harriet and Hugh glanced at each other. "We're not celebrities," Harriet objected. "Neither of us can understand why the media is making such a fuss about us. We're just a couple of kids from the low end of the arcology."

Mamsen Scrivener patted Harriet's arm. "You're too modest, Harriet. Your science project last year was nothing less than amazing. You figured out what hosts of experts couldn't. Principal McBride is so happy that your parents decided to send you here to our school. You know you could have gone somewhere better. I heard that the Martian Institute of Technology made you an offer."

"Well, yes," Harriet admitted, embarrassed. "They did, but we didn't want to leave our families. I'm only 16, and Hugh's 15."

"Well, we here at the Westfald Academy are very glad you two decided on our school." Mamsen Scrivener noticed a woman taking the stage. "Oops," she said hurriedly, "there's Mamsen McBride now. It looks like she's about ready to start. After the orientation, could you two please meet me out in the foyer with your families?" They nodded their agreement and Mamsen Scrivener scooted off toward the stairs that ascended onto the stage. She took her place near the pear-shaped Mamsen McBride.

"Welcome new and returning Westfald Academy students," Mamsen McBride gushed. "We're so happy to see all of you—especially our two new students Harriet Brighway and Hubert Benson. Stand up, please, both of you."

Harriet and Hugh stood, both flushing with embarrassment. Spotlights drifted down from the ceiling and focused on the both of them. A camerabot wafted toward them and aimed its lens right into Harriet's face. It was all Harriet could to do keep herself from crawling under her seat.

Mamsen McBride continued, "A big hand everyone for the two individuals who solved the mystery of the tragic wormhole collapse two years ago." She clapped enthusiastically while the crowd copied her with a polite smattering of applause.

Hugh sat quickly back in his seat, so Harriet sat down too. "I don't want to be here," Harriet heard Hugh mutter. Silently, Harriet agreed.

"We hope you'll all find the Westfald Academy to be everything you were looking for in an educational institution," Mamsen McBride continued as she gazed at them almost adoringly. Harriet forced a stiff smile back at her.

"And now, our Accelerated Program instructor, Mamsen Scrivener, will provide a special presentation introducing the Westfald Academy to all of our incoming students."

Mamsen Scrivener stood and began a 3D video presentation about the school. It started with an overview of the campus. "...and here is the astrophysics lab. Right next to that is our robotics lab. Those of you taking robotics and neurocomputing classes will do your courses here. Just down the corridor is our music department." Too nervous to concentrate, Harriet stopped listening.

After Mamsen Scrivener's presentation, a stick-like female teacher talked about the uniforms, dress code, and behavior code.

'The Westfald Academy sounds like a pretty strict school,' Harriet fretted.

The next presentation, given by a square-jawed male teacher in sweats, covered the recreational and physical education facilities. "Our students can go out for virtually any sport," he told the gathering as he gestured enthusiastically with his meaty hands. "We have artificial reality programs that cover pretty much every known sport or exercise. We currently have 180 AR pods in our PE department's three AR suites. Our pods come with a special feature that tells the occupant's body to release the master hormone that humans produce when they exercise. The occupant's body then responds by building muscle tissue, burning fat, and giving the occupant all of the other benefits of real exercise. So the more you work out in our programs, the better shape you'll be in." He waited for everyone to be impressed. When no one was, he droned on, but Harriet didn't listen.

"At least there's something worth coming to this school for," Hugh muttered. "People like us could never afford time in an AR suite."

Harriet didn't want to tell him that she'd been in an AR suite a few times when her family went on virtual vacations.

Another teacher gave a presentation on what to do on their first day of school. "Your first and most important task is to find your homeroom. That's where your Supervising Instructor and learning group will meet every morning before you start your various classes. Your Supervising Instructor will help you with your adjustment to the Westfald Academy. In addition, he or she will assist you with your homework, guide you in your selection of classes each semester, and be your primary instructor for your Core classes. Supervising Instructors have three to five learning groups in their homerooms. Each learning group has one male and one female group leader. Your learning group is composed of students with similar abilities and interests. You'll be in a lot of the same classes with your group members. Everyone in a learning group works together for the common good of all, and your groups will succeed together. So it's important that you do your best to contribute to all of the group's learning activities."

"That doesn't sound good to me," Hugh complained quietly.

'I've never known him to be this negative,' Harriet thought. 'He's usually so upbeat about everything.' But Harriet remembered that when Hugh skipped a grade in Junior High he became a target for a bully named Dirk Highborne. 'I guess that kind of experience can make anyone afraid of moving up in school,' Harriet mused.

The teachers droned on, giving presentation after presentation. Harriet felt overwhelmed. Glancing at her father, she saw him look over and give a reassuring smile. Somehow that made things seem better.

It took an hour and a half, but the orientation finally ended. With their families, Harriet and Hugh made their way out of the Assembly Hall and into the foyer. Mamsen Scrivener arrived promptly, with two students in tow.

"I'd like you to meet Leonardo de Medici and Tiffany Montague," she said to Harriet and Hugh. "They'll be your learning group leaders for this school year."

"I'm very glad to meet both of you," Leonardo said, his crystal blue eyes gazing directly into Harriet's. "It's amazing to be in the same study group with you. I hope we can all get along really well." He offered his muscular hand, which she shook somewhat timidly. Leonardo then shook hands with Hugh rather quickly.

"Uh ... yes," Harriet stammered, trying to be polite. "I'm sure we'll do our best to help the group be successful. Won't we Hugh?" Hugh nodded silently.

"Is it true that you have an IQ of 235?" Tiffany broke in, directing her question at Hugh.

Hugh looked as if he was about to have a heart attack. Other than Harriet, girls rarely spoke to him—especially not girls as stunning as Tiffany. "It ... it's not that big of a deal," he replied almost apologetically.

"Hubert doesn't like to boast," Hugh's mother interjected, "But it's true, he's been tested as having the highest IQ of anyone alive." She beamed proudly. "But, Harriet is almost the same, aren't you dear? Isn't your IQ 200?"

"215," Harriet's father announced proudly. Harriet wished she could disappear.

"215? Wow," remarked Leonardo. "That's way more than you, isn't it Tiff? Weren't you telling us at the end of last year that you were tested at 166? Didn't that make you the smartest girl in the school until Harriet showed up?"

Tiffany's face went hard. Leonardo smiled slyly.

Mamsen Scrivener interrupted, "Well, Leo, that's not really all that important, is it? What's important is that you and Tiffany do your best to help Harriet and Hugh to adjust and succeed." She sounded very stern.

"Yes, Mamsen Scrivener," Leonardo replied almost meekly. But he winked and smiled a secret smile at Harriet when Mamsen Scrivener turned to talk to the adults.

"If you wouldn't mind," she said to the four parents, "I'd like to briefly discuss a few things about your children's educations. Leonardo and Tiffany can show Hugh and Harriet around the school. We'll all meet back here in about forty minutes. Ok, Leonardo?"

"Sure Mamsen Scrivener. We'll be glad to give them a tour," he agreed. To Harriet, he said, "Let's go to the Student Commons first." He pointed off to the left. Harriet glanced at her father, who gave a small nod.

Harriet took a hesitant step in the direction Leonardo indicated. Hugh and Tiffany moved to follow her as Leonardo walked beside her. She smiled up at him, admiring his broad muscular shoulders.

As they walked, Harriet observed that Tiffany was tall, nearly six feet. Literally looking down at Harriet, Tiffany demanded, "So Harriet, why did you and Hugh decide to do an analysis of the hypergate failure for your school science project? That's a little out of the league of schools that far down in the arcology isn't it?"

Harriet saw a sour look pass briefly across Leonardo's face. She answered, "We had a friend go missing in the wormhole collapse. It ... motivated us to find out what really happened."

Leonardo gazed down at her sympathetically. "Was this a close friend?" he queried gently.

Hugh answered for her, "He started the robot club we were all in. We were repairing and selling robots to buy lessons we couldn't get at school."

Harriet added, "Yes, he was a really close friend. His name was Jeff Bowman. Without him, we never would have made it into a place like this."

"Well then I guess it's lucky for us that you had such a good friend," Leonardo commented warmly. "Did you ever find out what happened to him?"

Dropping her face downward, Harriet tried to answer, but couldn't. Hugh jumped in, "No. He was lost in the disaster. A lot of rescue ships and unmanned probes have been sent out. Every couple of months, they find more survivors scattered around on planets or in space in cryogenic stasis. But they never found anyone from Jeff's ship."

"So you decided to find out for yourselves what caused the hypergate to fail and the wormhole to collapse?" Leonardo

11

prompted the silent Harriet, but she still couldn't answer through the weight of her emotions.

Nodding, again Hugh replied for her, "Yeah. The news reports just didn't make sense. Hypergates generate stable artificial wormholes that are kind of like a tunnel through hyperspace. The experts all said the collapse was a failure in the hypergate. But once it's generated, there's no reason for a wormhole to break apart into so many fragments. Our science project showed that it couldn't have been a gate failure. The only thing that could cause what happened would be a series of gravitational bombs inside the wormhole."

"I don't see why they put you on the news for that," Tiffany snipped, ruffling her perfectly styled curls.

Glancing sourly at her over his shoulder, Leonardo told her, "Because it means that it was sabotage, Tiffany. Nearly 28,000 people were lost in the wormhole collapse. Less than a quarter of them have been found. Harriet and Hugh's science project showed it was some kind of attack. The Federated Alliance reopened their investigation because of these two. They have Rangers all over Alliance space trying to track down who did it. There's a Congressional committee and everything."

Tiffany accused, "I guess you two are pretty happy."

"Happy?" Harriet shot back hotly. "Jeff is gone. His whole family is gone with him. Lots of other people are gone too. Some of them have been found dead. There's nothing to be happy about."

"It got you into this school," Tiffany retorted.

Hugh countered, "I think we would both trade away the chance to go to this school if we could have our friend back."

Tiffany's lips compressed and her eyes narrowed. She asked, "But you were on all the 3V news shows. I think you liked that pretty well."

'I think I'm going to strangle her if she doesn't shut up,' thought Harriet hotly. Not trusting herself to answer, she silently clenched her teeth.

Hugh retorted, "Like I said, we'd trade it all away if we could have our friend back. Being on the 3V isn't anything great."

"How noble," Tiffany commented dryly.

Leonardo interjected, "Colored your hair lately Tiff?"

"What do you mean?" Tiffany demanded acidly, "This is my natural color."

"Oh yeah," Leonardo replied, "I keep forgetting that. It just seems to me that it was darker when we were in elementary school."

"No," Tiffany denied heatedly, "It's always been this color."

"My mistake," Leonardo apologized insincerely. Harriet saw Tiffany turn away and fume silently.

"Here we are," Leonardo said as he indicated the scene in front of them. "This is the Student Commons. The food court is over there. You can buy almost anything there that you could want to eat."

The Student Commons looked more like a luxury café than a part of a school. The wide room sported a high, vaulted ceiling that was bathed with brightness from recessed lights simulating natural sunlight. Chairs, tables, benches, and real, live potted plants were scattered across the wide room. Around the outer wall were booths with holographic signs displaying menus and ads. The scene was trimmed with large potted plants and trees.

"All of the corridors in the school radiate out from the Student Commons," Leonardo informed them. "The administration offices are down that way. The science classes are over there. PE, art, and stuff like that are down that green corridor. Music classes are down the light blue one. You probably won't get lost."

They were interrupted by a tinkling from Tiffany's purse. "Oops. There's my comPod," she said. Pulling out a thin, flat, rectangular object that was about 5 inches long and 3 inches wide, Tiffany cradled the device in her hand and the object displayed the image of a crisp, middle-aged woman. "What?" Tiffany asked the woman. "Oh, sure Alice, I'll be right there."

Harriet was surprised because there was no sound, just the image of the woman talking. She wondered how Tiffany could hear what the woman was saying. Glancing questioningly at Hugh, Harriet saw him tap the lower part of his ear and then point at Tiffany. Looking back at Tiffany, Harriet noticed that she was wearing colorful, but oddly-shaped, earrings. Then she understood. The earrings had tiny speakers in them that only Tiffany could hear.

Returning the comPod to her purse, Tiffany told them dryly, "It's been great, but I gotta go. Daddy's treating us to a quick vacation in the Biodome Belt before school starts and our housekeeper's taking me shopping first. Later." Tiffany shot them a tight-lipped, stilted smile and pranced airily away.

As they watched her go, Harriet asked Leonardo, "Is she always like that?"

"Not always," he replied. "She's laying it on thick for you. Until you showed up, she was the smartest person in school and she made sure everyone knew it. She's not the kind of girl that takes well to being second best."

"I guess not," Harriet commented dourly. Then she asked, "She has a human housekeeper? Not an android or robot?"

Leo answered, "Most people around here own some robots, but they also have some humans working for them. Usually the servants' families have been working for their employer's families for generations."

Apparently Hugh was more interested in her device. "What was that thing?" he asked. "Some kind of gridPhone?"

Obviously attempting to hide his surprise, Leo replied, "It's a comPod. They've been popular for a long time. It's smarter than a gridPhone. You don't run apps on it. Each one comes with its own AI. So the AI does everything you tell it to instead of you running apps like on a gridPhone. That was her family's AI there on the screen."

Surprised, Harriet exclaimed, "It wasn't a real person?"

"Naw," Leo drawled, "her family's AI has had that avatar forever. But Tiffany doesn't change it because her mother picked it out." He seemed to think that explained everything.

Harriet flushed red. 'Leo probably thinks we're from the Stone Age,' she thought.

Hugh, however, seemed unfazed and very interested in the technology available in this part of the arcology. He abruptly asked Leonardo, "What about the AR suites? They talked about AR classes in the orientation meeting. If they have so many AR classes here, why do they use human teachers instead of cyberteachers?"

"At the Westfald Academy," Leonardo explained, "they think that you get the best education when you have human teachers. Humans can react to your needs better, interact better, and all that stuff. That's what they say anyway. I don't know. It wouldn't much matter to me, but all the good colleges look for people with both AR and human-taught classes. So my parents put me here."

"Leonardo?" Hugh asked, abruptly changing the subject. "Do you know that guy over there?"

The boy he was pointing at leaned against a wall on the other side of the Student Commons. He seemed intently interested in something in his hand. What struck Harriet as unusual was the long, ratty overcoat he wore. People who lived in arcologies neither needed nor wore coats. Other than in 3V programs, she had never actually seen anyone wearing a heavy coat like that. Even if he hadn't been wearing the faded tan coat, his shoulder length, white-blond hair would have made him stand out in this crowd.

"No," Leonardo told Hugh. "I've never seen him before. The way he looks, I doubt he's a student here. Why do you ask?"

"I think I saw him scanning us with a handheld scanner," Hugh informed them.

Before Leonardo could answer, the blond youth glanced over his shoulder at them and then disappeared around a corner.

Leonardo pulled a small round object out of his pocket and put it to his ear. Harriet heard the beep-bee-booping of dialing emanating from the device.

"Hi, Security? This is Leonardo de Medici. I think we've got someone on campus that isn't a student. A description? Male. About 17 or 18. Shoulder length blond hair that's really blond—almost white. He's wearing a beat-up, light tan overcoat. Yeah, an overcoat. Seriously. I don't know, maybe he's from Outside. And we think he just scanned us with a scanner. Huh? No, it isn't a joke. Look, I remember the noodle incident too but I was in 7th grade then. I swear we saw this guy. Can't you send someone to check it out? Thanks." He returned the device to his pocket.

"Was that thing a comPod?" Hugh blurted out.

"Kind of," Leonardo replied pulling the device from his pocket again.

"How do you dial it?"

"You don't. It's one of the new mindpods."

Both Harriet and Hugh stared at him blankly.

"You haven't heard of a mindpod? It's the latest thing. It scans the brain of its owner and figures out what the electrical impulses mean. All you have to do is think of the name of the person or place you want to call and it calls them for you. And it comes with an AI that talks to you and does things for you, just like a comPod. But the AI talks to you in your head and you can think your orders to it. It's almost as good as having a datacrown."

'A datacrown?' Harriet wondered silently. But she didn't ask Leonardo about it for fear of embarrassment.

Hugh was fascinated with the gadget. He seemed to want to ask more about it, but he was interrupted by the sound of shouting. Across the Student Commons, a group of guys were pushing a younger student around. Taunting the slender boy they surrounded, the older students pulled at a box he carried. When they knocked it out of his hands, it burst open, causing art supplies to cascade onto the ground. Laughing, the boy's tormentors scooped up the supplies and began throwing them across the courtyard.

Before she knew what she was doing, Harriet was in motion. Anger flaring inside her, she stomped over to the group of bullies. But just when she was about to start yelling at them, an idea struck her. Changing to a nonchalant gait, Harriet sidled up to the group.

"Wow," she said to the younger student. "You must be quite a fighter if all these guys are afraid of you."

The boy froze, staring at her in confusion.

"We're not afraid of that little throodworm," one of the older students snapped at her.

"You must be," Harriet countered. "None of you will stand up to him alone."

Now the group zeroed in on her.

"What are you," one demanded, "his girlfriend?"

"Well," Harriet quipped coyly, "I'm always interested in strong guys. Not guys that have to run in packs like little Delarian sharkrats."

One of the group strode toward her menacingly. "Listen you little riklet. You better mind your own business if you know what's good for you."

"Riklet?" Harriet mocked. "Isn't a riklet a small bird that digs into your skull and eats your brains? I'd think someone from the fancy Westfald Academy would be smart enough to come up with something better than that."

"Shut up."

"Shut up? Wow, what a stunning comeback," Harriet flounced her long, red mane of wavy hair. "What are you going to do about it anyway? Hit me? What you're saying is that you're so big and brave that you're going to push around a girl that's a foot shorter than you and probably ninety pounds lighter? What do you do when someone your own size comes around, hide behind your mommy's skirt?"

One of the guys grabbed Harriet by the arm. Behind her, she heard Leonardo's determined footsteps approaching. Before Leonardo could intervene, one of the bullies spoke. "Let go of her, Jack. That's the girl that was on the news."

"That's right," Harriet shot back. "What do you think's going to happen if you do anything to me? Won't that get you thrown out of here permanently? At the very least, your name and picture will be all over the 3V news. Can you hear the headlines? 'Westfald Academy Student Assaults the Smartest Girl Alive on Her First Visit to School.' Kind of makes you wonder what company would ever hire a guy who got in the news for beating up a girl, doesn't it? But I guess you're not worrying about what will happen to you after you graduate, are you? Let me tell you, there's plenty of room on the streets Outside the arcology for a guy like you."

Jack released her arm. Her mention of Outside shocked him. He backed away. His friends followed him, leaving the courtyard.

The young art student stood frozen for a moment or two after they left. Then he offered his hand. "Thanks. Thanks a lot. I'm Will Ellis. I know who you are."

Harriet shook Will's hand. Forcing a smile, she replied, "I'm glad to help out Will. Now I've got to go."

Abruptly turning, she strode hurriedly past Hugh and Leonardo. They trailed after her. When they got around the corner, Harriet stopped and leaned against a wall. She folded her arms around herself and stared at the ground. Then slowly, she let herself slide downward until she was sitting. Silently, she started shaking. Leonardo and Hugh flanked her on either side.

"Are you all right?" Leonardo demanded.

In a tight, hushed voice, Harriet answered. "I'm ok." She let her hair fall around her face so he couldn't see that she was crying. "I need to get out of here." Shaking, she climbed to her feet, but staggered a little.

"Harriet, let me help you," Leonardo offered reassuringly. He put his arm around her to steady her. "You were so amazing. It was like you were on fire. You made *those* guys look like a bunch of throodworms."

He surprised Harriet by laughing briefly. "I grew up with those guys. They go after anyone new. I've never seen anyone handle them like you did. You're amazing, Harriet."

Steadied by Leonardo, Harriet tottered back toward the Assembly Hall with Hugh in tow. About halfway there, she felt better. Wiping away her tears, she told Leonardo, "I'm ok. I don't need any more help walking. But thanks."

Leonardo smiled and released her.

"I think it's probably time to go back to your parents," Leonardo suggested.

"Yeah ... I guess you're right," Harriet agreed.

Leonardo guided them to back to the large foyer in front of the Assembly Hall. Their parents were still deep in discussion with Mamsen Scrivener, so Harriet and Hugh sat on one of the benches scattered here and there.

Leonardo told them, "I've got to go, but it was great meeting you two. I'll see you Monday in homeroom."

Harriet, still shaken, forced a smile and replied, "Thanks for showing us around Leonardo."

Returning her smile, Leonardo said, "Call me Leo. Everyone does." He waved his goodbyes and left.

Their parents approached. "How was the tour?" Mamsen Scrivener asked.

Harriet and Hugh glanced at each other. "Fine," Harriet told her tightly. "It was just fine."

"Well, Harriet," her father said, "I think it's time for us to head home."

"Home. That would be really nice."

2

Harriet stood dreamily on a wide beach covered with red sand. The endless cascade of light purple waves slid over the gently-curving shore as it stretched into the distance. Above her, the similarly light purple sky was dotted with fluffy lavender-white clouds. A steady, warm breeze wafted over her as she gazed around herself. Looking out across the purple sea to her left, she saw a mammoth red sun brooding over most of the sky.

'I think I've been here before,' Harriet recalled hazily. But she couldn't remember when.

Turning toward her right, Harriet observed a manically colored jungle filled with an explosion of plant life. Seeing a gap in the forest, Harriet ambled in that direction. As she drew closer, she could see a path leading up from the beach. It connected the beach to a large castle-like structure made of pale blue crystal. With a growing feeling of familiarity, Harriet followed the path.

As she drew near to the castle, two people emerged from the large entrance. Harriet stopped, watching as the couple approached. She realized that she knew one of them. 'That's Madison Burke!' she thought.

"Madison!" Harriet called out. "Where are we? What are you doing here? What am I doing here?"

"Hello, Harriet," the girl said. "It's good to see you again. But please call me Eden now, not Madison."

Puzzled, Harriet asked, "Why?"

"Because I am no longer just Madison Burke. I've changed, Harriet."

It came to Harriet that Madison and her family were lost in the wormhole collapse like Jeff and his family.

"Madison, you're alive!" Harriet exclaimed. "Is Jeff alive too?"

"Yes, Harriet, he is. But I have not yet made contact with him. He's sleeping."

"Sleeping?"

"Harriet, don't worry about Jeff right now. He's safe. I need you to concentrate on what I'm telling you. The telepathic link between us could be lost very easily. It's hard to maintain it."

"Harriet," Madison continued, "I am no longer the person you knew. When the wormhole collapsed, I was on a ship going to the California system. Our ship was thrown far across the galaxy. Few survived the initial disaster. In the end, only Allen and I were left alive." She indicated the boy standing next to her. "We would have died too, but we came into contact with two aliens named Senthil and Jex. They were energy beings. To survive, we merged with them. I am now called Eden. Allen is called Genesis. The aliens we merged with were also a couple. Now we are all together. We need each other to survive."

"Aliens? Madison ... er ... Eden, no one's ever found any aliens."

"Humanity has not yet explored enough to come into contact with other intelligent species, Harriet. But the wormhole collapse sent us much farther than any human has ever gone before. It sent us to Senthil and Jex. I know everything Madison knew, and everything Senthil knew. I am reborn. Now I am Eden."

"And ... you brought me here ... how?" she asked.

"This is nothing more than a vision created by a telepathic link between you and I. You're seeing the planet that Genesis and I live on now. However, it's just a vision. You're really lying in your bed at home. But all that is unimportant. Harriet, there is a great danger facing the human race. To protect yourself, you must bring a ship to us. We will help you protect humanity."

"How in the universe am I supposed to get a ship to you?" Harriet asked.

"You must find a way, Harriet. I know you are still young. As you get older, you must go into a profession that enables you to get a ship. You must bring that ship to us. I will be with you through the years, and I will show you how to modify your ship to come here. For now, just focus your efforts on the gifts I've given you."

"Gifts?"

"Yes Harriet, gifts. Surely you wondered why you and Hugh suddenly became so much smarter?"

"Well ... yes, but I thought it was because of the lessons we were buying and all the studying we were doing."

"Of course those helped, Harriet. But it is primarily because of the gifts I gave you and Hugh that you have accomplished so much more than everyone around you. Can you remember being here before and receiving those gifts from me?"

Eden's question *did* trigger a memory. Harriet remembered a dream she'd had two years ago. Or at least, she thought it was a dream at the time. It was not long after Jeff was lost in the wormhole collapse. She recollected being in this same place talking with Madison. 'No ... she's Eden now,' she told herself. With gathering clarity, she recalled how Eden had touched her finger to both of Harriet's palms and forehead, one after the other. The tip of Eden's finger had been glowing. Strange glowing symbols had briefly appeared where Eden touched Harriet as the thick light seeped into her skin.

"You have power over fire, Harriet. You have great intelligence. There are many other things you can do. You must learn to use these gifts. It is critical to your survival. I have given you these abilities so that you can come to me."

Everything around Harriet shimmered and faded. "Eden?" Harriet called, but it was too late. It was all gone. Harriet opened her eyes and sat up. After a few moments of confusion, she told herself, "It was just a dream." But she wasn't so sure. She got up to get something to eat.

After breakfast, Harriet sat on her bed in the room she shared with her sister and examined the contents of the purple and gold box she received at the Westfald Academy orientation the day before. The box contained a welcoming letter that was actually printed out on fancy parchment-like synthpaper. The lettering was in a flowery, old-style script.

Deciding to save the letter in her scrapbook, Harriet found that her box contained two smaller boxes. Like the box that held them, the smaller boxes were also done in the Westfald Academy's school colors of purple and gold. Inside the smaller boxes she found an uninteresting rectangular object about the size of the palm of her hand and something else she couldn't identify. The card in one of the small boxes told her that these were her standard-issue autolibrary and dataglasses.

'What in the universe are these?' she wondered.

Harriet grabbed her old datapad from under her bed. Datapad technology was centuries old, so she was keenly aware that the Westfald students would probably laugh at her if they could see her using it.

Harriet turned her datapad on and connected to the grid, which was the arcology's network. She looked up "autolibrary" in the online encyclopedia. The entry said:

> **Autolibrary**—A device, usually small and portable, containing an entire library of information. Autolibraries first came into popular use in about 2690 AD (2690 CE) and have been steadily growing in content and shrinking in size since that time. Autolibraries are obsolescing older technologies such as datapads, databands, and most types of handheld

and wearable computing devices. Only high-end <u>datacrowns</u> store as much information as autolibraries.

Typically, autolibraries do not have user interfaces built into them. Instead, they are often paired with data access devices such as <u>dataglasses</u> and datacrowns.

Harriet touched the dataglasses link and read:

Dataglasses—A user interface device styled after <u>glasses</u> (a device used until the early 23rd century for the purpose of correcting vision problems that have since been resolved by other methods). Dataglasses typically do not store or process any data. Instead, they are used to access and manipulate data stored on other computers, such as <u>autolibraries</u>.

Figure 1 shows how dataglasses are worn. The stems, which extend over the top of the ears, contain scanning devices that examine the electrical impulses in certain centers of the wearer's brain. The scanned data is sent to the autolibrary or other computing device and analyzed for commands. This enables the wearer to "think" commands to the computer connected to the dataglasses. Responses from the computer are sent back to the dataglasses and transmitted directly to the wearer's optic nerves by the clear <u>plasticrystal</u> lenses mounted on the front. The transmitted images are seen only by the wearer. Audio data is sent by electronics in the rear part of the stems directly to the wearer's auditory nerves. As with the visual feedback, only the wearer can hear the audio output.

"I have to walk around with that thing on my face?" Harriet groaned as she looked at the picture. "And why is it called 'glasses' when there's only one?"

The letter from the Westfald Academy said that no other data access, storage, or processing devices were allowed on school premises. "This includes, but is not limited to, phones, comPods, datacrowns, databands, and all other electronic and optronic devices."

Harriet's datapad played a few flute-like notes to indicate that she had an incoming call. Checking her pad, she saw that it was from Hugh. Sliding a little panel on the bottom of the pad, she opened a compartment and removed a small earpiece. Placing it in her ear, she touched a button on the pad to answer the call.

"Hi, Harriet," Hugh greeted. "Are we still going surfing this morning?"

"Sure," Harriet replied, "I'll get changed and see you at the water park in half an hour."

They hung up and Harriet put her swimming suit on. Then she pulled a pair of shorts and a shirt on over her suit. Grabbing her towel, Harriet went to the nearest elevator and rode it to the water park. After checking out a surfboard from a vending machine, she made her way to the surfing area where she found Hugh in the Medium Surf Pool. He saw her and waved as she approached.

Catching the next wave, Hugh rode steadily toward the shallow end where Harriet stood. 'He's not a bad surfer considering he's only been doing it a year,' Harriet thought. But she often longed for a more skilled surfing companion. She reminisced about the times when she, Jeff, and Akio used to surf at this park together. Akio, whose family had left Earth to colonize the planet Yokohama in the New Tokyo system, rarely sent her video mail any more. It seemed he had nearly forgotten her.

As Harriet watched Hugh glide stiffly toward her, she remembered that Jeff was never as good a surfer as she and Akio. Nevertheless, he had been able to handle the waves in the Heavy Surf Pool. She knew Hugh had no hope of ever being able to do that.

'Oh well,' Harriet thought, 'Hugh is a good friend too.'

Hugh slid neatly toward Harriet as he skimmed across the top of the pool. He came to a halt almost directly in front of her and sank into the 3-foot-deep water. Smiling, Hugh asked, "Are you coming in?"

"Yeah," Harriet replied, "but I have to put my towel in a locker first."

"Here," Hugh said as he tossed her an orange key. "I already rented one."

After placing her towel in the locker, Harriet pulled off her shirt and shorts. She put them in the locker with her towel and returned to the pool to surf with Hugh. Catching a wave, Harriet zig-zagged on its crest with her long, braided red hair whipping back and forth as she went. Arriving at the shallow end, she waited for Hugh as he rode a straight course on the wave behind hers.

The pair surfed until nearly noon. Then they sat out for a while in the light of the sunlamps on the high ceiling. In the warmth of the simulated sunlight, their suits dried quickly. "Let's stop at my place for some lunch," Harriet offered as they chatted.

"We always stop at your flat for lunch."

Harriet shrugged. She didn't want to say that she knew that Hugh's parents were having a hard time making ends meet. Her mother had instructed her to bring Hugh by as often as possible for meals so that the Bensons could stretch their budget a bit farther. "It's on the way," she replied simply. "We can eat at your place if you want," Harriet offered. "All we're having at my place is ready-to-eat synthpaste."

"Ready-to-eat synthpaste is *all* we eat at my flat," Hugh commented sourly. "I *like* eating with your family. You eat *together*. I don't think I've ever had a sit-down dinner with my family, especially with my parents always at work."

"It's hard to make ends meet, Hugh. Our parents all struggle. So many jobs are being done by robots now, people are lucky to have any job at all."

"Maybe my family should colonize. I hear there's lots of opportunities outside the Solar System. New Cambridge University has a program for advanced high school students."

"I suppose, but are you really ready to leave the arcology and go to another star system?"

"Absolutely. I'm so tired of being poor. I'm tired of my parents having to work so hard."

Harriet had to agree. "That's true. But when we graduate college, we'll be able to get jobs anywhere. You'll probably be so rich that you'll be able to buy this whole arcology."

Silent for a moment, Hugh gazed distantly at the surfers still in the pool. "I suppose," he agreed at last. "But my parents are teachers. And they can hardly make ends meet. They could both get good jobs on Cambridge. My mom's cousin lives there. She does really well. It's humiliating for Mom and Dad here."

Harriet smiled and assured him, "Well, Hugh, someday you can buy them tickets to Cambridge."

"I will," Hugh insisted firmly.

They fell silent for a while, watching the surfers go by. Then Hugh resumed, "I had a weird dream last night."

"Oh?" Harriet asked warily, remembering her own dream.

"It was about Madison Burke. You remember her? She and her family were lost in the wormhole collapse."

Guardedly, Harriet replied, "I remember her."

"Well I dreamed she was still alive and living with some guy on a planet going around a red giant star. I liked the sky. It was purple of course."

"Why 'of course?' Why should the sky be purple?"

Surprised, Hugh commented, "After all the physics we studied together, I would think you'd know. Our sky is blue because of Rayleigh scattering. But if a habitable planet is going around a red giant star, then the increased red in the light gives it a really light purple color."

"Oh. I guess you're right. I should have known that."

"Anyway, Madison was living there on this jungle world in a blue crystal castle. It was great. I wanted to go inside, but she kept talking to me about coming to her planet. Finally she got upset with me and told me to tell you about it. She kept calling it a 'telepathic vision' and said you had them too. Then she told me I had super powers."

"What did you do?"

"I laughed, of course. I'm not a super powers kind of guy."

"Uh ... Hugh."

"What? Don't you think that's funny? Me, with super powers? I could dress in tights and call myself Captain America," he scoffed.

"That name's been taken," Harriet replied. "There was an old comic called Captain America. I read about it in one of the lessons we bought called 'Cultural Iconography.' It said he was an old symbol of America."

Hugh shrugged. "Ok, maybe I could call myself Superman or something."

"That name's been taken too."

Hugh sighed. "You don't seem to have much of a sense of humor today."

"Uh ... Hugh," Harriet repeated.

"What?"

"I had a dream about Madison Burke too."

"Huh?"

"It's true; she was on that planet with the purple sky. And the beach was red. There was a jungle along the shore with plants that were all different colors. And Madison called herself ..."

"...Eden," Hugh finished for her.

The two gazed at each other in electrified silence. In spite of the warmth of the sun lamps overhead, Harriet felt a chill run through her.

"How ..." Hugh asked, "how could we both have the same dream?"

"I don't know. Unless it really *was* a telepathic vision."

"Harriet, don't be nuts!"

"How else do you explain it?"

"I don't know!" Hugh shot back. "But telepathic visions? Come on! And super powers? What about those?"

Harriet just shook her head and shrugged.

"Harriet, she told me she was part alien now. Are you trying to tell me that that's true too? How long has humanity been looking for aliens? 700 years? Has anybody ever found even *one* alien? I know a lot of famous actors sorta *seem* like aliens but ..."

"Hugh," Harriet replied patiently, "I don't know what this means, but I do know that I had the same dream as you. And that's not normal. I also know that Madison told me that we're so smart because she gave us some kind of special gifts."

"Humph!" Hugh said disdainfully.

"You've got to admit, we did get a lot smarter after the wormhole collapse."

Hugh made a disgusted sound and said, "That was nothing but *hard work.*"

"The others in the group studied the same lessons we did," Harriet reminded him. "But they didn't change like we did. Hugh, on the Westfald entrance exams, they found that I read eleven times faster than the average human being. Eleven times!"

"I know, for me it was fourteen times faster than normal."

"Something is happening to us, Hugh. I don't know what it is, but I have a feeling that these dreams are part of it."

Hugh still wasn't convinced. He changed the subject. "It's probably time to get down to the community center for our study group."

"I suppose."

Surprised, Hugh commented, "You don't seem very anxious to go."

Harriet shrugged. "I guess I'm not. Ever since we got into Westfald, the group doesn't seem to like us as much anymore."

"They're just jealous."

"Hugh! They're our friends!"

"Yeah? Then you'd think they'd be happy for us."

Shaking her head, Harriet replied, "I think it's natural. They have to go to a school that's not nearly as good. Even with all the extra studying they do, they'll never get much more than five or six sectors higher in the arcology than they're at now. Life will always be more of a struggle for them, Hugh. You and I are having the best education possible handed to us on a silver platter."

"Well," Hugh commented, "if we're going, we should go now or we'll be late."

Gathering their things and putting their clothes on over their swimsuits, the pair returned their surfboards and left the water park. They rode an elevator down to the floor Harriet's flat was on. After eating a quick lunch together, Harriet scooped up her datapad, and the two of them took an elevator down to the floor Hugh lived on. Like Harriet, Hugh grabbed his datapad and headed then they both toward the community center.

After Jeff disappeared, Harriet occasionally reflected on the days when he started the group. It all began when Jeff was walking in the park located on the top of the arcology. Because the arcology was more than ten miles high, the park was covered by a clear dome supported by strong beams set into triangular shapes.

When Harriet, Jeff, and Akio were 12, Jeff used his robot, which was shaped like a small monkey, to find an access door to into the dome's support structure. The door was an entrance for maintenance robots and it led to a series of ramps. The ramps extended up among the giant support beams that held up the half-mile tall dome on top of the arcology. These days, the ramps were no longer used. Jeff observed that each day the ramps were bathed in sunlight. So he came up with the idea of growing food on them. He gathered his friends and they composted food scraps from their homes and the school cafeteria to make soil. They had their robots spread the composted soil over the ramps and plant seeds that they bought. When their harvest came, they sold their produce to a storeowner high in the arcology. The storeowner didn't ask a lot of questions. He was just happy to get cheap produce.

Everyone outside the group thought it was a club for kids to build, repair, and sell robots. Although the group did repair and sell robots, the robots were not the main source of their income. Instead, the group used the money from their "farm," as they called it, to buy themselves lessons that gave them a better education. Knowing that their farm would be shut down if anyone ever found out about it, they kept it a secret from everyone outside the group.

Harriet and Hugh arrived at the community center where, each Saturday afternoon, the entire group studied their lessons together. As Harriet entered, she saw that the group was already hard at their schooling. As soon as the pair came into the room, however, everyone stopped and stared. Harriet was caught off guard. 'They've never acted like this before,' she thought warily.

Ally Wilson got up and approached them. "Harriet, can I talk with you two outside?" she requested in a hushed voice. They followed her out.

"What's going on Ally?"

"Harriet," she began awkwardly. "Harriet ... I'm sorry. This wasn't my idea."

Harriet queried warily, "*What* wasn't your idea?"

"Well, Jeff started the group," Ally said, apparently as an excuse, "and he was the leader until he … until the wormhole collapse. Since Akio left too, you've been running things. But now that you and Hugh are going to school in the top sector …" She didn't seem to want to continue.

Harriet urged her on.

"This wasn't my idea," Ally repeated. "We're friends, Harriet. We have been since third grade."

"Ally," Harriet asked, "what's the matter?"

"They want me to be the leader now," Ally blurted out.

Harriet thought indignantly, 'After all I've done to keep things together and keep the farm producing?'

To Ally she said, "Well Ally, if that's what everyone wants, I guess it's ok with me too. I know you'll keep things going well."

"And …" Ally continued.

Guardedly, Harriet asked, "And what?"

"And they don't want you two to come study here any more. They say that you're so far ahead of them that you're just a distraction. Everyone thinks that you should keep farming. But … they … don't want to study with you any more."

Harriet burned inside. Before she could answer, Hugh said coolly, "That's fine Ally. I think we can manage the studying on our own now. And it's *really nice* that everyone says it's ok for us to keep working on *our parts* of the farm that *we* started with our *own* work and money. It's *especially great* because if it wasn't for *Harriet*, Akio, and Jeff, they wouldn't have their plots in the first place so *not one of them* would have *any* lessons to study. What a *really* great bunch they all are."

Ally recoiled, "I'm so sorry Hugh. Harriet, you've got to believe me. This isn't what I want at all."

Through clenched teeth Harriet replied, "I believe you, Ally. You and I are still friends."

With that, she turned and walked away. Hugh trailed after her. Behind her, Harriet heard him say, "I can't believe it! After all you've done for them. I can't believe it."

With a firm stride, Harriet kept moving toward the elevator. "It doesn't matter, Hugh," she told him as she tried to convince herself that her words were true. "We're starting a new life now. I guess we have to leave the old one behind." Still fuming, Harriet stepped into an elevator and spoke the number of her floor. The elevator doors slid closed and carried her upwards.

3

Hugh sat on a folding chair facing one corner of the single-room flat his family shared. Behind him, he could hear his older sister playing a game on her datapad. His parents were sitting at the foldout kitchen table talking together in low voices.

'They think I can't hear them when I use my dataglasses,' he thought as he read through an article on robotics.

"Do you think we're really doing the right thing, sending him up to that school?" his mother asked his father in a near whisper.

"Of course we are," his father shot back testily. "Do you want a kid like him to be limited in life by the few opportunities we can provide him? You know how smart he is. He doesn't belong this far down in the arcology."

"Neither do we," his mother replied wryly. "But we get by."

"I want him to do more than get by. He has the chance to do great things. He's Hubert Einstein Benson, named after the greatest genius since World War III. I named him that because I knew he'd be smart from the day he was born. I just had a feeling in my bones. It's the same now. We *have* to send him up to that school for him to reach his full potential. I feel it in my bones right now this minute."

"Well," his mother commented wryly, "I hope your bones are right. The last time we moved him up, that Highborne kid beat him up and put him in the hospital."

"Hmph," his father snorted. "That kid is gone, lost in space where he can't hurt anyone—if he's alive at all."

Hugh felt a stab of sadness. 'Jeff was lost in that wormhole collapse too,' he thought.

"Anyway," Hugh's father continued, "his new school has its own security force. He'll probably safer there than here."

Hugh's mother continued to express her reservations, but Hugh stopped listening. He'd heard it all before.

Returning to the robotics article, Hugh studied information on robotic command recognition matrices. As the evening passed, he read several more articles on robotics, some on gravitonics, and a few on spaceship design. By the time he was done, it was time for bed.

Hugh folded his chair, put it in a drawer, and lowered his bed from the ceiling. Grabbing his pajamas, he went into the bathroom. 'I really don't need that school,' he thought as he brushed his teeth and changed into his nightclothes. 'All I need is my dataglasses and autolibrary. What could that school offer me that isn't in the autolibrary?'

Climbing into bed, Hugh wished he didn't have to face the next day. Experience taught him that his mother was right. There would probably be someone at his new school that would start pushing him around.

'One day I'll learn to fight,' he thought. 'Then I'll never have to worry about being attacked.' Warmed by that thought, Hugh drifted off to sleep.

4

Harriet stood in the bustling Student Commons waiting for Hugh. Nervously watching the chattering influx of students, she shifted from foot to foot as she scanned the crowd.

From behind her, Harriet heard a friendly voice call, "Harriet! You made it." Turning around, she saw Leo smiling and waving. He strode confidently toward her.

"I was looking for you," he told her. "I was supposed to show you our homeroom the other day, but we didn't get to it. So I thought I'd come early and make sure you got to the right place."

A warm glow spread through Harriet as she replied, "That's really thoughtful Leo. Thanks." Her appreciative words made his face light up.

Hugh approached, fiddling with his necktie. Without preamble, he requested, "Leo, could you help me with this? I went onto the grid to find out how to tie it, but I can't get it right. Why do we have to wear these things anyway? They've been out of style for hundreds of years."

Leo nodded, "Yah, all the guys say that. But the Westfald Academy worries about its image. And ties are coming back into style in the upper levels of most arcologies."

Hugh made a disgusted sound.

Laughing, Leo said, "I made that same sound when I found out we had to wear ties."

"I think you two look very handsome," Harriet praised them. "Your uniforms are a lot better than the girls'. This is the first skirt I've ever owned. No one wears them where we come from."

"The girls wear them a lot up here," Leo commented. "At least the ones over 16. They're always getting themselves into trouble with the Sector Council by wearing them too short."

Surprised, Harriet asked, "You mean the Sector Council checks girls' skirt lengths?"

"Absolutely," Leo assured her. "Well, not the Council, but the female teachers will actually pull the girls out of class and measure the length of their skirts if they think it's too short. They have to enforce the 'no provocative clothing' parts of the Reproductive Allowance Laws or the school gets in trouble."

Worried, Harriet fussed, "I didn't know. I didn't measure mine. What if it's too short?"

Leo assured her, "Yours is below your knees when you stand up, so it's fine. Don't worry. And besides, you make that uniform look good."

Harriet beamed, but she saw Hugh roll his eyes and turn away. "Shouldn't we be getting to homeroom?" Hugh moaned.

Harriet and Leo agreed, so Leo led the way. He showed them that their study room, which he had pointed out on the day of the orientation assembly, backed onto their classroom. The front door of the class was in the next corridor over. Since they were back to back, there was a door and some windows between the classroom and the study room.

On the way to homeroom, Harriet noticed a group of guys eyeing them. Feeling self-conscious, she scurried quickly after Leo. Inside their class, Mamsen Scrivener rose from her desk and greeted them. "All ready for your first day?" she asked.

Harriet smiled and nodded. Hugh just nodded.

"Did you bring your autolibraries and dataglasses?" Mamsen Scrivener asked.

Harriet pulled hers out of her backpack. Hugh pointed to the autolibrary clipped to his belt. He retrieved his dataglasses from his shirt pocket and put them on.

Mamsen Scrivener questioned, "Have either of you ever used dataglasses before?"

Hugh replied, "I spent most of yesterday using them. It was great. They're *way* better than datapads."

Smiling approvingly, Mamsen Scrivener turned to Harriet. Weakly, Harriet admitted, "I haven't tried them yet. I don't know how to use them at all."

Suddenly, Tiffany's voice blurted out from the doorway, "You don't know how to use dataglasses?" she tittered. "You two really *do* come from the low end of the arcology."

"Tiffany, that will be quite enough," Mamsen Scrivener scolded. "Another outburst like that and you'll find yourself in detention."

Tiffany flushed and scowled darkly. She flounced to one of the chairs and plopped herself down.

"Leo," Mamsen Scrivener instructed, "why don't you take Harriet and Hugh into the study room and show them how we use dataglasses here."

Leo nodded and led them toward the door to their study room. He led them to the long table in the center. "This is where we do all of our group work," he explained. "Put on your dataglasses and I'll show you how it's done."

Harriet clipped her autolibrary to her belt and put on her dataglasses. Nothing happened. Hugh noticed her confusion. "You have to want them to turn on. The glasses read your mind and turn on the library."

"It doesn't actually read your mind," Leo countered. "It just scans for patterns in the electrical impulses in your brain that it recognizes as commands."

Hugh shrugged. "It amounts to the same thing."

Continuing, Leo told them, "Remember the old pictures of the first Mars landing? We've all seen them, right?" Harriet and Hugh nodded. "Well you just have to want to see them lying on the table, and they'll be there."

Harriet tried it. Leo was right. The pictures appeared to be laying flat on the table with white frames around them. One of them contained 3D video. As it started to play, Harriet heard the familiar voice of Raylene Bradbury, the first astronaut on Mars, as she intoned, "With this small step, all humankind takes the next giant leap on the path to the stars." Harriet could see the blurry figure of Bradbury in her bulky spacesuit stepping off the lander and onto the dusty Martian surface.

Leo pulled her attention back to the present by saying, "Only you can see the pictures right now. If you want me to see them, your autolibraries will contact mine across the network and share them. Good, Hugh. Harriet and I can see the pictures you just shared."

Leo was right. Another pile of pictures appeared on the table. Around her pile was a white circle with the words, "Seen only by Harriet," in it. The new pile was in a blue circle with the words, "Shared by Hugh with Harriet and Leonardo." Harriet willed her pictures to be shared too.

"Good," Leo praised. "I can see your pictures too, Harriet. You can do this kind of stuff without your dataglasses if you want to. The table's surface is also a display and the table has a computer in it. The walls in this room are the same way. So you can use any data or program stored in the table or walls without needing your autolibraries at all."

Gesturing toward the classroom, Leo continued, "And you can use your dataglasses this way in the classroom too. You can leave data on the table or the walls for anyone, anytime. Only the people you leave data for will be able to see it. We share data like that a lot when we work together on projects. Your chairs in the class are the same way. You use your dataglasses to want the desk, and it folds itself out of the arm. When you do, you'll see a folder with Mamsen

Scrivener's name on it. It only exists in the chair's computer. You use that folder to turn in assignments; just drop your work into the folder and she'll get it. And by the way, she can see any data that anyone shares. She can even take a look at what you're working on any time you're in the classroom or study room. All the teachers can. So it's not a good idea to try and pass notes and stuff. They can see you doing it and you get detention. Oh, and they can hear anything you're listening to if they want to. The only time Tiffany's ever been in detention was when we were in fourth grade. She recorded some smart-aleck comments and played them to her friends during class to make fun of the teacher. The teacher heard everything."

"Some things are the same wherever you go to school," Hugh commented. Leo grinned and nodded.

Hugh asked, "Do I really need surfaces like the table or the walls to draw on? Lots of holographic interfaces work without them."

"You don't need them," Leo confirmed. "If you want to display data right in the air in front of you, you can. You can swipe it to turn pages or use your finger to draw in the air or whatever. But most people don't do that unless they're alone. It looks funny. The dataglasses can let you draw or write with just your mind. Everyone around here learns to do it that way."

Glancing through the window to the classroom, Leo commented, "We'd better get back. Class is about to start."

Going back into the classroom, Harriet observed that the dataglasses were displaying her name in large letters that hovered above a sophisticated-looking chair. She made her way to the chair and sat down. Seeing other students put their backpacks in a compartment in the bottom of their chairs, Harriet did the same. She waited nervously for class to start.

Looking around the room, Harriet saw that the wall panels were colored a neutral shade of sky blue. As Mamsen Scrivener sat at her desk at the front of the classroom, she seemed to be using her dataglasses intently. Suddenly, several of the wall panels changed to landscapes of Mars. One of them displayed the flags of the Federated Alliance, the USA, and the state. The remaining panels displayed a grassy field under a sunny sky dotted with fluffy white clouds.

A bell rang. "Welcome back, everyone," Mamsen Scrivener greeted the class as she stood. "And welcome to our new students, Harriet Brightway and Hugh Benson. I hope *everyone* will do their best to make them feel part of our class," she said casting a rather withering glance in Tiffany's direction. Harriet saw Tiffany look downward and squirm in her seat.

They quickly moved into their lessons, which for everyone but Harriet and Hugh was a review of where they left off at the end of the previous school year. Harriet rapidly adjusted to using the dataglasses. When she wanted to take notes, a piece of virtual paper appeared on the desk. Of course, because the image was projected on her optic nerves by the dataglasses, she was the only one who could see the page. 'Well, with the exception of Mamsen Scrivener,' she thought.

Harriet opened a compartment in the padded arm of the chair and picked up a plastic stylus. She used it to write on the virtual paper. As she did, the dataglasses projected her writing onto the paper's image just as if she was writing with a real pen. Harriet found that the autolibrary had a place to file all of her notes by subject. She could also look up information as the lecture progressed and attach it to her notes.

'I think I'm *really* going to like using these,' Harriet thought, 'even if they do look funny on me.'

Homeroom was an hour long. Harriet settled into the class while Mamsen Scrivener began to lecture about someone named Shake Spear. 'How could anyone have a first name like Shake?' Harriet wondered. When Mamsen Scrivener talked about a play called Hamlet, Harriet was able to look it up. She found the author was, in fact, named William Shakespeare. And contrary to Harriet's expectations, Hamlet was not about a pig.

'I wonder why I've never heard of Shakespeare before.' Harriet mused. 'I guess when you're from the low end of the arcology, they don't bother to teach you about things like that.'

Deciding to rectify the situation there and then, Harriet spent the rest of the hour reading Hamlet. At first, she had to look up most of the words. 'But I guess I shouldn't be surprised at that. This stuff was written 1100 years ago.' In spite of the difficulty, she was able to get through the entire play by the time the lecture was finished.

At the end of the period, Mamsen Scrivener called Harriet and Hugh up to her desk at the front of the class. "Do you two *always* work that fast?" she asked them. "I've never seen *any* human beings access and process information as fast as the two of you did today. It was amazing. I could hardly see the data flash by. I've reviewed the test results on you two, but it really didn't prepare me for this."

Blushing, Harriet said, "I hope we didn't do anything wrong. We were paying attention, weren't we Hugh?" Hugh nodded vigorously.

Chuckling, Mamsen Scrivener told them, "Of course you didn't do anything wrong. I was just surprised, that's all. With you two in the class, I'll have to rethink everything about the way I teach."

"Our teachers at our old school," Hugh offered helpfully, "just did what they normally do and gave us extra work to do while they were lecturing. But we still paid attention to them at the same time."

"Well I think I can do more for the two of you than that. However, you'll have to be a little understanding of the situation here. Everyone else is going to be working *much* slower than the two of you. But I'll try to find a way to keep things interesting for you."

They both thanked her and left. As soon as Harriet wondered what her next class was, her schedule appeared in the air in front of her. 'Physics. Room C–15,' she read. 'Where is room C–15?' she thought. Her dataglasses displayed a green 3D arrow in the air in front of her, pointing the way.

Following the arrow's directions, Harriet wended her way to her physics class. The lecture was an introduction to motion in a 2D plane. It didn't take long for Harriet to get bored. 'Hugh and I did *much* harder physics than this for our science project last year,' she thought. She decided to look up information on gravitational anomalies in four dimensions. At the end of the period, she was called up to the teacher's desk again.

"Harriet," Sirsen Bigley told her. "I'm putting you into an advanced physics course."

"You're changing my schedule?"

"Oh no," Sirsen Bigley assured her. "I'm just changing the material you'll study while you're in here. From now on, just go directly to an AR pod when you come in. You'll be taking a post-graduate course in quantum hyperspacial theory. There'll be a simulated classroom with students and a teacher to interact with."

"But don't I need *this* class to graduate from high school?"

Sirsen Bigley chuckled. "Harriet, I'm the head of the physics department at Westfald. I reviewed your work on the wormhole collapse over the summer. You have no need of this class. I'm going to give you credit for this and all other physics classes we teach here. You'll be taking cyberuniversity physics from now on."

"Uh ... thanks Sirsen Bigley." Harriet left for art class, which was next on her schedule. She found that Hugh had art with her as well, so she sat next to him. They very quickly discovered that everyone else had been taking drawing and painting classes since they were little. They were the only two in the class who could not draw or paint at all.

While the others were working on their first drawing of the semester, the teacher, Mamsen Knightly, took them to the back of the class to show them some of the basics of drawing. Tiffany, who was also in the class, smirked openly at them. Mamsen Knightly handed Harriet and Hugh some funny styluses and showed them how to make marks on real drawing paper.

Harriet saw that the other students were producing realistic pictures of the bowl of plastic fruit that was on the table at the front of the class. She was frustrated. Neither she nor Hugh could make anything that looked remotely real. "Why do we have to do art?" she asked the teacher. "We *never* had any art classes in our old school."

Mamsen Knight was patient. "At the Westfald Academy, we believe that art and music stimulate our students to better creativity. They're required. Don't you *like* to draw?"

Harriet shrugged. "I used to fingerpaint on my datapad when I was little. And I drew a little with a stylus. But we never had any synthpaper or anything like these things to draw with. What are these things anyway?"

"They're colored pencils, Harriet. They're commonly used in drawing. Be patient with yourselves. You have to learn to handle the pencil and to draw some basic shapes first. Then you can move on to more realistic drawing."

Hugh complained, "Isn't there a class for beginners?"

"Not at the Academy," Mamsen Knightly replied. "Our students normally come from schools that require art and music like we do."

"So we're the only ones in the *entire* school that can't do this?" Hugh moaned. "Great."

Gently, Mamsen Knightly told him, "Hugh, you two are the smartest human beings alive. You've done amazing things in physics and math all on your own. You can be proud of what you've accomplished. But you can't expect to be the best at everything. Art is new for you. I'm sure you'll pick it up and learn to enjoy it."

"Maybe," Hugh replied doubtfully. "But it's really embarrassing to be doing baby stuff like this where everyone can see."

Mamsen Knightly brightened. "I can fix that," she told them. "I normally like to have students use real art materials, but you can do your practice with the program in your autolibrary. Just think about having a page to draw on."

Harriet thought, 'I want drawing paper.' The autolibrary used her dataglasses to display a piece of virtual paper.

"Good," Mamsen Knightly complimented. "Now I suggest you let each other see your papers. And instead of real pencils, use these styluses." She handed them each a plastic stylus, and explained how the paint program worked. It didn't take long for her to get the two of them drawing simple figures and color splotches on their virtual papers.

"Until you catch up," Mamsen Knightly told them, "you can practice with your drawing program. Put it into tutorial mode and it will teach you the basics. No one will see your work but you."

After class, Tiffany approached them. "I guess you two don't know *everything* do you?"

Dismayed, Harriet shot back, "We never said we did, Tiffany. *You're* the only one who worries about stuff like that."

Tiffany just smiled loftily and walked away.

"That raving riklet is going to get her hair torn off if she doesn't watch it," Harriet growled.

Hugh chuckled. "Harriet, she just wants to jerk you around. As soon as you get mad, she wins. Do what Leo does; turn the tables on her. Remember when he asked her about coloring her hair? She just deflated like a Greltan heliumfish under water. If you want to deal with her, you've got to do the same. Or just ignore her."

Sighing, Harriet mumbled, "I suppose."

Hugh smiled reassuringly and went to class. As he departed, Harriet noticed several boys gawking at her. Embarrassed, she left for her next class, which she discovered was orchestra.

"I've never played with a group before," Harriet told the teacher, Mamsen Chong. "I taught myself how to play the flute."

"I'm impressed, Harriet," Mamsen Chong replied. "Tiffany Montague is my teaching assistant, so I'll have her get the class going on their first song of the new school year."

'Oh great,' Harriet thought. 'I can't get rid of Tiffany no matter *where* I go.'

"While they're working on the song," Mamsen Chong continued, "You and I will do a few musical exercises that will help me understand your needs."

Mamsen Chong showed her to a small practice room with a piano. She left Harriet there while she and Tiffany got the rest of the class going. Harriet pulled her flute out of her backpack and tuned up.

"I wish I could just do what everyone else is doing," she murmured to herself. "Why do I have to be separated from the others in *every* class?" She heaved a sigh.

When Mamsen Chong returned, she put Harriet through her paces. With a lot of struggle, Harriet managed to play most of the music Mamsen Chong gave her. After half an hour, she said, "Very good, Harriet. You've taught yourself well. You're certainly good enough to play with the rest of the class. Come with me."

Mamsen Chong had Harriet sit in the last chair of the last row of flute players. "Ok, Tiffany. You can take your place now." Tiffany promptly went to the first chair of the flute section, picked up her flute from the chair, and sat down. She sneered in Harriet's direction.

"Alright class," Mamsen Chong instructed, "let's take it from the top." And with that, they played their way through the song. Harriet struggled, making lots of mistakes. A few times, she saw Tiffany glance over snidely when she heard Harriet's louder slip-ups. Harriet played softer.

It was a difficult hour, but Harriet got through it. At lunch, she went to the Student Commons to eat with Hugh. Pulling a tube of ready-to-eat synthpaste out of her backpack, she saw that all the students around them were sitting at the tables ordering food from small robots hovering next to them.

Mortified, Harriet said softly, "Hugh, we're the only ones not buying food!"

"We have synthpaste. We *don't* have money."

"I can't eat this in front of everyone!"

"Eat or go hungry; it's your choice."

At that moment, Leo approached. "Hi guys. Can I eat with you?" Harriet saw a flash of surprise cross his face when he noticed the synthpaste. She quickly slipped it into her backpack. Leo continued as if nothing had happened, "I was hoping you'd let me buy you lunch."

Harriet reddened. "Uh … thanks, but I'm not really hungry. I was just going to go to our study room and … practice some art. I'm really bad at art." She let out a nervous giggle.

"Well," Leo told her uncertainly, "if that's what you really want. But they're serving Mongolian Hot Pot today, and I really wanted someone to try it with me. Are you sure you guys won't eat with me?"

"Well …" Harriet said hesitantly.

"Ok," Hugh cut in.

"Great! It's settled," Leo announced. "Let's go get a table."

They found an empty table, plopped down their backpacks, and sat down. The table automatically displayed various menus on its surface. Leo told them, "I gotta duck out to the can. I'll be right back." Before they could reply, he strode away.

True to his word, Leo was only gone a few minutes. By that time, a robot waiter was floating toward them, ready to take their orders. Harriet's dataglasses told her she had urgent mail. Opening the message, she found that it was from the school administration. It read:

> Dear Harriet:
>
> As a way of saying thank you for choosing to attend the Westfald Academy, you are hereby gifted a daily food allowance. Please feel free to order any food from the vendors in the food court that you can eat on the school's premises.
>
> Thanks again for choosing the Westfald Academy for your educational needs. We hope you will find your time here rewarding and enjoyable.
>
> Sincerely,
> Ester McBride
> Principal
> Westfald Academy

Harriet was shocked. 'This *has* to be Leo's doing,' she thought. 'He didn't go to the bathroom just now, he called the principal.'

The waiterbot hovered next to Harriet and asked, "May I take your lunch order, Mamsen Brightway?"

Still not sure she believed the mail, Harriet hesitantly said, "Mongolian Hot Pot."

"Would you care for anything to drink? Orange soda is popular."

"Yes," agreed Harriet hastily. "I'll have that."

"Thank you," the robot replied, "Please say 'yes' to authorize payment for your food."

"Yes," she croaked, her mouth dry with nervousness.

"Payment received," the register said.

Harriet felt so relieved she was almost dizzy.

"Hey!" Leo cajoled. "You were supposed to let *me* pay for that. Oh, well. Next time."

Hugh and Leo ordered their food as well. The waiterbot returned with their meals within a minute. "Thank you and enjoy your meals," it intoned as it floated away.

Leo quickly said, "I don't know about you guys, but I really don't care to eat with chopsticks today. I'm getting a fork." He waved at one of the robots and demanded a fork. Copying Leo, Harriet agreed, "Me too. I prefer a fork." But she was thinking, 'I don't even know what chopsticks *are*.' The waiterbot quickly brought their forks.

They discussed the classes they'd had that morning as they ate. Both Harriet and Hugh said that this was the best Mongolian Hot Pot they'd ever had. 'Leo's probably figured out that we've never eaten this before,' she thought as she sipped her drink.

After lunch, all three had a study period with their group. When they arrived, Harriet saw photos left out on the study room table. As she drew closer, she saw that they were of her. Someone had taken pictures of her with the tube of synthpaste in her hand. Horrified, she saw that the pictures were inside a circle that had the words, "Seen by Everyone."

"Who did that?" Leo demanded angrily. Immediately, he strode into Mamsen Scrivener's classroom. Through the window, Harriet saw him talking to Mamsen Scrivener angrily. At that moment, the rest of the study group entered the room, with Tiffany in the rear. As they gathered around the table and sat down, they stared at the photos and snickered. Harriet wished she was dead.

Mamsen Scrivener followed Leo back to the study room. "There they are," Leo stated heatedly. "They're obviously faked."

"They look real to *me*," Tiffany commented loftily.

Leo gave her an accusing stare as he said, "I'd like to know who left them there."

"That information is stored in the table," Mamsen Scrivener interjected. "Let's just retrieve it, shall we?" The words, "Uploaded by Tiffany Montague" appeared on the table next to the pictures.

"Tiffany," Mamsen Scrivener commanded in a low, dangerously quiet voice, "Come with me." The pictures on the table disappeared. Tiffany did not return for the rest of the study period.

When Tiffany and Mamsen Scrivener were gone, Leo announced to the group, "Let's break into groups of three and work on the literature lesson we got this morning in homeroom. Hugh and Harriet, you're with me."

As Harriet watched, the others in the group dutifully arranged themselves into clusters of three and began studying at the tables or in the plush chairs arranged around the room. After half an hour of reviewing with Harriet and Hugh, Leo called a halt to their efforts. "You guys are amazing," he told them. "You read fast and remember everything. From what I hear, you're also way beyond me in math. Would either of you mind tutoring me?"

Hugh replied, "We *both* will, if you'll help us with art and music. I had to start learning piano today. I was so bad at it that the teacher had to put me in a little practice room by myself and send his teaching assistant to work with me."

Shyly, Harriet agreed. "I was drawing stick figures in art. It was *so* embarrassing."

"It's a deal then," Leo said. "In fact, since our study group is supposed to work as a team ..." Leo turned to face the rest of the room. "Hey you guys," he called out. The others looked up from their work. "Harriet and Hugh are *way* ahead of us in math and physics. Who wants them to tutor us?" Immediately hands were raised. "Well, if you do, you have to help them with art and music. We're ahead of them in those classes. If everyone agrees, I'll make up a schedule and we'll get started right away." The others murmured their agreement. "Hey Tanika," Leo called to a short girl with chocolate-colored skin and deep brown eyes. "You're the best artist here. Can you start by giving them some help?"

Tanika smiled at the compliment and nodded. As she stepped over to where Harriet and Hugh were sitting, Leo said, "I'm gonna change places with her. They're still working on Hamlet and I need to work on it." He rose and took a place in the trio that Tanika had left behind.

"We really appreciate this," Harriet greeted Tanika as she sat down. She noticed Hugh was suddenly very quiet.

"No problem," Tanika replied, tossing her long, straight black hair. "How much do you know about art?" she asked, flashing a bright smile. Hugh looked as if he were melting.

Seeing that Hugh wasn't likely to answer, Harriet replied, "Well, we've never really done any art before." She decided to be honest. "We never had much to draw with or on. And we never learned stuff like this in school."

Tanika didn't laugh. Instead, her whole face lit up with a smile that appeared to dazzle Hugh again. Harriet had to force herself not to giggle.

"That's ok," Tanika told them. "We can start with easy stuff and go from there. It's fun."

After obtaining styluses for each of them, Tanika had them start up the drawing program in their autolibraries. "We'll start with 2D pictures. They're easier." By the end of the study session, she had them drawing simple pictures of people and animals. "Tomorrow, we'll start with close-up views of faces," she told them as they went together into Mamsen Scrivener's classroom.

The rest of the day went reasonably well. After her study period, Harriet went to Biology class. The teacher, Sirsen Webb, began the class by enthusiastically announcing that he was a world expert on freshwater tubeworms. That didn't sound very exciting to Harriet. But luckily, Sirsen Webb seemed to realize that sophomores in high school aren't usually interested in freshwater tubeworms. Instead, he talked about food chains. It was fascinating.

Harriet's final class of the day was French, which she enjoyed immensely. It was especially nice because it was completely Tiffany-free.

After school, Harriet met Hugh in the Student Commons. 'In spite of Tiffany, it's not been too bad of a day,' Harriet thought as they walked together toward an elevator. "I think I may like it here," she told Hugh.

"Mmm," was his only reply.

"What's the matter, Hugh?"

"Tiffany was in my Chinese class," he replied as they rode downward. "She's mad at us. And she's *really* mad at *you*. I'd watch out for her tomorrow."

'I wish he hadn't told me that until tomorrow,' she fretted silently.

5

Strange blue and yellow bird-like creatures danced on the wind as they darted over Harriet's head.

"Where am I?" she murmured.

Gazing peacefully around herself, she saw that she was standing on a red sand beach. The surf lapped the shore in gentle playfulness under a lilac sky. Realizing that she was dreaming again, Harriet turned and walked to the castle she knew would be there.

"Hello, Harriet," Eden greeted as she approached. Hugh, Leo, and Tiffany were standing there.

"What ... what's she doing here?" Harriet demanded.

"You need her."

"No, I do NOT!"

"Yes," Eden replied patiently, "yes, you do. She's got a strong will to survive and she's extremely bright. All of you are. I need you and you all need each other."

Hugh broke in, "Why? What's this 'great danger' you keep talking about?"

Eden sighed, "I told you that I've merged with an energy being named Senthil. Her people are not the only energy beings that exist. You see, having a physical form is a very wonderful thing. Being solid and human lets you feel and perceive things we never could as just energy beings. Those who live in Senthil's universe have great knowledge and power. But they do not obtain a fullness of being unless they have a body. There is a passage into your universe that people from Senthil's realm could use if they knew it existed. Right now, I'm guarding this end of it. Senthil set a guardian on the other end before she came here. If the others found out about you, they would flood into your galaxy and take over every human being."

"Take over?" Hugh asked.

"Yes, Hugh. They would not merge with you as Senthil did with Madison. They would consume your life force, thereby obtaining all of your memories."

"You mean," Leo interrupted, "They would eat our souls?"

"Yes, Leonardo. That is exactly what I mean. And having a physical form gives energy beings great power. The other races would use your bodies to conquer and dominate Senthil's people.

So you see your danger is their danger. It's important that you work with Genesis and I to save both races."

With no further explanation, Eden turned and touched Tiffany's forehead. "Tiffany, I give you intelligence, as I have Harriet and Hugh. A bright white pool of light formed on Tiffany's forehead. It distorted itself into a symbol of some sort and absorbed into her skin. Seemingly in a daze, Tiffany held out her hands. Eden touched her right palm and pronounced, "I give you power over lightning and an affinity with the sky. You will be most powerful when you are in the heavens." A sky blue spot appeared on her palm, formed a symbol, and then sank into her skin. Touching Tiffany's left palm, Eden told her, "I give you power over the physical world around you; use it to keep yourself safe."

Remembering the vision she'd had not long after the wormhole collapse, Harriet thought, 'She said that to me too, when she touched my left palm.'

Turning to Leonardo, Eden intoned, "Just as I gave to the others, I give you intelligence." Like Tiffany, a pool of white light formed on Leo's forehead, changed into a symbol, and soaked into his skin. Eden touched his right hand. "I give you earth affinity. You shall have great strength as well as control over rock, metal, minerals, and water. You will be strongest when you are in contact with earth and water." Touching his left hand she told him, "I give you power over the physical world around you."

Eden stood and faced the four of them. "Now you have all you need to protect your people. Soon, I will begin to teach you to use these gifts. We will work together to save everything we hold dear."

Tiffany made a disgusted noise. No longer dazed, she appeared scornful. "I am so not getting involved in this. I've got more important things to do. Like shopping. This isn't even real."

Eden looked at her severely. "You do not have a choice, Tiffany. If you do not learn to work with the others, you will not survive. Someone else will take your body and use it to live in. You will be gone forever."

They fell silent as her words sank in.

"I will teach you," Eden said firmly. "You will gain great powers and use them to come to where I am. Together, we will make everyone safe."

"I can't think of a reason in the universe to trust you," Leo stated bluntly. "Senthil's people would want to take over our bodies too. You belong to the very people who want to destroy us—if they even exist."

Nodding, Eden agreed, "I understand your distrust, Leonardo. You're right. In a way, I'm one of them. But, you see, if I allowed Senthil's people or any other race from her universe to flood into this universe and take over every human, her race would be destroyed too."

"Why?"

"Long ago Senthil's universe was filled with violence. Laws and governments were put in place to keep order. I know this is difficult to understand, but if Senthil's people were allowed to come here and take the bodies of all humans, all that keeps their universe in order would be gone. There would be war that would destroy all people in both universes. No one would survive. Everyone is in danger until the gateway is properly controlled."

Leo seemed unconvinced. "I think I'm done talking to you," he said. Immediately, he disappeared.

Startled, Harriet demanded, "What did you do to Leo?"

"Nothing," Eden replied. "He simply broke the link. I cannot force you to link telepathically with me as I can with Senthil's people. Your minds are not compatible enough for that. And I would not force a link even if I could. I need your willing cooperation. Harriet, you must convince Leo to help. You need him and so do I. All of humanity does."

The vision faded. Harriet sat up in bed, staring wildly into the dark. She heard her sister roll over in her sleep on the upper bunk. Lying back, Harriet wondered, "It seems so real. Could it be more than just a dream?"

6

Tiffany seemed unusually subdued the next day. She did not appear during the study period. "She has detention," Leo informed Harriet. "Her dad got really mad. She can't go shopping until she's done with it. For Tiffany, that's like cutting off her oxygen."

"How do you know all this?" Harriet asked.

Surprised, Leo replied, "She lives on my floor. Her brother and I are good friends."

Harriet was embarrassed. 'Of course he would know a lot about her,' she thought. 'He's probably known Tiffany and her family most of his life.' She felt like such an outsider.

In orchestra class, Tiffany managed to corner Harriet in one of the practice rooms. Without preamble, Tiffany said, "I'm gonna crush and throw you away like the little piece of trash that you are."

Instantly, Harriet's temper flared, "Don't be so stupid, Tiffany. You have no one to blame but yourself." She turned back to her music and lifted her flute, preparing to resume playing.

Tiffany grabbed at Harriet's flute and hissed, "You *don't* turn your back on your betters when they talk to you, you little piece of garbage!"

Whacking Tiffany's arm away, Harriet jumped up and got right into Tiffany's face. "You keep away from me you psycho," she hissed, "or I'll have you dragged out of here by the police and locked in a cage where you belong."

Looking down her nose at Harriet, Tiffany smiled disdainfully and airily replied, "If you had any guts you'd take care of me yourself. That's the difference between me and a gutter rat like you. *I* can handle anything *myself*. And that's what's gonna let me walk all over you. Do yourself a favor and keep away from Leo. He's mine."

Harriet hissed scornfully, "Oh really? I didn't see your name printed anywhere on him. And *he* doesn't seem to think he belongs to you. I think you're just imagining it. Why don't you go back to your stupid little dream world and not burden those of us who are *smarter* than you?"

If looks could kill, Harriet would have been nothing but a pile of smoking ash. Tiffany repeated, "I'm gonna *crush* you. You asked for it." She stomped out of the practice room.

In spite of the threat, the rest of the week passed with no more incidents from Tiffany. School went well. PE turned out to be more fun than Harriet thought possible. Every day, they got to choose a sport or activity in the artificial reality suite.

Harriet tried a program that deposited her in a vast green valley. Standing not far from her was a group of winged horses. Harriet cautiously approached a pure white mare. As she drew near, the mare gently bowed its head in greeting. Carefully, Harriet climbed onto the mare's back and took hold of the reins of the golden bridle it wore.

"What do I do now?" Harriet wondered out loud.

A young woman in a flowing toga appeared next to Harriet. "I'm the tutor for this program," she announced. The tutor spent about ten minutes giving Harriet instructions on how to handle the horse on the ground and in the air. Then she told Harriet, "It's time for you to take your mount for a quick spin."

Nodding apprehensively, Harriet nudged the horse's sides with her heels. The mare sprang forward, galloping across the meadow as it flapped its wings. Slowly and gracefully, the exquisite creature lifted itself into the air. Harriet's heart raced as the ground fell away.

It didn't take long for Harriet to get the knack of flying. Before the end of the period, she was whirling and spiraling through the sky like an expert. It quickly became her favorite program. Unfortunately, Tiffany also liked the program and invited herself along when Harriet, Hugh, Leo, and Tanika decided to use it during their PE period on Thursday. Somehow, wherever Harriet flew, Tiffany always "accidentally" ended up in the way.

After the fifth time that she nearly collided with Tiffany, Harriet was fuming. Then she thought, 'This is an AR program. You can't get hurt here no matter what.' The next time that Tiffany got in the way, Harriet dove straight at her. To keep them from hitting each other, the program automatically moved Tiffany far across the valley from where Harriet and the others were. Harriet was pleased with herself.

As they flew over the verdant valley below, Harriet couldn't help noticing that Hugh and Tanika seemed to fly close to each other a lot. With Tanika's attentive help, it didn't take long for Hugh to become a proficient flyer. At the end of the period, Harriet was on her way to French when Leo stopped her. "Hey Harriet," he called.

"Hey yourself," she replied playfully.

"Wanna do something this weekend?"

Surprised, Harriet was momentarily speechless. "You ... you mean like a date?"

Nodding, Leo replied, "I mean like a date. Radioactive Waste is putting on a concert on Saturday night. Do you like them?"

'Who?' Harriet wondered. "Sure," she replied brightly. "What floor will they be performing on?"

Leo's eyebrows shot up. "The concert isn't in this arcology. It's in the Gigadome."

"The Gigadome! Clear down at the south end of the state?"

"Sure, but the skytrain will get us there in less than an hour."

"Um ... ok, that sounds nice."

"Great!" Leo said. "I'll pick you up at your place at 5:00 on Saturday. We'll take the skytrain and have dinner at a restaurant at the Gigadome."

Harriet blushed. "My place? Maybe we could meet at school."

Gently, Leo replied, "Your place will be fine, Harriet. Your dad will probably want to meet me before I take you out anyway."

"But that's so old-fashioned!"

"Yeah," Leo agreed. "But dads still like to meet the guys that take their daughters out. I've found I get along much better with girls' dads if I meet them on the first date."

'*First* date?' Harriet thought hopefully.

Leo repeated, "I'll pick you up at 5:00 on Saturday." Pausing a moment, he appeared to turn an idea over in his head. "My younger sister came back from Venus yesterday," he continued. "Her school has a different schedule than ours, so she's here on vacation for four weeks. Want to come to my place after school and meet her?"

'Go to his home?' Harriet thought in wild panic. 'What will his family think? They probably won't even like me.'

"Well ..." she began.

"Come on," Leo urged. "You'll have a good time. The three of us can go hypersailing in our AR pods."

"*Your* AR pods?"

"Yeah," Leo replied hesitantly. "My family has four."

'They have their *own* artificial reality pods? Just *how* rich are they?' Harriet wondered. "I guess that would be ok," she told him. "I'll send my mom a voice mail to let her know I'll be late."

"Sounds great," Leo replied. "I'll meet you in the Commons right after school." He waved as he walked away. Harriet turned to go to class and found Tiffany standing not far behind her, staring and smoldering with hate.

'I wonder how long that riklet has been standing there listening?' Harriet wondered angrily. She decided to ignore Tiffany as she brushed past and went to class.

But all through the remainder of the day, Harriet struggled to keep herself from panicking. What would Leo's family think of a girl from so low in the arcology? As she tried to concentrate on her schoolwork, she had visions of Leo's mother horrified at the pathetic little poor girl he had brought home. In her mind, she could see his sister laughing at the idea that *she* should be friendly to someone like Harriet. 'I wouldn't be surprised if Leo's father physically picked me up and threw me out,' she worried.

At the end of the day, Harriet was so worked up that she stood trembling in the Commons as she waited for Leo. She heard a voice from behind her say, "Harriet?" Turning around, Harriet saw a younger boy. She had the feeling she had met him somewhere before.

"Harriet?" the boy repeated. "Do you remember me?"

Blushing, Harriet admitted, "You look familiar."

"I'm Will Ellis. We met a few days before school started. You … you helped me out." He became suddenly awkward. The memory of that day clearly embarrassed him.

"Oh yeah," Harriet said quickly. "I do remember you. You're the one who likes art."

Will brightened. "Yeah, that's me. My parents try to get me to focus on things they say are 'more practical.' But somehow I always seem to go back to art."

"You're lucky," Harriet told him. "I'm terrible at art."

After hesitating for a moment, Will changed the subject abruptly. "Harriet, I saw a guy that I think was scanning you just a few minutes ago."

"Scanning me?"

"Yeah. He had what looked like a hand-held scanner and it was pointed at you."

"Who was he, a student?"

Shaking his head Will replied, "I don't think so. He wasn't wearing a uniform. He had on a long, beat-up overcoat."

Harriet remembered the blond boy who scanned her and Hugh the first day they visited the school. "Was he blond?" she asked.

"Yeah. Real blond. His hair was almost white."

"Is he still around?"

"Naw. He saw me looking at him so he shoved his scanner in his coat pocket and ran off. I think maybe you should let School Security know so they can keep a lookout for him."

Nodding, Harriet said, "I think I will." She thought ominously, 'That's creepy. I wonder why he's so interested in me?'

Before she could give it any further thought, Leo arrived. "Hi Harriet," he greeted, shifting his gaze from her to Will.

Harriet replied quickly, "Well, thanks Will. I appreciate you letting me know."

Will took the hint. "No problem. See ya around." He scooted away.

"You know him?" Leo asked as he jerked his thumb at Will's retreating back.

"We met him the first day we came here, remember? He was the guy the others were picking on."

Leo smiled, "Oh yeah. The artist guy. He's kinda famous, you know."

"No. I didn't know."

"Yeah, he started showing his artwork when he was in grade school. He was all over the news for a while. Haven't heard anything about him recently though. I hear his parents want him to take over the family business."

"Do you know him?"

"Not him, but I know his family. One of his mother's cousins is married to my cousin's cousin."

"So ... so you're kind of related to him."

Leo shrugged. "Kind of, I guess. But in this part of the arcology a lot of people are related like that. Probably half the people in this school have relatives that married into one generation or another of my family, or someone from my family married into theirs. Most of the families in our sector lived together in one of the big habitation complexes before the arcology was built. We go back probably two or three hundred years."

"Two or three *hundred* years? You've all been marrying into the same families?"

He nodded. Then he shook his head. "Not all, but a lot of us have. And new families marry into ours in every generation. Our families all own groups of companies together. It's called a conglomerate. When there's a marriage, it's more like a corporate merger."

Harriet was dumfounded. "Huh?"

"About half of our marriages are arranged for business reasons. We don't always pick who we marry. The other half tend to be kids that aren't in the family businesses. Parents usually don't care so much who they marry."

"Leo, that's horrible! I thought people stopped arranging marriages hundreds and hundreds of years ago."

Shrugging again, Leo stated matter-of-factly, "Not really. People with money have always been doing that kind of thing."

Harriet thought it sounded like something out of the Dark Ages. But Leo appeared unperturbed by the whole idea. He changed the subject. "Are you ready to go?" he asked.

Harriet's heart fluttered. "I ... I guess so."

"Great, I've got my hoverbike parked right near the school entrance."

"A hoverbike? I didn't know you ride a hoverbike."

Smiling broadly, Leo replied, "Sure. But we can't go fast on it. My dad's still mad at me for all the tickets I got over vacation." He strutted toward the entrance to the school.

As Harriet scurried to keep up, she told Leo, "I don't know how to ride something like that Leo. I've never been on a hovercycle before."

Leo dismissed her concerns with a wave of his hand. "No worries," he reassured her. "All you have to do is sit on the back and I'll do the rest. Here we are," he said as they arrived at the rack of hovercycles. The red bike that Leo pulled from the rack more resembled a bullet than a vehicle. Throwing a leg over, he climbed on.

"Hop on," he directed.

"Um ... Leo. You may not have noticed it, but I'm wearing a skirt. I can't just toss a leg over that thing like you do."

"That's ok. Just sit sideways. All the girls do. It'll be ok, I promise."

Harriet did not like the way things were shaping up at all. However, she plucked up her courage, turned her backside to the hovercycle, and scooted gingerly onto the black leather seat. As she did, she held her skirt so that it stayed down.

"I'm not so sure I like this Leo."

"It'll be ok. You'll see." With that, Leo started the engine. Amid more noise than Harriet had ever heard a vehicle make, the hovercycle drifted upward about a foot. Harriet placed her feet on a small cylindrical footrest and tried to balance herself.

"Hold on," Leo commanded as he revved the engine.

"Hold onto what?"

"Me of course!"

Harriet tucked the loose parts of her skirt under her legs and slid her arms around Leonardo. She had to move closer to him to get a good grip, which she didn't think was a bad thing. Without a word, Leo launched the hovercycle forward at a surprising speed. Harriet gasped and clutched Leo as hard as she could, which, when she thought about it, was also not a bad thing. Together, they shot down the wide corridor and up a large ramp.

"I don't use the vehicle elevators," Leo shouted to her as they sped upward to the next floor.

'Now's a good time to start,' Harriet thought, but she didn't say anything out loud.

After going up about ten levels, Harriet noticed that the corridors were much wider. After a few more floors, Leo turned the bike away from the ramps and they zipped down a passageway. Harriet could see that the doors to people's homes were much farther apart than on her level. 'These people must have *huge* flats,' she thought. She reminded herself that in this part of the arcology, the residents called them condominiums, rather than flats or apartments.

Leo pulled up to a particularly large door that opened automatically as they approached. He guided his bike into an alcove and parked it. After helping Harriet hop down, he opened the alcove's inner door. "This is the family entrance," Leo explained. "That's why it's so small. The main entrance is in another corridor."

'This is the *small* entrance?' Harriet thought, astounded.

"Elena!" Leo called. "Elena we're here."

No answer.

"She might be in the hypersailing program already," Leo commented. He guided her down a wide hallway that connected a series of huge rooms. Harriet had never seen such splendor. One large room was filled with plants. It resembled the pictures that Harriet had seen of jungles. Other rooms contained opulent furniture, thick carpets, and real paintings. Decorative vases seemed to be everywhere. The more she saw, the more Harriet dreaded meeting Leo's family.

"Are your parents here?" Harriet asked.

"Probably not," Leo replied. "They're not around that much. Mostly Angelo takes care of us."

"Angelo?"

"Yeah. He's kind of a combination of butler and family manager. He and his wife Anna take care of most things around here. When my parents are gone, that includes my sister and me."

"Are your parents gone a lot?"

Leo nodded. "They run the family companies, so they have to travel a lot. I think Mom's still somewhere near Jupiter. I'm pretty sure Dad's not back from London yet."

'How sad,' Harriet thought. It was so different for her family. Their two-bedroom flat was so small that they spent a lot of time close together. They never traveled, so Harriet couldn't remember a time in her life when she was apart from her family for the whole day. The more she thought about it, the more she liked it. 'I could never be so alone,' she thought. 'I just couldn't live without my family.'

"Here we are," Leo said. "This is our AR suite." He pulled open a pair of large sliding doors that appeared to be made from *real* wood. "Yup, there she is," Leo stated as he peered into the curved window of one of the four artificial reality pods.

Harriet followed his gaze to a girl a year or so younger than herself. Elena's short black hair framed her pretty face.

Leo indicated an empty pod. "Hop in. We'll join her." He touched the side of the cylindrical pod and the curved door on top opened. Harriet got in and lay down. As soon she closed her eyes, she found herself standing on a long golden beach near a battered wooden dock. Seagulls squawked to each other as they danced on the constant breeze. The cloudless sky was a deeper blue than Harriet had ever seen.

"It's a simulation of the planet San Juan, in the Cordova system."

Harriet turned around to find Leo standing behind her. They were both in bathing suits.

"Hey!" Harriet heard from behind them. Turning, she saw Leo's sister guiding a small sailboat toward the dock. It skimmed delicately above the water on a sleek, flat foil as she adjusted its oddly angular sails.

Leo strode onto the dock, so Harriet trailed along behind, her hair fluttering in the wind. He reached the end and extended his hands. His sister tossed a rope into his waiting grasp. As she did, the foil sank into the water and the slender boat settled downward, its hull bobbing in the gentle waves. Leo tied the boat to the dock as his sister hopped lightly onto the dock. She turned to Harriet.

"You must be Harriet. I'm Elena."

Casting a sly glance at her brother, Elena told him, "You know how to pick 'em. She's pretty." Harriet flushed a bright red and Elena giggled at her discomfort.

"I hear she's smart too," Elena continued, eyeing Harriet. "It was on the news."

Harriet wished she could disappear. Seeing her embarrassment, Leo said, "Don't pay any attention to her. She likes to get a reaction. Be nice Elena. Harriet's not like the girls from around here."

"What do you mean by that? *I'm* one of the girls from around here!"

Harriet instantly joined in, "Yes, Leo. What *do* you mean by that?"

Alarmed, Leo stammered, "Well ... uh ... Harriet ... It's just that ..."

"Yes?"

"It's just that, except for my sister here, who is the single most wonderful girl I've ever met in my entire life," he glanced warily at Elena, "the girls around here tend to be ..."

"... spoiled rotten," Elena finished for him.

"Well yeah," Leo agreed.

"He's right," Elena told Harriet. "That's one of the reasons I don't go to school here any more. Can't stand how the other girls are so in orbit around themselves. Anna raised us not to be that way."

"Anna, raised you?"

Nodding, Leo interjected, "Yeah, it's like I told you. Our parents aren't around much." He continued quickly, "So you wanna hypersail?"

Harriet nodded and Leo said, "Let's go!"

Without a word, Elena glided gracefully back into the boat. Leo stepped in after her and extended his hand for Harriet. She took it and hopped gingerly in after them. As the boat tipped back and forth, Leo steadied her with one hand and slipped the other around her waist. He guided her gently to one of the seats. "Thanks," Harriet murmured warmly.

Leo untied the boat and shoved off. As it slipped away from the dock, Elena worked the sails, which immediately caught the wind. Sprawling backward across her seat, she controlled the tiller with her foot while her hands flew over the sail's ropes. The boat rapidly picked up speed and rose up on its foil.

"She's lots better at this than I am," Leo remarked as he sat down next to Harriet.

Before Harriet could comment, Elena thrust a rope into her right hand. "Here. Pull this when I tell you." Putting another rope in Harriet's left hand, she instructed, "Don't pull these at the same time. I'll just say 'right' or 'left' to tell you which one I want you to pull." She sat up in her seat and took the tiller in her right hand.

Harriet held the ropes with some trepidation. 'I hope I don't make an idiot out of myself,' she thought.

Elena piloted the boat not far from the shore, following the coastline as she went. "Left!" she called. Harriet jerked hard on the rope. The sail went tight and the boat tipped frighteningly.

"Not so hard!" Elena commanded, "Just pull gently."

Embarrassed, Harriet gave the rope some slack. "Better," Elena encouraged as the boat straightened itself out.

Harriet nervously waited for Elena's next command while Leo chatted happily. Harriet did her best to appear relaxed and keep up her end of the conversation. All that came from Elena was an occasional "right!" or "left" as she piloted the boat.

Harriet quickly became better at managing the ropes she was holding. By the time they were out of the bay and into the open ocean, she was anticipating Elena's instructions.

Leo continued talking and after a while, Elena joined in. Leo seemed quite curious about Harriet's family, wanting to talk endlessly about her parents. 'He's surprised that I'm so close to my parents,' she realized. It was clear he wished for the same kind of relationship himself. 'We have something that he doesn't.' She felt rather sad for Leo and Elena.

Time passed more quickly than Harriet realized. A man's voice, seemingly from the sky, announced, "Dinner is served." The scene around them dissolved and Harriet opened her eyes in the AR pod. As she climbed out, she heard the man's voice again say, "Dinner is served in the outer dining room."

"The outer dining room?" Leo repeated, apparently puzzled. "Why there?" He stepped out of the AR suite with the girls following in his wake.

When they reached the dining room, a man and a woman were there waiting. The room was longer than Harriet could believe. And it had an outside window. Natural sunlight streamed in as the sun set across the vast city. Harriet was amazed. She didn't know *anyone* with an actual window.

The man held Elena's chair as she sat down. He glanced sharply at Leo and cleared his throat. Taking the hint, Leo held the chair for Harriet and then went to the other end of the table and sat down. An unhappy expression crossed his face, then Leo said, "Angelo."

"Yes, Master Leonardo?" the man responded.

"Since when do you call me *Master* Leonardo?"

"Aha aha," Angelo drolled. "Young Master Leonardo jests well. However, we must observe the rules of propriety when we have guests."

Feeling as if a bright white spotlight had suddenly turned on her, Harriet shrank a little in her chair. Leo sighed, seeming a bit frustrated. "Angelo, I think we would prefer to eat in the kitchen like we always do. I don't think I've even *been* in this room before. I can hardly see Harriet. She looks like she's in a different time zone."

Standing, Leo walked the long distance down to Harriet's end of the table. "Come on," he said, offering his hand. "Let's go eat somewhere more normal."

"Sounds good to me," agreed Elena.

Harriet smiled, took Leo's hand, and stood. He guided her through several hallways still holding her hand. When they reached the kitchen, Leo led her to a round table that was perfectly sized for four people. He held Harriet's chair as she sat down and then took a seat beside her. Elena sat opposite from Harriet.

Angelo, somewhat flustered, burst into the kitchen behind them with a floating food cart following close behind him. The woman, who Harriet assumed was his wife Anna, brought up the rear. Together, the two of them served dinner for Leo, Elena, and Harriet.

Leo instructed, "Angelo, please stop fussing over us. It feels too weird. Grab some chairs from the other room for you and Anna. Anna, get a plate, and sit down like always."

Soon the five of them were squeezed together at the table and eating Anna's cooking. As she dug into her dinner, Elena told Harriet, "Anna's probably the best cook I've met in my entire life."

Harriet nibbled her food. She had no idea what it was, but it was *good*. "Wow," she replied, "I think you're right."

Anna beamed. "So," she said to Leo, "You finally brought home a girl with some sense."

At the end of the meal, as Angelo and Anna were clearing away the dishes, Elena burst out with, "Harriet, you need to come with me." She stood and gazed at Harriet.

"Um ... ok," Harriet replied, "But where are we going?"

"My room," Elena stated flatly. Harriet shot a questioning look at Leo, but he just shrugged. Grabbing Harriet by the wrist, Elena towed her out of the kitchen and down a series of hallways.

Elena's bedroom was vast. In the center was a huge, four-poster bed with gauzy curtains hanging from it. Elena guided Harriet toward the rear wall and said, "Closet."

Immediately a large door slid open revealing a closet that was more than twice the size of the living room in Harriet's flat. It was filled with every kind, style, and color of clothing imaginable.

"Ok, here's the thing," Elena said, speaking rapidly. "Leo told me he's taking you to the Radioactive Waste concert on Saturday. I don't want you to be embarrassed, but I know where you come from, and I know you haven't got anything to wear to a concert like that. I have so many clothes, and you and I are pretty much the same size, and Leo *really* likes you, and *I* really like you, so I want you to help yourself to anything in my closet. Not to borrow, to keep."

Harriet couldn't believe her ears. She looked at Elena. She looked at all of the clothes that seemed to overflow from the endless closet. She looked at Elena again and, before she realized what was happening, she hugged Elena and cried.

Elena hugged her back and then enthusiastically started digging through the closet. She had Harriet try on outfit after outfit. Finally, she found one she seemed satisfied with. Gazing at the sleek, multi-colored dress that Harriet now wore, Elena smiled. "That's the one. It looks really good on you and it's not out of style yet. Now we need to get you some shoes. Have you ever worn high heels?"

Harriet shook her head. Elena retrieved the tallest pair of sandals that Harriet had ever seen. "High heels are back in style. Women haven't worn them for almost a hundred years, but *everyone's* wearing them now. These are called platform shoes."

Stepping into the sandals, Harriet fastened the straps and stood shakily. She stumbled and almost fell.

Chuckling, Elena told her, "Don't feel bad. I did the same thing when I first tried to wear them. Hold my hand and walk around. I'll steady you until you get used to them."

Harriet tottered around the room clutching tightly to Elena's hand.

"Just practice," Elena reassured her. "It doesn't take long to get used to them."

"But why do I want to wear these?"

"*Everyone* is wearing them now. If you don't, you'll look old-fashioned. Besides, these are nice shoes. The platform soles are made with real wood."

Harriet froze. "*Real* wood?" she gasped. "In a pair of shoes? Aren't they expensive then?"

Elena shrugged. "Beats me," she replied nonchalantly. "But I don't wear them any more."

Elena pulled a drawer open. After rummaging around a bit, she found a small purse to go with the dress. Next, she gathered a few bracelets and some earrings. Finally, Elena grabbed a bag off the shelf and tossed in the purse and jewelry. "Here," she said, thrusting the bag at Harriet. "Put your outfit in here."

Gratefully, Harriet accepted. After she changed back to her own clothes, she put the outfit Elena gave her into the bag. "I really don't know what to say," Harriet told Elena. "This is *really* nice of you."

"I'm glad to do it," Elena replied, smiling. "You're so much nicer than Tiffany."

Again, Harriet froze. "Tiffany?" she asked warily. "Has Leo dated Tiffany?"

Elena shook her head. "Not yet," she answered. "But with their marriage being arranged already ..."

"WHAT?"

"Oh ... didn't Leo tell you?"

"No!"

"I'm sorry Harriet. I assumed he had. Our parents and Tiffany's arranged their marriage for business reasons before they were born. They even planned who would have the boy and who would have the girl."

"Then ... then why is Leo taking me out?"

Elena shrugged, "I thought it was because he'd seen some sense. No one can *make* you marry someone you don't want to, even if your parents put a lot of pressure on you. I figured he was finally getting up enough guts to choose someone decent, someone *he* likes."

Harriet was stunned. "But I'm only 16 and he's only 17. That's too young to choose someone to marry."

"Yeah," Elena agreed. "But dating someone your parents didn't pick is a good start."

Seeing that Harriet was at a loss for words, Elena continued, "Look Harriet. I don't want to ruin this for you. Just go and have a good time. You're right. We're way too young to worry about who to marry. You and Leo may just decide to be friends and never get serious. Or you might fall in love and get married and live happily ever after. Either way, you just need to give it some time and not worry about things right now."

"I ... I guess you're right."

"Let's go back and find Leo. He's got to get you home anyway." Elena led Harriet back to the kitchen. As they walked, Harriet's thoughts raced through her head. 'He's engaged to Tiffany. He was *born* to marry her. I don't belong here. What am I doing here anyway?'

In the kitchen, Leo had apparently been chatting with Angelo while Harriet and Elena were gone. "It's about time," Leo commented as they returned. "I thought you two got lost."

Harriet smiled, trying not to let Leo know how she felt. "I think I'd better get home," she told him. Jumping to his feet, Leo offered, "I'll take you. We'll ride my hoverbike again."

Following him to the alcove, Harriet scooped up her backpack from where she had left it when they had arrived. After Leo mounted the hovercycle, she hopped on the back behind him.

"Hang on," Leo reminded her. Harriet slid her arms around him and hugged him tightly. She smiled and sighed with a purring sort of sound, letting her doubts and fears dissolve. Leo spilled the hovercycle out of the alcove door and sped down the huge corridor. This time, Leo didn't use the ramps to get from floor to floor. Instead, he glided into a vehicle elevator and told it to go to Harriet's floor.

As the elevator dropped, Harriet still hung onto Leo. Snuggling up to his back, she felt calmer.

"You can let go for a while," Leo said. Harriet released him as he turned and looked back at her. He warmed her with a smile. It took more than 15 minutes to reach her floor. They spent the time happily chatting about nothing in particular. All the while, Harriet couldn't help thinking, 'Am I the sort of girl that could make you go against your parents' wishes and not marry Tiffany? What do you really feel when you look at me?'

When the elevator arrived on her floor, Harriet again hugged Leo tightly as they sped toward her flat. She gave directions to him while they slid down the much narrower corridors. They pulled up to her front door and Harriet slid off the back of the bike.

"Thanks for the ride Leo," she cooed shyly.

"Any time," he replied cheerfully. To her surprise, Leo leaned toward her and gave her a quick kiss. She flushed happily. Before she could say anything more, Leo zipped away on his hovercycle.

It wasn't until he was around the corner and gone that Harriet realized that there was quite a crowd staring at her. Harriet was horrified, 'Of course they're staring,' she thought. 'No one down here has a hovercycle.' Realizing what a spectacle she'd just made, Harriet quickly turned to go inside.

"Harriet," a familiar voice called from behind her. Harriet turned to find Ally Wilson approaching. Awkwardly, Harriet responded, "Oh, hi Ally."

"I haven't seen much of you lately. Not since … not since the others asked you not to come to study group." Ally paused guardedly. "Are you still mad at me?"

Ashamed, Harriet realized that she hadn't even talked to Ally since that day. 'I guess I *was* mad at her.'

"No Ally," Harriet told her. "I don't blame you. I like your hair. When did you cut it?"

Ally proudly fluffed her short hairstyle. "My cousin is here for a visit. She cut it yesterday. I was getting tired of long hair. Maybe you could try short hair too. She'd cut it for you if I asked her to."

"Thanks," Harriet replied, "but I like my hair long." She hesitated a moment and then asked, "Why don't you come in for a while?"

Pleased, Ally smiled and nodded. "Is that your boyfriend?" she blurted out.

"I don't know yet."

"But he sure likes you."

"I guess."

"What's it like to ride on his hovercycle?"

"Fun."

"I'll bet," Ally agreed slyly. "I noticed you were hanging onto him real tight. I'll bet that was nice too."

"Maybe," Harriet said as she grinned and opened the door to let Ally go in first.

7

Friday passed quickly. But Saturday seemed to crawl by. Harriet spent most of the morning practicing walking in her platform shoes with the help of her sister. After lunch, she started getting ready. Ruth Ann tried putting Harriet's hair into three different styles before they were both satisfied. At last, Harriet dressed in the outfit Elena gave her and waited nervously for Leo to arrive.

Harriet's mother chatted with Ruth Ann while her father pretended to read the news on his datapad. But Harriet could see that he was glancing a lot at the front door.

As time crawled by, Harriet began to worry that Leo wasn't coming. 'Maybe it was all just a joke,' she worried. 'Maybe he's up there with Elena right now laughing at the dumb little poor girl who's going to wait all night for a date that never comes.' The more time passed, the more Harriet was sure that it was all a terrible prank. Her sense of dread was smothering. She just wanted to crawl away and hide somewhere.

The doorbell rang. Glancing at the clock, Harriet saw that Leo was five minutes early. She quavered, unsure whether she could get up to answer the door. Her mother could see Harriet's nervousness, so she rose and answered the door for her. Harriet almost cried with joy to see Leo stride confidently in with a bunch of flowers in his hand.

Harriet stood shakily. Smiling shyly, she approached Leo who was dressed immaculately in a sleek, knee-length burgundy suit jacket and slacks, with a powder blue high-collared shirt. Such bold colors were uncommon in the clothing of people on Harriet's level. As she stepped up next to him, his fashionable, confident appearance made her feel a bit awestruck.

Leo surprised her by hugging her as he greeted, "Hi Harriet." Releasing her, he extended the flowers to her. Harriet was so ecstatic that she hardly heard her mother exclaim, "Oh how lovely, real flowers!"

Taking the flowers gratefully, Harriet said, "Thank you Leo. You didn't have to do that." She put the flowers to her face and inhaled their sweet fragrances deeply. Harriet's mother quickly took them from her hands and busied herself by searching for a vase to put them in.

Harriet's father cleared his throat as he approached and extended his hand. "So you're Leonardo," he said.

"Yes Sirsen," Leo replied respectfully as he shook her father's hand. Harriet saw that that really pleased her dad.

"And where will you be going tonight?"

'Oh please Daddy, don't be so old-fashioned,' Harriet thought.

Smiling, Leo replied, "Well, Sirsen Brightway, I thought I'd take Harriet on the skytrain to the Gigadome. We'll be having dinner there and then we'll go to the concert. We'll be back about midnight."

Harriet's father seemed satisfied. He nodded and shook Leo's hand again. Giving Harriet a quick hug and kiss on the forehead, he said, "Have fun." He slipped his gridPhone into her small purse. "In case you need to call," he told her.

Harriet was moved by the gesture. 'That's the only phone our family has,' she thought. 'He'll have to take all his calls on his datapad.'

"Thanks, Daddy, but I have my autolibrary."

Her father smiled and insisted gently, "Take the phone, it's easier to use."

Leo asked, "Shall we go?" He extended his hand.

Smiling warmly, Harriet slipped her hand into his and waved goodbye to her family. The door closed behind them as they walked away. As he led them toward the nearest elevator, Leo pulled her close and commented, "You look really great."

"Thanks," she replied as a glow of happiness rippled through her.

Harriet and Leo chatted blissfully while the elevator rose to level 1500. There, they entered the station and went to the platform to catch their skytrain. Leo slipped his arm around Harriet's waist as they stood watching the trains float into the station through the openings in the sides of the arcology. Each opening had a force field over it that kept air from flooding out of the building. Harriet watched the fields shimmer as the trains moved through them.

Soon, their train arrived. Leo led Harriet onto the skytrain and found seats for them near the front. When the doors closed, the train pulled out of the arcology and into the clear, blue sky. The skytrain's engines hummed deeply as it arrowed away. Harriet watched the arcology fall rapidly behind. 'This doesn't seem real,' she thought. 'I can't believe I'm actually going Outside.'

The skytrain got them to the Gigadome in less an hour. As they drew close to their destination, the train descended. It darted into an opening in the side of the massive entertainment complex and pulled into the station. After leaving the station, they climbed into a waiting robocab.

"Thank you for choosing Western Robotix Robocabs. Where would you like to go tonight?" the cab's robotic driver asked.

Leo gave the name of a French restaurant and the cab whooshed away. "I thought since you're taking French you might like French food," he told Harriet.

"Sounds great," she replied, her face glowing with warmth and happiness.

The Gigadome was crammed full of shops, restaurants, hotels, conference centers, and entertainment venues of all kinds. Robocabs whisked crisply along in special lanes dedicated to nothing but vehicle traffic. Harriet had never seen anything so spacious. She was mesmerized by the busyness, the crowded walkways, the constant motion, and the deluge of holographic signs and ads.

Feeling like a butterfly that had just left its cocoon, Harriet snuggled closer to Leo for comfort. He smiled warmly in return.

Arriving at the restaurant, Harriet was astonished by its opulence. It was fancier than anything Harriet had ever seen—other than Leo's home. As soon as they entered, they were whisked to a candlelit table near the back by an actual human waiter. When the waiter handed them menus, Leo looked at Harriet and asked, "I've been here before, so I have an idea what's good. Do you mind if I order for both of us?"

"Ok," Harriet replied. To Harriet's amazement, Leo immediately started ordering in fluent French. In no time, their dinner arrived. The food was amazingly good. Leo chatted happily to Harriet about something he was having done to his hovercycle that would make the bike go faster. Or make more noise. Harriet wasn't sure which, but she smiled and tried to listen. After a while, he hesitantly asked Harriet about her family again.

"What do you guys do together?"

"Mostly, we talk."

"Just talk? Together? For a long time?"

"Sure."

"What about?"

"Oh, anything. The shows we watch. Things we hear on the news. Dad complains about the taxes and politics and stuff. He always asks about what we do each day."

"Every day?"

"Sure."

Leo was incredulous. "So he pretty much knows all about your life?"

"Sure."

"Wow, you have a great family."

Harriet was pleased at his praise.

After dinner, they took another cab to one of the many entertainment venues the Gigadome contained. "This is the main concert hall," Leo told Harriet as they entered the vast arena. "Our seats are down there, near the front."

When they descended to their seats, Harriet found an odd globe resting in a receptacle in the arm of her chair. "What's this?" she asked, pointing. The object was a clear sphere slightly larger than a softball. It contained a much smaller green sphere in the center.

"That's a sonic imager. They put it there so you can participate," Leo informed her.

"Participate? In what?"

"In the concert. Everyone who sits down here gets one. When the band plays, you can use these to play along. If the band likes what you play, they turn over instruments to you for you to play by yourself. The more they like what you do, the more instruments you get to control. That's why Radioactive Waste's concerts are so popular. In the live shows, the songs are always played differently each time they perform."

Harriet wasn't sure she understood. But she took her seat and waited for the show to start.

Leo asked, "So are you having a good time so far?"

Smiling up at him, Harriet replied, "Of course. The skytrain ride was fun and the dinner was amazing."

"What about the company?" Leo queried.

"The company is wonderful," Harriet murmured, dropping her eyes. Leo slipped his arm around her and drew her closer. Just then, the lights in the arena dimmed. The crowd started to clap, shout, and whistle. Harriet gazed at the stage expectantly. Leo instructed, "Pick up your sonic imager."

"But I don't know how to use it."

"It's easy. If it lights up, it means the band is taking input from you. You'll see things inside it. If you touch the outside of the imager, the things inside react. That changes the music."

"What kinds of things does it display?"

"It's different every time. That's part of what makes it fun. You have to figure out how it works fast."

Harriet shot him a worried look.

"Just wait, you'll see," he reassured her.

The band members, each one standing on a small circular floating platform, rose through holes in the stage. The audience went wild. Harriet clapped uncertainly. Leo whistled loudly and let out a huge whoop. A large opening appeared in the stage behind the band. One of the band members danced his hands across a set of holographic controls that hovered in the air in front of him. Loud drums started beating.

Harriet watched as a strange object rose from the hole. It was made up of a horizontal circle of thick tubing. All around the inside of the circle were drums and other percussion instruments. In the center of the circle was small spherical robot with long arms. In its very human-like hands, it had a pair of drumsticks and it was playing one of the drums. The drums, with their mechanized drummer, floated upward over the band.

Doors swung open in a huge panel at the very back of the stage. Tall stringed instruments, similar to vertical guitars, floated out and danced through the air around the drums. Each instrument had robotic arms attached. On the end of each arm was a tube with a small ball on the end. The instruments' arms started to beat the little balls up and down on their strings, producing musical notes.

Harriet was astounded. She'd never seen anything like it. She watched the band members controlling the strange instruments that wafted overhead. Two of them moved to the same holographic interface as the drummer and started sending commands. From the large hole in the stage, two more circles containing percussion instruments and robot drummers emerged and glided into place around the first drum set. It became a series of circles within circles, each layer containing dozens of drums and at least one pair of mechanized arms.

Panels opened up in the high ceiling. Squares of various sizes descended through them. Harriet observed that more squares were rising through the same hole that the drums came from. The lower squares positioned themselves below the upper squares that matched their sizes. Harriet was surprised when the upper squares lit up one or two at a time and dropped what appeared to be a solid slab of light on the lower squares. When a slab hit the lower square, it produced a deep, booming musical note.

A large, cone-shaped metal tower slid forward out of the stage's back panel. Just in front of the tower were two silver tubes, one on its left side and the other on its right, which projected forward from its top and curved down to its base. A purple laser stabbed out from somewhere at the back of the arena near the roof. When its beam hit the left tube, it produced a garbled wail. A red laser fired at the right tube, letting out a thunderous screech. Rings on the metal tower lit up, each emitting a booming note.

Horns of various types ascended from beneath the stage, each blown by an accordion-like pump. Instruments similar to flutes came forward from the doors in the stage's back panel. Circular xylophones, played by robotic arms, descended from the ceiling. Violins, each with their own mechanical arms, emerged from nowhere and joined the onslaught of music.

Harriet was overwhelmed. The noise, the lights, and the constant motion were almost more than she could handle. Her quiet world in the lower part of the arcology contained nothing like this assault on her senses.

"Isn't this great?" Leo yelled to her, beaming. She could hardly make out what he was saying, but she managed a smile and a nod. Harriet saw the sonic imager in the hands of a man a few rows in front of them light up. He frantically poked his fingers at its surface. One of the drum machines changed its beat. Apparently the band didn't like the man's rhythm; his sonic imager went dim and others lit up around the arena.

With a feeling of rising fear, Harriet dreaded the possibility that her imager might light up. 'If it does, I'll make an idiot of myself in front of Leo,' she agonized.

Just then, Leo's globe glowed brightly. Harriet gazed into his imager as small planets appeared around a yellow sun. Leo quickly touched each of the planets one after the other, and zipped his finger across the surface of the globe. As he did, each planet went flying in the direction his finger traced. They bounced off of each other randomly. At the same time, several of the horns changed their tunes. Leo touched the sun lightly, turning it pink. An instrument that sounded similar to a clarinet moved toward the front of the stage. It played a wild tune. Leo pressed the sun hard, turning it a deep purple. The rings around the tower boomed out frantically.

Most of the sonic imagers around the arena went dark. Harriet immediately understood that the band was giving Leo control of more instruments. Out of the corner of her eye, she noticed that another globe was lit behind them. Glancing backward, Harriet saw Tiffany confidently manipulating the pictures on her imager. Few other imagers were still active.

Harriet blazed with anger as she thought, 'She heard Leo ask me out. She followed us here to spoil our date. That's so pathetic.'

Tiffany, seeing that Harriet was looking at her, flashed an arrogant and derisive sneer. Suddenly, Harriet's imager lit up. Inside, she saw flocks of birds swirl around the upper half. In the lower half, a school of strange and colorful fish appeared to dart through water.

Immediately, Harriet took control of the flock and guided it in smooth arcs and figure eights. The music decreased its frantic pace as she did. Leo's imager was still active. He guided some of the planets into smooth paths. More of the instruments matched Harriet's gentle sounds.

One group of instruments thundered out a frenzied wall of music. 'That's gotta be Tiffany,' Harriet thought. She noticed that Leo sent a few of his planets off at wild angles. Some of his instruments matched Tiffany's aggressive beat. Several more globes around the arena went dark.

Harriet took control of the fish, dividing them into groups and sending them in spirals, circles, and waves. She matched the movements of the birds to those of the fish. Soothing sounds wafted over the arena. Leo aligned his planets into graceful circles and his music blended beautifully with Harriet's. Tiffany's music grew increasingly harsh and wild. 'She's getting angry,' Harriet realized with pleasure.

Leo's globe went dark. As far as Harriet could tell, it was just her and Tiffany now. Increasing in her confidence, Harriet's swiftly sorted out the relationships of the pictures in the globe with the individual instruments above her.

Dolphins and whales appeared at the surface of the water, leaping and diving. She guided the sea mammals and interwove their movements with those of the fish. Grabbing one of the whales, Harriet made it leap into the air while a group of birds swirled around it. The music rose to a crescendo that drew applause from the audience.

Stars appeared across the top of her globe. Tiffany's burning wall of music ceased. Harriet glanced around her. No other globes in the entire arena were lit. Most of the band was standing on the stage, just looking at her.

Fighting to stay focused, Harriet guided the stars into gentle patterns to match the movements of the animals below. A thrill of excitement ran through her as she took total control of the music.

Harriet settled all of the images into stillness, causing the corresponding instruments to fall silent. The only thing playing was a flute that bobbed near the ceiling. Controlling a small blue bird, she input a new melody. It was a song she had composed on her flute after Jeff had been lost in the wormhole collapse. Its haunting sadness echoed through the now-subdued arena. Harriet closed her eyes as she let herself be carried away in the memory of her old and familiar grief.

The song ended and Harriet opened her eyes. To her horror, she saw that a bright white spotlight was pointed directly at her, lighting her up for the whole audience to see. The arena exploded into applause. The voice of one of the band members boomed through the arena saying, "Stand up. Stand up and take a bow."

Alarmed, she looked to Leo for guidance. "Stand up," he urged. Awkwardly, Harriet stood and received a fresh round of applause. She smiled tentatively and waved timidly. Turning to face the rear of the arena, Harriet saw Tiffany stomping up the aisle toward the exit.

Harriet sat down jubilantly. "That was great," Leo said as he hugged her.

Someone screamed. Harriet looked up in time to see a man jumping out from behind the stage with a plasma pistol. He pointed it directly at her and fired as Leo jerked her out of the way. The blast hit a woman behind Harriet, killing her instantly.

With his arm still around her, Leo lurched to the side, desperately trying to get himself and Harriet to the end of the row. They tumbled into the aisle as the man shot at them again, killing the boy next to them.

Before she knew what she was doing, Harriet scrambled to her feet and raised her arms. Pointing her hands directly at the man, Harriet exploded into flame. Instinctively, she sent two fiery columns at the man, one from each hand.

The audience, already panicking, erupted into sheer terror. Everyone was trying to flee in every direction. Harriet gazed at herself as the flames broiled around her. She was completely unhurt by the fire. Not even her clothes were singed.

The fire sprinklers came on, raining water down on everyone.

Looking back at her attacker, Harriet saw that he had been knocked down by the flames when they hit him, but he was otherwise unhurt. Nearly everything around him was on fire. He raised his pistol again.

Leo stood and faced the man on the abandoned stage. The seething mass of panicked humanity screamed its way out of every exit. Harriet saw that Leo's anger was about to explode. The temperature near him went suddenly down; Harriet could feel it in spite of the flames that engulfed her. She saw water from the sprinklers gather around him and turn into razor-sharp daggers of ice. With a wave of his hand, Leo sent the ice knives hurtling at their attacker before he could fire his pistol again. A couple of them hit the man, but bounced off him. He fired at Leo, but Leo dove out of the way.

Raising her arms again, Harriet was about to blast the man with fire again when Tiffany appeared next to her. Before Harriet could react, Tiffany let loose a blast of lightning from her hands that knocked the man to the back of the stage.

"LEAVE HIM ALONE!" Tiffany screamed as she let loose another volley.

Harriet heard Eden's distant voice say, "Attack again, Harriet. If you make him use his powers, I can force a telepathic connection to him and find out who he is." Harriet had no idea what Eden was talking about, or even if her voice was real. But she attacked as Tiffany fired off another wave of lightning.

The man rose into the air, encircled by a semi-transparent yellow sphere. Leo concentrated all of the water coming down from above into a single huge blob and froze it. He let it drop on the man. It bounced off harmlessly. Harriet and Tiffany continued their attacks. Nothing they did had any effect.

"He has a shield!" Harriet yelled.

Suddenly, a needle of energy came from high in the arena. It cut through the man's shield, barely missing his face. Looking up, Harriet saw a blond boy about her age with a tattered overcoat. He had a rifle unlike any that Harriet had ever seen. The boy fired again as the man dodged and dove through the large hole in the stage.

The boy yelled down at Harriet, Tiffany, and Leo. "Get out of here!" he shouted. "He won't stop until you're dead. Run *now*!"

Not needing to be told twice, Leo grabbed Harriet and Tiffany by the hand and sprinted for the exit. Harriet could hardly keep up. She had to pause momentarily to pull off the platform sandals.

Taking a cue from Harriet, Tiffany pulled off her spike-heeled shoes as well. Then, as fast as they could go, the three of them scrambled for the skytrain station. Jostling through the crowd, they forced their way down onto a platform. Leo dragged them onto the first train they encountered. The doors closed and the train rocketed away.

"What just happened?" Tiffany shouted. She was trembling visibly.

"How the jark should I know?" Leo shot back shakily.

Harriet was still panting from their sprint to the station. "Does anybody know where we're going?"

Seeming to get a grip on himself, Leo looked up at a display on the wall. "In exactly the wrong direction," he told her. "But we can get off at the next stop and take an express back to the arcology."

Leo looked at Tiffany and then at Harriet. "Did anyone else hear that girl talking to us?" he asked.

Harriet questioned, "What did you hear?"

"She was telling me to make that guy use his powers. What does that mean?"

Collecting herself, Harriet replied, "I think we saw what it meant. He flew in the air and had a shield of some kind. He had powers. So did we. We got them from..."

"From that jarking veech Eden of yours!" Tiffany shouted at Harriet. "*She* did this to us."

Harriet had no idea what a jarking veech was, but she imagined it wasn't a compliment. Unbelievably, Leo chuckled. "I didn't know you knew street words like that, Tiff." Tiffany scowled, but didn't reply. She plopped herself into an empty seat.

"Who ... who was that man?" Harriet asked no one in particular.

Leo shrugged and sat down. "Beats me, but he sure wanted us dead."

Harriet wailed, "But why? Why would someone want to kill us? To kill *me*? I'm nobody."

"Apparently that guy doesn't agree," Leo countered. "He fired at you first."

"Me? He wants to kill just me?" Harriet demanded, feeling sick with fear. Everything around her spun momentarily. Gripping the back of a seat, Harriet steadied herself and then sat down. After a moment, Harriet told the other two, "Maybe ... maybe you two shouldn't be near me. If he wants to kill only me..."

"Oh, quit being so noble," Tiffany shot back, sneeringly. "He fired at Leo too. The universe isn't all about you, you know."

"We'll stick together," Leo stated. The train slowed. "This is our stop. Let's get off." He strode toward a door, waiting for it to open. The girls followed.

It took only a few minutes to transfer trains, and then they were on the way back to their arcology. Harriet gazed out of the window at the lights of the city below while the train rose into the air. "What's happening?" she questioned softly.

Leo slid into the seat next to her and put his arm around her. Tiffany planted herself in the seat on the other side of Leo. He put his arm around her as well. Harriet didn't bother to be angry. Fighting with Tiffany over Leo seemed silly now.

'I need to get home,' Harriet thought. 'I need to get to Daddy. He'll know what to do.' Remembering the gridPhone, Harriet pulled it from her purse and called home. Her father answered on his datapad.

As soon as she heard her father's voice, Harriet's emotions flooded out of her. "Daddy?" she sobbed into the phone.

"What's the matter, baby girl?"

"Daddy, a man tried to shoot us!"

"What? What are you talking about?"

"In the concert ... a man with a pistol. He shot at us, but we're ok now. We're on the skytrain back to the arcology."

"Harriet, are you serious?"

"Yes, Daddy, yes," she wept. "It's real. He really shot at us. Leo saved me. Then a boy with a rifle shot at the man and we ran away. We're coming home soon. Leo's bringing me home."

There was silence on the phone for a moment. Then her father instructed, "Alright. You're on the train? I'll meet you at the station. Tell me what train you're on."

"The northbound 114, we're on the 114."

"Alright, I'll meet you at the platform. Then we can decide what to do."

"Thank you, Daddy. I love you so much."

"I love you too, baby girl. See you soon." She hung up.

Leo and Tiffany were staring at her. "What?" she asked. "Aren't you going to call your parents?"

Tiffany rolled her eyes. "My mom hasn't been home in two years. She's too busy chasing her next husband. Dad just left for Mars."

"I probably should call Angelo," Leo said. "He'll know how to contact my parents." He pulled out his mindpod and called home. When he hung up, he put his arms around the girls again. The three of them lapsed into silence as their train sped on through the night.

8

Hugh sat very close to Tanika, watching her draw. Her thick, straight hair cascaded over his arm, which encircled her shoulders. 'I don't think I've ever been this happy before,' he thought.

Tanika put the finishing touches on her drawing of the rose bush across the path from the bench they sat on. She warmed Hugh with a smile and tore the page off her pad. "It's for you," she told him. "To thank you for bringing me to the park. I don't get up here all that much."

"I come at this time every other week," Hugh informed her. "This park has always been my favorite place in the world." He turned his gaze up at the dome that arched high over their heads. 'What would she say,' he wondered, 'if she knew I was growing food in the beams that hold up that dome?' To Tanika, he said, "Can I ask you a question?"

"Sure."

"Why did you say yes to a date in the park with me? You could go out with any guy in that school. And all of them are richer than me."

Tanika seemed surprised and a little insulted. "Is that what you think matters to me? Money?"

"No! Well ... I don't know. When you haven't got much money, it seems to be a bigger deal. I mean, I can't even afford to buy you a lousy donut."

"I don't care, Hugh. I don't care about that at all."

"What do you care about?"

"You mean, why do I like you?"

"Yeah, I guess I do."

"You really don't know?"

Hugh shrugged.

"Hugh, you're the nicest guy I've ever met. You're smart and funny and sweet. You're not like the other guys I've dated. They're fussier about their looks than most girls are. I get so tired of guys that are just all about themselves. You really talk to me and you really *listen* to me. And you make me laugh."

Hugh smiled, then bashfully asked, "Tanika ... can I kiss you?"

"If you don't, I'll be mad. I've been waiting for you to kiss me all evening."

Now that he had her permission, Hugh wasn't sure he could go through with it. During his whole life, he'd been raised with the fear of punishments from the Reproductive Allowance Laws. Tanika didn't know it yet, but he was a year younger than her. He had skipped a grade two years previously. Being still 15, Hugh wasn't allowed by law to date or kiss girls yet. 'Maybe I'd better tell her,' he thought.

Before he could react, Tanika reached her hand around his head, grabbed the back of it, leaned forward, and kissed him. Hugh decided he didn't care if he spent an entire year in jail for this. It was worth it.

Hugh's autolibrary beeped. It beeped again. Tanika let go of him and he took a deep breath. When the autolibrary beeped a third time, Hugh pulled it from his pocket along with his dataglasses. He answered the call and his sister's image appeared in the air in front of him. "What?" he demanded.

"Hugh, you'd better check the news," she instructed.

"Why?"

"Your friend Harriet is on it."

"What?"

"Harriet is on the news. They say there was some kind of gunfight at the Gigadome tonight and she's involved, along with a guy and a girl. They're still talking about it. I think you'd better take a look."

Hugh hung up and connected to a free news service.

"What's the matter?" Tanika questioned.

"Harriet and Leo got into some kind of trouble at the concert tonight. My sister says they're talking about it on the news."

Tanika retrieved her autolibrary and dataglasses from her art bag and connected to a news service. They watched as the news displayed images of a man shooting at Harriet and Leo. Tanika caught her breath when Harriet burst into flames and shot them at the man with the gun.

"What in the universe?" demanded Hugh.

"Tiffany?" Tanika gasped. "Lightning came from Tiffany?"

"That man is flying!" Hugh exclaimed. "We've got to find out what's going on." He attempted to call Harriet but got no answer. "She must not have her autolibrary with her."

"Or it's turned off. Let's go to her place," Tanika suggested. "Maybe she went home after the attack."

"That's a good idea," Hugh agreed.

They trotted hurriedly down the path toward an elevator.

9

As the train pulled up to the platform and opened its doors, Harriet saw her father and mother. Running through the crowd, she tumbled into her father's arms and sobbed with relief. Her father stroked her hair and held her tightly as she trembled. "Are you hurt?" he demanded.

It took a few moments before she could compose herself enough to speak. Leo and Tiffany approached. Harriet's mother hugged her tightly.

"We're ok," Harriet told her parents as she wiped her tears. "But a man was shooting at us Daddy. Why us?"

"I don't know, but let's get you home. Then we can figure this out."

Leo interjected. "Since you're with your parents, I'm going to take Tiffany back to her place. I don't think she should go alone."

"That's a good idea," Harriet's father replied. "Call us if anything more happens." Leo nodded, took Tiffany's hand and walked away.

Harriet's father led her toward the exit. "Harriet, tell us exactly what happened."

"Richard," her mother objected, "let's get her home first. We can talk about this when she's calmed down more."

He nodded his agreement and guided Harriet into an elevator. Harriet clung to her father and held her mother's hand as the elevator descended rapidly. When they arrived at their flat, her father sat her on the couch while her mother retrieved a blanket and wrapped it around her. She placed a pillow on the couch and gently commanded, "Lie down, dear. You're shaking." Harriet let herself plop onto her side, and her mother lifted her feet onto the couch.

"Where's Ruthie?" Harriet asked.

"On a date," her mother answered. "She doesn't know anything's happened yet."

The doorbell rang. "Who could that be?" Harriet's father muttered as he answered the door.

As soon as the door opened, Hugh and Tanika burst in. Hugh spotted Harriet lying on the couch.

"Harriet!" he shouted. "It was on the news. It's on screens in public areas all over the arcology. A man shooting at you! And you were on fire!"

"On fire?" Harriet's father asked incredulously.

Pulling the blanket tighter around her, Harriet just nodded. In a small voice, she told them, "I was on fire, but I didn't burn up. Eden did it. She made us different."

"Eden?" Hugh countered. "That wasn't real. It was just a dream."

"We all had the same dream. It was real. She made us different."

Harriet's father questioned, "What do you mean, Harriet? Who's Eden? How did she make you different?"

"I don't know, Daddy. We're just different. She did something to us. She gave us these things that glowed. And now we can do things."

"Who's we? You and Hugh?"

"Yes. And Tiffany and Leo."

"Where did you meet this person?"

"She came into our dreams. But she talked to us when we were being attacked. We all heard her voice."

"From where?"

"From another planet. Far away. There's a purple sky and a big red sun."

"A purple sky? Harriet, that has to be a dream. There is no planet with a purple sky."

Hugh explained, "Its light purple. Dark lavender, really. The planet goes around a red giant. Normally, the sky would be blue, but with the increased red sunlight, it's shifted to purple."

Harriet's father was incredulous. "You believe this, Hugh?"

Hugh wagged his head in a so-so sort of way and shrugged his shoulders. "I don't know," he replied. "But Harriet and I did have the same dream. I don't know about the other two."

"Richard?" Harriet's mother asked. "What does it all mean?"

Her father paused a moment, then said, "I ... I think the dream part is just a coincidence. I don't know about the rest. I have to see it to believe it."

"Turn on your datapad," Hugh suggested. "It's all over the news."

Harriet's father warily retrieved his datapad. He connected to a news service.

"You see?" Hugh said, pointing to the pad. "They're showing it over and over. Here's where Harriet catches on fire."

"Oh dear lord!" her mother gasped.

"If you watch," Hugh continued, "Leo does some stuff with the water and Tiffany shoots lightning."

Harriet's parents observed in shocked silence. After watching the replay a few times, her father plunked heavily down into a chair. He leaned forward, placing his head between his hands. "I ... I don't know what to think," he muttered. "I don't know what to believe. I can't understand this. What's happening? *What's happening*?"

The doorbell rang several times. Someone pounded on the door. Harriet's parents didn't move. Hugh looked from one to the other, and then opened the door.

Leo shoved Tiffany into the room. Both were gasping. "He was there. He was waiting for us! He tried to kill us at Tiffany's. We've got to get out of here, now."

Harriet's father sat bolt upright. "WHO? Who are you talking about?"

Still panting, Leo answered, "The guy with the pistol. The one who was shooting at us at the concert. He was waiting at Tiffany's. He almost got us. But that guy with the rifle saved us."

Tiffany broke in, "They ran away! The servants ran away. They've been taking care of me all my life and they didn't even *try* to help me."

Leo overrode her, "I think we need to get away. My family has a shuttle at the spaceport. We have a place on the Moon. We can all go there and hide."

Sitting up, Harriet noticed the blond boy with the long overcoat standing in the doorway. "Who are you?" she demanded.

"I could ask you the same thing," he replied. "Why is that Creature after you?"

"The man with the pistol?" she queried. "How would we know?"

"Are you human?"

"Of course!"

"No," he countered. "Not 'of course.' You did things no human can do."

Harriet, Hugh, Leo, and Tiffany looked at each other almost guiltily. "Well ..." Harriet told him, "that's a long story."

"I'll bet. But if that thing wants you dead, you'd better run. It's powerful—very powerful. And it never stops coming."

Harriet's father broke in, "Who are you? What are you talking about? Who is that man?"

"It's not a man. It takes over human bodies. The only thing that cuts through its shield is this rifle." The boy opened his coat to show a rifle in a holster that was sewn into the coat's lining.

Harriet's father instantly rose to his feet and positioned himself in front of the blond boy with his wife and daughter behind. "Is that ...? It can't be! That's ... those are illegal. Since the War they've been illegal."

The boy smiled humorlessly. "Yes, I know. But they were in common use on my planet when I left. It's the only thing that can hurt that Creature."

"What is it, Richard?" Harriet's mother asked.

In a low, tight voice, her father replied, "It's a QID—a quantum implosion disruptor. They've been illegal since World War III. Getting hit by a blast from that thing is considered the most painful and horrific way to die in the universe."

"Yes," the boy replied simply. His eyes narrowed to slits as he watched them intently. His right hand seemed frozen at his side, poised and ready.

"You get out of here with that," Harriet's father hissed. "We'll call the police."

"You don't understand," the boy stated in a near whisper. "This is the only thing that can hurt that Creature. It's the only thing that can protect your daughter. If it was waiting at her condo," he jerked his thumb at Tiffany, "then you can be sure it's on the way here. It's coming for her." He pointed at Harriet. "You can't stop that thing if you send me away."

"We'll call the police!" Richard shouted again.

"The police can't protect you. They don't have the right kind of weapons. Plasma blasters won't hurt it at all. Without this rifle, that thing can't be stopped. Even if you kill its host, the human it's in, it just jumps to another host. It's fast, really fast. I've killed its host three times. Once I wounded it while it was between hosts. I think that's the only way to kill it. It has to be outside a human and I have to get a direct hit."

"I've had enough of this!" Richard stated definitely. Grabbing his datapad, he started to dial for emergency services.

A loud beeping sound erupted from the boy's pocket. "IT'S HERE!" he screamed as he stepped quickly inside and slammed the door shut. He drew his rifle and dove toward a wall. "Get away from the door!"

BOOM!

The door flew off its frame, rocketing across the room. A volley of plasma blasts pelted inside. The boy fired several times with his rifle. Harriet leaped to her feet in terror and erupted into flame. Reacting instinctively, she blindly sent a column of flame through the doorway. Tiffany, who was knocked down by the initial blast, scrambled to her feet and let loose with wildly-aimed peals of lightning. Leo grabbed the door from off the floor as if it was as light as a feather. He hurled it through the empty doorframe. Everyone else threw themselves against the walls to get away from the doorway. The boy fired again.

"I hit it!" the boy yelled. He dashed out of the room. Harriet heard his rifle discharge several more times. Smoke billowed in from the corridor. Harriet heard screaming in the corridor outside.

Looking around desperately, Harriet was horrified to see that Tanika lay crumpled against the far wall. 'The door must have hit her when it blew off its frame,' Harriet realized. Hugh was kneeling beside her, crying. He cradled her head tenderly in his hands. Outside, the boy continued to shoot his rifle. Harriet heard him run screaming down the corridor.

Harriet froze in horror. Her mother was lying on the floor beside her father. A plasma burn covered most of her right side.

"Nooooo," Richard wailed as he picked his wife up and held her tightly. "Noooo," he sobbed.

It dawned on Harriet that she was wet. The thought, 'fire sprinklers" came distantly into her mind. Slowly, she knelt down next to her mother and picked up her hand.

"Mama," she heard herself call in a little girl's voice. "Mama, are you alright? Mama?"

Everything seemed to be moving in slow motion. Nothing around her looked real. Even her father appeared to be far, far away. She took her mother's hand and put it to her own cheek. Once more, she heard her own voice softly call, "Mama?"

"LOOK OUT!" Leo screamed.

Springing to her feet, Harriet whirled around. Something was coming through the wall. It pulsated with an ugly yellowish-green glow. Tentacle-like projections waved outward from its body, as if it was seeking for something or reaching out for something to hold onto. They writhed toward Leo, but pulled back. The thing slid through the air toward Hugh, its feelers reaching. Again it pulled back.

No one moved. No one spoke.

The boy ran back into the room, saw the Creature, and fired. Moving almost too fast to see, the Creature leapt at Harriet's father and entered his body. He shuddered and quavered for a moment.

Then, in a blur, he jumped straight at the boy and knocked him down.

Harriet heard Eden's voice. "I can sense him. Your minds won't let me see him when he's out of his host, so I can't tell who he his. Get him to use his powers! It lets me find him and force a connection. Then I can control him. Quickly!"

Richard turned toward her. His face was twisted and contorted into a look of hatred that Harriet had never seen. She froze in fear.

"Don't listen to her Harriet," her father commanded in a voice that wasn't quite his. "You have to come with me. All of you do. I'll keep you safe."

Harriet took a step backward. A bolt of lightning exploded through the room, knocking Harriet's father into the corridor. The blond boy got up, grabbed his rifle and shot at Harriet's father. But Richard, recovering himself, dodged so fast that the boy couldn't hit him. He streaked away.

"NO!" Harriet screamed. "DON'T SHOOT MY DADDY!"

"It's not your father!" the boy yelled back. "Your father's dead! That thing killed him and took his body. Run! It's our only chance. RUN!"

Harriet felt Leo's strong hand clamp on her arm. He pulled her out into the corridor. "Tiffany!" he yelled over his shoulder, "Bring Hugh!"

"NO!" Harriet screamed. "No I can't go! My mom's dead! I have to wait for my dad to come back!"

Grabbing both her arms, Leo shook Harriet, but not hard. Harriet stared up into his fierce eyes. "HARRIET! Get a grip on yourself! You saw that thing. It went into your father. You saw Tiffany hit your dad with that blast. A human can't survive that. That guy's right. Your father's dead. That Creature's in him now. We've got to run! I can get us to somewhere safe."

In shock, Harriet let him drag her away. She cast a glance backwards. Tiffany was pushing a sobbing Hugh along the corridor. Everywhere the walls were burning. The front door of Harriet's flat was embedded in the wall across the corridor. Fire crews were arriving and fighting the blaze. Bodies were scattered around, blackened bodies. Police were all over the place. Lights shined at them.

"Stop!" a man commanded. "Police! Don't move."

Leo halted, stopping Harriet. Tiffany and Hugh nearly bumped into them.

"Drop your weapons!" someone yelled. "Drop that rifle!"

The blond boy stepped up beside them. His gazed flitted wildly around him.

"Drop it or we'll shoot!"

Harriet saw her father striding mechanically toward them through the billowing smoke.

Blackness engulfed Harriet. She seemed to be falling in every direction at once. There was no air in her lungs. Then suddenly, she was gasping and panting in front of Hugh's flat.

"Wha ... what happened?" she heard the blond boy ask.

Hugh stammered, "I ... I think I did that. I just wanted us to be here, and ... we were."

"Move!" Leo commanded. He took Harriet's hand, grabbed Tiffany's hand, and started them moving toward an elevator. "Hugh, come," he ordered.

Hugh hesitated, gesturing toward his flat.

"No!" Leo shouted over his shoulder. "Think of your family!"

Hugh, visibly shaken, clearly realized what could happen to his parents and sister. Erupting into motion, Hugh bolted forward. The blond boy sprinted along behind.

They boarded an elevator. "Level 1500," Leo commanded. The elevator rose rapidly.

No one spoke.

When the doors opened, they ran for the skytrain station. Harriet heard someone yell, "It's them! Those kids on the news! Call the police!"

They ran faster, panting up to the entry. Leo moved to the scanner so that it could identify him. "Central Spaceport," he told it. "Five tickets."

"Payment received," the machine replied. The entry opened.

They ran to the platform. "The spaceport trains come through every thirty minutes," Leo explained as he gazed at a display on the wall. "There should be one in eight minutes."

Harriet's heart pounded. 'Eight minutes,' she thought. 'That thing could be here in eight minutes. We could die in eight minutes.' An image of her father flashed through her mind. Nauseated, she began to tremble. Everything around her started to spin. But then she felt Leo's strong arms around her.

"Hang on Harriet," he urged. "You have to hang on. We'll get to my shuttle and I'll fly us to the Moon. We'll be safe there. I'll arrange for my family's private security company to protect us. We just have to make it to the spaceport."

Harriet let Leo lead her to a chair against a wall and settle her into it. He sat down on her right. She saw Hugh standing in front of her, crying silently.

"It killed her," he murmured. "Just killed her." Hugh sat shakily in the chair on Harriet's left. Wordlessly, Tiffany sat on the other side of Hugh.

The blond boy, a scanner in his hand, strode up and down the platform with his face pulled into a tight, blank expression. With darting eyes he inspected the few other travelers that were waiting for the train. Red lights flashed on his scanner and it wailed out a hysterical beeping.

"It's coming," he hissed at them. "We can't wait for the train. We'll have to drop down to street level. I have a zipcraft not far from here. We'll take that."

Leo rose, pulled Harriet into a standing position, and then did the same for Hugh and Tiffany. Fearfully, they skittered toward the exit.

"There he is!" called the blond boy, pointing far across the station to the entrance.

Turning, Harriet's heart stopped as she saw her father moving toward them cautiously. "Daddy," she moaned softly, hurrying behind the others.

They ran out the station exit, and scurried toward the nearest bank elevators. None were working. A red light flashed above each elevator in the bank, indicating an emergency.

"They've locked down the elevators," Hugh said. "The police are locking down the arcology! We won't be able to get out."

Harriet saw her father grinding toward them robotically. From the distance, he stared at them unblinkingly. Harriet shuddered.

"Run!" Leo commanded. "We'll use the vehicle ramps." He grabbed a massive vending machine and tossed it lightly at Richard, who dodged easily.

They sprinted away. It did no good. Richard moved fast. He was closing the distance between them. Then Hugh surged forward, but his feet weren't moving. Incredibly, he was surfing a foot above the floor.

"I just wanted to get away!" he called as he skimmed down the corridor. "I just imagined a wave carrying me away!"

Harriet wished she could do the same, and immediately she could. To her surprise, she was riding a surfboard that looked just like a real board. She glided over the floor.

"I can't do that!" Tiffany screamed, "I don't know how to surf."

Harriet pulled Tiffany onto the back of her board and willed it to move forward. With Tiffany hanging on for dear life, she shooshed speedily along the corridor, scattering screaming people in every direction. Glancing behind herself, Harriet saw Leo on a surfboard with the blond boy hanging on behind him. Richard was still following, closing in.

Drawing near to a vehicle ramp, they saw that it was blocked off. "Follow me!" Hugh yelled, turning down a side corridor. He glided toward the building's central shaft. Halting at a maintenance door, he stepped off his surfboard. It disappeared. Harriet pulled up beside him and made her board disappear, surprising Tiffany and causing her to stumble. Flushed with anger, she glared at Harriet. Leo and the blond boy arrived and dismounted from their board.

Quickly, Hugh entered a number code into the door's keypad. The door slid open and Hugh strode in with the others close behind. Hugh closed the door and locked it.

"There's an old robot ladder in here. I've had my dogbot use it a lot over the years. We can climb down it," he told them.

Leo snorted. "All the way to street level? That's 1500 floors. We'd never make it."

"You got a better idea?" Hugh challenged.

Stymied, Leo admitted, "Not really. Ok, we'll use the ladder to go down a couple floors so we can lose that ... that thing. Then we'll find another way out."

They entered the central shaft. The deep emptiness in front of them stopped them cold. Maintenance robots drifted slowly up and down the yawning gulf.

"The ... the ladder's right here," he told them, pointing. He gazed downward at the seemingly infinite drop.

"I'm not going down that," Tiffany stated, unequivocally folding her arms.

"We can't stay here," the blond boy countered. "It'll find us sooner or later."

"I'm not going down that," Tiffany repeated.

Hugh stared into the shaft. "Wait a minute," he said, "I have an idea."

As a chunky, cylindrical maintenance robot glided down the shaft, Hugh jumped. Harriet let out a yelp of startled surprise. But Hugh was safe. He was sitting on the robot's large, flat head as it descended.

"Jump on one," Hugh exclaimed. He pulled his autolibrary and dataglasses from his pocket and put them on. Seconds later, the robot he was sitting on stopped in midair.

Hugh explained, "I've hacked into the bot. I'll get one for each of you."

Harriet saw four more robots, one after the other, come to a stop. They sailed toward where she was standing and waited for them to climb on.

"Why can't you hack the elevators instead?" Tiffany queried.

Hugh shook his head. "I can't break the police security codes. They don't expect people to ride maintenance robots, so the security isn't as strong here. Besides, I've been hacking the maintenance system in this arcology for years. Just get on."

Deciding to trust Hugh, Harriet edged warily up to a robot and scooted herself onto the top of it. She looked back at Leo. "It ... it's ok," she said. "I think this will work."

Leo clamored onto a robot. The blond boy did the same. Tiffany stared down into the shaft's abyss. Shuddering, she gingerly mounted her blocky, mechanized steed.

Hugh's robot descended. Harriet reached down and held onto the robot's head as it followed smoothly after his. The others trailed behind.

The trip took over an hour. The entire time, Harriet tried to concentrate on staying still and holding on. Images of her mother lying in blood kept pushing their way into her mind. With great effort, she kept herself focused.

At last, they were at street level. Sliding off their robotic mounts, they exited the shaft through a maintenance door. The halls were empty as they wended toward the arcology's main entrances. They stepped out into a main corridor.

Police were everywhere. Hurriedly, they drew back into a side hallway.

"They've blocked all the exits," Tiffany wailed. "That thing will find us and kill us."

Leo interjected, "Maybe we should let the police take us. That would be safer."

"No. It wouldn't," the blond boy disagreed. "That thing can take over anyone's body. That means it can become a cop, the chief of police, or the highest government official. Once it does, we'd never be safe in the hands of the police. The only way we're going to live is to stay free."

Frustrated, Leo growled, "We can see the exit right over there." He pointed across the main lobby. "If only we could ... hey Hugh.

Can you do that teleport thing again? Look through the outside windows. All you have to do is teleport us over to that alley across the street there."

Hugh cringed as they all looked expectantly at him. "I … I don't know. I don't really know how I did it before. I just wanted to get away."

The blond boy said, "Well it would be a good idea if you *really* wanted to get away right now."

"I'll … I'll try."

Hugh faced the windows across the vast lobby. He closed his eyes. Nothing happened. He opened his eyes and stared. Nothing continued to happen.

Suddenly, from behind them, a woman's voice shouted, "There they are! Don't move! We've got you covered!"

Once again, blackness engulfed Harriet as she fell in every direction at once. Her lungs ached, but then there was air. They were standing in front of the alley. Harriet looked back across the street at the main entrance to the arcology. She was Outside.

They slipped into the darkness of the alley. No lights showed from the buildings around the arcology. The air was cold, damp, and dank. Everything stank like death and decay. Harriet shivered.

The blond boy pulled a small flashlight out of his coat and turned it on. "This way," he indicated. They followed after him into the oppressive darkness.

Part 2

Nightmares and Dreams

"There are a few fundamental forces that drive history. One of them is basic survival. Others are things like love, greed, power, freedom, or a longing for something better. These things can turn the flow of history into a raging storm. When such times come upon us, we naturally seek a peaceful refuge. But all too often, those refuges are nothing but an illusion or a dream." *The Human Race in the Second Age*, Hugh Benson, p. 109.

10

"We've got to get to the spaceport," Leo stated firmly as he stumbled along behind the blond boy. "Maybe we can call a hovercab."

The boy didn't answer. He guided them through long alleyways strewn with junk and trash.

'Everything Outside stinks,' Harriet thought. 'There aren't near this many smells inside the arcology.'

"I'm going to call us a cab," Leo insisted.

The blond boy stopped dead. Turning, he shined his flashlight into Leo's face. "You can't do that," he said ominously.

Defiantly, Leo shot back, "Oh yeah? Why not?"

"You told her father about your shuttle and your place on the Moon," he jerked his thumb in Harriet's direction. "That thing has all of her father's memories. It'll know that's where we're headed, so we can't go there. You can't even contact anyone you know. The Creature will find right where you are. It can hack into almost any computer system and get almost any information it wants."

Leo was shaken, but still combative. "You got a better idea?"

"Maybe. We'll see if we can use an old trick that once got me out of a tight situation. But first you guys will need money—lots of it. Then we need to get to my ship." He turned and walked determinedly on. The others followed.

"I can get us money," Leo asserted.

The boy shook his head. "Probably not. They've identified the four of you by now. They'll close down your bank accounts."

That brought Leo and Tiffany to a standstill.

"What ... what are we going to do?" demanded Tiffany. "We have to call someone. We have to get help."

Shaking his head, the blond boy replied, "You saw what could happen to your family members if you go to them for help. Is that what you want?"

No one answered. Harriet felt another wave of nausea wash over her. Her heart felt like it was being squeezed by an iron fist. For a moment, she felt dizzy with grief. She willed herself to stay focused and her head cleared.

"I'll take that as a no," the blond boy said. "If you're going to survive, you have to do it on your own. I'll help. Come with me."

With no further discussion, they followed him down several long alleys. At last, he led them into a dark, dank building. The walls dripped with slimy moisture. Mold and green slime battled with the explosion of graffiti for wall space. The oppressive hallway was lit only by the blond boy's flashlight. Guiding them toward the center of the building, the boy found an elevator with a glowing communications panel next to it. An ailing light shone above the elevator door.

"Why are we going up this elevator?" Hugh asked.

The boy replied, "We have to get up above level 10. Then we'll find an AR suite. There are gathering places online where you can do business."

Harriet was puzzled. "What kind of business could we do?"

Pointing to the autolibrary still clipped to Hugh's belt, the boy answered, "You can sell the data in that. It's worth a lot."

Hugh agreed, "Data piracy? All of the data in these libraries is encoded with the owner's ID number. If I sell the data, the police will track it back to me. They'll put me in jail."

The boy shrugged. "Sell the data or die. You choose." Hugh scowled.

The boy pressed a button on a communications panel. A gruff man's face appeared on the screen. "Wayoh?" he barked.

"We want in. We've got business," the boy replied.

"Choong," the man snapped. "10 farthings. Each."

"I'm paying," the boy told him, holding up an ID.

There was a pause. The man grunted, "Pau. Skajee 'yes' to authorize payment."

"Yes," the boy said clearly. The door slid open and the five of them went inside.

The elevator ascended to level 20. When they stepped out, they found it was completely different than the dark, moldy floors below. The wide corridors were lighted and the air was clean and warm. Even though it was late, people walked up and down along the level's main boulevard. There were shops and nightclubs with brightly-lit signs. Music came out of several of the restaurants and stores.

The boy strode up to a wall information panel displaying a map of the building. "I want to know where the nearest AR suites are," he told it.

A soft, female voice said, "There are two establishments on this level. They are indicated by the green arrows. The red arrow indicates your current position. Thank you for choosing an

Infocenter Interstellar Corporation Information Kiosk for your information needs."

The boy made a beeline for the nearest AR suite. He strode crisply inside with the others trailing behind. The fat, grungy man behind the counter eyed them suspiciously. "Vachoo Vahn?"

"AR shitai," the boy replied. "Cinco." He held up five fingers.

"Choong 15 talents each."

"AR pods yo mei yo dataport ma?"

The man's eyes narrowed. "Yo. Choong 200 farthings each."

The boy nodded and paid. The man jerked his thumb down a long hallway lined on either side with AR pods. Near the end were five empty AR pods. The boy indicated that they should get in.

Hugh hesitated. "I'm not sure we should do this," he said. Besides, even if we find someone to buy the data, how do we get it to them?"

"These AR pods have dataports on them. Didn't you hear me ask the guy?"

"I didn't understand it. What language was that?"

"It was a mix of a lot of languages. That's the way things are on the streets. Hardly anyone here speaks pure English like you do in the arcologies."

Shaking his head and clutching his autolibrary tightly, Hugh asserted, "I'm not going to do it. There has to be another way."

"If there is, you tell me what it is," the boy challenged.

Harriet could see he was right. She also saw an increasingly stubborn expression on Hugh's face.

"I'll do it," she blurted out. Harriet reached into her small handbag and pulled out her autolibrary.

"Do you all have these on you?" he asked. Leo and Tiffany both nodded. Leo pointed at his pocket. Tiffany indicated her purse.

"Must be nice," he said as he took Harriet's proffered autolibrary. He pulled a small cable from a pocket in his coat and plugged one end into the autolibrary. Stooping down, he inserted the other end into the dataport on the side of the AR pod. "Get in," he ordered as he climbed into the pod.

Harriet climbed into the AP pod next to the boy. The others lay down in the remaining pods. Harriet closed her eyes.

She found herself standing in a large town square under a bright sun shining in a clear blue sky. Surrounding her were people, shops, and amusements of all kinds. She could hear a band down a street. People were flying overhead.

"Where are we?" she asked the blond boy, who was standing next to her.

"Just a public recreation world. Lots of people use this program because a lot of things in it are free. Hang on a second." A computer panel appeared in front of the boy. He input some data, and suddenly changed into a man in his twenties.

"This is an avatar that I use a lot," the boy explained. "You guys need them too. We don't want you to get spotted."

He input some more data, and Harriet, Hugh, Leo, and Tiffany all changed into men that looked extremely similar to the boy's avatar.

"I don't want to be a man!" Tiffany wailed.

The boy shot back, "No one will recognize you. Let's go. We need to get to a teleporter." He pointed to a platform near the edge of the square and strode toward it. Harriet and the others followed.

Glancing over his shoulder at them, the boy suddenly stopped and pointed at Tiffany. "You," he said, "Blondie. Stop walking like a girl."

"What do you mean?"

"Don't bend your wrist up like that; just let your arms hang. And don't wiggle your behind. Men don't do that."

Tiffany growled, "I never asked to be a man." She stomped toward the teleporter.

The boy stepped onto the teleporter pad and said, "Let's go."

A thought struck Harriet, "Hey. We don't even know your name."

The boy hesitated. "My name is Foi," he replied.

"Foi?"

"Yes, Foi. It's short for a long Polynesian name."

Harriet stared at him. "Poly ... what?"

Hugh interjected, "Polynesian; people from the islands in the Pacific Ocean. You don't look very Polynesian. Polynesians have dark hair and skin. They're not white-blond like you."

Without answering, Foi tapped an address into the teleporter. Instantly they found themselves in a wide plaza under a dark sky. The floor glowed with a dim neon blue shimmer. Tall buildings trimmed in blue light rose above her.

"This way," Foi instructed as he walked away. The others followed.

They reached a shop run by a young woman in tight pants and a blouse that sagged off one of her shoulders. Her straight brown hair drooped down her back. "Yes?" she asked politely as they entered. When she saw Foi, her expression changed. She looked suddenly cagey and secretive. "Oh it's you again."

"Yeah. It's me. But it's not me that has business for you. It's my friend here." Foi indicated Harriet.

"What kind of business?" the woman asked.

"The same kind we did last time I was here."

She nodded. "Let me see what you have."

Foi shook his head. "Offer first. It's an autolibrary. A Dataplus Dynamics GX 1000."

Shocked, the woman hissed, "You're jarking kidding! There'll be an extra fee. The security on those things are tight."

Confidently, Foi replied, "I'm sure you can make it worthwhile for my friend."

The shopowner shot him a cautious look, cocked her head to one side, and said, "Well … maybe. How does 50,000 talents sound to you?"

Stonily, Foi replied, "50,000 talents sounds like a joke. We should leave." He turned away.

Hastily, the woman called out, "Don't be so touchy! I'm sure we can work something out. How about 75,000?"

"Goodbye," Foi answered, not bothering to turn around. He was almost to the door when the woman shouted, "125,000!"

Foi stopped, but didn't turn around. They continued dickering for several minutes that way, but Foi hardly budged.

At last the woman heaved an exaggerated sigh and said, "Ok, you win. 350,000 talents. Where do you want it deposited?"

Foi turned around and gave her a card with some writing on it.

The woman eyed him slyly. "A numbered Swiss account? My, my. Those are hard to get these days." Foi stared unblinkingly at her.

The woman instructed, "Open the connection to the autolibrary so I can download the data."

Foi handed Harriet a small, glowing sphere that he produced from nowhere. As she took it in her hand, he instructed, "You have to log onto your autolibrary. Think your username and password. Then give her this ball."

Harriet did as she was told. As soon as the woman took the sphere into her hand, a display appeared next to her in the air. Data flashed across its surface. The woman's jaw dropped as she stared at the autolibrary's contents.

"Boy, you just financed my retirement!" she exclaimed. "This thing is fully loaded."

A mechanical voice from the small sphere said, "Download complete."

A screen appeared in the air next to Foi. There was a number pad along the bottom. Foi entered some numbers and waited. Information displayed on the screen. A voice from the screen said, "Deposit confirmed." Foi nodded, satisfied.

Turning to the others, Foi said, "We need to get out of this program." He disappeared. Harriet willed herself to exit the program and opened her eyes as the door to her AR pod slid back. She climbed out. Foi was already standing next to his AR pod, disconnecting the autolibrary. He handed it to Harriet.

"You're a data pirate now," he told her. "You've got to get out of Alliance space fast. It'll be about 24 hours before the owner of that shop puts the data out for sale. Then they'll be after you."

"They're already after me," Harriet mumbled glumly. "And I haven't done anything."

Foi told her, "Your money is in a numbered Swiss account. They're very private. When we get off of Earth, we'll transfer it to a bank account on the planet Quinault. They're universally accessible and even more private than a Swiss account."

Pointing toward the exit, Foi instructed, "Let's go. We need to get to my zipcraft. It's not far." He led the way with the others trailing behind.

"Harriet," Hugh whispered to her as they walked, "why did you do that?"

"We needed the money Hugh. We need to get away. My parents are dead. I can't let that thing get Ruthie."

"I ... I'm sorry about your parents, Harriet. But you shouldn't have sold your data. Things are already bad enough for you. You should have made me go ahead and do it."

"I wasn't going force you."

"Thank you Harriet. You're the best friend I've ever had." He reached out and gave her hand a squeeze.

They rode the elevator back down to street level. Foi guided them through the smothering darkness. Suddenly, a ball of fire exploded a few blocks ahead. They flattened themselves against the nearest building.

Gunfire echoed down the streets and several vehicles with flashing red lights zipped by. There was another explosion. A male voice cursed, "I'll kill you chongpeths!" It was followed by laughter and the sound of a hovercar speeding away with its headlights off. Harriet briefly wondered what a chongpeth was, but then decided she'd rather not know.

From the direction of the fighting, Harriet heard the sound of a small child crying. Without hesitation, she ran toward the sound.

Near a building with a large burn mark in the side, she found a ragged boy about 12 years old lying on the sidewalk. He was bleeding badly. Next to him was a small girl who looked about 5 or 6 years old.

"We've got to call an ambulance," Harriet gasped as Hugh, Leo, Tiffany, and Foi drew alongside her.

Foi shook his head. "No ambulance will come here," he stated.

Angry, Harriet shot back, "He'll die if we don't do something!"

"Every day in this city thousands of people die in attacks like this or in street crime," Foi told her, irritated. "If that doesn't get them, starvation does. No one cares."

Gasping, the injured boy said, "Please. We were trying ... to get across the street to find ... work and food. My sister ... please. We don't have anyone to help."

"Where are your parents and relatives?" Harriet asked as she knelt beside the bleeding boy.

"Dead. All dead. Please ... don't let Celeste die." The boy passed out.

"Wake up!" Harriet cried. "You can't die. We can't take care of your sister."

But the boy didn't wake up. Foi drew his scanner from his pocket. "He's dead," he informed them blandly. "Let's go."

Harriet gasped, "We can't leave Celeste!"

"Yes, we can," Foi disagreed. "Like I said, thousands of people die on these streets every day. No one cares. This is the way everyone wants things. If they didn't, they'd make it different."

Without another word, Foi turned and retraced their steps up the street. Leo, Tiffany, and Hugh gazed sadly at Harriet for a moment and then followed Foi. Harriet scooped Celeste up in her arms and went after them. As they turned the next corner, Hugh asked, "What was that fight all about anyway?"

"It was probably just a fight between a couple of rival police tribes," Foi commented in an offhand way.

"Police tribes?" Hugh questioned. "What are police tribes?"

Without turning around, Foi answered, "That's who runs things out here. They're like warlords. There used to be street gangs, but the government gave them each a territory and turned them into police to keep order. They rule everything from the street level to the 10th floor of each of these buildings. That's where the real towns and governments start. Below level 10, they just let people live in the buildings if they want to. It's where they dump the poor. There's free water and sewer, but no electricity unless you pay. Most people live near the centers of the buildings because the police tribes tend to try and expand their territories. It usually leads to fights."

"That's horrible!" Harriet declared.

Foi just kept walking. After they covered a couple of miles, Tiffany grumbled, "I thought you said your ship wasn't far. These heels are killing me."

Hugh had his dataglasses so he could monitor the news broadcasts. "They've figured out we're Outside the arcology," he informed them. "They're widening their search. And by the way, it's morning."

"Morning?" questioned Harriet. "How can that be? It's still dark."

"It's only dark on the street level," Foi explained. "All around us are buildings that are 300 stories tall. The smallest building is one entire city block. Most cover ten blocks or more. The streets are too narrow to let much light get down here. It's also why it's always damp and rainy. The air down here doesn't move much."

They arrived at an ancient warehouse. Foi led them inside. There they found his small spaceship among various piles of rubble and garbage.

"You fly around in this?" Tiffany asked. "Does it actually get off the ground?"

"I came from outside Alliance space in this," Foi replied, tight-lipped. He opened the hatch and they got inside. A door on the outside of the building slid open. Foi sat down in the zipcraft's bubble cockpit and started the engines. They quickly took off and sailed upwards between the buildings until they emerged into the bright, cheery dawn. The small craft gently skimmed above the habitation complexes and merged with the morning traffic. After a couple of hours, they were near the spaceport. Foi landed.

"What is this place?" Leo asked gazing over the top of Foi's head. Harriet peeked around Leo. She saw an open field with large numbers of ruined ships.

"A ship junkyard," Foi replied absently as he typed information into his ship's computer. "We're going to find ... aah there it is. Just what we need."

He took off again, sailing low over the vast field of rubbish. When he arrived at the wreck of a medium-sized freighter, he nosed his zipcraft inside through a large, gaping hole.

"We're here," he told them as they landed.

"Where?" Leo asked.

"Some kinds of junk are not worth recycling on Earth," Foi said. "They can't make enough money off of it to justify recycling it and it's too expensive to just cut it up, process it so it's safe, and then throw it in a fusion generator. So they ship it to other star systems to be recycled there if it has more value, or dumped there if it doesn't. This wreck is scheduled to be moved in a few hours. It'll be sent with some other junked ships to Venus. From there, it'll go out of the Solar System. But we won't be with it. Once we get off Earth, I have a better way for us to travel."

Harriet asked, "So ... so we just wait here until they come get the wreck?"

"Kind of," Foi replied. "I'll run out and get us the supplies we need. Then we wait. If they notice my zipcraft, they'll just think that it's something that goes with this old wreck."

True to his word, Foi went out for about two hours. He came back with a large floating cart full of supplies in containers. "We'll hide these in one of the freighter's cabins," he told them, "and then wait inside the zipcraft."

In another hour, the wreck shuddered. They felt it rise shakily upward. The gravity gradually diminished down to zero so Harriet knew they were in space. It was her first time in zero gravity. It might have been fun under other circumstances. Hugh looked like he was going to be sick.

After another half hour, they felt the ship bump its way into the cargo bay of a megafreighter. The artificial gravity came on, making everything and everyone settle to the floor. When the cargo bay's doors closed and the bay pressurized, they opened the hatch of the zipcraft.

"Ok," Foi said, "we need to set up quarters for each of you in the cabins. I can even tap into my zipcraft's power grid and get electricity to them. It'll take a week to get to Venus, so we need to make ourselves comfortable as fast as possible. Let's get started."

It took hours. But following Foi's directions, they got power flowing to four cabins that were still functional. Foi tapped into the zipcraft's plumbing and got water to their cabins as well. They set up a kitchen in a fifth cabin. Foi had food, clothes, mattresses, bedding, and virtually everything else they needed for the trip.

When all the preparations were complete, Foi cooked them a meal. While he did, each of them showered in their own cabins' bathrooms and changed their clothes. Harriet cast aside the outfit Elena gave her.

"Somehow, I don't think I'll be needing it again," she told herself. Her heart ached as she recalled the day before. She had shined like a star at the concert. Standing there in the spotlight with Leo smiling up at her and Tiffany stomping away was the greatest moment in her life. 'So of course the universe chose that moment to reach out and crush me,' she thought bitterly. Her mind went back to the sight of her mother bleeding on the floor. Dizziness and grief swept over her.

Then she saw Celeste sitting on the mattress. The pale child was filthy, dressed in rags, and very thin. She stared wide-eyed at Harriet.

"Celeste," Harriet said gently, "I'm going to take you someplace safe. But first, we need to get you cleaned up."

Celeste let Harriet take her hand, lead her to the shower, and clean her. Wrapping a towel around the small girl, Harriet searched for some items of clothing that might fit. She found that Foi had bought a couple of outfits for Celeste to wear. 'I guess he's not quite as uncaring as he seems,' Harriet thought as she dressed Celeste.

Taking Celeste's hand, Harriet went back to the makeshift kitchen to eat. She fed the girl and then herself. They ate in silence, too exhausted and shell-shocked to talk. 'Besides,' Harriet thought emptily. 'What is there to talk about?'

After they cleaned up the dishes, Harriet went to her cabin. Her mattress lay in the middle of the floor. Foi bought them each a king-sized bed because he got a "special price" on them. Harriet suspected they were stolen. It was the largest bed she had ever seen.

Harriet tucked Celeste into one side of the bed, and then crawled slowly to the other side of the mattress. She pulled the covers up to her neck.

It was then that reality set in—the attacks, the fire, the lightning, the deaths of her parents and Tanika—everything. She could no longer block it out. The grief was devastating. Harriet clung to her pillow and let herself sob. In spite of the tiny girl next to her, she felt completely alone in the universe.

11

Hugh woke up alone for the first time in his life. He had to sit up and stare around himself for a few moments to remember where he was. Then sadness and fear swept over him. He got up skittishly. The old, nearly empty cabin seemed to cast a hard stare at him and demand to know why he was trespassing.

Hugh dressed quickly and went into the kitchen. Foi was there, cooking. "You're up," Foi said. Hugh nodded.

Watching Foi fry up some synthbeef, Hugh decided to ask, "How did you learn to do all that stuff?"

Foi paused questioningly. "What stuff?"

"Like shoot a gun. And cook. And hook into plumbing and electrical systems. All that stuff."

Foi shrugged slightly and said, "I was like you guys when I started out. I didn't know anything about taking care of myself. I had to learn or die. The universe isn't a friendly place. At least, not for me." He returned to his cooking.

"But," Hugh persisted, "how did you learn?"

Still facing the cookstove, Foi answered, "Books. My ship has a large message buffer built in for delivering mail. I used part of it to start a library. If you're going to live in space you practically have to know how to build a ship from scratch. You have to learn to feed yourself and keep yourself clean."

"Cleaning? That can't be that important."

"Wrong," For retorted. "In a small closed environment like a ship, a little mold can spread through the whole cabin and make it too toxic to live in. Plenty of people have died in ships because they were slobs. You want to know how to survive in space? Look back in history and find out how other people did it. Out here, it's not the survival of the fittest; it's the survival of the smartest. You can't be stupid and live."

There and then Hugh decided, 'I want to know as much as Foi. More. I'm going to learn everything about everything. If I'm going to get through this, I need to be able to outthink that Creature.'

Leaving Foi to his cooking, Hugh went back to his cabin and retrieved his autolibrary and dataglasses. He returned to the kitchen and sat in a chair, reading a book about space survival.

Foi finished the breakfast and dished himself up. He covered the pot and left it on the table for the others. Hugh saw Foi glance at him occasionally as he sat reading. After a while, Foi stated, "Those autolibraries have a lot of data in them."

"Yup," Hugh replied.

Foi continued, "I know a few tricks that the data dealers use. Like how to get past the security interlocks on those things."

"Mmm."

"In return for me helping you guys out, maybe you could let me have a copy of your autolibrary."

"Fair enough," Hugh replied. 'After all,' he rationalized, 'I can't let Harriet take all the risks.'

They fell silent.

Hugh finished his book and then read through two more. Hours passed. Leo came in, looking sullen, and silently ate. After a while, Tiffany also appeared and had some breakfast. She looked like she had been crying. There was no sign of Harriet.

Celeste peeked out of Harriet's room. She approached Hugh cautiously, not saying a word. When she reached where he was sitting, she simply stared at him.

"Are you hungry?" he asked. Celeste nodded. Hugh dished her some food, and placed it on the table. Wordlessly, Celeste climbed into a chair and sat happily swinging her feet as she ate.

Hugh decided to go see if Harriet was ok. He went to her cabin and knocked on the door gently. No reply. "Harriet?" he called. Silence. "Harriet, I'm coming in." Hugh slid the door open.

Harriet was awake, but still curled up in bed. She was crying and probably had been for a long time. Hugh went over and lay down on top of the covers behind her. He put his hand on her shoulder. Her hand appeared from under the covers. She grabbed his wrist and pulled his arm around her waist. He scooted closer and held her tight. Hugh heard Harriet weeping.

"Oh Hugh, they're dead! Both of my parents are dead! And that thing has Daddy's body. It's walking around in him. He's dead but his body is still walking around! It's so awful I can hardly stand it. That thing's out there, trying to kill us! Why, Hugh, why?"

Harriet's entire body shook with spasms of grief. Hugh held her tight. The only thing he could think of to say was, "I'm so sorry, Harriet. I'm so sorry."

After a while, she calmed down some. Hugh told her, "Harriet, we'll find a way to get though this. We'll find a way to kill that thing and then we'll go home. You'll see. It'll come out right."

In a small, small voice, Harriet told him, "No Hugh, it'll never be all right. They're gone. My parents are gone. What's Ruth Ann going to do? How will she live? How will *we* live?"

"Your aunt still lives in the arcology, remember? And your cousin, Savannah? They'll take care of Ruth Ann, Harriet. She'll be ok. And we have each other, Harriet. We're friends. We always have been since the day we met. I'll stick by you no matter what."

"Oh, Hugh," Harriet whispered. She turned over and hugged him tightly, then kissed his cheek.

He hugged her back, and then said, "Harriet, you need to keep up your strength. You have to come out and eat."

Hugh stood and reached down. Harriet let him take her hand and pull her to her feet. They walked together into the kitchen. Hugh dished them both some breakfast and they sat down to eat.

Foi wasn't in the room. 'Probably went back to his zipcraft,' Hugh thought. Tiffany watched the news on her autolibrary. Periodically, she gave them updates.

"We're still the big story," she informed them. "They keep showing the video of us at the concert. There's more at Harriet's flat. Disappearing in front of everyone is a big hit. The reporters can't get enough of it. They've even got pictures of us surfing away from the skytrain station. The police are looking for us. The commentators have 'experts' on their shows. Some of them say we're terrorists, others say we're criminals. Leo's parents have posted a reward for his safe return. So has my father. They ... they haven't been able to contact my mother yet."

Leo stared at the wall. No one said anything.

Foi returned.

Watching him cautiously, Hugh decided he needed to know more about what was going on. "It's time," he told Foi, "for you to do some explaining."

"Explaining?" he asked.

Leo looked up. Tiffany glanced at him questioningly.

"Yes," Hugh said, "some explaining. Like ... who are you? Why were you following us and scanning us? Why do you carry a QID rifle? Why are you helping us? What is that Creature? Where did it come from? And why are you hunting it?"

Foi eyed him suspiciously. Then he answered, "Ok, but it'll have to be a trade. You have to tell me who you are and why you can do what you can do."

"It's a deal," Hugh agreed.

So Foi began his story.

12

He landed on our world two days before my 13th birthday. Like most days after school, I was playing hoopball in the big circular driveway out in front of the small inn my mother and grandparents ran. There wasn't much traffic to our planet, so it was normal for me to stop and watch when a ship came in. Our inn was the closest to the spaceport, so most offworlders stayed with us.

When I saw his tiny zipcraft come down from the pale greenish-blue sky, I wondered, "How can a little ship like that make it all the way out here?" But the zipcraft descended and lightly landed next to one of the long white buildings at the other end of the spaceport. The pilot got out of his ship and went inside.

A long time passed. I was about to go inside for dinner when I saw the cab bringing him to the inn. I set down my hoop and my ball and went to help him with his luggage.

I had never seen anyone like him. His hair was black, not white-blond or red like most people on our world. And his skin was brown. I even didn't know there *were* people with brown skin.

"What was that game you were playing?" he asked as we went inside.

"Hoopball," I told him. "You saw me?"

"Sure," he replied, smiling. "The cockpit on a zipcraft is just a big clear bubble. You get a good view from there. Maybe tomorrow you could teach me to play."

That made me stop dead. "Play?" I asked. "Adults don't play. They work."

He looked at me oddly. "Even adults play sometimes," he said.

"I've never seen one play," I told him.

"Never?"

"Never."

He had a puzzled look on his face, but he didn't say anything else until we reached the front desk. My grandfather took his information and payment for five days. I carried his bag to his room and went to our quarters for dinner.

I didn't see him until late the next afternoon. I was playing hoopball by myself again and I turned around to see him with his arms overflowing with groceries. He set his stuff down and came over to me.

"What's your name?" he asked. My name is Foi."

"Foi?" I asked. "What kind of a name is that?" I didn't realize that I was being impolite.

"It's a short version of a long Polynesian name. Most people can't pronounce my whole name, so I just go by Foi."

"Poly-what?"

He chuckled. "Polynesian. How about showing me how to play your game?"

"Really?"

"Really."

So I showed him how to play hoopball. It was nice to play with two. I didn't get a chance to do that much because most people lived in town, not out near the spaceport like us. We played for a couple of hours. Then we rode my powerscooter over to the spaceport and took his groceries over to his ship.

The zipcraft sat alone in the hangar where it was parked. It was like any other zipcraft, except that it had two long, large tubes running from back to front along its top. "What are those?" I asked Foi. There were two smaller ones that pointed backwards and could swivel.

"Weapons," he answered. "I sometimes get attacked out there. The one on the left is a laser cannon. The other one is a p-wave disruptor. The ones in the rear are pulse blasters."

I was glad we didn't have to worry about such primitive things on our planet. I felt lucky to live in a place where everyone was reasonable and rational. We never had a need for weapons so the government took them all away long ago. Only the police and the soldiers carried weapons.

"It must take a long time to get anywhere in a ship this small," I commented as we put the groceries away. He chuckled.

"Oh yeah," Foi agreed. "This little hummer is slow, but it's mine."

"But this small amount of food can't last you your whole trip," I objected.

Shaking his head, Foi replied, "It doesn't. I go into cryostasis for most of the trip. That's the unit over there." He pointed to a long box against the back wall.

I was astounded. "You came all this way in cryo? Why?"

"I deliver mail. I've got a special, large-capacity message storage buffer for the computer on this ship. I get paid to travel out to where hardly any ships go and deliver mail. I didn't want to be a fisherman like the rest of my family. So I bought this ship and set out to see the universe."

"Why?" I asked.

"I really don't know," Foi answered. "I just felt like seeing it."

I changed the subject. "Can I see the cockpit?"

Foi smiled and replied, "Sure. But don't touch anything."

I slipped into the cockpit and sat in the pilot's chair. Looking over the controls, I warned him, "Hey, you left yourself logged into the computer. Someone could steal your ship."

"Who would want to?" Foi countered. "It's too old."

The next day was both a holiday and my birthday. I was born on First Landing Day in 100AL. 100AL is 100 years After Landing, when our ancestors landed on our world.

Foi came up to the front desk early the next morning just as I was asking my mother if we could go to town for the First Landing Celebrations. "I can't get away," she told me as she worked on the inn's books. "Why don't you ask Grandpa and Grandma?"

"They always say they're too old for such things," I replied. "They won't take me."

"I'm going to town," Foi told my mom. "It won't cost anything extra if he rides in my cab."

My mom made polite noises about not wanting to put him out. "No problem," he said. Then he told me, "I'll be in town until about four. You'll have to come back with me then. Is that ok?"

"Sure," I answered. "Most of the celebrations are done by then anyway."

So we went to town and I showed him around. He seemed like he had a good time. We stopped at a candy shop and he bought us both yenickcicles to cool us off from the summer heat. As we sat eating and watching the celebrations, he asked, "What are these made of anyway?"

"Frozen yenick, of course."

"What's a yenick?"

"A type of worm."

"A what?" he shot back, eyeing his yenickcicle as if it was poison.

"It's a giant worm with big claws and fangs. You take out their insides and make a mush from them. Then you freeze it. It tastes sweet. It's my favorite. Don't you like yours?"

"Well, I did before I found out it was made from worms."

"What difference does it make what it's made from?" I asked, "As long as it's ok to eat and tastes good, does it matter?"

He smiled and said, "A reasonable attitude. I suppose you're right." Gingerly, he started licking his yenickcicle again. After a while, he asked me another question. "The man inside the shop asked me if that was the artist's son I was with. I said I didn't know, but that you're the son of the woman who runs the inn at the spaceport. Is your father an artist?"

I hung my head in shame. "He was," I answered, but he killed himself two weeks before I was born."

Foi flushed red. "I'm sorry."

Sadly, I shrugged. "It's ok. You didn't know. He was a very popular artist from the time he was five years old. Everyone said he was a child prodigy. After he became an adult, he couldn't seem to do his art any more. My mom said he got really sad. He started doing irrational things. One day he just killed himself."

There were a few moments of awkward silence. Eventually, Foi asked, "How come only the kids are celebrating? Don't the adults want to have some fun too?"

I couldn't believe he asked me that. "Adults don't have fun," I said. "Only kids."

He was puzzled, but he accepted my answer. When we got back to the inn, he thanked me for going around with him. Then he asked, "Does your family celebrate at home? Or are the celebrations all done?"

"It's mostly done," I said. "But today's still special. It's my 13th birthday."

"Will your mom make you something special for dinner?" he asked.

"No," I shook my head. "She can't. I won't be home at dinnertime. Today's my 13th birthday."

"So what do you do, stay out and party all night?"

I didn't understand. "You're not like any adult I've ever met. You're grown up, but you play like a kid. Why?"

Foi smiled and shrugged. "Some adults are just like that I guess."

"Not here," I stated. "Here the adults work. Kids learn and play. When kids become adults, they work. They don't play. Tonight I'll go to the hospital and become an adult."

Foi was stunned. "The hospital? Why do you go to the hospital on your birthday?"

"That's how you become an adult, of course. You go to the hospital and they put you to sleep. You float in a tank of fluid for a while with tubes stuck into you. When you come out of the tank and wake up, you're a full-grown adult. You work."

He surprised me by blurting out, "You're kidding, right?"

"No. That's how it works. It's reasonable and rational. And you get to live 150 years. It's the best way. That's what our Great Leader tells us."

"Aaaah," he said slowly. "You have a Great Leader, do you?"

"Of course," I told him proudly. "He's the one who built our world out of a small band of warring colonies after the sleeper ship landed here. Now we live in peace through reason and science. He taught us a better way."

"I see. So this Great Leader tells you how to live, and you all do it."

I was glad he was finally understanding. "Right," I assured him. "He tells us what to do and we do it. It's the only rational way to live."

"I think I need to check out," he told me suddenly.

"Check out?" I asked. "I thought you were staying five days."

"I was," he replied. "But I just realized I need to go. Right now." Abruptly, he went inside, almost running to his room.

My grandfather and I were just about to leave for the hospital when he came back out with his bag. He saw us standing at the desk, dressed for going into town.

"I'd like to check out," Foi said hesitantly.

"You're leaving early?" my grandfather asked. "Ah well, I hope we see you again sometime."

My grandfather checked him out, and then we waited for my mother and my grandmother to finish getting ready. Foi sat at the other end of the lobby waiting for his cab. While we sat, I asked, "Grandpa? Is there another way to become an adult besides getting the Operation?"

My grandfather turned pale. "Why are you asking such a thing?"

"I ... I don't know," I stammered. "I just wondered, that's all. I didn't mean anything by it."

That only seemed to make him angrier. "Who put such ideas into your head?" he hissed. "Who?"

I couldn't help it. Without thinking, I glanced at Foi. My grandfather looked at him with narrow, cruel eyes. "Stay here," he commanded as he stood and when into the inn's office.

Within minutes, a small aircraft descended from the sky and landed in our large, circular driveway. A man in a grey uniform got out. I could see he was a Checker for the State. He entered and said, "I'm here to check that everyone is in compliance." Looking at my grandfather, he asked, "Is this the boy?"

"Yes, Sir. Thank you for coming so quickly."

The Checker strode up to me and told me, "You are not in compliance. This is not rational or reasonable. You will be adjusted." He drew out a disruptor pistol. Just as he fired, Foi exploded into motion and leaped between the Checker and I. He was dead before he hit the floor.

My grandfather, my grandmother, my mother, and the Checker stood as if frozen. They stared at Foi, lying lifeless on the floor, his body dissolving. Finally, the Checker said, "That was irrational."

"What shall we do?" my grandfather asked. "He was an off-worlder. Won't that cause problems?"

The Checker appeared puzzled. "I don't think so. It seems to me that it was his fault, not ours. He deliberately put himself in the path of the disruptor blast. Either he was out of his mind or it was an accident. For the sake of simplicity in dealing with off-world authorities, I rule his death an accident. It will be reported as such."

The adults agreed among themselves that this was a rational solution.

"And now," the Checker continued as he turned toward me, "We must take care of this boy." He raised his disruptor.

"Wait!" I shouted, terrified. "I didn't mean anything. I want to become an adult. Take me to the hospital. Please!"

The Checker shook his head sadly. "I'm sorry. I sympathize with your position. But once someone is out of compliance my duty is clear. Adjustment is the only rational thing to do."

I completely panicked. I stumbled backwards, bumping into the front desk. At that time, our planet still had a mail service that carried real paper letters. When I threw out my arms to catch my balance, my right hand came down on my grandfather's long, fancy letter opener on the desk. Instinctively, I grabbed it.

Knowing that the Checker was about to fire, I threw the letter opener at him. It hit him dead in the throat, sinking in deeply. I was horrified. He clawed at his throat trying to get the letter opener out. Falling to his knees, the Checker struggled for breath as his blood gushed out over the carpet and my grandmother's antique furniture.

I was frozen. I couldn't do anything but watch him topple backwards. Everything was happening so slowly. My grandfather stood rubbing his chin. My grandmother walked up and stared at the Checker's body thoughtfully. At last she commented, "I'm going to have trouble getting that stain out of the carpet."

Nodding, my grandfather told her, "And I'll probably have to call another Checker. This is very non-compliant behavior." His eyes settled on me.

"Grandpa," I pleaded, "it was an accident. I didn't mean to hurt him. Please don't let them kill me."

"I'm sorry," he sympathized, "but that would not be rational or reasonable behavior. I'm sure you see that it's best to be in compliance."

"I can be in compliance!"

He smiled gently and replied, "It's too late for that. Don't worry; we can get this taken care of quite quickly. Just wait here." He went into the office behind the front desk.

I felt like someone had dumped ice in my veins. Bolting for the door, I ran outside and hopped onto my powerscooter. I started it up and shot away at full speed. Not knowing where I was going, my eyes fell on the spaceport's hangar. An idea flared into my mind. I headed for Foi's ship.

When I reached the hangar, I tossed the scooter aside and climbed in the zipcraft.

"Foi?" the zipcraft's computer asked.

"Yes," I replied. The small computer wasn't smart enough to detect my lie. Because Foi was still logged in, it accepted me as him.

"Take me to Capital City," I ordered.

"Would you like me to engage the autopilot?"

"Yes! Take off now!"

"Have we received clearance?"

"Yes! Go! Go!"

Luckily, the hangar doors were open. The ship lifted slightly, floated outside and swooshed into the sky. My family didn't live far from Capitol City, so the trip took only a few minutes. From the bubble-like cockpit I could see the Great Leader's palace. I instructed the computer to land there.

As the ship glided gracefully downward, I saw the Great Leader himself walking toward the wide main stairs of the palace with his Wise Advisors. I had the computer land the ship a few yards ahead of him. The small group froze as the ship descended and armed guards ran toward us. I clamored out of the ship as fast as I could and dashed to the Great Leader. Dropping down on my knees, I called out to him, "Great Leader, you who protect and guide us, help me please."

The Great Leader stood like a statue. I suppose I was the first person in the history of our planet who ever did anything like this. When he didn't say anything, I kept going.

"Great Leader, a stranger stayed at our inn. He told me about other ways to grow up on other planets. I didn't know questions like that weren't allowed. My grandfather called a Checker and the Checker wanted to erase me. Please, Great Leader, please let me grow up. Take me to a hospital now so I can become an adult."

I waited hopefully, sure that the Great Leader would understand. I knew he would be merciful.

Gazing at me, the Great Leader said to the guards who were now standing next to him, "Kill him."

It was like lightning hit me. I sprang toward the Great Leader just as the guards raised their guns. I don't know really what I was trying to do. I think I was just going to grab onto his feet and beg for mercy. But one of the guards fired, and hit the Great Leader instead of me.

The Great Leader fell backwards, his body slowly dissolving into an angry, boiling red goo. Then ... then something came out of him. Something yellowish-green and glowing harshly. Not quite pure energy, but not quite solid—something in between. It had a squid-like head on the top with tentacle-like arms below. There was a band of flashing colors around the middle of its head. The band turned red, then orange.

The thing floated in the air above where the Great Leader had been. No one moved but me. Somehow I sensed that the thing was evil. To this day, I don't know why, but I scrambled to my feet and yanked a rifle out of the hands of one of the stunned guards as she stared at the creature in the air.

I fired at it. Its entire body flushed fiery red as it recoiled, looking like it was wounded. It leapt at one of the Wise Advisors, passing right into his body. The advisor stumbled momentarily, appearing disoriented. Then with a fierce, cold gaze, he turned his attention to me.

"I'm the Great Leader now," he declared. "Kill that boy."

No one moved. One of the Wise Advisors stated, "We have no guidelines or protocols for replacing the Great Leader. We will have to determine them ourselves and then execute them accordingly. Until then, it is clear that all decisions must be reached together. We are the Quorum of Wise Advisors. We must act as a unified group for now. This is the reasonable and rational thing to do."

"Fine, I propose that we kill the boy."

"As Senior Advisor, I will take the motion under consideration. Let us repair to the Council Chamber to discuss the motion and take a vote."

"No! No! Kill that little monster!" He stomped to a flabbergasted guard and jerked a rifle from his hands.

I didn't wait; I shot directly at his face.

He dodged far faster than a human being should be able to. I missed him completely. I shot again. He zipped away, moving like a streak. He was little more than a blur. But I got off one more lucky shot. I hit him dead on and the thing came out of him. Without pausing, it flew away.

I turned and ran back to the zipcraft, still clutching the rifle. Pulling the hatch closed, I screamed at the computer, "Get me out of here! Get us into space!"

Obediently, the ship sailed into the sky. It took me three months of dodging the cops to get out to where interstellar traffic left our system. Our star system doesn't have its own hypergate. We have to wait until someone else uses their hypergate to open a wormhole to our system and go through that. The wormhole only opened once every other month. When it did, I was there. I attached my zipcraft to the docking port of a large freighter without their knowing it. My ship looked like one of their shuttles. When we got through to the other side, I detached and went my way.

Since then, I've used Foi's name, identity, and ship. I found that he had been traveling for nearly eighty years, spending most of his time in stasis. I've done the same. All this happened thirty-nine years ago. But for me, it's only been four years.

I've been chasing the Creature ever since I first encountered it. It took over another host and left our planet. Recently, I traced it from the Normandy system in French space as it went to Earth. That was right after the all those news stories about you two. I couldn't understand why it suddenly left Normandy. I guess now I know why. It came here to kill you.

13

Foi stared intently at Harriet, Hugh, Tiffany, and Leo.

Harriet asked, "Thirty-nine years? You've been chasing that thing for thirty-nine years?"

"Yes," Foi affirmed.

"How did you get money to live on?" Leo demanded.

"I stole it."

"You STOLE it?"

"Of course," Foi answered calmly. "I'm far better with computers than the real Foi was. I was able to hack into the government accounts for my home world and take all the money I needed. I live on that."

His admission was so casual and frank that the others simply stared at him in surprised silence.

"What?" he asked. "I'm doing them a favor. I'm hunting down that thing. It stole everything that was human from the people of my world. Now I'm making sure it doesn't do that to anyone else. I *should* be paid for that."

For the first time since the attack, Leonardo smiled. "Foi," he announced, "You're a complete freak. But you're just the kind of freak I like."

Harriet hit Leo on the arm. "Don't say that," she objected.

"Harriet," Leo replied gently, "We've got an alien thing running around human space doing all kinds of nasty things to the human race. It killed a bunch of people, chased us away from the only life we ever knew, and it's hunting us. It's up to us to kill it. Right now, I'm not going to worry about Foi stealing from a government that performs operations on kids to make them into almost mindless robots."

Turning away, Harriet flushed with anger. "I suppose," she grumbled in reply. But Hugh could see that she was still disappointed with Leo's words. Turning back to Foi, Harriet asked, "Why does that thing want to kill us?"

"That's pretty obvious," Hugh answered instead. "It considers us a threat."

Foi nodded. "Which brings me to my question; how can you do the things you do? Like the lightning and the fire. And that teleportation trick really kills. I can think of a lot of times when I could have used that."

Harriet answered, "It all started with a friend of ours."

"Jeff," Hugh broke in.

"Yes," Harriet agreed. She explained about their farm on the ramps inside the dome's supporting structure. "We had a group of thirty-seven friends. We all grew food there together to make money to buy lessons. We were trying to get into better schools."

Tiffany emitted a scornful sound, causing everyone to turn and look. But she ignored them and continued to watch the news.

Irritated, Harriet continued, "One of the people in our group was a girl named Madison Burke. She and Jeff and Akio all colonized about the same time, just after school ended. Madison and Jeff were on different ships, but they were both in the wormhole that collapsed two years ago. You heard about that?"

Foi nodded.

"A few weeks later, I had a dream. I saw Madison and some guy. She said that they'd merged with aliens from another universe. Energy beings, she said. Hugh was in the dream too. She touched my forehead, then both of my palms. When she did, these glowing things appeared and went inside me. She said I'd be able to do things. Then she said that the human race was in danger. She told us to come find her on the planet she's on. When I woke up, I just ignored it because I thought it was all a dream. Then a week or so before the attack, I had another dream about Madison. Hugh, Leo, and Tiffany were all there. I found out later that we all had the same dream, but I still didn't believe it was real."

Foi, clearly doubtful, asked, "And now you do?"

"I suppose," Harriet replied. "We've all heard her voice talking to us."

Foi's eyes widened. "When?" he demanded.

"During the attacks," Harriet replied. Hugh and Leo nodded.

"You mean it can read your minds?" Foi asked.

"Kind of," Harriet told him. "She says she can connect to us telepathically. Not all the time, because we can break the connection. I saw Leo do it." Hugh nodded his agreement. "When we use our powers—that's when she seems to be able to connect with us the best," Harriet explained.

"It's not looking at us now?"

Harriet shook her head, "No. I don't think so. Now that I look back, I realize that I could feel her connection to me when she was talking and when we were using our powers. I think if she were watching us, we'd know." Again, Hugh and Leo nodded.

"How do I know you're telling the truth? Maybe you're aliens too," Foi postulated.

Hugh countered, "How do we know you're telling the truth? Maybe that story was completely made up and you're working with whatever's chasing us."

"I wouldn't hide you if I was," Foi retorted.

"Well we have as much reason to trust you as you have to trust us. It works both ways," Hugh asserted.

Foi walked to the doorway and stood gazing out for a few moments as he leaned against the doorframe. The silence was broken by Hugh. "By the way, how does your scanner detect when that thing's near?"

"Brain patterns," Foi muttered. "When it's in a human, the host's brain patterns are different than a normal human's. The scanner is programmed to sound an alarm when it detects the Creature's brain patterns. That's why I was scanning you. I wanted to see if you had the same brain patterns as that thing."

Turning to Hugh, Harriet asked, "Do you think you could make one of those Hugh?"

"Yeah, Hugh replied. "I just need a scanner and the pattern to look for. Next chance we get, I'll make one for each of us."

Leo broke in, "What I want to know is where we can get some of those QID rifles."

Foi looked at him sharply, "The only place I know is on my home planet, New Caledonia."

"New Caledonia?" asked Leo, puzzled. "In Scottish space?"

"No," Foi replied, "Our planet has the same name. We were the descendants of Scottish colonists in sleeper ships that left before the Alliance was formed. My ancestors left Earth in 2432. Our planet is a Frontier World way outside Alliance territory. We named our system Scottshaven. On your star maps, our system is labeled Delta Sigma 8."

"What I want to know," Tiffany broke in suddenly, "is what we're going to do now? If our families can't protect us and the police can't protect us, what are we going to do?"

Hugh saw Harriet slump in her chair at Tiffany's mention of their families. He didn't want to let her fall into hopelessness again, so he quickly said, "The way I see it, we've got two choices. We can run away and hide, or we can fight that thing and kill it."

"Or we can do both," Leo countered. "We need time to regroup. We should go someplace where we can make some preparations and plans and get some of those QID rifles. Then I say we track that thing down and kill it."

"I don't think we have to track it down," Hugh speculated. "I think if we just don't hide, it will come to us."

Leo agreed, "You're probably right."

"That doesn't sound like much of a plan to me," Tiffany snapped. "Where are we going to go? Where are we going to get QID rifles? What about money? What we've got isn't going to last long if we keep tramping around space. We can't hide in wrecks every time we need to go somewhere."

"I know where you can hide for a while," Foi said. "The relatives of the first Foi live on planet Nason in the Gamma Epsilon 21 system. It's out in the Edge Worlds just beyond Alliance space. I tracked them down to tell them what had happened to him. They moved there ... after he left. Every time I've gone there, they've treated me good. They act like I'm the real Foi."

Hugh agreed, "Ok, we go to planet Nason. But how do we get there? Tiffany's right, we can't keep traveling in wrecks."

"I can take care of that," Foi answered. "But it'll cost you some money. Actually, it'll cost a lot of money."

'Hmm,' thought Hugh, 'I don't know if I like the sound of that.'

14

It took a week to get to Venus. Harriet passed the time by learning as much from her autolibrary as she could and by playing with Celeste, who warmed up to her quickly. Everyone took at least one turn cooking, even though Leo had to yell at Tiffany to get her to do it. But Harriet noticed that Tiffany was pleased when everyone complimented the result. After that, she didn't complain as much when she was asked to do chores.

When they reached Venus, the megafreighter dumped the wreck they were in, leaving it floating in orbit. "Other freighters will dump more junk here," Foi told them, "and when the clump gets big enough, it'll all be hauled to another system."

They waited until the megafreighter slipped away, and then jetted out of the wreck and down to the planet's surface.

"Venus is hot," Tiffany complained when they landed and stepped outside the zipcraft. "And it smells bad." The others ignored her.

As they rode a taxi from the spaceport into the city, Harriet thought that Venus pulsed with life. Everything was clean and bright. The buildings were slender compared to those on Earth and they weren't so high, so sunlight got down to the street. Busy people hurried briskly along the wide sidewalks. The broad, grass-covered streets flowed with hovercars. Holographic billboards floated by flashing advertisements.

"What are those black things people wear on their faces?" Harriet asked the others. "They look like dataglasses."

"They're sunglasses," replied Foi. "People wear them to protect their eyes from the sun when it's too strong. They're common here. Hats are too."

Leo said, "I think we should all buy hats and sunglasses. It'll help keep us from being recognized."

Harriet observed that Foi was right. Most people wore sunglasses. And almost all of the women wore big, floppy hats. So when they got out of the taxi, Harriet quickly bought herself a big hat and some sunglasses. She also bought a hat and sunglasses for Celeste, who was far too pale to handle the sunlight well.

Tiffany put up a fuss. "I'm not wearing them," she objected, "they make me look old." But Leo insisted. Eventually she was able to find a hat she liked. Leo picked out sunglasses for her. After that, she was so nice it almost made Harriet sick. 'Boy,' Harriet thought, 'a little shopping sure makes her easier to be around. Or maybe it was the attention from Leo.'

"We need to get rid of the little girl," Foi stated as the stood on the street outside the shop. "We can't take care of her."

Harriet cradled Celeste protectively. "I won't just dump her on the street," she hissed. "Celeste's lost her parents. She's lost everyone."

Gazing at Harriet woodenly, Foi told her, "I know a place for her."

They hailed a cab and went to a large building that looked like a school. "This is a church orphanage," Foi explained. "They'll take good care of her. I'll take her inside, Harriet. You might be recognized."

Harriet hugged Celeste tightly and said, "Celeste, Foi is going to take you to some people who will take good care of you. You'll be happy here. Can you go with him?" Celeste nodded.

Taking Celeste's hand, Foi led her inside. He returned a few minutes later alone. "It's time for us to get out of Federated Alliance space," he said matter-of-factly. Harriet sighed and glanced back at the orphanage once more as they rode away in a robocab.

Foi had them withdraw a large amount of cash from the money that Harriet had gotten for selling the data. He stuffed it into several large pockets on the inside of his coat. Satisfied, he led them down a side street and into a small store selling used robots. He sauntered up to the old man at the counter and offhandedly said, "Sirsen Slate sent me. He said you could get me something good."

The man eyed him narrowly. "I don't know no Sirsen Slate. You wanna robot? I got good deals."

Foi glanced around the room, not seeming to look at anything in particular. "I see many fine robots here. But they all look so … artificial. Can you show me something that looks more natural? Sirsen Slate highly recommended your services in that area. He said you were the best."

"I keep tellin' ya, I don' know no Sirsen Slate."

"That surprises me," Foi told the man as he inspected the sleeve of his tattered overcoat. He brushed away some non-existent lint. "He said he was your regular customer. Didn't he, Mary?"

Realizing that Foi was addressing her, Harriet played along. "Yes. I distinctly remember him saying that."

"I ain't got time for a buncha kids," the shopowner growled.

"Hmmm," Foi sighed, seemingly disappointed. "That's too bad. All four of my friends here are interested in your merchandise. They're willing to pay for the very best you have."

The man perked up. "All four?" He eyed them suspiciously. "Ya got money? I only take cash."

Foi showed him the cash. After another suspicious glance, the man pointed at a doorway and said, "In the back. The wife will show ya what you're looking for."

They filed through the door and down a long hall. At the end of the hall was a dimly lit room with a large mirror. A saggy, potato-like old woman with ratty hair appeared from a doorway wearing a faded green dress. "So what are we talking here?" she asked without any preamble. "Just faces or the whole nine yards?"

Foi replied, "Faces, hands, and IDs."

"It won't fool spaceport scanners, if that's what you're up to," she said bluntly.

"We're on our way out of town," Foi replied. "We'll be taking a long nap."

That seemed to brighten the woman up quite a bit.

"Gotta be careful," she grunted as she waddled to a cabinet. "Buncha kids comin' in here. Don't know what to think. But I called Slate. He vouched for Blond Boy there. And since you're takin' the big sleep, I guess they can't trace nuthin' back here."

The woman pulled out a hand-held scanner, and rapidly scanned Leo, Tiffany, Harriet, and then Hugh. "I got just the thing," she told them. "You, boy," she pointed a thick finger at Leo. "Take your shirt off."

Taken aback, Leo glanced questioningly at Foi, who nodded. Hesitantly, Leo pulled off his shirt. The stout woman retrieved a box from a cabinet. Opening the box, the woman took out what looked like the skin from someone's head and arms. She handed it to Leo, who slipped it over his head, hands, and arms. Instantly, the fake skin reacted by fitting itself to Leo. Leo was startled, but he stayed calm.

Where the false skin covered his head, arms, and hands, Leo looked like a 40-year-old man. It was perfectly fitted to every contour of his face. Harriet could see that the eyes were still Leo's, but that was about it. Leo now had a thick mustache and thick grey hair.

Leo examined himself in the mirror. "Not bad," he said. "Not bad at all."

The woman objected, "Waddya mean 'not bad?' These are the best plastifaces you can find!"

"It's just an expression," Leo told her. "It's really good. My own mother wouldn't know me." That satisfied her.

Tiffany commented, "His voice is different."

The woman replied, "There's a distorter in the neck that sits against your throat. It adjusts your voice so that you sound the same age as you look. Can't have a bunch of kids' voices coming out of old faces, ya know? People would know right away you're wearing plastifaces."

The old woman turned and pointed to Harriet. "Red," she said, "You're next."

Harriet stepped cautiously toward the woman, who handed her a box. "Just got this in yesterday. It'll fit real good on you. Go in there and change." She pointed to a door on the other side of the room.

Leo asked huffily, "Why didn't you tell me you had a changing room?"

The woman cackled, "I don't get to see young guys as good lookin' as you. Of course I wan' you to pull off your shirt here instead of in there." Her hacking laugh seemed to slap him across his face. Leo smoldered quietly.

Harriet pulled open the door the woman indicated and found a small, dirty bathroom. She took the box and went inside. When she emerged, she demanded, "What's this? I'm old." She angrily gazed in the mirror. There stood a woman of at least 65 in her clothes.

The woman cackled again. "Hey, you wan' to change your looks, they're changed. You're his mother now." She pointed at Leo. "You," she said, pointing to Tiffany, "take this." She handed Tiffany a box.

When Tiffany emerged from the bathroom, she was an attractive 40-year-old woman. She smiled at her reflection.

"How come you didn't give me that one?" Harriet demanded.

The woman retorted huffily, "The one you got fits you better. Don't complain. Somebody's got to be the mother."

Tiffany smirked and said, "You'll need new clothes, Mother. Those are *definitely* not you." Harriet turned away and fumed silently.

"You, Skinny," the woman commanded pointing at Hugh. "Put this on." She plunked a box on the floor. "Stay in here, go in the other room, I don't care." She turned away.

Hugh angrily snatched up the box and stomped into the bathroom. He emerged moments later with the face and hands of a 65-year-old.

The old woman passed out their new IDs. "You're Francis and Jane Kronkmeyer," she told Leo and Tiffany. "And you two are Henry and Lilly Kronkmeyer, his father and mother. You got what you want, now pay." Foi handed over the cash. Harriet hated to see so much money disappear in one transaction.

Outside on the street, Foi told them. "Tiffany's … uh … Jane's right about your clothes, Lilly. Go buy something that looks like what older people wear. You just need one or two outfits. You can buy more when we get to Nason."

Foi pulled out a very old-fashioned gridPhone and instructed, "Hugh, I mean Henry, I'm sending my number to your autolibrary. You guys go get yourselves a hotel and call me to let me know where you are. I've got to go back to the spaceport and arrange for our passage and for my zipcraft to be shipped."

"Why don't you just fly it to Nason?" Hugh asked

Foi shook his head. "This small ship goes slow. It would take me years. Somehow, I don't think we have that kind of time." So saying, Foi hailed a cab and left.

Tiffany asserted, "If we're going to get a hotel, I want something nice."

Nodding, Leo agreed, "Yes, nice but not expensive."

"I think I've found someplace good," Hugh said as he scanned through hotel listings with his autolibrary and dataglasses. "And it's not too far away."

They took a cab to the hotel, which was next to a giant shopping mall. Of course, Tiffany wanted to go there immediately, so they all went together. Harriet soon selected a couple of outfits for herself and Hugh to put on when they were wearing the plastifaces. But she also bought herself something fashionable and nice. 'For when I'm not wearing this awful old face,' she told herself. They all bought suitcases to put their clothes in.

Tiffany, of course, bought more clothes than she needed. Leo picked out a nice suit and some casual clothes. "This is something my dad would wear," he commented.

Foi returned and booked a room in the same hotel. They decided to treat themselves to an expensive dinner. As they ate, he told them, "It's all set. The four of you will be shipping out tomorrow as cryopassengers on a ship called the Bajan. My zipcraft will be in one of the cargo holds and I'll use my cryostasis unit inside."

Tiffany moaned, "Why do we have to go in cryostais?"

Irritated, Foi explained, "First, it's a long trip. We'd waste a lot of money on food and stuff if we weren't in cryostasis. Second, it's a long trip and I don't want to have to listen to you whine all the way there." Tiffany bristled, but Foi ignored her and continued, "Third, they don't scan cryopassengers at the spaceport."

"What do you mean?" Leo wondered. "You always get scanned at the spaceport."

"Not here. Not if you're a cryopassenger going outside Alliance space."

Harriet asked, "Why?"

Foi said, "The planetary government of Venus decided a long time ago that they don't want to become as overcrowded as Earth. Unlike Earth, they allow cryopassengers here so that even the very poor can leave. If you're being shipped out of Alliance space, they don't bother to do background checks or scan for people wearing plastifaces. Anyone wanted for crimes or with unpaid debts can run away to someplace outside Alliance space by putting on a plastiface and leaving as a cryopassenger. They get rid of the poor and the criminals that way."

"That's just plain mean," Harriet told him. Foi shrugged and continued eating.

When they returned to their hotel rooms, the five of them gathered together to review their plans for the next day. Afterward, Harriet said, "I want to call my sister before I go."

Foi disagreed, "You shouldn't do that. The Creature is really good with computers. It can trace your call. It'll find out right where we are. You wouldn't want it to be there waiting when we arrive on Nason, would you?"

"We can record video mail," Hugh countered. "And set it for a time delay. It takes 5 months to get to Nason. We'll set the messages to be delivered in 5 months. By the time anyone hears from us, we'll be completely out of Alliance space."

Agreeing, Foi said, "That works. Record your messages and forward them to my zipcraft. It's got special equipment and programs for delivering mail. I'll set it to stealth route the messages into a computer that I know of on Callisto, one of the moons of Jupiter. They'll look like they came from there. That way, no one will ever be able to trace them back to this hotel."

"Can we send money too?" Harriet asked.

Dismayed, Foi answered, "Sure, I can package an electronic funds transfer into the message. But you should hang onto your money."

"My sister needs some way to live," Harriet told him. Foi shrugged.

Hugh said to Harriet, "If it's ok with you, I think I'm going to send my family enough money for some tickets to Cambridge." Harriet nodded.

They left the restaurant and returned to their hotel suites. Harriet went into the bedroom of one suite while Hugh used the living room.

15

"Hi Ruthie. I'm sorry I haven't been able to contact you sooner. I'm recording this a week after the attack. Please don't let anyone know you've heard from me. By the time you get this, five months will have passed. I know they've said bad things about us on the news, but don't believe it. We're not terrorists or criminals."

"Ruthie, someone's trying to kill us. He's very, very dangerous. I ... I had to run away so you wouldn't be killed like Mom and Dad. I know the news said Dad was seen leaving the arcology, but don't believe it. That isn't Dad. Don't go near him. No matter how much he looks and acts like Dad, he *isn't* Dad. You've *got* to believe me Ruthie. He *killed* Mom and Dad. If you get near him, he'll kill you too. Just stay away from him, Ruthie, just stay away."

"I don't know when we'll be back, Ruthie. I don't know if we can ever come back. I ... I just want you to know that I love you so much. Please find a way to have a happy life. I know that's hard with Mom and Dad dead. But please try. I'm transferring some money to you to help you live. Please don't tell anyone. I'll send you another message later if I can. Goodbye, Ruth Ann. I love you."

16

Harriet turned off the recorder. She forwarded her message to Foi's ship and then went into the other room. Hugh was just finishing his message to his family. She could see that he was crying and realized that her face was covered with tears as well. When Hugh was done, Harriet hugged him tightly.

"We'll find a way out of this, Hugh," she reassured him. "We'll find a way."

Not long afterward, Tiffany came over from the other room and Hugh left. Harriet told her, "This couch folds out into a bed. One of us can sleep here and one in the bedroom. How do you want to decide?"

"I'm taking the bedroom," Tiffany stated flatly.

Irritated and exasperated, Harriet glared at Tiffany. But then she decided, 'This isn't worth fighting over.' So she said, "Fine, Tiffany. Be that way. Take the bedroom." She retrieved her suitcase from the bedroom and Tiffany hauled hers in.

As Harriet changed into pajamas and got into bed, she muttered to herself, "We had better find a way out of this soon or I'll strangle that girl before all this is done."

The following morning, wearing their plastifaces, they met Foi in the lobby and went to breakfast together. After they ate, they checked out of the hotel and rode a taxi back to the spaceport.

"You're on your own from here," Foi told them. "I have to fly my zipcraft up and meet the Bajan. You guys take the space elevator to Gateway 5 and board the Bajan there." He left them at the spaceport entrance.

"How come our spaceport back home didn't have a space elevator?" Hugh wondered out loud.

"It wasn't big enough," Leo answered as he lifted his and Tiffany's suitcases. To Tiffany he grumbled, "What have you got in here 'Jane?' It feels like you loaded this with rocks."

"I need everything in there," Tiffany retorted. "Besides, we should have gotten suitcases that float along behind you and are smart enough to know how to follow you."

"Those are way too expensive for simple folks like us, Janie dear," Harriet said.

Dripping with sarcasm, Tiffany sighed and replied, "Oh thank you Mommy Dearest. I hope you and Father aren't bothered by this heat. You're not as young as you used to be." Blue sparks danced across Tiffany's hands.

"Cool it Tiff," hissed Leo. "The last thing we need right now is for you to cut loose with a blast of lightning."

"I didn't mean to," Tiffany wailed. "I got mad and my hands just started to spark."

Leo cut off further discussion, "Let's go. We need to get up to our ship. Father, could you carry Mother's bag?"

Hugh nodded and picked up his and Harriet's bags. Inside, Leo quickly found a roboporter to handle their suitcases for them. There was a special gate for cryopassengers that led to a large waiting area. Just as Foi told them, there were no security scans.

After a half hour wait, they boarded the space elevator. The walls of the large circular car were clear and all the seats faced outward so the passengers could watch it ascend. Their seatbelts slid around them automatically when they sat down.

Another five minutes passed and then the elevator started to climb. It rose along a cable that was thousands of miles long and stretched from the ground into space. The cable, which was made of superstrong plastic, was attached at the top to a space station called Gateway 5.

The trip took nearly two hours. Watching the planet slowly fall away beneath them was nothing less than breathtaking.

"Look," Hugh said to Harriet as he pointed into space. "You can see the Venusian Blinds."

"The what?"

"The Venusian Blinds. They're huge, flat bands of superplastic that orbit completely around Venus. Each one is about 500 miles wide. They block out some of the sunlight so that Venus has a livable temperature. Before they were built, Venus was too hot to live on."

"I think I need to study more about space," Harriet murmured.

When they reached the top, their seatbelts automatically released and the doors opened. It didn't take long to find the Bajan. Once they were aboard the ship, a robot showed them to their cryostasis units. "Here are your medications," it said, handing them each a small green pill.

"Don't people going into cryostasis usually get shots?" Leo asked the robot.

It answered, "You can have shots if you prefer, but there's an extra fee."

"We'll take the pills," Leo replied, scowling.

The robot took Leo's suitcase and stowed it in a compartment in the bottom of the cryostasis unit. It did the same for the other three.

After the robot observed them swallowing their pills and settled them into their cryostasis units, it told them, "Your medications will take effect in about 10 minutes. In the meantime, please enjoy some relaxing music played to you by your SuperSleep Corporation GS2100 Cryostasis Unit. And thank you for choosing the SuperSleep GS2100. We hope you'll choose SuperSleep again in the future for your cryostasis needs. Have a pleasant trip." It turned and walked away.

Lying in her cryostasis unit, Harriet heard Tiffany ask, "Leo, are we doing the right thing?"

"Yes Tiffany," Leo assured her, "we're doing the right thing."

As she listened to the soft music her cryostasis unit played to her, Harriet thought, 'I really hope he's right.'

Nervous minutes passed, and then Harriet felt herself start to relax. It was hard to keep her eyes open. She drifted off to sleep.

Unbeknownst to Harriet or any of the others, robots moved through the rows of sleeping cryopassengers to check that each one was ready for stasis. When they were finished, the door on each cryostasis pod slid closed. The lights dimmed. Not long afterward, the Bajan got under way.

17

"Lilly, Lilly dear. Time to wake up."

Harriet heard a male voice talking near her, but she was too sleepy to pay attention.

"Harriet!" hissed the voice quietly in her ear. "Wake up!"

Harriet groaned and opened her eyes. A strange old man hovered over her as she gazed blankly upward. "Go way," she told him. "I don't know you."

A robot's face appeared above her. "Don't worry Sirsen. There's sometimes a momentary lapse of memory upon waking from a long cryostasis sleep. She'll remember everything in no more than 1.7 minutes."

Harriet didn't like the robot. She wanted it to go away. It did.

Blinking and rubbing her eyes, Harriet slowly sat up. Glancing blearily around, she wondered where she was. The strange old man looked at her expectantly. She wished he would go away too. He didn't.

The fog in Harriet's mind lifted, and she realized that the strange old man was Hugh. "Where's L ... where's Francis and Jane?" she asked.

"Behind you, Mother," came Tiffany's answer. She turned around. Tiffany, in her plastiface, was standing next to Leo's cryostasis unit trying to rouse him. Like Harriet, he didn't want to get up.

None of the other cryopassengers were up. 'I guess we're the only ones getting off at Nason,' Harriet thought as she got out of the cryostasis pod.

When Leo was finally on his feet, the robot returned and gathered their suitcases for them. It guided them through some rather narrow passages in the ship to an airlock, which was open. Foi's ship was docked there.

"Here's your shuttle down to the planet Nason," the robot told them as it loaded their luggage into the zipcraft. They boarded Foi's ship, and the airlock sealed behind them.

"You know," Tiffany told Foi, who was sitting in the small craft's bubble cockpit, "this ship smells bad."

"Nice to see you too," Foi replied, not bothering to turn around. He completed his preflight checks and then the Bajan released its docking clamps. The zipcraft floated free.

Foi gunned the little ship, plunging straight for the planet. "How was the nap?" he asked them casually.

Hanging on for dear life, none of the others seemed to want to answer. Finally, Leo managed to say, "Just fine. Look, do you have to go that fast?"

Foi glanced over his shoulder, expressionless. "This isn't fast," he replied, turning forward again.

When they reached the planet's surface, they landed at a small spaceport. A scruffy attendant checked their IDs. "Ok," he grunted. They returned to Foi's ship.

"My ship has a bathroom in there," Foi told them, pointing at a door. "Use it to take off your plastifaces and change your clothes."

One by one, each of them entered the small bathroom and changed. The zipcraft sailed over green, rolling countryside. A row of gorgeous mountains lined the horizon to the right. To the left was a vast open plain.

"Where are all the cities and people?" Harriet asked Foi.

"There are no cities here," he replied. "At least, not the kind of cities you're thinking of."

"What do you mean?"

"You'll see when we get there." Foi wouldn't say anything more.

Foi brought the zipcraft to a landing in a wide, grassy valley near a river. He took out a thin rod with a pulley and a string on it. The others followed him outside.

"What?" Foi asked when everyone else stared at the rod he was carrying. "Haven't you ever seen a fishing pole before?"

"No," Leo replied for them. "We live in a giant can, remember?"

"Well then, I'll teach you all how to fish while we wait."

Harriet asked, "What are we waiting for anyway?"

"Kailua," Foi answered. "You'll see." He walked down to the river with Harriet, Hugh, and Leo in tow, baited his hook with a bit of food, and dropped his line into the river.

Harriet, Hugh, and Leo sat down on the bank to watch Foi fish. 'It doesn't seem very exciting,' Harriet thought. But she sat between Leo and Hugh and just enjoyed the sunshine. Tiffany sat on the grass next to Leo. A couple of hours passed. During that time, Foi managed to catch a few large, yellow fish.

Suddenly, Hugh got a puzzled look on his face. He turned his head in different directions, apparently straining to hear something. "Do you hear that?" he asked the others.

"What?" Harriet queried.

"That real low thump-thump, thump-thump. Can't you hear it?"

Harriet listened intently. "Yeah," she said. "It's coming from the forest across the river."

Leo was apprehensive. "Maybe we better get back to the ship."

"We're fine here," Foi told them.

That didn't satisfy Leo. "What's coming at us?" he demanded.

"Kailua."

"What's a Kailua?"

"It's a village. Just wait. You'll see."

About twenty minutes later, something gigantic crested a low hill across the river. It resembled a fat lizard, with four thick legs and a stubby round head.

"Is that alive?" Hugh asked as he watched it follow a wide, grassy path through the trees. "It looks like it's got a house on its back!"

Foi briefly flashed a knowing look that almost seemed to be a smile.

"It looks like a big robot," Leo commented. Foi pulled another fish out of the water.

'He's right,' Harriet thought as the thing drew closer. 'It's a walking machine.'

"Hey!" Hugh exclaimed, "Those aren't eyes on its head. They're windows. And there's someone inside!"

"You have sharp eyes," Foi commented casually as another walking machine crested the hill.

"Those things have to be 250 feet long," Leo estimated. "How can something that big walk?"

They watched the first machine arrive at the wide river and easily wade across. It stopped about 30 yards from where they were standing. A door in the side of the head opened and a balcony extended outward. A young woman stepped out onto it.

"Foi?" the woman asked. "Is that you?" Foi pulled his fishing line out of the water and waved briefly.

The woman turned back inside the machine and called out, "Foi's home! And it looks like he brought company." Turning to outward again, she yelled, "Foi, bring your ship inside."

Foi nodded to her and told the others, "Come on. We need to get into the zipcraft."

Back in the ship, Foi fired up the engines and flew in a wide circle around the gargantuan walking machine. As the zipcraft drew near, the walking machine opened its mouth. Foi flew straight inside and landed. The massive jaw closed.

"Come on," Foi commanded, "They're waiting for us."

The five of them exited the zipcraft and stepped toward a set of double doors that were in a wall at the back of the machine's head.

"Weird," Hugh said. "I feel like we're walking down its throat."

Inside, they were greeted by a young man. "Hey Foi, howzit? Takin' a break from your big adventures?"

"Hi Paki," Foi replied. Surprisingly, he was smiling. "This is Harriet, Hugh, Leo, and Tiffany. I brought you some fish." He held up the fish he had caught.

Paki accepted the gift and welcomed them with a warm, "Hi guys. What you doin' hangin' around with this spacebum, eh?" He gave Foi a friendly punch on the shoulder. Uncharacteristically, Foi chuckled.

Looking at Paki, Harriet saw that he was probably not more than about 28 years old. He was tall and strongly built. His jet-black hair was short and stood straight up on the top of his head, and his eyes and skin were both a deep brown. Smiling easily, Paki greeted each of them with a hearty handshake.

Harriet observed that the room they were in was strewn about with machine parts of various types. There were also two hovercycles parked against one wall.

Through a hole in the ceiling, the woman descended a ladder and scolded, "Paki, whatchoo doin'? The tail's down. Put the animals out."

"She Who Must Be Obeyed," Paki joked to Foi as he exited through a door in the rear of the room.

"Guys, this is Nalani Latu," Foi introduced. "Nalani, this is Harriet, Hugh, Leo, and Tiffany. They need a place to stay for a while. It's after them."

Nalani's eyebrows arched. Growing suddenly serious, she asked, "You mean the Creature? What does it want with them?"

Leo answered instead, "It wants us dead. It attacked us." Pointing at Harriet, he continued, "We got away but both her parents both got killed."

Nalani gasped. She stepped forward and hugged Harriet. "You poor little thing. So you're all alone in the universe?"

"She has us," Hugh asserted.

Nalani smiled at him and nodded. "Of course she does."

"My sister is still alive too," Harriet told her. "She wasn't home during the attack."

"Foi," asked Nalani, "are you sure that thing didn't follow you here?"

"No way. We covered our tracks way too well."

"Good boy. Ok, get everyone inside and we'll get dinner going. We'll talk more later."

The five of them followed Nalani through a door and into the kitchen. Like Paki, her skin and eyes were a deep brown. She pulled a band from her pocket and used it to tie her long, straight black hair into a ponytail.

Under Nalani's supervision, they were soon cutting fruits and vegetables for the meal. She pulled a chicken out of the stasis freezer and shoved it into an ultrawave oven.

Paki returned. "Hey! What you girls doing? Don't you know cooking is man's work?"

Nalani kissed him and replied, "That's only in Samoan families, Honey. Don't worry, we're not taking over your kitchen. We were just helping while you were doing the animals."

"You keep animals?" Harriet asked.

Paki nodded and suggested, "Nani, why don't you take the girls out to see the animals while the guys and I finish dinner?"

Smiling, Nalani agreed, "Ok, you girls come with me. We'll leave the men to their work." Grabbing a bucket and a stool, Nalani handed a tall can to Harriet and another to Tiffany. Waving for them to follow her, she led them through the building. The three of them emerged from an arched doorway onto the back of the walking house. Its flat, stubby tail was extended down to the ground, forming a wide ramp. Harriet and Tiffany trailed after Nalani as she guided them down to the ground. There they found a group of goats, two cows, some chickens, and a family of ducks. The animals were exploring the river.

Harriet was surprised to see about sixty of the walking houses scattered across the grassland on both sides of the river. Everywhere people were shooing animals outside. Children played in the shallow spots in the water under their parents' watchful eyes. Several teenagers chased each other around on horses. A man on a hovercycle sped by as he zipped up the river.

"Wow," Harriet commented. "Just a little while ago, this was an empty grassland. Now it looks like a whole town."

"It is," Nalani told her. "It's the village of Kailua."

"A walking village?"

Nalani chuckled. "Yes. All of the villages on this planet are like that."

"All of them?"

"Most of them. There are a few mining towns here and there."

"Where did you get these machines?" she questioned as she made a sweeping gesture toward the walking houses.

"We made them. See that really big walker over there? It's not a house. It's a factory. That's where we synthesize all the parts we need to build and maintain our homes. We can almost make anything we need from whatever's around us. And anything we can't make is made by some other village somewhere else. We all trade and everyone has everything they need. We keep moving so that the resources around us never get used up. And we always clean up behind ourselves so we don't mess up things for other villages. They do the same."

Harriet was impressed. "This is like paradise."

"That's the idea," Nalani replied. She held out the bucket. "Want to help me milk the cows?"

"What does that mean?"

Surprised, Nalani gently chided, "Where you from girl? Don't you know where milk comes from?"

"I'm from Earth. I lived in an arcology. I don't even know what milk is."

"It's something you drink. You get it from cows."

Tiffany broke in, "Are you kidding? You actually drink something that comes out of an animal? That's just gross."

Nalani didn't take offence. "People been drinking milk for thousands and thousands of years. Haven't you ever eaten yogurt or cheese?"

"Of course," Tiffany replied airily. "What's that got do to with anything? You're not telling me they come out of a cow too?"

Nalani laughed so hard it brought tears to her eyes. Tiffany got mad. "I'm sorry dear," Nalani guffawed. "No, yogurt and cheese are made from milk." Still chuckling, she told them, "Don't worry about it, we'll teach you all you need to know to get by around here. Come on, those cows aren't going to milk themselves."

Turning to the cows, Nalani called, "Nonesuch, Nonesuch, time for milking, Nonesuch." A black and while spotted cow responded by ambling toward Nalani in the most relaxed way possible. It stepped up beside her, chewing the grass contentedly. Nalani set the stool beside the cow, put the bucket under the large animal, and commenced milking.

"That has got to be the weirdest thing I've ever seen," Tiffany said. "I mean, how did humans start getting milk from cows anyway? Did someone way back in history say, 'Gee, look at those dangly things under that animal. I'm gonna squeeze them and drink whatever comes out?' It's just weird." She dropped the can, wandered back up the ramp, and stared impatiently over the scenery.

Harriet was fascinated. "Can you teach me to do that?" she asked.

"Sure, come sit here on the stool," Nalani encouraged as she stood up.

With some instruction from Nalani, Harriet was able to get a few squirts of milk. Other than that her efforts didn't yield much. Nonesuch turned her head and fixed Harriet with an unhappy stare. Harriet flushed red under the animal's reproachful gaze.

"It's normal to not get much the first time," Nalani assured her. "You'll learn."

"Nalani?" Harriet asked as Nalani resumed the milking. "Did I hear Paki call you Nani? Is that a nickname?"

Nalani nodded. "Yeah. It's short for Nalani, but it's also 'beautiful' in Hawaiian. I'm Hawaiian, Chinese, and Martian. Paki is Samoan and Venusian."

Harriet continued to watch her work. Then she asked, "What's going to happen to us? Is there a place for us here in your village?"

"Of course, Harriet! We wouldn't turn you away. You and Tiffany can share one of our spare bedrooms. Hugh and Leo can sleep in the other for now. Foi always sleeps in his ship. Tomorrow, we'll go talk to old Russell Akina. He's been looking for someone to help out at his place since his kids left and his wife died. Maybe he'll take Leo and Hugh in with him. You and Tiffany can stay here with Paki and me."

Nalani stood. Her bucket was full, so she poured its contents into the large can. Then she stuck the bucket back underneath the cow and resumed her milking.

"What are you kids planning on doing?" Nalani continued. "You can stay here as long as you want, you know."

Apprehensively, Harriet replied, "We're trying to think of a way to kill the Creature. Foi has a special gun ..."

Nalani broke in with a reproachful, "Humph! Yeah, I know about that gun of his. That boy is half wild, I think. He goes around chasing that Creature and usually only comes back here when he's nearly dead. I remember when I was just a little girl and he showed up with one arm missing. Our village doctor had to grow him a new one."

"Why does he chase the Creature?"

"I don't know, Harriet. I really don't. My grandfather asked him that years ago, when he first contacted the family to let us know that the first Foi was dead. The boy never gave a clear answer. Maybe it's for his people. Maybe it's for the first Foi. Doesn't make sense to me. Revenge never gets anyone anywhere."

"Who was Foi? I mean the first one."

"He was my great-grandfather's younger brother. But because he spent so much time in cryostasis, my grandfather, who was his nephew, was his closest living relative when he died. My grandfather made my mother promise to always take care of the haole Foi like he was a real family member."

"What does 'haole' mean?"

"Anglo. White. When we're talking about both Fois, we usually call the new Foi 'the haole Foi.' We actually don't know his real name. He never told anyone."

"He hasn't told us either."

Nalani stood again, dumped another bucket of milk into the milk can and called to the other cow. "Nonsense, Nonsense, come get milked." Like the first cow, Nonsense responded by walking up next to her and waiting.

While Nalani milked Nonsense, Harriet said, "I don't know about Foi, but the rest of us don't want to kill it for revenge. We just want our old lives back."

"Can you get that, Harriet?"

"What do you mean?"

"Even if you kill that thing and go back to Earth, will you get your old life back?"

Harriet hung her head. "No," she answered quietly. "My parents are dead. I can never have my old life back."

"Then maybe," Nalani responded, "killing the Creature isn't the best thing for you to do."

Harriet didn't answer. When Nalani finished the milking, Harriet carried one of the full milk cans back into the house. Nalani got Tiffany to carry the other.

As soon as they arrived inside, Paki told them, "Dinner's ready. Everyone have a seat." He gestured toward the table. They all sat down and dug in. The food was great, and there was plenty of it. Paki kept urging them to eat more. By the time she waddled away from the table, Harriet thought she would burst.

After dinner, Harriet, Tiffany, and Nalani cleaned the dishes. "The men cooked, we clean. It's only fair," Nalani told them.

The sun was sliding below the horizon when Nalani showed Harriet and Tiffany to their room. Tiffany changed in the bathroom and then got straight into bed. Harriet could tell she was mad about something.

"Tiffany?"

"What?" Tiffany replied woodenly.

"Are you ok?"

Tiffany sat up in her bed. "How can you even ask that after all you've done to me?"

"What have I done to you?"

"Everything! You completely destroyed my life!"

"I did not!"

"We're here because of you! That thing is chasing us because of you and your stupid alien friend! Everything I've ever worked for is gone because of *you*. You destroyed everything! I was supposed to marry Leo. He's mine! He's always been mine! But you show up and Leo and every other guy at school are following you around trying to sneak a look at you. They were all chasing you instead of *me*! All my life everyone expected me to fail just like my mother. Everyone was always against her because she was poor. They thought she married my father for his money so they treated her like trash until she started drinking all the time. Now my parents are divorced and I haven't seen my mother in two years!"

Tears ran down Tiffany's face. "You don't know what it's like. You had so much. Everyone just handed everything to you. You had parents. You had a family. You're the smartest girl alive. You had everything! I was the best at everything. Everything! I worked *hard* for that. I had to be the best at everything just so I could get people to treat me decent. Then you showed up and it was like I was invisible. And all I've ever had to make me happy was shopping. And now I'm on the only planet in the universe where there isn't a single store!" She turned away.

Harriet was stunned. "You can't be serious, Tiffany. No one was chasing me at school. There were no boys following me around." But then she remembered catching groups of guys looking at her from time to time.

"You're so stupid! They were all trying to meet you! No one paid any attention to me."

"I ... I never knew. But Tiffany, you can't think I wanted things this way. My parents are dead, Tiffany, *dead*! You haven't lost anyone you love. I didn't want these things Eden gave me. And you heard me when she chose you. I told her not to, but she did it anyway. When she was Madson Burke, she wasn't even my friend. She was always trying to steal my boyfriend."

Turning back toward Harriet, Tiffany countered, "So you stole mine!" Blue sparks flicked across Tiffany's hands.

"Well I didn't know that when I accepted the date. And I don't know why he asked me out. He just did. And anyway, if you want to hang onto him, maybe you should try being nice to him for a change. He seems to like that." Harriet could feel her hands starting to flame.

"You two are LOUD!" a voice from the doorway interrupted them. Startled, they both turned toward the sound, and then guiltily looked at their hands. Tiffany's hands were no longer sparking, and Harriet's looked normal as well.

Nalani stood in the doorway. "I thought you two were going to bed."

Harriet glanced at Tiffany, who turned away and wiped her tears. "We are," she told Nalani. "With no more noise," she added as she saw Tiffany lie down and pull her covers up to her head.

Harriet got into her bed and pulled her blankets up. Her head was spinning. 'How could those things be true?' she wondered. 'How could all the guys have been after me and I didn't even know it? I guess I was too busy feeling like everyone looked down on me because I was poor. I guess I didn't see that things weren't so bad after all.'

'Maybe,' Harriet thought, 'it's the same now. Maybe there's a way out of this and things aren't as bad as they seem. Maybe I just can't see it now.' But no matter how she tried to make herself more hopeful, the memory of her parents' deaths still dominated her thoughts.

18

"Harriet."

Harriet opened her eyes and looked out over the red sand beach. Eden stood in front of her. Beside her were Hugh, Leo, and Tiffany.

Dismayed, Harriet asked, "What do you want?"

"Why so hostile Harriet?" Eden queried, apparently puzzled.

Harriet put her hands on her hips. "It's your fault all of this happened. If you hadn't ..."

Tiffany exploded into motion, jumping at Eden with her hands outstretched like claws. She grabbed at Eden's throat, but Eden disappeared, only to reappear a few feet away. Tiffany made another lunge at her, but Eden disappeared and reappeared out of reach once again.

Calmly, she said, "Tiffany, this won't help you. You've got to get control of yourself. This is only a telepathic vision. We are not really in the same place at all. There is no way you can hurt me."

Tiffany slapped Eden, but her hand went right through her. Eden signed. "I am very sorry for what's happened to the four of you. But worse things will happen to your entire race if we don't act together. We must work together for everyone's survival."

Leo demanded, "What is it you want us to do?"

"I need you to bring a ship to me," Eden answered.

Leo told her, "There is absolutely no possibility we can do that now that the Creature is after us."

"He's right," Hugh agreed. "It's all we can do to survive now. Do you know who or what that Creature is and how he got to Earth?"

Shaking her head, Eden replied, "No. I know it must be an energy being like Senthil and Jex, but I couldn't see it when it was outside its host. Your minds wouldn't let me. We're not compatible enough. I don't know how it got to Earth or even how it got into your universe. The fact that it's there means that someone from the other universe knows about the passageway and is trying to take control of it."

Leo countered, "If that's true, how come there aren't more of your kind here?"

"He may not be of my kind, Leo," Eden explained. "There are many different intelligent species where I'm from."

Leo spat, "You think that makes any difference to us?"

Serenely, Eden told him, "Leonardo, I understand you're upset and untrusting of me. But you have to believe that I'm doing everything I can to help you. I will teach you to use the abilities I've given you so that you can better defend yourselves. You must learn all of the technology of your people that you can. I've given you great intelligence so that you can do just that. Once you have learned what you can from humanity, I will teach you much of our technology so that you can build a ship that will reach me. The four of you must do this. There is no other way."

No one replied to Eden, so she continued. "I have been unable to observe your surroundings lately. Are you in a safe place now?" The four of them nodded. "Then settle in. When you are ready, contact me. You will know how. Then we will begin your lessons. Don't wait long to get in touch. You must get ready to defend yourselves as soon as you can. Do you understand?" All four nodded again grimly.

"It ... it took over my father's body," Harriet stammered. "Is there any chance he's still alive?"

"No, Harriet," Eden told her regretfully. "He's dead. There's nothing left of him but his memories. I'm sorry."

"I have a question," Hugh blurted out. "Why didn't it take over one of us? It looked like it was trying to get Leo and me. It didn't even seem to notice Harriet or Tiffany."

Eden explained, "It can't take over females. Our species has genders, like yours. Our reproduction doesn't work quite the same way, but there's a gender that corresponds to what you know as male and another that corresponds to female. The being that attacked you is male, so it can only take over the bodies of males. And it can't take over you and Leo because the creatures I put inside you protect you from that. All four of you are safe in that respect."

"I must go now," Eden concluded. She repeated, "But don't wait too long to get in touch with me."

The dream faded and Harriet sat up in bed. Tiffany also sat up and looked at her. "I don't much like your friend," she said, "But I think she's right."

'She's not my friend,' Harriet thought as she got out of bed. To Tiffany, she said, "Mind if I take the first shower?"

Harriet went to the kitchen and found that Leo was already there helping Paki with breakfast. "Can I help too?" she asked. Paki showed her how to cook eggs and sausages, so she cooked enough for everyone.

At breakfast, Paki bluntly asked, "So what's the plan, you guys? Are you staying here or what?"

Foi answered, "We're not sure. We have to come up with a plan for killing the Creature."

"You been tryin' to do that for years," Paki countered. "What makes you think anything's gonna be different now?"

"I've almost killed it before," Foi replied somewhat indignantly. "Besides, I've got these four to help me now."

"What makes you think these guys are gonna be any help? They're not soldiers or cops or anything." To Harriet, Hugh, Leo, and Tiffany he quickly added, "No offense kids."

Foi's face became mask-like. "I've seen them in action. They're better than any cops or soldiers. With all of us working, I think we can win."

"We just hafta get more guns like Foi's," Leo interjected.

Paki darkened, "Those guns are bad news all the way around. Where do you think you can get more of those?"

No one had an answer.

Gently, Nalani advised them, "You kids should rethink this. Whatever that thing is, it's very dangerous. Trying to kill the Creature isn't a game. Why do you need to kill it anyway? You can make lives for yourselves here."

Hotly, Tiffany shot back, "I could never make a life here. I want to go home."

Leo agreed, "We have families back there, Nalani. So much has been taken away from us. We're willing to fight to get it back."

"And are you willing to die for what you want?" Paki countered.

Hugh asked, "What makes you think we will? Maybe we'll win and get exactly what we want."

Nalani sighed. "You're young. You think you're indestructible, like Paki. He thinks he can do anything. That's why he's had so many broken bones."

Paki huffed, "I haven't had that many broken bones. Besides, Doc Manutai is good at fixing them or growing them back."

"Paki, that's not the point! What they want to do is too dangerous. Look, you kids, you need to take some time and think about all this. I called old Russ Akina and he says he's willing to take Leo and Hugh in. Harriet and Tiffany can stay here."

"Can't we all stay together?" Harriet asked. "There are enough bedrooms, aren't there?"

Paki smiled proudly. A gentle expression passed over Nalani's face. "There are enough rooms now," she agreed, "but there won't be in a few months. I'm not showing yet, but I'm going to have a baby."

The news lightened the mood considerably. After congratulations from everyone, Nalani continued, "So you see, we can only take two of you. And Russ would rather have a couple of boys living with him. He says he needs some good strong backs for the work he's got around his place." To Hugh and Leo, she added, "He'll be good to you boys."

"Well," Leo ventured, "I guess we could move in and see how it goes. What kind of work does he want us to do?"

"Mostly help with the animals. He's getting older, so he probably needs help in his greenhouses too."

"Greenhouses?" Hugh asked. "He grows his own food?"

"We all do," Nalani said. We have two greenhouses on board. Russ has three. We do well trading food and the stuff that we make to the mining towns."

Tiffany asked, "Mining towns?"

"Yup. We use minerals and metals the miners dig up to manufacture the things we need. We provide them with food and manufactured goods."

Hugh questioned, "They don't grow their own food?"

"They grow a little food," Nalani explained, "But most of the mining towns are up in the mountains. It's hard to grow anything up there so they get a lot of their food from us. It works out well for everyone."

Finishing breakfast, they cleaned up the dishes. Leo and Hugh packed their things and left with Paki. Foi muttered something about getting some maintenance done on his zipcraft. "I'll be back tonight," he told them. Moments later, he flew off toward the spaceport.

"Ok, girls," Nalani said as soon as the guys left. "Let's get to work."

"Work?" Tiffany asked, horrified. She put her hands over her mouth as if she had just uttered a dirty word. "What work?"

"Tiffany, we talked about this at breakfast. We make everything we use here. We grow all our own food. Now that there are more mouths to feed, we need more animals and we need to plant more in our greenhouses."

"But I don't work," Tiffany objected, "I pay people to do that stuff. Can't we just pay you for our food and things?"

Kindly, Nalani told her, "Paki and I aren't servants. That's not the way we live, Tiffany. If you don't work, you don't eat. I know that's harsh, but that's the way the universe works."

Tiffany fell into a sullen pout. But she followed Nalani and Harriet into one of the greenhouses. "Ok girls, the first thing we need to do is plant more food. We'll need more of everything. Let's start with brainfruit."

Nalani stepped to a blue bush that was planted in a large pot and picked an ugly black fruit that looked exactly like a small human brain. She set it on a small workbench. Cutting it open, she extracted its many seeds. She had Harriet bring her containers that were stacked along the far wall. When each pot had its share of seeds, Nalani pointed and said, "See that hovercart? Turn it on, put the containers on that, and grab some shovels. Go outside and fill the containers with dirt. The cart will follow you. When you're done, come back in here and put the pots on those empty shelves there by the windows. Let me know when you're done. I have to go put some eggs in an incubator so we get more chickens. We'll need them with you two here."

Harriet and Tiffany moved to obey. As Harriet filled her first pot with dirt, she thought, 'This isn't too bad.'

Tiffany, on the other hand, let out a steady stream of complaints from the first shovelful. By the time Harriet's pots were full, she was already sick of hearing it. Since Tiffany was still working on her second pot, Harriet decided to ask Nalani what else she could do while she was waiting. She put on her dataglasses and called Nalani using her autolibrary.

"We could use more fourlips," Nalani told her. "They're big, bushy, orange plants that grow down by the river. Dig at the bottom and you'll find red bulbs. Gather up a bunch of those. But stay near the other people. There's a lot of rivercats along there. They stay away when there's lots of people around. They almost never attack. But they can get dangerous if you're alone and you accidentally step on one. If you get one mad, don't move. It can't find you if you're still."

Nalani's warning caused Harriet some trepidation, but she took a shovel and walked to the river. There were plenty of people around, so she felt better. Quickly finding a fourlip plant, Harriet dug at its base. It didn't take her long to pull up several plump, juicy bulbs. They smelled sweet and good. Harriet moved to the next bush and gathered more.

The third bush was a little way down the river in a clump of tall, thick grass. As Harriet dug, she suddenly felt something brush her leg. Jumping in surprise and dropping her shovel, she saw a creature with the body and tail of a fish. It had stubby appendages that looked like a cross between front legs and fins. The animal's blunt head had a wide mouth sporting lots of fangs. It had no eyes.

The creature hissed at her. Remembering Nalani's words, Harriet froze. Sure enough, the rivercat was unable to detect her. It waved its head back and forth, as if listening. Harriet was sure it could hear her wild heartbeat, but the creature was clearly confused. It crawled toward her on its two, stubby front legs, thrashing its tail as it moved. The rivercat had no back legs.

The slimy animal brushed against Harriet's leg again as it searched for her. 'I can't stand this,' she thought as revulsion and fear welled inside her. The rivercat seemed to suspect something. It nudged her leg with its snout. Impulsively, Harriet recoiled.

The rivercat hissed and struck, but Harriet jumped away before it could get its double rows of fangs into her. Instinctively, Harriet shot a fireball at it from her right hand. The rivercat screeched and scurried away.

Harriet looked up. Several people along the riverbank were staring at her and at the smoldering grass. 'The grass is up to my shoulders,' she thought, 'so they couldn't have seen the fire come from my hands.' She picked up her shovel, gathered her fourlip bulbs, and hurried back to Tiffany.

"What's wrong?" Tiffany asked.

"Nothing. Are you done yet?"

"I just finished my last pot."

"Then let's go in," Harriet said forcefully. She dumped her fourlip bulbs onto the hovercart and scurried inside.

Harriet and Tiffany spent the rest of the morning planting, caring for animals, and gathering food from the surrounding countryside. By evening, they were exhausted and dirty.

"I need to wash my clothes," Harriet told Nalani.

"Already? You must not have much to wear."

"We don't. We had to run for our lives after the attack. We bought a few things on the way here, but none of us has much to wear."

"Well, let's go over to the factory after dinner and get you some more. We'll get Leo and Hugh and take them along."

So when dinner was done, they walked over to Sirsen Akina's house, gathered up Leo and Hugh, and went to the factory. A middle-aged woman met them there. Nalani introduced her as Evelyn. Evelyn showed them how to operate the synthesizer used for spraying out clothes. Harriet tried it first. She was pleased with the work clothes she produced.

"Spray yourself out a swimsuit, Harriet," Nalani advised. "You'll need it for the hot tub."

"Hot tub? What's that?"

"A very old invention, but a very nice one. You'll see later, just get yourself a swimsuit."

After they all sprayed out the clothes they needed, Hugh commented in a way that Harriet found overly casual, "Hey guys, I think we should take this opportunity to get ourselves some handheld scanners. You never know when they might come in handy."

"Uh, yeah Hugh," Leo agreed in a somewhat strained voice. "Let's do that."

Nalani eyed them both suspiciously.

"You want electronics?" Evelyn asked. "You need that synthesizer over there." She pointed to machine in the middle of the room. Hugh sprayed out their scanners. Afterward, they paid Evelyn, and then Nalani escorted them back to her house. "Get into your swimsuits and I'll fire up the hot tub," she instructed.

Once they were changed, Nalani led them up to a terrace on an upper floor. "Hop in," she said, pointing at a round tub filled with bubbling water. "I'll turn on the water jets. Sit in front of them. It makes your back feel good."

"Ah," Hugh said as he happily clamored in. "Hot. Tub. Just exactly what it sounds like. Oooooh, I really need this."

Harriet slid herself into the warm water. It eased the soreness of her muscles. "Did you work hard?"

"Are you kidding?" Hugh asked. "Russ—he asked us to call him Russ—Russ worked us like crazy. I'm so sore I can hardly move. But he was really happy. He said we got more work done today than he could do in a week. Then he told us getting old is a complete waste, so we should stay young. I said I'd see what I could do. He likes it when we joke with him."

They fell silent for quite a while. At last, Harriet said, "You know. It isn't bad here."

"No it isn't," Leo agreed. "But I still want my life back."

Tiffany turned away. "Me too," she said quietly.

"Are you crying, Tiff?" Leo asked. She didn't reply. Leo gathered her in his arms and told her, "It'll be alright. We'll get home." Harriet cringed. Deciding she couldn't continue to watch, she got out of the hot tub, dried off, wrapped her towel around herself, and went downstairs.

When she drew near to the kitchen, she heard voices arguing. "What have you brought among us Foi?" Paki was saying. "What are they? We're having a baby, you know. We can't have them here if they're dangerous."

"They're not dangerous!" Foi snapped. "They're kids. Just like me. They can just do some things that most people can't, that's all. I think they can be trusted."

"But Nalani saw fire coming from Harriet's hands when she was fighting with Tiffany! And sparks of electricity from Tiffany's hands. You call that safe?"

Foi chuckled, "Well, Tiffany can get on anyone's nerves. Look, I'll talk to the two of them and tell them they need to get along better. And you can tell the other villagers that Harriet was carrying a plasma pistol. The rivercat surprised her and she shot at it. She's sorry and she won't carry the pistol around any more. End of story."

"Is that thing coming here after them?" Paki demanded.

"If it does," Foi answered, "you'll know a long time before it gets here. Remember that I programmed its brain patterns into your house's scanners a long time ago. It'll sound an alarm."

"That's not much of a comfort. I've still got a wife to think about, and a baby coming."

"Paki, if that thing comes, we'll all run. We'll draw it far away from here. It doesn't want any of you. It would only want us."

They fell silent for a time. Then Paki said, "I don't think they should stay here, Honey."

Quietly, almost too quietly to hear, Nalani answered, "I won't turn them away, Paki. They're just kids, and they're alone and so very far from home. How could we make them leave? Could you really put Harriet out on her own? She's such a sweet girl—so full of life—even after all she's been through. Her parents were murdered right in front of her. What could be more terrible than that? I just can't send them away when they can hardly take care of themselves."

Unable to contain herself any longer, Harriet stepped into the room. Silence immediately fell on the kitchen. Paki, Nalani, and Foi stared at her.

"We ... we can leave, Nalani," Harriet said. "We don't want to put you in any danger. We'll just get in the way anyway. You'll have a baby soon to think about. We'll find someplace else to hide."

Tears came to Nalani's eyes. "No," Nalani told Harriet as she rose and gathered Harriet gently into her arms. "You'll stay right here," she whispered. "For the rest of your life if you want to."

19

Something was bothering Hugh. He couldn't put his finger on what it was. There was something that was odd that kept nagging at him somewhere in the back of his mind. It was something that should be obvious.

'It's not this place,' he thought. 'This place is good, and the people are too.' Nalani was right about Russ Akina. He took Hugh and Leo in gladly. In the two months that had passed since then, they had gotten along really well with him. His ready smile and gentle manner went a long way toward helping them recover from the horror they experienced in their last days on Earth.

Still, Hugh had days when he was so depressed that he just didn't want to get out of bed. The other three had times like that too. 'Well, it's hard to get Tiffany to get up and doing anything on *any* day,' Hugh thought, 'but that's just Tiffany.' To be fair, Hugh had to admit that Tiffany was getting better. Having so much of Nalani's time and attention seemed to help her quite a bit. Tiffany was even nice to Hugh—once.

Harriet seemed to be especially struggling. But Hugh thought, 'I guess that's natural, given what's happened to her.' Twice Nalani had called Hugh over to their place in the morning to help Harriet. Mostly, he just went over and held her for a while. His presence seemed comforting to her, which made him happy. 'She's the best friend I've ever had,' he mused. He was glad to be there for her when she needed someone to lean on. But then he thought wryly, 'Of course, being around Leo really cheers her up too.'

As the days had gone by, Russ had worked Hugh and Leo quite hard. They helped with planting and harvesting in the greenhouses, with gathering food from the surrounding countryside, and with the cleaning and maintenance of his walking home. The old contraption had fallen into considerable disrepair in the years since Russ's wife had died, so there was a lot to do.

Hugh had found that he had a knack for working on the walking house. He had to use his autolibrary to look up a lot of information about how it worked, but he enjoyed that. 'I'm learning a lot,' he told himself as he studied.

Leo seemed to be doing reasonably well. There had been only one day so far when he seemed to struggle. But he got onto Russ's ancient hovercycle and rode up the river for the day. Hugh had been a little worried about him as he watched him skim away over the water, but Leo came back late that night in reasonable spirits.

Hugh and Leo took Russ's hovercycle on as a project. They spent a little time each day fixing it up. Hugh often wondered how such a broken-down vehicle could keep running at all. Under their ministrations, the antique cycle began to look and run much better. After a couple of weeks, Russ told them, "That bike hasn't run that well since my youngest son left. He loved riding that thing." Hugh liked riding it too. Leo taught him how. Hugh now thought of Leo as a friend.

When Hugh showed the restored hovercycle to Harriet, she also wanted to learn to drive one. Hugh advised Tiffany to learn too, but she immediately turned up her nose. "I don't drive," she replied disdainfully, "I have people drive me."

Of course, she changed her attitude immediately when she saw Leo teaching Harriet to drive. Hugh could hardly contain his laughter as he and Tiffany watched Harriet and Leo during their first lesson. Harriet was sitting on the front holding onto the handlebars with Leo on the back. Leo had his left arm tightly around Harriet's waist and was holding onto her right hand with his right hand as he helped her work the throttle. Hugh noticed that Leo was snuggled up quite close to Harriet as he explained how the bike worked. Harriet was happier than Hugh had seen her since the attack. Hugh gazed at Tiffany when Harriet and Leo glided away on the hovercycle. 'I think her head is going to explode,' he chuckled.

The next day, Tiffany insisted that Leo teach her to ride the hovercycle. In the end, they each decided to buy one for themselves. Fortunately, one of the villagers was willing to sell the hovercycles her children had left behind when they had gone off to a university in another star system. Hugh, Harriet, Leo, and Tiffany often spent the warm evenings zipping over the landscape together.

But each day, the nagging feeling would come back to Hugh. 'There's something important that I've missed,' he kept telling himself.

For a day or so, Hugh thought it might have something to do with Foi. 'After all,' Hugh wondered, 'what do we really know about him? He doesn't say anything about himself.'

When Hugh asked Paki about Foi, Paki just shrugged and said, "I don't really know what to tell you Hugh. Foi has never really opened up to us much either. I don't know if he can. All the adults where he grew up had some sort of mind control operation performed on them. I kinda think they were unable to express a lot of emotion as a result. If that's the case, then Foi is just being like them, which is natural." He shrugged again and repeated, "I don't really know."

Foi spent a lot of time fishing. It seemed to be the one thing in the universe that enabled him to relax and be happy. Hugh couldn't understand it. 'He just sits there holding that pole and dangling the string into the water,' Hugh marveled. 'How can that be fun?'

One day, Foi gathered the four of them together and said, "I've been sending messages to some of my contacts. I think I've found an arms dealer who can supply us with the guns we need."

"That's great!" beamed Leo. "When can we get them?"

"It's not that easy," Foi explained. "This isn't some mail order outfit on the grid. I'll have to go see him myself. It'll take a couple of months to get there and do the deal, then another couple of months to get back."

"Months!" screeched Tiffany. "What are we supposed to do in the meantime?"

"You should probably use those autolibraries to learn everything you can," Foi advised. "You need to know as much as you can about the universe to get by. The only thing that kept me alive when I left home was learning a lot, as fast as I could."

"I think he's right," Hugh agreed. "In fact, I've been thinking we should get a cyberschool program for our autolibraries to help us. We've got enough money."

"No you don't," Foi disagreed. "You need to give all of it to me to buy weapons."

"All of it?" the four of them asked with one voice.

Foi nodded. "If we're going to buy these guns, it's going to take all of your money plus all of mine. None of us will have anything left."

"How will we live?" Tiffany wailed. "What do we do for money?"

"You sell your autolibrary data."

"Ok," Tiffany agreed abruptly.

Hugh was surprised. "It doesn't bother you that selling your data will make you a criminal?" he asked.

"Of course not," Tiffany replied disdainfully. "I'm a minor. Kids do that kind of thing. Besides, my Daddy's got lots of lawyers. They'll take care of it."

Harriet objected, "Even with your fancy lawyers, it's still wrong. They even send minors to jail for that."

"They send *poor* minors to jail for that. I'm rich. I'll never see the inside of a cell."

Leo interrupted, "The data is encoded with her unique ID. If we sell the data to a local dealer, won't the Creature be able to find out that we're here?"

Foi shook his head. "Nope. I'll make it seem like the data originated on the other side of Alliance space."

"How?" Leo queried.

Foi flashed one of his rare grins. "I've got my ways. We'll probably get payment in two or three weeks."

Tiffany countered, "What do you mean 'we?' It's not your data, it's mine."

Foi's expression stiffened, "I'm using all of my money to get your guns and arranging the sale of your data. You're not going to share with me so I can live too?"

Leo broke in forcefully, "Yes, we are. You get half. And when we get back to Earth, my father will give you triple that."

Surprised, Foi brightened. "You sure?" he asked.

"Absolutely," Leo assured him. My family will pay a lot to get me back. And in spite of the way Tiffany acts," Leo shot her a fiery glance causing her to cringe, "her family will too. Between my family and hers, you'll get enough money to last you the rest of your life."

"Good," Foi said. He left in his zipcraft the next day.

The more Hugh thought about it, the more he decided that he trusted Foi. 'Whatever's bothering me has nothing to do with Foi,' he finally concluded.

'Could it be the other villagers?' Hugh speculated. He, Harriet, Leo, and Tiffany were meeting many of the people who lived in Kailua. They were all very warm and welcoming. Hugh decided, 'Whatever the problem is, it isn't the villagers.'

As the weeks passed, Hugh occasionally felt Eden reaching out to them across the void of space. He mentioned it to the others. "We feel it too," they assured him.

"Maybe it's time we contacted Eden," Harriet suggested one night as they sat on one of the terraces of Paki and Nalani's house.

"Why?" Leo questioned suspiciously.

Harriet answered, "If we're going to get home, we have to know what she can teach us. I think we can trust her. When she was Madison Burke, she was a nice girl. And she's helped us a lot."

Leo was doubtful. "We don't *have* to trust her," he mused. "We just have to find out how to kill that Creature. Then she can holler till she's blue in the face, but we don't have to pay attention."

The others agreed. The next day, they rode their hovercycles far from the village and found some large rocks to sit on in a sparsely-vegetated spot.

"So what do we do?" demanded Tiffany. "It's not like we know her phone number."

"She said we'd know how to get in touch," Harriet reminded them. "Maybe we should just sit here and think about her and see what happens."

Silently, the four of them sat and concentrated on Eden.

Time went by. Tiffany complained, "Nothing's happening."

"We need to keep at it," Harriet encouraged. So they kept at it.

More time went by. Exasperated, Tiffany finally conceded, "I give up. This isn't going to work anyway."

"Tiffany," Eden said, "please be more patient."

Startled, the four of them whirled around. There stood Eden.

"I'm not really here," she explained to their astounded expressions. "This is just a telepathic image. It's only in your minds. No one else can see me."

"Neat trick," Leo commented distantly. "So what is it that you want to teach us?"

"Not much for small talk, are you Leonardo?" Eden remarked patiently. "So you've decided to trust me."

Leo replied, "No, we've decided to listen to you. We'll decide about trust later."

"If you would trust me more and open your minds," Eden persuaded, "I could give you much more knowledge much more quickly."

"Knowledge first," insisted Leo, "and *maybe* trust later."

"Fair enough," Eden told them. "All right, let's get to it. There are some things that all of you can do, and there are some gifts that you each have that are yours individually. First, we'll work on the things that all of you can do. Everyone stand in a line side by side about 10 feet apart."

They spread themselves out and faced her.

"Ok, what I want you to do now is to try to emit enough force to gently push each other back. Just imagine that you're throwing your will in a circle around you. Go ahead Hugh. Give it a try first."

Hugh was unhappy. 'How do you throw your will?' he wondered. He stood still and imagined pushing Leo, who was immediately to his left. Nothing happened.

Eden advised, "Just clear your mind and picture a wave of force emanating from you. Believe that you are power itself. Focus your power—yourself—with your mind like light through a magnifying lens. Then gently throw it from you outward in all directions."

Hugh closed his eyes.

WHUMP!

"Hugh!" Harriet yelled as she, Leo, and Tiffany picked themselves up from the ground. "Be careful!" She dusted herself off.

Eden reminded, "Remember, Hugh, that I used the word 'gently.' I do not think that what you just did fits into the definition of 'gently.' At least not as I understand the word."

Leo suggested, "Let's move farther apart."

When they had doubled the distance between themselves, Eden continued, "Now all of you follow Hugh's highly successful attempt and try it together."

WHUMP! WHUMP! WHUMP! WHUMP!

"Excellent, all of you. I can see this is going to go very well. Next, I want you to try telekinesis, moving things without touching them. Everyone select one of the smaller stones here on the ground. Imagine that your will is a hand that can reach out and pick up the stone. Draw the stone to you and catch it in your real hand."

Hugh picked a rock about three feet in front of him and concentrated. The rock stayed stubbornly still. He glanced sideways at the others. None of them seemed to be successful either.

"That's all right," Eden encouraged, "Keep trying."

After about ten minutes of effort, Tiffany managed to get a rock to skitter across the ground and come to rest at her feet. She smiled triumphantly.

"Very good Tiffany. You see everyone? It can be done. Keep trying."

They didn't make much progress on telekinesis. Hugh suggested, "Let's take a break." He sat on a large rock. The other three joined him.

Leo told Eden, "This doesn't seem like it will help us much against that Creature."

"Don't be easily discouraged Leo," she replied. "You have to master the basics before you get to the harder things."

"What about surfing?" Hugh interjected. "We made surfboards appear and we flew on them. That's how we got away from it. How did we do that?"

Eden smiled, "The life forms inside you, which are called *korei*, are symbiotic. That means they do something for you and you do something for them. They like living in your bodies and minds."

"Can they read our minds?" interrupted Hugh.

"They're not really intelligent enough for that. But they understand your will and feel your emotions. But as I was saying, the *korei* like you. They're actively trying to help you learn what you can do."

Hugh broke in again, "So when they sensed our fear, they helped us get away."

"Yes, Hugh. But your minds are like lenses that focus their powers. They can only give you power in ways that your mind understands. The surfboards are a metaphor, a symbol. You don't really need them. Your actual power is flight. Your minds manifested the power of flight as surfboards because it was something you know and are familiar with. It could have just as easily been something else. It's your mind's way of giving yourself permission to fly. When you become used to your powers, you won't need such metaphors, you'll just fly."

"We can really fly?" asked Tiffany. "All of us?"

"Yes, Tiffany. You just need to find the power within yourself."

Leo wanted to know, "What else can we do? I know Hugh can teleport. Can the rest of us do that?"

"No, Leo. That's a gift for him alone. Just as you have power over earth and rock, Harriet has power over fire, and Tiffany has power over lightning."

Leo objected, "But those things didn't do much at the concert. None of our attacks got through the Creature's shield."

"That's true, Leo. But when you combine your attacks, you can defeat him. And, of course, I'll help. All you have to do is attack him enough to make him use his powers. Then I'll force a telepathic connection and take him over."

"We don't want him taken over," Leo blurted out. "We want him dead. That way, we get our lives back."

Eden continued, ignoring Leo's interruption, "The more aggressive he is, the more likely it is that I'll be able to make the connection. So attack him with everything you've got and do it all together. He'll have to respond with more than just his shield."

'Hmm,' Hugh thought, 'she really doesn't want that thing dead. Is it because she knows that if it dies, we don't have to listen to her or do what she says any more?' To Eden he said, "If we make him aggressive, we could die."

"You are much more resilient to damage now," Eden explained.

That nagging feeling was back. Hugh realized that whatever was bothering him had something to do with Eden. There was something important about her that he was missing. On impulse he asked, "Eden, how did Senthil meet Madison Burke?"

"Why do you ask?"

"Oh, I just wondered. Since we're taking a break, I was hoping you might tell us about the wormhole collapse and how Senthil met Madison."

Eden considered it a moment and then said, "There's not that much to tell, Hugh. The ship Madison was on was heavily damaged. She and Allen were the only survivors. Madison dragged Allen into a shuttle and tried to get to the planet I'm on now. Unfortunately, it was her first time piloting a real shuttle, rather than a simulator. The shuttle crashed. Both Madison and Allen were dying when Senthil and Jex found them. Beings from their universe can't survive in your universe for long without a host. Senthil and Jex merged with Madison and Allen. All four were saved. We became Eden and Genesis."

"But why were you in the wormhole in the first place?" Hugh pursued.

"What do you mean?" Eden questioned. "Madison was on the way to the California system with her family."

"But Madison should have been nearly there already," Hugh objected. "She shouldn't have been in that particular wormhole at that particular time."

Eden nodded. "You're right," she agreed. "The ship Madison was on had an outbreak of Kalaran swinepox. It was quarantined for two months. That's why Madison was in the wormhole when she was."

"Kalaran swinepox?" Hugh asked, incredulous. "That's a really rare disease. So rare that it's one of the few that they don't inoculate against. It's one of the few diseases that can quarantine a ship these days."

Eden shrugged. "They never did figure out how the infection started. But once it did, we had to be isolated outside the star system until the disease ran its course."

Pausing, Eden asked, "Does that satisfy your curiosity, Hugh?" Hugh nodded. "Well then, let's get back to our lessons. Since you seem to like surfing, let's do that for a while."

Hugh, Harriet, and Leo were immediately able to recreate the surfboards they produced when they were running away from the

Creature. Soon they were skimming across the rolling terrain. However, none of them seemed to be able to get more than about twenty feet off the ground.

Tiffany had more trouble. After a lot of struggle, she decided, "Surfing is stupid! That's why I don't do it."

Eden instructed, "You can use any metaphor that works, Tiffany. Try imagining that you're riding a hovercycle."

Instantly, Tiffany made a silver hovercycle appear. She climbed on and chased after the other three.

Under Eden's patient guidance, they spent the rest of the day improving their force throws and flying. By the time they were ready to return to the village, all four of them had learned to focus the force throw in a single direction. They could stand next to each other and all aim at the same target without knocking each other down.

When they got back to Kailua, they talked briefly before returning to the walking houses.

"We've got to keep taking lessons from her," Leo stated. "I think the best thing to do is learn everything Eden will teach us, and get help from Foi. That should give us the best chance we have against the Creature."

The other three agreed. Then Harriet asked, "Hugh, why did you ask her about Madison?"

"I'm not sure," he replied. "But for some reason I think it's important. Maybe everything about Eden's important. The more we know about her and about that Creature, the better chance we have of coming out of this alive."

Thoughtfully, the four of them returned to the walking houses.

20

"Hi girls," greeted Nalani, as Harriet and Tiffany sat in the living room one morning a few weeks later. "You two need to stay away from Paki for a few days. He's got the Melorian flu. It's going around the Edge Worlds. It's not serious, but it makes all your hair fall out. So I wouldn't want either of you to get it."

"We can't," Harriet replied.

Puzzled, Nalani asked, "What do you mean?"

"They inoculate us in the arcology," Harriet told her. "We can't get most diseases or allergies because they give us a shot that makes us immune."

"You're kidding."

Harriet shook her head. "Nope. They tell us that if they didn't, they'd have epidemics in the arcology like they do in the streets."

"Would you mind going over with me to the village doctor's place later? He might be able to use antibodies from your blood to help Paki."

Harriet replied, "Sure. We'd be glad to help Paki, especially after all you two have done for us. Won't we Tiffany?"

"I suppose," Tiffany moaned.

Nalani said, "Thanks girls. Let's go right after breakfast."

"I'll cook something for us to eat," Harriet volunteered. Harriet was getting pretty good at cooking lately.

After breakfast, they got out their hovercycles. Harriet asked, "Nalani, the four of us were planning another outing later today, if you can spare us."

"Hmmm ... you kids have been going on a lot of those 'outings' lately. Does this have anything to do with the newly burned-out area to the south of here?"

"Well ..." Harriet hesitated.

"You two girls haven't been fighting again, have you?"

"No, no," Harriet answered quickly. "We're just ..."

"Practicing," Tiffany interjected.

Nalani's eyebrows went up. "Practicing?" she asked. "Are you kids still planning on killing that Creature?"

"Yes," Tiffany answered.

"I'm surprised you're that open about it Tiffany."

For the first time since Harriet had known her, Tiffany's face genuinely softened. "We trust you, Nalani," Tiffany said.

"Thanks, girls. But I wish you'd also take my advice and stay away from that Creature."

Tiffany shrugged. Harriet didn't know what to say. With no further comments, they each mounted a hovercycle and drove to meet Dr. Manutai, the village physician. It only took the doctor a few minutes to draw some blood from Harriet and Tiffany.

"I think we should invest in the same shots these girls have had," he commented to Nalani. "It would be nice to get everyone in the village inoculated. This shows just how out of touch I am these days. I hadn't even heard that such inoculations were available."

"It'll probably cost some serious money. We can bring it up at the next village council meeting," Nalani suggested.

The doctor nodded his agreement. "I've just got a few things to do around here. I'll be by in an hour or so to give Paki his shot. He may even be well enough by tomorrow to drive your walker."

They said their goodbyes and walked down the ramp from the doctor's house to their waiting hovercycles.

"What did he mean," Harriet asked, "about driving the walker?"

"The village is moving tomorrow," Nalani explained. "We're getting underway first thing in the morning. Paki won't drive, he needs rest. I'll do it so he can take the day off tomorrow. Shall we go home? We've got a lot to do before we leave tomorrow."

They mounted their hovercycles. 'Guess we won't be meeting Eden today,' Harriet thought as they drove home. 'We'll have to contact her when we get a chance and let her know.'

Preparations for the move kept them busy the entire day. As he promised, Dr. Manutai dropped by and gave Paki his shot. Paki was up and around by dinnertime, but there were large empty patches on his head where his thick, black hair had fallen out.

"I'll just go ahead and shave it all off," he told them at dinner as he ate some soup Nalani made. "It'll grow back."

Harriet was glad she didn't have to worry about getting sick.

In the morning, the walking houses got under way not long after dawn. The gentle rumble of the engines woke Harriet, so she got dressed and went up to the pilothouse in the walker's head. Nalani was at the controls.

"Morning Harriet. You're up early."

"I wanted to see the house walk. It doesn't feel like we're moving."

"The house has an inertial dampening field, like a spaceship. It reduces the feeling of movement."

Harriet observed their progress across the vast, green landscape for a while, and then went down to the kitchen to cook breakfast. Just as she started, Hugh called her on her autolibrary.

"I've found him," Hugh blurted out.

"Found who?"

"The Creature. He's been on Earth for a long, long time."

"How do you know?"

"I've been studying history. Remember, we talked about getting more education?"

Harriet had completely forgotten about the conversation. In the intervening months, she had only used her autolibrary occasionally. Guiltily, Harriet replied, "Oh, of course. What did you find?"

Excitedly, Hugh replied, "I'm sending you a link to the data. But to make a long story short, the Creature tried to attack Leo's family a long time ago. Leo and I will come over later and we'll talk."

"Hugh, we're moving! You can't come over."

"Sure we can. We'll just have Nalani let the tail down low enough so that we can drive up on our hovercycles. Russ says people here do it all the time."

Hugh hung up and Harriet returned to her cooking.

"Don't you ever get tired of that?" Tiffany's voice asked from behind her. Startled, Harriet turned around to see Tiffany blearily entering the kitchen.

Harriet asked, "Get tired of what?"

"Cooking."

"Of course not. I like cooking. I'm not as good as I'd like to be yet. But I'm getting there. Don't you want to learn?"

Tiffany surprised her by answering, "I suppose."

"Well then, why don't you cut up some bell peppers?"

Tiffany stepped to the counter and picked up a knife. "Whatever. How do you cut these?" Harriet demonstrated and Tiffany was soon cutting the bell peppers into tiny pieces.

"Tiffany?"

"What?"

"Are we actually getting along?"

"I wouldn't go that far. At least, not until you get your own boyfriend and leave mine alone."

Harriet chuckled and cut up some green onions.

It wasn't until later that afternoon that Hugh and Leo showed up. The four of them gathered on a terrace on top of the walker's head to talk.

"It all started with Leo's family," Hugh began.

Leo nodded in agreement and said, "One of my ancestors was a man called Lorenzo de Medici. He was one of the most important people in the Renaissance."

Harriet asked, "The what?"

Irritated, Tiffany interrupted, "The Renaissance, the Renaissance! Didn't they teach you anything in that school you went to before the Academy?"

"I don't need your help," Leo snapped before Harriet could reply. Tiffany sulked.

Leo continued, "The Renaissance was the time when Europe discovered science and technology by relearning what the ancient Greeks and Romans knew. My ancestors ruled a city in Italy called Florence from the 1200's to the 1600's. The most important of all of them was a guy named Lorenzo de Medici. There were also two rival families, the Salviatis and the Pazzis. They wanted to take over power in Florence, so they put together a plot to kill Lorenzo."

"That's a pretty subtle way to get yourself put in charge," Tiffany remarked sarcastically.

Leo ignored her, "Here's the interesting part. The conspiracy was put together by a wizard that the Salviatis introduced to the Pazzis. It was said that this wizard could fly, shoot flames, and throw lightning. Sound familiar?"

Harriet asked, "Did he kill Lorenzo?"

"No, the plot didn't succeed. The wizard didn't participate. He wouldn't move openly because he was afraid of a she-demon who lived in the sky."

"A she-demon?" Harriet puzzled. "You mean Eden?"

Leo nodded meaningfully. "I think our friend Eden has been around a lot longer than she's letting on."

"But Leo! You're talking about things that happened over a thousand years ago. It couldn't be Eden and the same Creature. They'd be dead by now."

Leo countered, "Do we know how long they live? Is it possible they live a lot longer than humans?"

Harriet shrugged. "I guess it's possible. We don't really know."

"Exactly," Leo emphasized. "We know almost nothing about Eden or the Creature. She hasn't told us hardly anything."

"But Leo," Harriet objected, "Look at all she's been teaching us. We've made real progress."

Leo dismissed her words with, "The point is, we know now that there's more to the story than Eden's telling us."

"Do we?" Harriet challenged. "Do we really know that the Creature has been on Earth for a thousand years? If he has, why hasn't he done more damage?"

"According to the legends," Leo answered, "Lorenzo de Medici had four demons that served him. They taught him something called the Spell of the Medici that sealed the wizard in a cursed urn."

"What's an urn?" Harriet asked.

"Did you see the big vases in my condo?" Leo asked. "My mother loves collecting them." Harriet nodded. "An urn is kinda like a vase."

Harriet questioned, "What happened to the urn?"

"There's lots of different legends about it," Leo told her. "They all say something a little different than the others. But several of them talk about it being in a secret chamber in the Sistine Chapel."

"What's that?"

"It's a big church in Rome. An artist named Michelangelo painted these really famous pictures on the ceiling. As it turns out, the person that Michelangelo worked for most of his life was Lorenzo de Medici."

Inserting herself once again into the conversation, Tiffany asked, "So how does any of this help us?"

"Well," Leo replied, "Hugh tells me that a lot of historians say that legends are usually based on fact. So it might be possible that the Spell of the Medici and the cursed urn are real."

Tiffany looked doubtful, "It all sounds like magic and old fairy tales to me."

"Maybe," Leo said, "but so do things like throwing lightning and fire from your hands."

Tiffany admitted that he had a point.

Leo continued, "And there are actually stories in my family about a special urn that was hidden somewhere in Italy that could be used for fighting off evil spirits. My great-grandfather told me about it when I was little. He said it was a source of magic for our family that made us great."

Tiffany repeated, "So how does any of this help us?"

"I think we need to find out what happened to that urn and learn the spell that made it work."

"Leo, are you serious?"

"Look Tiff, if the urn exists, it isn't really magic. It's technology."

"What makes you think so?"

"Because the wizard wasn't a wizard. He was the Creature. And the Creature is an alien life form. The four demons that served Lorenzo de Medici, if they existed, weren't demons. They were probably aliens too. They brought some kind of technology to Earth that made it so Lorenzo de Medici could capture the Creature. We need that technology. But the catch is, we'd have to go back to Earth to get it."

"Going back to Earth is not a good idea."

Startled, the four of them turned around to see Nalani standing in the doorway behind them. She came out on the terrace, pulled up a chair, and sat down.

"How long have you been listening?" Hugh asked.

"Long enough to know that you kids are going to try something stupid and dangerous," Nalani answered curtly.

"Nalani," Harriet appealed, "we have to do something. We can't live the rest of our lives running from that Creature."

"Hey!" Hugh exclaimed to Nalani. "If you're up here and Paki's in bed, who's driving the house?"

"It's on autopilot. Don't worry. This terrain is pretty smooth. The autopilot can handle it just fine. I'll take over when we get closer to the foothills."

"Foothills?" Hugh asked. "Are we going into the mountains?"

"Yes. We're headed to a mining town. We're going for the annual Fall Gathering. A lot of the villages in the area will be there. It's a time when we all get together and trade things that we grow and things that we make. We buy our annual supply of fuel for our walkers from the miners there. It's also a big celebration. All the young guys try to meet girls from the other villages."

"It sounds fun," Harriet commented.

"It is. And you kids should stick around for it. We'll be there in about a month. Foi should be getting back about then. He'll probably join us there. You think you'll stay?"

"Sure," Harriet told her. "We'll be here at least that long."

Gazing at Harriet and Tiffany, Nalani teased, "It might even be a chance for one of you to meet a guy so both of you aren't chasing Leo."

"Nalani!" Harriet squealed.

"Don't worry," Nalani chuckled, "Leo likes having both of you after him. But it's better for the rest of us if one of you finds another boyfriend—less accidental fire and lightning."

Harriet wasn't sure whether or not she had just been insulted.

Nalani asked, "It's better just to stay here, don't you think? You kids have been through so much already. That Creature won't find you here. Just stay with us."

Decisively, Leo told her "We can't take the chance, Nalani. If the Creature does find us here, you could all be killed." Harriet and Tiffany nodded in agreement.

Nalani sat back down in her chair and wiped tears from her eyes. "You're just kids," she wept. "You shouldn't have to face this."

They fell into silence as the giant walking house made its lumbering way across the green countryside.

Part 3

Yes, Virginia, There Really Are Monsters

"First Contact with alien races changed our perceptions of both ourselves and the universe in which we live. It was the dawn of the Second Age of Humanity, when we knew without a doubt that we are not alone. The Second Age brought in a time when we started to see ourselves as having truly limitless potential. It also brought a time when we started to see both the fantastic beauties and the utter horrors that the universes contain." *The Human Race in the Second Age*, Hugh Benson, p. 401.

21

Harriet stood on the barren, rocky hillside with a whirlwind of fire spinning around her. Hands over her head, she struggled to keep the current of flame flowing in a stable pattern. The air immediately around her was blistering hot as it flowed with the firestorm. But to Harriet, it was nothing but a comfortable glow of warmth. Her long, red hair danced carelessly on the intense wind.

"Very good Harriet," Eden encouraged. "Now throw it forward."

Snapping her hands downward so that they pointed straight ahead of her, she pushed the firestorm forward. It shot away from her, scorching everything in its path, and slowly dissipated as it progressed toward the bottom of the hill.

Watching from the top of the hill, Hugh called down, "Wow, Harriet. That's great!"

Harriet was pleased with herself. But Eden didn't let her rest. "Now try your fireball," she directed.

Holding her right hand out to her side with the palm upward, Harriet summoned fire and spun it into a sphere. She felt the fireball's pleasant heat as it spun in her hand. When she tossed it forward with all her might, it rocketed straight across the gully to the next hillside and exploded.

Eden congratulated, "Well done, Harriet. Take a break. Hugh, come down and show me how you're doing."

Hugh teleported and appeared next to Harriet, who climbed the hill to where Leo and Tiffany were waiting. Behind her, Harriet heard her own voice call, "Hey Harriet!"

Surprised, Harriet turned to see herself standing next to Hugh and Eden.

"Very good Hugh," Eden praised. "Can you do Leo?"

Hugh smiled and Leo appeared next to him. From the top of the hill, Harriet heard Leo call, "Hey! I'm taller than that."

The Leo standing next to Hugh grew to nearly twenty feet tall. "Is this tall enough?" the giant illusion boomed.

"Almost," Leo answered from the hilltop.

Harriet drew near to Leo and Tiffany and sat on a rock to watch Hugh. Ten Hughs stood in a circle around Eden. They all disappeared, and then Hughs appeared and disappeared at random. Harriet wasn't sure which was the real Hugh.

From behind them, Harriet heard Eden's voice say, "Leo, pick up that boulder to your left and throw it at Hugh."

'I hate it when she's in one place and throws her voice to somewhere else,' Harriet thought. 'It creeps me out.'

The boulder Leo lifted was easily twice as tall as he was. Hefting the massive rock as if it had no weight at all, Leo tossed it down the hill. The big stone bounced once about thirty feet in front of Eden and Hugh. Startled, all ten Hughs yelled and scattered in every direction.

"Alright Tiffany, your turn," Eden called.

Tiffany stood. A gorgeously silken pair of golden wings appeared on her back. She lifted them to the gentle breeze and let it carry her effortlessly skyward. As she rose, she flapped her wings slightly to gain altitude and speed. Wheeling and dancing over the stony landscape, Tiffany let loose with a blast of lightning that pulverized a boulder on a nearby hill.

'I have to learn to fly like that,' Harriet thought a little enviously. So far, Tiffany was the only one who could truly fly. The best the other three could do was to skim over the ground on the surfboards they created.

Her long blond hair streaming behind her, Tiffany ascended while the others watched.

"Throw a fireball at her Harriet," Eden directed. "Leo, throw a rock at her."

The fireball Harriet threw streaked at Tiffany like a rocket. She watched as Tiffany neatly dodged. Crossing her hands, Tiffany erected a powerful sheet of energy in front of her that caused the next fireball to bounce harmlessly off. The shield faded away after a few moments.

Leo appeared bored. Harriet wondered what he was up to as she watched him stretch out his hand. A group of large rocks pulled themselves together to form the body, head, arms, and legs of a giant rock man. It thumped down the hill, kicking boulders as it went. When it arrived at the bottom of the gully, it fell apart.

From above, a blast of cold wind circled itself around Tiffany, keeping her suspended in the air. The icy whirlwind blew into her wings and lifted her higher as it gathered strength. Lightning flashed outward. Then Tiffany flapped her way above the storm and sent it careening across the sky. She descended to the hillside and made her wings disappear.

"I think we'd better get back to the village," Leo advised. "We don't want to get so far behind them that we can't get back by nightfall."

Appearing in front of them, Eden said, "You're probably right. We can continue this later. But well done, all of you."

A couple of hours later, the four of them pulled their hovercycles into Kailua as the houses plodded along. Using her autolibrary, Harriet called Paki and asked him to let down the walker's tail. Waving to Hugh and Leo, she drove her hovercycle up the ramp. Tiffany followed behind. Hugh and Leo waved back and turned toward Russ Akina's house.

Inside, Paki and Nalani greeted Harriet as she climbed the ladder into the pilot's cabin in the walker's head. "Nalani," Harriet reprimanded, "You shouldn't be climbing the ladder. What if you fell?"

"Thanks Harriet," Nalani said, "but I'm ok. I may be eight and a half months pregnant, but I'm not going to be stopped by something as simple as that ladder."

Harriet asked, "But I bet you don't want to be on your feet a lot. Since Paki's driving, can I cook dinner tonight?"

"Sure. Thanks."

Harriet popped happily down the ladder.

Tiffany was sitting in the kitchen using her autolibrary. "Some ship just brought a batch of news broadcasts into the star system," she told Harriet.

"You're watching the news?"

Nodding, Tiffany said, "I figured it was about time one of us did. There's nothing about us any more. But there's a war on."

"A war?" Harriet gasped. "A real war?"

"Yup," Tiffany answered. "It started when we were on our way here."

"That's almost six months ago!" Harriet said. "There's been a war going on all this time and we didn't know it? How come nobody told us?"

"I'm not surprised," Tiffany told her. "The news services only deliver news to this system once a month. The war started right after we went into cryostasis, so by the time we got here it was old news."

"Who's fighting?"

"The French are attacking everyone. They invaded the New Tokyo system first, then went to Kamakura and Shikoku. From there, they took over the Rhineland and Rio Bravo systems. There's rumors that they're going after the Hindustan system next."

"New Tokyo? They invaded New Tokyo? I've got a friend there."

Harriet put on her dataglasses and anxiously tore into the news feeds. What she read made her heart sink. She called Hugh.

"Hugh, there's a war on," she announced as soon as he answered. "The French in the Normandy system invaded the New Tokyo system. I think Akio is dead."

"No way!"

"Look at the news feeds."

Together, they went through all the information they could get. They discovered that Normandy declared its independence from the French government on Earth. The other French systems were officially refusing to have anything to do with the Normans, but the Burgundy system was suspected of smuggling weapons and supplies into Norman-controlled space.

Leo and Tiffany joined Harriet and Hugh in a four-way call.

"You never know," Hugh consoled Harriet. "He might be alive. It says the Japanese are putting up a pretty good resistance."

"I can't imagine why the Space Corps doesn't stop the war!" Harriet declared.

"They're a police force, Harriet, not a military. They're set up to chase pirates and smugglers. You saw the news. The Alliance is building ships and starting to draft soldiers."

"Yes, but it'll be at least another year before they can do anything about the Normans. Even if Akio's alive, how can he hold on that long before help comes?"

Hugh was at a loss. "I don't know Harriet. We just have to hope he's ok. The best way we can help him is to solve our own problems first." Then he said, "Hey, wait a minute. Didn't Foi tell us that just before the Creature came after us, it was in the Normandy system?"

"That's right," Harriet recalled. "It came from Normandy right after we were in the news. Hugh, what does this mean?"

Leo answered for him, "I think it's pretty clear what it means. We've all been assuming it was the Creature that set the gravity bombs in the wormhole a few years ago, right?" The other three agreed. "We think it may have attacked my family a thousand years ago. I'm wondering if it did that to somehow destroy me."

"How could it know you were going to be born?" Harriet asked.

"I don't know," Leo admitted, "but there's got to be a connection. You two said your friend Jeff was in the wormhole collapse, right? Could that be why the Creature set the bombs? To kill Jeff?"

"That doesn't work," Harriet countered. "Madison didn't become Eden until after the collapse. So Eden couldn't have given

Jeff any *korei* before the collapse. He wasn't a threat and he was totally defenseless. If the Creature was trying to kill Jeff, he could have just killed Jeff. I think it was up to something else. There's a bigger picture we're not seeing yet."

Leo agreed. He added, "And now the Creature may have started the first war in six hundred years. Whatever the bigger picture is, it includes that as well. I wonder ... what if Eden also contacted your friend in New Tokyo? What if your friend has *korei* in him like us? And what if Eden gave them to some of his friends, like she did to Tiffany and me? What if the Creature started this war to kill him and his friends just like he's trying to kill us? The French are normally peaceful. Until now, everyone got along with them. It's just plain weird for them to attack anyone."

"I don't know, Leo," Harriet mused. "It seems like overkill to start a whole war just to kill a small group of people. It came after us by itself. Why wouldn't it do the same to Akio?"

"Well, maybe it's also got another reason to have a war," Leo conceded. "But I don't think it's a coincidence that the first system that was attacked is the only one that has a close friend of yours in it. Something big is happening here—something that the Creature doesn't want anyone with a *korei* to interfere with. And it will do anything it needs to in order to make sure we don't."

"Hold on," Hugh broke in.

"What?" Leo responded.

"Something you said earlier reminded me of something," Hugh told him. "Remember when I asked Eden about how Senthil and Madison met?"

"Yeah, so?"

"She told us that Madison's ship got delayed by an outbreak of Kalaran swinepox."

"Yeah, so?" Leo repeated.

"So that's a rare disease. So rare that they don't inoculate for it on Earth. I wonder ... you said you thought the Creature was trying to get you by attacking your family a thousand years ago. But it would have to know the future to do that. And you wondered if it was trying to kill Jeff by collapsing the wormhole. But the only way that would make sense is if the Creature knew the future. So I'm thinking it wasn't a coincidence that Madison's ship was in the wormhole as well. Maybe the Creature caused the outbreak of Kalaran swinepox so that she'd be inside it. That way, it could make sure Madison and that other guy became Eden and Genesis *and* kill Jeff at the same time. If ... if it knew the future."

Harriet asked, "You think the Creature really has power to see the future?"

"Who knows?" Hugh answered. "We don't know what those aliens can really do."

Tiffany joined in with, "It would be really bad if that thing could see the future."

There seemed nothing more to say, so they hung up.

Nalani came into the kitchen. "Hey, what happened to dinner?"

Harriet flushed. "I'm sorry, Nalani. We just found out about the war between the Normans and the Japanese. Hugh and I have a close friend in the New Tokyo system."

Incredulous, Nalani asked, "You didn't know?" Harriet shook her head. More softly, Nalani asked, "Did your friend make it out?"

"We don't know. The news says that the Japanese, Germans, and Spanish have all formed resistance movements. But we don't know if Akio and his family made it to a safe place."

Nalani hugged Harriet. She consoled, "I hope your friend is ok."

Thinking of Eden, Harriet said, "Well, we may have a way of finding out if he's alive. A friend of ours might know. We'll contact her and see."

Releasing Harriet, Nalani asked, "Your friend can get news from the war zone?"

Awkwardly, Harriet replied, "Maybe. She's ... got ways of contacting people."

Nalani's expression grew sober. "Another one like you four, eh? Sometime, you have to tell me how you do such unusual things. In the meantime, I'll make dinner. Why don't you see what you can do about contacting your friend?"

Harriet went to the bedroom and concentrated hard on Eden, who appeared before her immediately.

"Is something wrong, Harriet?"

"Why didn't you tell me about the war?"

"I'm sorry, Harriet. I thought you knew."

"If I knew, I'd have asked about Akio!"

"Yes, well don't shout. Yes, I suppose I should have realized that. I'm sorry. Akio is fine, Harriet. Don't worry about him. I'm helping him like I'm helping you. Together, we can keep you all safe. I'll let you know if Akio needs your help. But Harriet, you need to stay focused on the task at hand. The Creature is still out there. It must be dealt with before you can do anything else."

"I suppose."

"It'll be alright in the end, Harriet. We just have to work together for the good of all."

Harriet repeated, "I suppose."

Eden smiled and nodded, then disappeared.

22

Another week passed with no additional news of the war. Harriet spent the time studying her autolibrary and trying to make up for all of the school she was missing. But she found it hard to focus. Her thoughts kept going back to Akio. She was glad when they finally arrived at Snohomish, the mining town where the Fall Gathering was being held.

It was early in the morning when Paki guided the walker into a large open space between thick groves of bluish-purple trees. All of the walking houses in the village were parked tightly together. "Lots of other villages are coming," Paki explained when Harriet asked him about it.

After lowering the walker's tail, Paki made some calls. When he hung up, he turned to Harriet and Tiffany and said, "I have to go into town and Nalani's asleep. Can you two stay here and wait for George Lightfoot? He's a local food distributor that we sell to. He buys our food and sells it to local stores and to the other villages that are here for the Gathering."

"Sure," Harriet agreed, "what do we need to do?"

"Just be here when he comes. He knows how to open the hatches and get the food." Paki waved to them as he left. Moments later, Harriet saw him on his hovercycle speeding down a grassy road through the forest. His hovercart obediently followed along behind the bike.

Harriet was just finishing breakfast when the comm system beeped. "It's George Lightfoot," a man's voice said when Harriet answered it. "I'm here to pick up the food."

"Just a moment," Harriet replied, "I'll let you in."

Harriet went to the walking house's door and opened it.

"Is Paki or Nalani here?" Sirsen Lightfoot asked, eyeing Harriet curiously. He pulled off his over-sized, floppy cowboy hat and held it casually in his large, brown, calloused hands. Towering over Harriet, Sirsen Lightfoot had an easy, reassuring air about him. The lines on his face told the universe that he had seen a lot of life and worked hard through all of it. But his eyes shone with a gentleness that made Harriet instantly comfortable around him.

"Paki went into town," Harriet explained, "and Nalani's sleeping. I'm ... a friend of theirs. I live with them now. Paki asked me to let you in."

Sirsen Lightfoot nodded and Harriet stepped back so he could enter. His black, braided hair swung from side to side as his heavy boots clunked on the hard floor. He went to a lower level in the walker's belly that Harriet had never been into. They entered a corridor that ran nearly the whole length of the walking house. Sirsen Lightfoot went to the first of several cylindrical stasis freezers that were stacked three high. Ambling down to the end of the corridor, he flipped two rows of switches on the wall. A hatch opened in the wall next to each stasis freezer. Sirsen Lightfoot went upstairs and then outside. Harriet trailed along behind.

Climbing into a large truck unlike any Harriet had ever seen, Sirsen Lightfoot appeared to type instructions into a device in its cab. Then one by one the stasis freezers slid gracefully out of the walker, emptied itself into his truck, and returned to its spot in the walker.

When all of the freezers were empty, he leaned out of the beat-up truck's cab and asked, "Can you go back inside and close the hatches for me? I've got to hurry. I've got a lot of pick-ups this morning. Three villages have come in since midnight."

"Sure Sirsen Lightfoot," Harriet agreed.

"Thanks. Tell Paki the money will be deposited this afternoon." He waved and slowly pulled away. The lumbering truck gingerly made its way through the parked houses toward the same road Paki used earlier.

Harriet went back inside and flipped the switches to shut the hatches. When she came back up into the kitchen, Harriet found that Nalani was up and sitting at the table.

"I swear," Nalani commented ruefully, "that truck of George's gets louder every year. Thanks for letting him in, Harriet. Do you and Tiffany want to go into town and spend the day at the fair?"

"What's a fair?"

"You've never been to a fair?"

Harriet shook her heard.

"Well, it's easier to go and see it for yourself. Just follow that road over there," Nalani instructed, pointing out the window at the road Paki and Sirsen Lightfoot used. "It goes straight to town. There are signs that show you how to get to the fairgrounds. Have some fun. If you and Tiffany go together, you'll probably meet a lot of very nice-looking young men. Leo can be jealous for a change. It's his turn."

Blushing, Harriet said, "I think I'd rather go with all of us."

Nalani smiled knowingly and agreed, "Well, gather up the other three and go have some fun. Try to be back before dark. Take your autolibrary so you can call home if you need to."

After giving Nalani a quick hug, Harriet went to get her hovercycle. She started it up and drifted slowly down the walker's tail. As she sat on the seat, she called Tiffany on her autolibrary.

"I'm on my way over to Russ Akina's to see if Hugh and Leo want to go to the Gathering in town. Want to come too?"

Tiffany's voice came back, "As if I'd let you spend the day with Leo without me there." She hung up. Harriet smiled wryly.

Hugh and Leo were finishing some chores when Harriet arrived. When she asked them about going into town, Leo replied, "Sure." But just as Tiffany arrived, Hugh pointed into the sky and said, "Look. It's Foi."

Harriet turned to see Foi's zipcraft descending. It landed near the Latu's walking house.

Eagerly, Leo suggested, "Let's go see if he got the guns."

"What about the Gathering?" Harriet asked.

"We can do that later. Let's go." Leo bounded onto his hovercycle and took off toward the Latu's. The other three followed.

When they arrived, Harriet saw that Foi hadn't bothered to park his zipcraft inside the walker's mouth. It rested on the ground next to the tail.

"I got the items we were interested in," he told them secretively as soon as they arrived. Looking even more ragged than usual, Foi glanced around hastily to see if anyone else was nearby. "I think we should go for a ride in my ship."

They boarded the zipcraft and took off. Foi vectored the ship away from town. In fifteen minutes, they were skimming low over a broad, rocky open area. Foi set the ship down and climbed out of the cockpit.

"They're stashed out of sight," he explained as he removed a wall panel next to his cryostasis unit. As Foi reached inside the bulkhead, Harriet heard a switch click. The cryostasis unit rose into the air. Underneath was a compartment containing a large crate. The others moved in close to see.

"Hand me that crowbar there, would you Hugh?" Foi requested. Hugh passed the tool and Foi jammed the curved end underneath the lid of the crate. Pulling backward, he levered the crate open.

"Whoa!" Leo exclaimed. "How many did you buy? It looks like you got enough QID rifles for a small army."

"Not quite. There's twenty-five of them in there."

Harriet asked, "How did you afford that many?"

"Things didn't quite go as planned. But in the end, I got what we need. Each of you grab one and I'll show you how to use them."

Tiffany objected, "Right now? We were going into town."

"Right now," Foi commanded intensely. "There are reports of aliens in a nearby system that are stealing people's organs. The Creature may be coming for us."

"Stealing people's organs? From inside their bodies?" Harriet gasped.

"Yes, now grab a rifle, each of you."

His words immediately sobered them all. Taking a rifle from the crate, they followed Foi outside. Without preamble, he pointed to the rifle and explained, "These things aren't like plasma rifles. There's only one setting. You can't stun someone with these. Anything you hit with this is going to start dissolving. Hard objects like buildings and vehicles will crumble. One shot can take out an entire wall. Soft things, like human bodies, will dissolve completely. There'll be nothing left but red goo."

Harriet shuddered as she stared at the weapon in her hands. She began to feel sick. 'I don't think I can do this,' she thought queasily. To Foi she said, "Now that I'm holding this, I really wonder if it's the best way."

"What do you mean?" he asked.

"There's got to be another solution to this besides guns."

"Tell me what it is," Foi shot back immediately.

Flustered, Harriet silently burned with confusion and embarrassment. "I don't know," she got out at last. "I just think that guns aren't the solution to every problem that people have."

Surprisingly, Foi agreed, "You're right. They're not the solution to *every* problem. But in *this* case, I don't see another way. If you come up with one, I'm willing to consider it. In the meantime, all four of you need to practice with these rifles."

Harriet had nothing to say to that, so she let Foi demonstrate how to fire the guns. "There's not really a lot to it," he told them. "You just hold it like this, point, and pull the trigger. The gun scans your eyes to see where you're looking. It can tell from your body's reactions who you consider hostile. With all that information it aims itself at your enemy. If you get the general direction right, the gun does the rest. The problem with hitting the Creature is that it's fast, really fast. Even with the self-aiming feature, the gun will have a hard time hitting it. You have to anticipate where it will be and shoot there. That's very hard to do."

Foi had them point their rifles at some large rocks. Harriet felt the gun's hard, cold muzzle squirm and writhe like a living, hunting creature. As she focused her attention on a particular rock, the gun settled in her grasp, twisting its barrel to its prey. With a shudder, Harriet laid her index finger as lightly as possible on the trigger. A blood-red targeting laser activated and stabbed at the rock with a tiny dot of light.

"Squeeze with your whole hand," instructed Foi. "Don't just jerk your index finger. It knocks your aim off."

With Foi's urging, Harriet fearfully pulled the trigger. An angry orange pulse of energy spat from the gun and hit the rock. The front half of the boulder blasted apart. The rest of it slowly crumbled.

Harriet turned and threw up. She sat down on a boulder to recover.

Leo and Hugh were thundering away with their rifles like they were born to it. They ooo'd and aaah'd at how powerful the guns were as they pulverized the landscape. Tiffany, cool and collected, shot like a precision machine, showing no emotion whatsoever.

Seeing Tiffany, Harriet thought, 'I have to be strong enough do this. If she can do it, so can I.' She stood shakily, took aim, and fired.

Under Foi's instruction, the four of them practiced all day with the rifles. They took only one break about midday to talk with Foi about the Creature having visited the Normandy system and their suspicions that it started the war.

"If it did," Foi observed, "then things are much worse than I thought. We have to kill it as soon as we can. And I think we should not let that alien friend of yours know what we're up to."

"Eden?" Harriet asked. "Why? She can help us."

"She can also help herself," Foi retorted. "All of you have told me that she wants to control the Creature, not kill it. We don't know how she'll react if she finds out what we're doing. It's better to keep her out of things unless we absolutely can't do otherwise. Agreed?"

Harriet wondered if they were being a bit too paranoid. After all, Eden was helping them as much as she could. But, like the other three, she reluctantly went along with Foi's suggestion.

They returned to their practice, finally stopping when the sun sank low on the horizon. Boarding Foi's ship, they flew back to Kailua. Leo and Hugh rode their hovercycles to Russ's place.

Going inside the Latu's house with Tiffany trailing along behind, Harriet was surprised to find Doctor Manutai and Paki sitting at the kitchen table eating a sandwich.

"There you are," Paki exclaimed. "We've been trying to call you all day. You must have had your autolibraries turned off. Nalani had the baby about one o'clock today. A girl. Seven pounds four ounces."

Together, Harriet and Tiffany squealed, "Nalani had the baby?" They hugged Paki.

"Her sister's with the two of them now," Paki informed them.

Harriet asked, "Her sister? I didn't know she had a sister."

"Yeah, Leilani lives in the village of Mililani. They're here for the Gathering too. Leilani will be staying in the baby's room for a few weeks. The baby will sleep in a bassinet in our room while Leilani's here. You girls want to see Nalani and the baby?"

"Can we?" Harriet asked.

"Sure, go on into our room."

Harriet and Tiffany went upstairs and cautiously approached the bedroom. Tiffany knocked softly. "Come in," Nalani's voice called from inside. They entered.

"Hi girls, meet my sister Leilani," Nalani introduced. They exchanged greetings and Harriet saw that Leilani and Nalani were near mirror images of each other. Leilani was clearly a year or two younger than Nalani and her hair was almost down to her knees. But otherwise, they were nearly identical.

As they stepped closer to the bed, they stared at the tiny form sleeping in Nalani's arms. "You want to hold her?" Nalani asked, extending the baby out toward Harriet. Gently, Harriet lifted the slumbering infant. Carefully, she cradled the baby.

"I think she likes to lie on your shoulder," Nalani told her. Harriet nestled the tiny girl against her shoulder.

"What's her name?" Tiffany asked.

Smiling broadly, Nalani replied, "Leilani Harriet Tiffany Latu."

Harriet gasped. "You named her after us? Oh, Nalani."

Tiffany was as pleased as Harriet. She hugged Nalani tightly and thanked her profusely. "Can I hold her now?" she softly asked Harriet.

'Wow, this is a side of Tiffany I haven't seen before,' Harriet thought as she passed the tiny infant to her.

After a while, Nalani's sister said, "I think we'd better go, girls. Nalani and little Leilani need to sleep."

They said their goodbyes and followed Leilani into the kitchen. The doctor was gone. Foi was sitting at the table chatting with Paki, who was cooking. They broke off as soon as the girls entered.

Paki said brightly, "There they are. Are you ready for a big, big dinner to celebrate? Leo and Hugh are on the way back over here to eat with us."

Leilani plopped unceremoniously into a chair across from Foi. She was clearly ill at ease. "You came back," she stated to him.

Cautiously, Foi answered, "Yes. I came back."

"It always scares me when you come here," Leilani stated. "That thing may follow you."

Foi told her, "It didn't follow me."

Paki tried to interrupt, "Leilani, let him alone now. We're celebrating the baby. Can't that be enough for tonight?"

Harriet interjected, "You know about the Creature?"

"We all know about the Creature. At least, all of us from Kailua and Mililani," Leilani replied. She pointed to Foi, "He first came here in my grandfather's time. Our families lived on the planet Lanai then. They were fishermen. He told us what happened to the first Foi, and a bunch of men from the village decided to hunt the Creature down and kill it. The only one to come back was him." She pointed again at Foi. "The rest were all dead. The Creature came to Lanai in my grandfather's body. It killed most of the village and some of the surrounding villages as well. Foi, this Foi," she pointed again, "got the survivors to safety. My mother, uncle, and grandmother were in the group. We've lived here ever since."

Paki scolded, "That was a long time ago, Leilani. It was their own fault. Foi warned them over and over not to go after it. They didn't listen. It wasn't Foi's fault."

"No," Leilani agreed tightly, "I don't suppose it was. But no one from Kailua or Mililani is really all that pleased when Foi shows up, except for you and Nalani."

Instead of answering, Foi stood stiffly and left the house. Paki shot a severe look at Leilani.

"I'm sorry," Leilani apologized to Paki. "I didn't mean to ruin your dinner."

Grumpily, Paki told her, "I'll take a plate for him to his ship later. I'd just appreciate it if you wouldn't keep going on about that when he's here. What's past is past. All of us who are left are alive because of him."

Leilani sighed and went to the baby's room. Harriet and Tiffany made themselves scarce by returning to their own room.

Paki went all out for the celebration dinner, which he finished about an hour later. Nalani brought the baby out to the kitchen and joined in. Hugh put away an amazing amount of food, which made Paki so happy that he managed to shake off his earlier crabbiness.

When everyone was done eating, Paki packed some food for Leo and Hugh to take with them. He also bundled up a big helping and asked Leo to pass it along to Russ Akina. Next Paki prepared a heaping plate for Foi. He walked outside with Leo and Hugh as Harriet and Tiffany followed behind. Foi was sitting outside at the bottom of the ramp.

"Something to eat," Paki said, handing the plate to Foi. Foi silently accepted the food, looking much older than his seventeen years.

As Leo and Hugh were getting onto their hovercycles, Foi told Paki, "You can't stay here."

"What?" Paki asked, startled. The other four stopped and stared at Foi.

"It may be coming."

Shocked, Paki demanded, "Here? It's coming here?"

"I'm not sure. But there are reports of aliens attacking people on the planet Alofi in the Niue system. That's not very far from here. It may be closing in on the five of us."

Doubtfully, Paki countered, "There are reports of aliens all over human space every year. They always turn out to be hoaxes."

Foi shook his head. "From the details in the news, I think this one is real."

Paki sat heavily on the edge of the walker's tail. "What are we going to do?" he muttered to no one.

"You have to leave," Foi commanded. "All of you. All of Kailua and all of Mililani. I can't be responsible for another massacre." Foi reached under the walker's tail and pulled out a QID rifle. He extended it to Paki.

Eyes wide, Paki said, "I don't want your gun."

"This isn't my gun, Paki. Mine's in my coat. This one's for you. There are twenty more in my ship for anyone in the village who wants one."

Paki stammered, "How ... how did you get QID weapons?"

"I found someone who was selling them to the Normans for their war."

"The Normans are using QIDs?"

Foi nodded and said, "Yes. The war is getting really ugly. And the five of us think that the Creature started it. We don't know why."

Paki put his head in his hands and stuttered, "This ... this can't be real. We just had a baby. What kind of a universe did we bring our daughter into?" He sat up, glared at Foi, and demanded, "How did you get so many QIDs?"

Foi's pressed his lips together tightly. After a moment, he answered, "I went to get four, one for each of them." He jerked his head toward Harriet, Tiffany, Hugh, and Leo. "The seller decided to take all my money and torture me instead. They wanted to know why I wanted QIDs rather than regular rifles. I got away, but I took a crate of QIDs from him and helped myself to everything in his bank accounts. He won't be dealing any more weapons to the Normans."

Glaring at him, Paki commented, "I suppose that's something good at least. And I hope you didn't kill anyone."

Foi shifted uncomfortably, and then said, "You have to go somewhere where we'll never find you, Paki. If the creature takes over one of us, it'll know everything about you."

Paki jumped to his feet. "What do you mean? Who's 'us?' The five of you? Are you going after it?"

"Yes, Paki, we are. We're leaving early tomorrow morning."

Paki shook with anger. Foi seemed not to notice. With a death-like calm, he stared into Paki's eyes and said, "It's going to take us two weeks to get to Alofi. You have that long to get off this planet. After that, I can't say how safe you'll be here. I still have my money and I've returned the money these four gave me. So we have enough for ourselves. I've put all the money I stole from the arms dealer into your bank account because you'll share with everyone else from Kailua and Mililani. You'll all have plenty of cash for the rest of your lives. That guy owned an entire moon. Now he's broke."

"I can't take stolen money," Paki hissed.

"You have to, Paki. You need it for your family and your friends. Don't worry about it being stolen. He was an arms dealer. Millions of people died because of the weapons he was selling. Not having him as a supplier will slow the war down a lot. Who knows how many lives it will save?"

Foi paused, but Paki didn't comment, so he continued, "There's a Leviathan-class megafreighter coming into the system next week. I checked. It's big enough to take both villages—walkers and all. With this money, you can afford passage to anywhere. Go someplace far away, someplace where you'll never see the five of us again. Be safe Paki. Keep your wife and baby safe."

Paki looked at Foi. Slowly, with trembling hands, he reached out and accepted the rifle. Foi told Paki, "I'll unload the crate before I go to bed and leave it here on the ramp." Hesitantly, Paki nodded.

Foi said, "Thanks for the food. Don't tell Nalani until after we're gone. She'll try and stop us if she finds out sooner. It's better for everyone if we just disappear." To Harriet, Hugh, Leo, and Tiffany, Foi said, "Pack tonight. Be up by five tomorrow morning. We leave at six. I've arranged for someone in town to buy your hovercycles." He strode to his ship.

23

Harriet drove her hovercycle through the early morning mist as she traveled with Leo, Hugh, and Tiffany toward town. Her jacket whipped behind her in the wind. No one spoke.

Following the directions Foi gave them, they arrived at a vehicle dealership. They saw that Foi was already there with his ship. After selling their hovercycles, they boarded the zipcraft. Foi lifted off as the other four watched from the windows.

Very softly, almost too softly to hear, Tiffany sighed, "I was happy here. For the first time in my life, I was happy." She turned away and went to lie down on Foi's bunk. Harriet wasn't sure, but she thought she could hear Tiffany crying.

The trip into space was spent in silence. They docked with a passenger liner and were taken to their cabins. Foi's ship was stored in a hold. Just before they boarded the ship, Foi handed them IDs. "You're April North," he told Harriet. "Hugh, you're Harry Kestler. Leo is Anthony Vincent and Tiffany is Candice Chandler."

"We don't need our plastifaces?" Harriet asked.

Foi shook his head. "I don't think so. We're too far out for anyone to be looking for you. And if anyone asks, we're all 18."

Harriet spent the first day in her cabin reading her autolibrary. The ship had AR suites, as well as other recreational facilities, but she didn't seem to want to use any of them. She just stayed in her room and had room service bring her meals.

"I didn't even get to say goodbye to Nalani and the baby," she complained to no one as she lay on her bed. She thought about little Leilani Harriet Tiffany Latu. "At least she'll be safe," Harriet told herself. That made things a little better. "That Creature won't be able to kill *everyone* I care about."

On the second day of the trip, Harriet came out of her cabin and went with Foi, Hugh, and Leo to one of the restaurants on board. Tiffany didn't want to join them.

"I think leaving Nason has hit Tiffany pretty hard," Leo commented as they ate breakfast.

"She said it was the first time in her life she was happy," Harriet stated.

Hugh agreed, "We were all happy there. It was a good place to be." He changed the subject, "Hey Foi. Why is such a fancy ship way out here in a backwater system like this?"

"It's a chartered sightseeing tour. There's some sort of asteroid cluster that they've come to see," Foi answered. "Apparently it lights up in a really spectacular way every few years. We arrive later today. The tourists watch the show from the ship's big observation deck. Next week, the ship will make the jump to the Niue system so the tourists can see the firewhales return from deep space. We'll be on the planet Alofi a week later."

"What are we gonna do for the next two weeks?" Harriet wondered.

Hugh answered, "I'm spending the time studying. I've almost finished a college degree in artificially intelligent matrix design."

"Wow, Hugh. I'm impressed," Harriet congratulated him.

Hugh smiled and told her, "I wanted to improve my computer programming skills."

Foi glanced at him knowingly and said, "I think you want to learn to crack into computer systems like I do."

"He does not," Harriet countered, "do you Hugh?"

"Well ..."

"Hugh!"

"You've got to admit, it's a survival skill in a situation like ours."

Foi answered for Hugh. "He has a point. It can make the difference between living and dying."

Harriet was smoldering. "We've already done too many things that are illegal. I thought we were going to get the Creature and go back to our lives, our legal lives."

"Well," Hugh agreed, "that's the goal. But we may have a hard road ahead of us. Foi, what do you use to get into computers, BlackHat?"

"Hugh!"

Acting as if he hadn't heard Harriet, Foi told Hugh, "Naw, that won't get you into all that many systems these days. I use BackDoor. Wanna come to my ship and get a look?"

"Sure," Hugh replied, "I'll even let you copy my autolibrary if you put BackDoor on it."

"Hugh!" Harriet objected again.

Hugh cast a guilty glance at her. "Sorry Harriet," he apologized, "but I think I should do this. Foi and I will meet you for dinner." Hugh and Foi made a hasty exit.

Harriet sat with her arms tightly folded, feeling as if Hugh had somehow turned against her. Leo consoled, "Look Harriet, don't be mad. It's his decision, and it's not up to us to try to control what he does. Besides, none of us *want* to do illegal things. If the circumstances weren't so extreme, we wouldn't break the law."

"I suppose," she groused. "I just think we should find better ways to deal with the situation."

"You're right," Leo agreed. "And from now on, we'll do our best to do that."

Leo's words took the edge off Harriet's anger.

"Looks like it's just you and me today," Leo told her. "What shall we do?"

Still a bit put out, Harriet mumbled, "Maybe we could try out the AR programs on this ship. How about going hypersailing?"

Nodding, Leo replied warmly, "That sounds perfect." He extended his hand, which surprised Harriet. In all of their time on Nason, Harriet and Leo never had time alone with each other. Harriet had begun to think Leo wasn't interested in her any more. Tentatively, she took his hand and they walked together to one of the AR suites. They found a hypersailing program and entered, appearing on the beach in bathing suits. Harriet went to a booth on the grass above the beach and got herself a pair of sunglasses while Leo picked out a boat for them. "Take the tiller," he instructed. "I'll handle the ropes."

Uncertainly, Harriet sat at the back of the boat and took a firm grip on the tiller. Leo cast them off from the dock and hoisted the sails. The boat slid forward.

"Point us toward the mouth of the bay," Leo said. Harriet turned the tiller and the boat lurched to the side, almost knocking Leo off his feet. He laughed. "You're trying to dump me into the water!" he accused jokingly.

Defensively, Harriet replied, "No I wasn't, I ..."

"I'm just kidding, Harriet. I know you didn't do it on purpose," Leo told her. "Relax. A hypersailer is a really touchy boat. It just takes a small movement of the tiller to turn it. Just do it gently and you'll be ok."

Leo tugged and pulled the ropes, moving the sails into a better position to catch the wind. The boat rose on its foils and whisked forward.

Harriet piloted them out of the bay and along the south coast of the AR program's tropical island. With Leo's help, Harriet quickly mastered the art of controlling the small craft. They sailed along for a couple of hours, chatting and enjoying the scenery. As they rounded a point of land, they found a long stretch of golden beach. Leo suggested they land the boat there.

While Harriet guided them toward the shore, Leo pulled down the sails. When the boat slowed enough for it to lower itself into the water, he turned a crank that retracted the foils. They glided into shallow water and nosed the boat onto the beach. Leo hopped out to steady it. Offering his hand to Harriet, he helped her out onto the sand. Harriet couldn't help but notice that he kept hold of her hand after she was out of the boat.

Wading in the warm seawater that lapped the shoreline, they walked hand in hand. A flock of white seagulls flew over them, cawing and calling to each other as they darted through the air. After a while, Harriet asked, "Leo?"

"What?"

"Do ... do really think this will turn out all right?"

"Yes, Harriet, I do."

"I ... I wonder."

"You wonder what?"

"We're not really fighters, you know—in spite of all the practice with the guns and everything Eden's taught us."

Leo stopped, bringing Harriet to a stop as well. He looked deep into her eyes, and then gently brushed away a lock of her hair that the breeze blew into her face. "If we need to be fighters," he said soothingly, "we'll be fighters."

"How can you be so sure of that?"

"Confidence is the first rule of business. That's what my father taught me."

"Did your father teach you a lot about business?"

"Yeah," Leo answered wistfully. Sadness passed across his face. "I was being raised to take over the conglomerate. I started learning about business when I was eight. I did my first hostile takeover when I was twelve. I should have finished my senior year and be starting college by now. I should be ..." Falling silent, Leo hung his head.

Harriet nestled closer to Leo and gazed up into his suddenly puppy-like blue eyes. "Don't be sad. You're right. We'll make this work out right. We'll get home and everything will be perfect for you, for us." She slid her arms around him and held him tightly. Leo stroked her long hair. Lifting Harriet's chin, he kissed her tenderly. Harriet's heart beat like it never had before.

Three ascending tones sounded. Startled, Harriet released Leo and looked around.

A man's voice from the sky said, "Attention Honored Guests. The ship is now approaching the Lewiston Vortex. We will be stopping here for exactly twenty-four hours to observe the Lighting of the Everlasting Brocade. The Lighting is the best opportunity to see the Dance of the Brocade Ghosts. We are humbly grateful for the opportunity to provide you with excellent viewing of the Lighting on our singular observation deck. A luncheon will also be served. Please enjoy our services. And thank you for flying Completely Celestial Voyages."

Harriet saw that Leo was still gazing affectionately down at her. She slid back into his embrace. 'I could hold you forever,' Harriet thought.

"Shall we go watch?" Leo asked. "I heard it was pretty spectacular."

Looking deeply into his wonderfully blue eyes, Harriet hesitated, kissed him lightly, and then softly cooed, "I guess. But let's come back here after lunch." They let go of each other.

"Actually," Leo said, "I was wondering if you wanted to go dancing this afternoon. They have night clubs and dance halls that open at 1 p.m. and go until 6 a.m. Do you know how to dance?"

"I know swing dancing and some types of ballroom dancing," Harriet told him. "I've actually been doing them for a while. I don't know the line dances that have been popular for years and years."

"That's ok," Leo assured her. "They're going out of style now anyway. After the swing dancing craze a couple of years ago, everyone decided that they like dancing together better than in lines. They're doing all the old-style ballroom dances from like, way, way back."

"I don't have any shoes that are good for dancing," Harriet said.

Chuckling, Leo observed, "Girls and their shoes. Ok, we'll stop and buy some in the ship's shopping center."

Leo disappeared. Harriet willed herself to be out of the program and sat up as the door of her AR pod opened. She took Leo's proffered hand and together they walked to the ship's shopping complex. Leo was patient while she bought her shoes, but she could see he was getting bored.

"Sorry for making you wait," Harriet told him, feeling a bit embarrassed.

He shrugged tolerantly as they approached the observation deck and said, "Look, we're just in time."

The observation deck flared with the light of the asteroids of the Everlasting Brocade entering the Lewiston Vortex. Morphing shapes, like living things, flowed from deep within each energy node of the Brocade. Harriet watched one as it shaped itself into a dolphin-like creature, swimming through the depths of space. Another resembled a netherworldly bird. Others had no distinct shape; they just spun and danced in the misty glow of the gaseous Vortex.

"Shall we have lunch and watch them?" Leo asked.

Harriet agreed and they found a table near a window. As Harriet ooo'd and aaah'd through the meal, Leo kept saying things like, "Yeah, it's really spectacular. Pass the spring rolls please."

After lunch, they went back to their rooms to change. Harriet put on a sleek, flattering dress she bought back on Venus and slipped into her new shoes.

When she met Leo again, he was dressed in an equally sleek, ankle-length suit jacket and slacks. "I got this yesterday," he told Harriet. "I don't know if I like the jacket this long, but it's what everyone's wearing now."

Harriet coyly told him, "You look very handsome in it."

Together, they went to the ship's nightclub section.

"Let's start with this one," Leo urged, pulling her toward a dance hall.

"The jitterbug!" Harriet exclaimed as they entered.

"You know the jitterbug?" Leo queried.

Harriet nodded. "Sure, it was really popular last year."

"It's like, a way old dance, you know," Leo said.

Shrugging, Harriet repeated, "Well it was popular last year."

"Well then," Leo encouraged, "let's jitterbug." He led her onto the dance floor where they stayed for hours, enjoying dance after dance.

"Harriet," Leo commented while they were holding each other closely during a slow song, "you're one of the best dance partners I've ever had."

Harriet glowed. "Thank you," she replied demurely. "And you're the absolutely best dance partner I've ever had."

"Do you think the universe would end if I kissed you right here on the dance floor?" Leo asked with a smile.

"There's only one way to find out," Harriet answered.

Leo leaned down and kissed her.

BOOM!

Harriet cast her eyes around wildly to see what happened. People screamed. The ship's sirens blared through the dance hall. A voice came from the ceiling, "Ladies and gentlemen, please exit the dance hall immediately."

Near one of the entrances to the hall, right next to a wall that was showering the room with electrical sparks and gushing fire, stood Tiffany. She was dressed like a girl ready for a night out, but her face was pure fury.

"Uh oh," Leo said. "I think you'd better just leave. I'll see if I can get Tiffany calmed down before she destroys the ship."

Deciding that Leo was probably right, Harriet left through a rear door. She went back to her room and changed. Almost immediately after she was back into her regular clothes, the doorbell rang.

"Door open," Harriet commanded. Foi and Hugh walked in.

Without preamble, Foi asked sharply, "Do you think you can stay away from Leo until we get off this ship? Tiffany caused a pretty major incident in that dance hall. We're lucky no one figured out that the electrical burst came from her."

Harriet asked, "What happened?"

"Leo got her calmed down," Hugh answered. "Like Foi said, no one figured out it was her. She was touching the wall when she saw you two, and she shorted out a power conduit. From now on, do us all a favor. Only hang out with Leo when the rest of us are there. Ok?"

"Humph," Harriet grumbled. "That girl just has to get control of herself."

"Harriet, please. Just until we're off the ship," Hugh begged.

Exasperated, she replied, "Oh, all right."

The silence at dinner that evening was very strained. For the rest of the trip, the five of them spent a lot of time together. Hugh and Foi made special efforts to ensure that neither of the girls was alone with Leo.

Foi encouraged them all to take some basic martial arts classes in the AR suites. "You all need the practice fighting," he explained. Hugh also suggested that they try some of the AR suite's shooter games. "We need the practice with guns."

So Harriet and the others tramped around in mud, ran down dark corridors, and pushed through thick jungles as they shot, punched, and kicked their way through game after game. After days and days of it, she complained to the others, "I'm getting so sick of this. It's so gross. There's blood and guts everywhere. I can't see why anyone would think this is fun."

Surprisingly, Tiffany agreed, "Yeah, why is this even a game?"

Foi, Leo, and Hugh stared at her blankly.

"Don't you see all the explosions?" Hugh asked.

"And the blood and guts?" Foi added.

"And the explosions?" Leo reiterated.

Putting her hands on her hips, Harriet challenged, "Yeah, so?"

"So, that's why it's fun!" the guys exclaimed in unison.

Tiffany looked at Harriet and demanded, "When are guys gonna stop being CAVEMEN?"

'At last,' Harriet thought, 'Tiff and I have found something we agree on.'

24

The lights from the city of Liku on the planet Alofi sparkled along the seacoast as Foi's zipcraft descended. When they landed, it was late at night. They quickly checked into a hotel, gathered in Foi's room, and began searching for information on the news services.

"Wow," Hugh commented to Foi, "you were right. The local news feeds are burning up with stories about aliens."

Foi shook his head. "Yeah," he agreed, "but they're the wrong kind. The short grey guys in this artist's rendition are definitely not what we're looking for. It must be another hoax of some kind. Sightings of these kinds of aliens have been reported for centuries."

Harriet disagreed, "Yeah but there's something going on here, Foi. The aliens, or whatever they are, keep taking specific organs out of people's bodies. They do it over and over. There's eight people dead so far."

"The attacks are always at night," Leo interjected. "There was another one last night. The police showed up and started firing at the aliens, but the aliens disappeared. The two people they attacked survived."

Hugh suggested, "Should we go to the hospital and scan the victims? Maybe we can get some information that way."

The others agreed that was worth a try. "But before we go anywhere," Foi said, "I think we should all buy ourselves some comPods."

"I've got a comPod," Tiffany objected.

"And we can make calls with our autolibraries," Harriet agreed.

Foi countered, "No, we need to be able to make fast, hands-free calls. We need minipods, the kind you clip to your ear."

Tiffany wrinkled her nose and said, "Those are out of style."

Foi gave her a hard stare. Tiffany blushed. Leo told Tiffany, "He's right. I'd say we should all get mindpods if the local planetary grid supported them. But since this place is too far behind the times for that, we should get minipods. Like Foi says, you can clip them onto your ear so they're always ready. All you've got to do is say the name of the person you're calling, and it will connect. It's fast and reliable. And if we get split up, we can regroup fast."

Foi continued, "We also need to get overcoats for all of you. We can sew some holsters inside. Then you can carry your rifles in your coats like I do."

"This planet is cold and kind of dreary anyway," Tiffany commented. "I could use a nice, warm overcoat. Oooo, I saw some really excellent leather coats in a store window on the way from the spaceport. Real leather. And they had really cute belts and matching shoes and ..."

"Uh Tiff," Leo interrupted.

"What?"

"Can we not change the subject please?"

"Humph," Tiffany pouted.

"It's still the middle of the night here," Leo said. "We need to try and adjust to local time. I say we all go back to our rooms and try to rest. We can go out and buy coats and minipods after dawn."

Agreeing that Leo's suggestion was a good idea, they returned to their rooms for the rest of the night. As Harriet lay on her bed, her thoughts went back to Nalani's warnings and to her parents' deaths.

'What are we getting ourselves into?' Harriet wondered. 'Do we really have a chance of killing that thing? But if we run away and hide, will we be better off? Nalani and her friends and relatives have been on the run from the Creature for decades. Now they have to leave their home behind for the second time. Is that what I want for myself?'

After lying in bed and worrying for a couple of hours, Harriet fell into a troubled sleep. She woke up when her room's computer sounded a chime and said, "Mamsen North, this is the wake-up call you asked for. Mamsen North?"

"Wha ... ?" Harriet stammered blearily. It took a moment to remember that she was using the name April North. "Yes," she told the computer. "I'm awake."

After gathering in the hotel's restaurant for breakfast together, Harriet and the others hopped a cab and went shopping. Tiffany insisted that they go to the store where she'd seen the real leather coats. She got so excited that she was about to buy several of them. Leo intervened. "You only need one, Tiff," he told her. "These are expensive and we have to be careful with our money."

"I can't do that. I just can't do it. Please Leo," she pleaded, "you can't make me buy just one. I at least have to have the black one and the red one."

Relenting, Leo sighed, "Oh all right. Two then. And you can pick one out for me." Happily, Tiffany pulled coat after coat off the men's rack. She tried each one of them on Leo as he repeatedly sighed and looked exasperated.

"I think he's going to sprain his eyes if he keeps rolling them like that," Hugh joked when he and Harriet were out of earshot of the other two.

"But he's sure making Tiffany happy," Harriet observed sourly.

"I suppose. Hey, wanna help me pick out a coat?"

"Ok," Harriet agreed. Then she had a thought. "Hey Foi!" she called waving him over to where they were standing. As he approached them, Harriet suggested, "Maybe it's time for you to buy a new coat too."

"That's ok," he demurred, "I'll stick with this one. It's just the way I like it."

"In other words," Hugh interpreted, "you've got too many pockets you've put into it for all the weapons you carry and you don't want to have to sew all those pockets into a new coat."

Shrugging, Foi nodded and returned to watching Tiffany and Leo. By the time Harriet and Hugh picked out coats for themselves, Leo was showing obvious impatience with Tiffany. "That one," he stated definitively as he pointed to a black coat. "I'll take that one. Let's pay right now and get out of here." Tiffany looked a little miffed, but she complied.

Buying minipods wasn't nearly as much trouble as getting the coats. But getting sewing supplies took some hunting around. Returning to the hotel, they spent the afternoon sewing their rifle holsters into their coats. Harriet tried hers on. The short, light rifle didn't weigh her down much as it hung in the coat's lining. But having the gun in her coat made Harriet nervous as they stepped out onto the street and hailed a cab. She was sure someone would notice. 'When this is over,' she thought, 'I'll never touch a gun again.'

At the hospital, Hugh used his autolibrary to break into the hospital's poorly-protected computer in spite of Harriet's objections. "We don't want to draw attention to ourselves by asking about the attack victims," he replied defensively. Harriet was not pleased.

After a few moments, Hugh told them, "One of the victims died already. The other is on the eighth floor. Room 811."

Riding the elevator, they wandered down the hall looking for room 811. When they found it, Foi extracted his scanner from his coat. He checked the room and said, "There's someone in there besides the victim, probably a relative." Scanning the neighboring room, he told them, "There's a patient in room 810, but she's unconscious. Let's go in there."

They entered room 810 and saw a girl of about 9 or 10 asleep on the bed. Foi scanned the patient in room 811 through the wall. "Hugh," he said, "I'm sending the data directly to your autolibrary. Upload it to the hospital diagnostic computer for analysis."

"Quiet," Leo cautioned, "we don't want to wake her up." He pointed at the small girl on the bed.

"We can't," Hugh told him. "I'm looking at her hospital records. She's comatose. She can't wake up."

"What happened to her?" Harriet asked.

"Shuttle crash," Hugh informed her. "Her parents were killed."

A noise came from the doorway as it slid open. Foi hastily jammed his scanner into his pocket.

A nurse entered. "Are you Carlene's aunt?" she asked Harriet.

Warily, Harriet answered, "Uh … yes. How did you know?"

The nurse smiled and said, "Well, we got your letter saying you were on the way, and you must admit that your hair makes it an easy guess." Harriet glanced at the girl on the bed and saw that she had flaming red hair too.

"She got the teddy bear you sent, poor dear," the nurse continued, looking down at the sleeping girl. Harriet saw the stuffed bear tucked into the girl's blankets. "But I'm so glad she has family here now. We've been worried, what with all the controversy that surrounded her parents." She glanced apprehensively back to Harriet. "Not that your sister and her husband weren't perfectly wonderful people. I always admired them, and I want to extend my condolences on your loss."

"Thank you," Harriet replied. "Um …"

"Yes?"

"How is she?"

"Well, as I mentioned in my vmail, the transplants you authorized from her parents saved her life. The organs are functioning perfectly. But for some reason, she just doesn't wake up. The doctors can't understand it."

"I see. Is there any hope for her?"

"At this point, Mamsen Wells, we just don't know. Well, I'll just leave you to visit," the nurse said as she exited the room.

Harriet asked Hugh, "Who is this girl?"

"She's Carlene Paloma, according to her records," Hugh answered. "Her parents were Enrique and Matilda Paloma. They were pronounced dead on arrival at the hospital. The doctors saved Carlene using organs from her parents. Carlene's only living relative is an aunt, Sheila Wells."

"None of that is important," Foi hissed. He was already scanning through the wall again. He asked Hugh, "What do the hospital's records say about the survivor in 811? And have you gotten anything from the diagnostic computer yet?"

"Hmm," Hugh said, "The records say he's Larry Brent, age 35. He was really cut up but it looks like he'll recover."

"What about the scans?" Foi demanded.

"Nothing unusual," Hugh replied, shrugging. "Normal brain patterns, normal everything."

"Dead end," Leo commented.

"Yeah," Foi agreed, "let's go back to the hotel. I need to get into the local police network. We'll wait until word comes in of another attack and then try to get there in time to see something."

As they left the hospital, Leo suggested, "Let's eat there." He pointed to a small Garlendian restaurant on the other side of the street. The others agreed. By the time they finished their meal, it was quite late. The grey, drizzly afternoon had turned into a black, drizzly night.

"I don't see any cabs," observed Foi as he gazed along the nearly empty streets.

Hugh still had his dataglasses on. He said, "I'm on the local public network. Everything in this town shuts down fairly early, especially with these attacks. There's no more cabs, but there's a train station a few blocks down that street. It's not even a skytrain. They use old-style maglev trains here." He pointed to a dark, wet boulevard.

"Let's get going," Leo urged, heading down the street. The others followed. As they walked, they discussed the news reports of the attacks.

"The news reports say that these 'aliens' or whatever they are, keep taking organs from people's bodies," Hugh remarked. "It's always the same organs too: the heart, lungs, liver, and eyes. I wonder why?"

Leo said, "I played an AR game once called 'Attack of the Zombie Aliens' where they took people's organs back to their planet for transplant because they all had a disease that turned them into zombies."

Tiffany hit Leo's upper arm and commanded, "Don't be gross! This isn't a game."

"Ok, Tiff, ok! I'm just saying, that's all."

Harriet stiffened. "Sh!" she hissed. "Did you hear that?"

They all froze. Harriet suddenly noticed that they were standing in the darkness between two widely separated streetlamps.

"I don't hear anything," Hugh said tensely.

"Sh!" Foi said. "She's right. Something's following us." He unholstered his gun.

Harriet's heart was pounding. She glanced around wildly, trying to find the source of the weird sound she had heard. The noise came again, this time from a pitch-black alleyway they were standing near. 'I can take care of that,' she realized.

Glancing up and down the street to ensure no one was around, Harriet lifted her right hand over her head and created a fireball. It bathed their surroundings in its bright light. Harriet was horrified to see two short, grey humanoids with large heads, large eyes, and only four fingers on each hand. They froze in the glare of her fireball, staring at her.

Foi fired, hitting one of the aliens directly in the chest. Its unearthly scream was like a dagger in their ears. The injured alien fell backwards, while its companion threw a force push at Harriet, flinging her to the ground. Harriet scrambled to her feet. Her entire body ached, but she wasn't seriously hurt. Angry, she erupted into a flame.

Leo grabbed a vehicle that was parked near them on the street and threw it at the pair of aliens. It hit the wounded one, but the other one dodged and shot a blast of freezing energy at Leo. Tiffany threw up her sheet-like shield between the alien and Leo, protecting him completely. Foi fired again at the injured alien. It fell dead and began to dissolve.

The uninjured alien froze, staring at its companion. Then it simply disappeared. Cautiously, they approached the dead alien. Suddenly, an orb-like ball of energy rose from the extraterrestrial. Across its middle was a blue band of color. Below that were six tentacle-like arms that flailed manically. Foi shot the energy creature.

When the blast hit it, the life form let out a wail, but didn't make a sound. 'I heard it in my head,' Harriet realized. 'That thing's telepathic.'

The energy creature dissipated into a glowing haze while the corpse it abandoned dissolved into a pool of grey muck.

25

"I think it was a different species than the Creature," Hugh surmised when they gathered for breakfast in the hotel restaurant the next day.

"So that means Eden was right," Harriet said. "There are more of them coming into our universe."

Foi stated, "Same species or different, we have to kill the other grey alien before it takes anyone else's organs."

Hugh and Foi immediately commenced hacking into the police's network. Leo exclaimed, "Hey! I want to help too. I'm good with computers." He pulled out his autolibrary and joined their huddle.

Harriet heaved a frustrated sigh. 'I wish they wouldn't act like it's all just a game instead of a crime,' she thought.

"This is interesting," Hugh told the others. "I'm looking at a map the police posted in their files on the attacks. Every attack is shown in red. They all occurred within two miles of the hospital we were at tonight. Four of them were within a few blocks."

"You mean five of them," Leo interjected, "counting the attack on us."

"Right," Hugh agreed. "Oh wait, this isn't good."

"What isn't good?" Harriet asked warily.

"The cops found the truck Leo tossed at the aliens. The report talks about scorch marks all over the place. They think it was another alien attack even though they didn't find bodies. They just got a shipment of hovercameras in. They plan to use the cameras to monitor the entire area around the hospital, starting tonight."

"That isn't good," Foi echoed. "With cameras floating around, we'll be spotted if anything happens."

"What do we do?" Harriet wondered aloud, "Get new plastifaces?"

Foi shook his head. "That kind of technology is hard to find out here. We'll just have to kill that thing as quickly and quietly as we can. But I think we should pack our stuff and load it into my ship this afternoon just in case we have to make a fast getaway."

They spent most of the day in their rooms, resting. In the late afternoon, they packed their belongings and took them to Foi's ship at the spaceport. After dinner, the five of them rode the train back to the hospital. Following their plan, they walked all the streets in a five-block area around the hospital. Several times, they saw the hovercams pass by.

"I'm logged onto the police network," Hugh told them. "I can see all the video inputs from the cameras. Nothing's happened so far."

"My feet are tired," Tiffany complained. "Since we're back at the hospital, let's go inside and sit down for a few minutes."

"I suppose we're not doing much good walking around like this," Leo agreed.

Hugh said, "Actually, it's probably better that we stay inside. The local police are starting to get suspicious of us. They've seen us on the cameras too many times. Let's wait in the hospital until something happens."

Inside the hospital lobby, they found some comfortable chairs to wait in. Foi plopped into one of them and queried, "Hugh, is there any way you can shut down the hovercams if an attack starts?"

"No problem," Hugh boasted. "I can control their entire network."

"Oh, Mamsen Wells, there you are," said a woman's voice from behind them.

Turning around, Harriet saw the nurse from the night before. She approached, smiling.

"I forgot to ask where you were staying," the nurse said. "Your niece is improving. The doctors say she has a good chance of waking up soon."

"Really?" Harriet asked. "That's great."

"Yes," the nurse continued, "you know it was strange. She's had the oddest brainwave patterns since the accident. But they improved significantly last night."

"Odd brainwave patterns?" Foi asked intently.

"Yes, but as I said, Carlene's much closer to normal now. If this continues, she should wake up within the next few days. Are you on your way up to see her?"

"Uh … yes," Harriet answered quickly. "My friends and I were just about to go up." She stood.

"Well," the nurse commented, "I was just on my way to the cafeteria. I'm on my break. But Tami, the nurse on duty up there now, will help you if you need anything." The nurse left.

With a thoughtful look in his eye, Foi said, "I think we should see these 'odd brainwave patterns' for ourselves."

"Foi's right," Harriet agreed. "Besides, the nurse will get suspicious if we don't visit Carlene."

Riding an elevator to the eighth floor, they went to Carlene's room. The tiny red-haired girl slept peacefully as Foi scanned her.

"Her brainwave patterns are odd," Foi told them. "Hugh, hook up to the hospital's computer and see what the doctors wrote in her patient records about them."

After a moment, Hugh said, "They have no idea why she's emitting patterns like that. They've never seen anything like it."

"Neither have I," Foi mumbled. "They're not like the Creature's, especially in the lower regions of the brain. I don't know what this means. Maybe it doesn't mean anything."

A thought struck Harriet. She asked, "Hugh, what time did her brainwave patterns improve yesterday? Do her patient records say?"

"9:44 last night."

"What time did we kill that alien?"

Foi stopped scanning Carlene and replied, "I think it was about that same time."

Harriet wondered, "Does anyone think that's a coincidence?"

"I don't believe in coincidences," Foi said in a wary voice. He started scanning in all directions.

Leo broke in, "We need information on this girl."

Tiffany surprised Harriet by already having her dataglasses on. She told Leo, "I'm already on it. There's actually not much about her, but there's a lot about her parents, Enrique and Matilda Paloma. They were big politicians in the Ceti Alpha 15 system, which is near here. Apparently, the Ceti Alpha 15 system and the Martinique system, which is also near here, are on the verge of war."

"War?" Harriet recoiled. "Another war?"

Tiffany nodded, "The Palomas were coming here for some kind of conference that was aimed at settling things. Now I see why the nurse said they were so controversial."

"Why?" Harriet asked.

"Several political commentators say that the movement the Palomas started is the reason for the war."

"What kind of movement?"

"I'm not really sure. It doesn't seem to make sense, but they got people hating each other over the weirdest stuff. Like politics."

"Two wars," Leo commented, "that can't be a coincidence."

Foi repeated, "I don't ..."

"... believe in coincidences, I know," Leo finished for him. "But if the Creature is responsible for this war too, there has to be a reason." Abruptly, his eyes shone with sudden understanding. "Of course!" he exclaimed, snapping his fingers. "I think I know why the Creature would start a war here. There are three star systems in this sector that mine minerals that are critical to the production of high-powered weapons for spaceships. One of our conglomerate's companies provides ship hulls for a small fighter the Space Corps uses. The main components of the weapons come from the Ceti Alpha 12 system. They get their raw materials from the Ceti Alpha 15 and Martinique systems."

"I don't like the sound of that," Hugh commented darkly.

Tiffany interjected, "Well, someone else decided to put a stop to the Palomas before a war could start. They put a bomb in the Palomas' shuttle. Enrique, Carlene's father, piloted it to the ground, but it crashed."

"Coincidences ..." Harriet muttered as she pondered. "Hugh," she asked, "what organs did Carlene receive from her parents?"

"She got a heart, lungs, liver, and eyes," Hugh said, reading the information from Carlene's hospital records.

"That's too many coincidences," Harriet stated.

"I'VE GOT SOMETHING!" Foi shouted. He stared intently at the scanner. "Over there!" He shouted, pointing toward the door.

There stood the small, grey alien, its eyes glowing with a furious green. It shot a bolt of cold energy at Tiffany, who was closest to it. Instantly, she threw a bolt of lightning at it, and the two forms of energy canceled each other out. The resulting blast flung her across the room where she bounced off the wall like a limp doll. As Tiffany scrambled to her feet, Leo lunged at the alien, grabbed it, and tossed it out the door. It slammed against the wall in the hallway, apparently unhurt.

The small humanoid flew down the corridor to the nurse's station, as everyone spilled out of Carlene's room. Two nurses, who were on duty there, screamed and ran. Hovering under the bright ceiling lamps, the alien created disks of light in its hands and tossed them down the hall. The first one nearly hit Foi, but he ducked, rolled, and drew his rifle in one fluid motion. Foi fired a blast at the alien, but the creature dodged too fast. Tiffany let loose with a lightning bolt, hitting the alien squarely in the chest.

Harriet saw that Leo had his rifle out and was firing. She drew hers as well. 'It's better to use the gun in here,' she thought quickly. 'If I use fire, I'll burn the place down.'

Floating above the floor, the alien zoomed down the corridor, turned along a hallway, and circled around. It came out a side hallway behind them and threw three disks of light. Hugh was closest to the creature. He hammered it with a force push that tossed it all the way down to the end of the corridor.

Patients were screaming from their rooms. Security guards arrived on the floor. Harriet heard shouting all around them. 'We've got to get that thing out of here,' she thought, 'or someone will get killed.'

Suddenly, the alien disappeared.

"Where did it go?" Leo demanded.

Hugh whipped out his scanner. "I don't see it," he answered. Then he said, "Wait. There's something going on back there." He pointed toward Carlene's room.

There, standing in the hallway staring at them, was Carlene Paloma. The grey humanoid alien stood behind her. It wrapped its long, stick-like fingers around her head. For a moment, nothing happened. Then Carlene dropped to the floor.

"Kill it!" Foi shouted. He shot the alien, but it jumped back into Carlene's room.

"NO!" Harriet shouted. "Don't shoot! You might hit Carlene!"

"She's dead, Harriet," Foi shot back. "That thing killed her already. It was using her as a host. Now it's got its own body."

Foi pulled his scanner back out, he advanced on Carlene's room.

"All of you freeze!" a voice shouted. Turning around, they found several armed security guards. "Drop your weapons, the police are on their way."

"Tiffany," Leo commanded, "make sure none of them shoots us. Hugh, get your gun out and come with me."

"Drop your guns!" the guard shouted again. Seeing Hugh drawing his rifle from his coat, the guard fired his plasma pistol. Instantly, Tiffany responded by throwing her lightning shield between themselves and the guard. The plasma bolts bounced off uselessly. The shield faded after a few moments.

Stunned, the guard shouted, "Fall back! Wait for the cops." He and the other guards ducked into a side corridor behind them.

Harriet turned to see Leo, Foi, and Hugh at the door of Carlene's room. A blast of white, cold fire erupted from inside, instantly freezing everything it touched. The three boys ducked. Then Leo held his gun in front of the doorway and fired randomly.

From inside the room, Harriet heard a ghastly scream.

"I hit it!" Leo shouted. Hugh and Foi fired into the room as well.

BOOM!

The explosion threw Leo, Foi, and Hugh down the corridor. Harriet ran to them to see if they were injured. Foi was crumpled against the corridor wall, bleeding from a gash in his head. Leo climbed to his feet.

At first, Hugh was nowhere to be found. But then he appeared next to Harriet. "Teleported," he muttered. "It was a reflex."

Clutching her gun tightly, Harriet peered into Carlene's room. A huge hole was blown into the outside wall. The alien was gone. Harriet acted swiftly. "Tiffany!" she shouted. "The alien's gone. It must have flown away. Go after it!"

Tiffany was still poised protectively between the still-cowering security guards and the five of them. She turned and ran down the hallway to Carlene's room. Without hesitation, she drew her rifle and jumped through the gaping hole. Her wings appeared and she flew out into the night.

Leo said, "Let's get after her. Hugh, can you teleport us down to street level?"

"I've got a better idea," he replied, stepping into Carlene's room with the rest following. "I can take us to the top of that building over there." So saying, Hugh teleported the four of them onto the roof of another building.

Harriet looked back. They were a couple of buildings away from the hospital. Tiffany was ahead of them, moving rapidly into the distance. Harriet's minipod, which was clipped to her ear, rang. So did everyone else's.

"I'm right behind it," Tiffany's voice sounded in Harriet's ear when she answered her minipod. "You guys better hurry; it's moving fast."

Hugh teleported them again, and again, and again. They were much closer to Tiffany now, who was circling near the alien. They teleported twice more. Harriet saw the alien hanging in the air almost directly above them. It emitted a green glow.

Police hovercars, with their sirens blaring, were approaching from everywhere. They shined their powerful spotlights up at the alien, bathing it in intense brightness. The alien gathered the light into disks and threw them at Tiffany, who fired her rifle. Foi, Leo, and Hugh fired at the alien, but it just rose higher into the sky.

Tiffany avoided all but one of the light disks. The last one hit her left wing. She screamed in pain and her wings disappeared, sending her plummeting downward. In a blur of motion, Harriet jumped into the air. A massive white tigress with wings of fire appeared underneath her, flapping its wings furiously. Harriet rose as Tiffany fell. She tried desperately to get under Tiffany, but was too slow. Tiffany plunged downward, unconscious.

Suddenly, Hugh appeared in midair. He wrapped his arms around Tiffany and disappeared. As Harriet rode through the air, she looked down to see Hugh and Tiffany on the roof below her with Leo and Foi. Tiffany was coming around.

A dragon appeared in the sky above them, surprising Harriet. It circled close to the alien, who watched it warily. When the dragon drew closer, the alien tossed its freezing energy at the lithe beast. The dragon was unaffected.

Harriet looked down. Foi and Leo were still firing at the alien. She could see that Hugh was concentrating intently, his gun dangling unused in his hands. 'Ah,' she thought, 'the dragon is one of Hugh's illusions. He's trying to distract the alien.'

Harriet aimed her gun and shot, but the alien was too fast. It deftly avoided their blasts and threw a mammoth bolt of freezing fire down at Leo, Foi, Hugh, and Tiffany. Hugh teleported them safely to another rooftop.

Harriet holstered her gun, grabbed the tigress's thick, striped neck fur, and willed it upward. It flapped its wings and rose rapidly, responding to her unspoken wishes. As she ascended, Harriet let herself burst into flames. Raising her hands over her head, she spun the fire in a funnel-shaped storm around herself and the flying tigress.

Harriet threw her firestorm toward the alien, who was still dodging a steady stream of QID blasts from Leo and Foi. Caught up in the firestorm, the alien screeched hideously as it flailed in the air. Harriet fired at the alien, but missed.

A blast of lightning arced through the sky. This time, it came from below. Harriet glanced down to see Tiffany rising rapidly with furiously-beating wings. She had murder in her face as she let go with another bolt of lightning. The alien dragged itself from the dissipating firestorm as Harriet shot at it again. With the fury of a wounded demon, the alien bellowed and flew toward Harriet.

Harriet banked away from the alien and plunged toward the ground. 'I've got to get it closer to the others,' she thought.

The alien closed in on Harriet, but was hit by lightning from Tiffany. It spun and fell. Turning, Harriet pulled out of her dive. Below her, she could see police cars everywhere. 'Did Hugh remember to turn off the police's hovercams?' she wondered with a sinking feeling.

Freezing energy struck Harriet, searing through her in a flood of pain. Her fire went out immediately and she fell limply from her tigress. The magnificent beast rolled downward, beat its wings frantically, and flew next to Harriet. Barely conscious, Harriet took weak hold of the fur of its neck. The tigress gently moved under her and slowly leveled out its fall. Harriet and the tigress skimmed close to the sea of police who watched with amazement in their upturned faces.

Harriet's head cleared. Her entire body was wracked with cold agony, but she wasn't hurt too badly. Looking upward, she saw Tiffany fighting the alien as Leo, Hugh, and Foi continued shooting. Harriet gained altitude as quickly as possible. Rising above the battling pair, she took careful aim at the alien and fired. It reeled and dove. Harriet saw that it was very, very angry.

Suddenly, Leo leapt upward from the rooftop in a perfect arc to where the alien hovered. The alien, whose attention was focused on Harriet, didn't see Leo coming. With the grace of an acrobat, Leo clamped his arm around the alien's neck as he reached it, placing it into a perfect headlock. The alien screamed and writhed wildly, trying to throw Leo off. They thrashed upward through the sky, locked in a deadly embrace.

Harriet turned the tigress back toward Leo and the alien. She heard Tiffany shout, "Leo!" Tiffany flew upwards. Harriet heard the blast of Leo's QID rifle. To her horror, Leo was plummeting downward. Seemingly unaware he was falling, Leo fired upward twice more.

Harriet's tigress immediately responded to her urgent thoughts. She gained altitude as fast as she could. But Tiffany got there first and wrapped her arms around Leo. She beat her wings against the air while Harriet drew alongside.

"Push him onto the tigress!" Harriet shouted to Tiffany. But Tiffany didn't respond. Resolutely, she fought to keep both herself and Leo airborne. At last, she slowed their fall and leveled out. Harriet saw Tiffany kiss Leo passionately, and then they landed on the rooftop near Foi and Hugh. Angrily, Harriet followed.

"The energy creature is dead," Leo announced. "It came out of that alien body and I shot it dead! I saw it dissolve."

Brimming with joy, Foi agreed, "I saw it too. It came out, and the second time you hit it, it completely dissolved. It's dead." He thumped Leo on the back and then hugged him. Tears streamed down his face.

"We've got to get out of here," Hugh urged them. "There are police air cruisers on the way."

Foi, still gushing with happiness, yelled out, "Spaceport! Let's get to the spaceport."

Harriet turned. Her giant tigress was behind her. Gently, it approached and nuzzled her. She tenderly stroked its neck. Then, the exquisite creature dissipated into a fog of fiery light that soaked into Harriet like an embracing wind of joy. It dissolved all of her anger at Tiffany. Harriet stood frozen in happiness.

"Harriet?" Hugh asked from behind her. "Harriet, we've got to leave."

Turning, Harriet softly said, "Yes, Hugh, we've got to leave."

26

Harriet was relieved when they finally arrived at the spaceport. After Hugh teleported them repeatedly from rooftop to rooftop to get there, she was feeling queasy. Harriet would be glad if she never experienced that airless falling feeling again.

As soon as they got into the zipcraft, Leo asked, "Hugh, can you do your invisibility thing and cover the whole ship?"

"I don't know," Hugh replied, "but I'll try."

With an expression of intense concentration, Hugh rendered the entire craft invisible. Foi took off. "We'll go to the Mutalau Shipping Station," he informed them. "It'll only take a couple of hours. Leo, use your autolibrary and see if you can find us a ship that's leaving this system right away."

"Are we sure all the aliens are dead?" Harriet asked.

Leo replied, "All the news reports said there were only two. Always two."

"I think it's safe to assume we got them all," Foi announced, still elated. "I can't believe it. After all this time, it's a relief to make real progress."

"We still haven't killed the thing that attacked us on Earth," Tiffany observed.

"We'll find it," Foi stated definitely, "and we'll kill it—just like we did these two."

Suddenly, Hugh burst out laughing. The others all stared at him in surprise.

"Sorry," Hugh chuckled, "But the police just identified us."

"Oh no!" Harriet gasped, "They know who we are? Why is that funny?"

Hugh laughed again and replied, "Yes, they've identified us. And they've put out arrest warrants for April North, Harry Kestler, Anthony Vincent, Candice Chandler, and an unknown accomplice."

"I don't think that's funny, Hugh," Tiffany told him.

Hugh's smile faded. "You guys have no sense of humor," he said dourly.

Foi asked, "What about a way out of this system?"

"I've already booked us passage to the Ceti Alpha 12 system on a freighter," Leo informed them. "They're docked at the Mutalau Shipping Station. Oh, and we all need to put on our plastifaces."

Harriet, Tiffany, and Leo all groaned. "Oh goody," Harriet commented sourly, "I get to be really old again."

Two hours later, Foi docked at the Mutalau Shipping Station. Harriet, Hugh, Leo, and Tiffany, all wearing their plastifaces, made their way to a ship called the Paula's Sanity. It was an ancient, dingy vessel captained by a broken-down, chunky, older woman named Paula Tillman. Her crew of five was just as ill-tempered and grungy as she was.

There were only two rooms for passengers, so Harriet and Tiffany shared one while Leo and Hugh shared the other. Foi stayed in his ship. Captain Tillman wouldn't allow them to cook, so they had to buy a two-week's supply of ready-to-eat synthpaste at the Mutalau Shipping Station just prior to departure.

"I can't eat this," Tiffany complained as they sat together for their first meal after takeoff.

"Then starve," Foi said flatly. Small bursts of electricity arced across Tiffany's fingertips, but she folded her arms and kept herself under control.

"What do we do now?" Harriet asked, hurriedly changing the subject.

Foi replied, "I think that's obvious. We track down the Creature and kill it."

"You know what?" Leo asked. "I don't want to talk about this now. I want to eat, shower, and go to bed. I've been blown up, tossed around, and I've saved an entire planet from evil aliens. I'm done for the day."

Harriet, Tiffany, and Hugh immediately agreed. But before they went to their rooms, Tiffany rose and stood in front of Hugh. "You saved me when that thing knocked me out," she stated.

Embarrassed, Hugh stammered, "Well ... yeah ... I suppose, but you know ..."

Before he could say anything else, Tiffany grabbed the front of Hugh's shirt, pulled his face to hers, and planted a huge kiss on him. When she was finished she said, "Thanks." Releasing his shirt, Tiffany left the room.

Dazed, Hugh continued stammering, "Uh ... welcome ... you're welcome ... uh."

"Goodnight, Hugh," Harriet said, amused. She followed Tiffany and went to the cramped room they shared. Tiffany already had her plastiface off. Harriet removed hers as well.

As she got ready for bed, Harriet had a foreboding feeling, as if she'd forgotten something important. She no sooner closed her eyes than she found herself standing on the red sand beach under the purple sky. Hugh, Leo, and Tiffany were there as well.

"You used your powers extensively," Eden stated. "You shouldn't do that without my help."

"We don't need your help," Leo boasted. "We killed two of your friends without any help from you at all."

"What do you mean?" Eden demanded. "Who did you kill?"

"Not, who, what," Leo shot back. "Two energy creatures." Proudly, Leo told Eden the entire story. Then he said, "And we're gonna find the other one and kill it too. We don't need you. I don't trust you. I never did. This is the last time you and I are gonna talk. I've had enough of you and your kind. I'm gonna get my life back."

Coolly, Eden replied, "Leonardo, by your description, I can tell that those beings you killed are not of the same species as I am. They're called *churei*. My species is *dairei*. We've had wars with the *churei*. Did it ever occur to you to wonder how they got into your universe in the first place?"

"I don't care. We killed them and we'll kill the other one too. Then I'm going home." Leo seemed punchy. Harriet could see that he was reckless and full of himself.

Eden asked, "Leonardo, what if more of them come? What will you do then?"

Leo froze. "What do you mean, more of them?" he demanded.

"If these two *churei* got into your universe," Eden explained, "more could get in as well. What will you do then?"

Glaring at Eden, Leo said, "I'm done talking to you." He disappeared. Without a word, Tiffany vanished as well.

Eden sighed. Turning to Harriet and Hugh, she said, "I understand his feelings. I really do. But there's so much more at stake than the lives of you four." She sighed again and advised, "Rest now. We can talk again later. Please contact me tomorrow."

Harriet nodded, and then everything dissolved away. She sat up in her bunk. Tiffany said, "Your friend really knows how to ruin things."

"She really does," Harriet agreed. She lay back down and went to sleep.

27

"You were all very foolish to attack the *churei* without me," Eden scolded as Harriet and Hugh sat with her on the red sand beach the next day. "You could have easily been killed. The *churei* are very powerful and dangerous."

"As powerful as you?" Hugh asked.

Eden replied, "No, we're a more advanced race."

Harriet queried, "Why were the *churei* here?"

Eden explained, "I believe they were under the control of a *dairei*. We can exercise mind control over them and bind them to our wills."

"That's terrible!" Harriet objected.

"Yes," Eden agreed. "It's not a power we use lightly. We're not monsters, Harriet. In any case, the person that was controlling the *churei* was probably the *dairei* that attacked you on Earth. As you guessed, he probably sent them to start a war. Somehow, he hopes to benefit from human wars."

"Why was the first one so easy to kill compared to the second one?" Hugh asked.

Eden answered. "There were two *churei*. Each one possessed the body of one of Carlene's parents. When the shuttle crashed, their hosts died. Our kind can't live in your universe long without a host. Rather than die, they shared Carlene as their host even though they were male and female. The male could enter her body and use her as a host because she wasn't an adult yet. But neither of them could take complete control of her without killing the other, so she didn't die but she couldn't wake up. The *churei* were not completely conscious themselves. They were acting out Carlene's nightmares."

Hugh prodded, "What do you mean?"

"They were taking the same organs from people that Carlene received from her parents. Carlene's unconscious mind must have heard the doctors talking about the transplants. It filled her nightmares. Acting out her fantasies, the *churei* grew those alien bodies from Carlene's tissues."

Astounded, Hugh demanded, "What?"

"Look, humans can get growths, like cancer, on their skin, right?"

"I guess. It's kinda gross but ..."

"The *churei* probably manifested themselves as growths that the doctors removed and threw away. But the growths lived and formed themselves into those aliens. They were the typical aliens that Carlene had seen in your entertainment media; more images from her nightmares."

Harriet broke in, "Does that mean that the *churei* were using those bodies as their hosts instead of Carlene?"

"No. They were connected to both those bodies and Carlene. When you first met the two *churei*, neither of them were truly conscious, so they couldn't use their full powers. That's why the first one was so easy to kill. Once it was dead, the other *churei* had Carlene's body all to itself so it was able to regain consciousness. But it didn't need her any more because it had the alien-form body. So it just let her die. By then it was completely conscious and able to use its full powers. You saw how much more difficult things got after that."

Harriet and Hugh nodded.

"You four are going to need me when you confront the *dairei*," Eden advised. "He'll be *much* harder to kill. Please, you two must help Leo and Tiffany to trust me. I really am trying to do what's best for everyone. Please try and convince them to talk to me again."

"I suppose we can try," Harriet replied cautiously. Eden nodded and the vision faded. Leo was standing over her, with Tiffany behind him. Harriet got out of her bunk. Hugh and Foi entered the room.

"Have you been talking to Eden?" Leo demanded.

Quietly, Harriet answered, "Yes, Leo, we have. We learned some important information."

"I've figured a few things out myself," Leo stated confidently.

Surprised, Harriet asked, "What do you mean?"

"I've been doing some research in my autolibrary," Leo explained, "and I really think that the cursed urn and the Spell of the Medici are real. The urn is mentioned in legends about my family for hundreds of years. If it can help kill the Creature, we need to try and find it."

"Leo, that's a wild goose chase," Harriet countered.

Stubbornly, Leo disagreed, "No, Harriet. I'm sure it's real. The legends even say that the Spell of the Medici is written on the outside of the urn. If we can find that thing, we can use the instructions to help us against the Creature."

Like a granite statue, Leo folded his arms and resolutely stated, "I've decided to go look for it, even if none of you comes along."

Before Harriet could object, Foi chimed in with, "Even if we don't find the urn, it won't hurt us to look for it. Whether we find it or don't find it, we can go after the Creature when we're done searching."

Angry, Harriet fumed, "It's way too dangerous! How are we going to get back into Alliance space?"

Foi answered, "Ceti Alpha 12 is used by a lot of smugglers. The entire system is controlled by eight corporations. They operate their own hypergates and they take bribes. So for a fee, smugglers can ride an illegal wormhole into one of the Border Systems just inside Alliance space. Once we're in, I'll hack a computer to create records showing that we entered legally."

Harriet shot back, "Is that your only answer to things— breaking the law?"

Unperturbed, Foi told her, "You don't have to come along, Harriet. No one's making you go."

Hugh interjected, "I think we should go, Harriet. Leo's got his mind made up, and I think we're safer together." Turning to Tiffany, he asked, "What about you, Tiff? What do you think?"

"I'll go where Leo goes," Tiffany answered simply.

Harriet sat seething on her bunk. Her hands danced with flame. Quickly, she folded her arms and tried to calm down. Through gritted teeth, she growled, "Oh all right. We'll all go. "

"But if we don't find the urn," she added hastily, "we'll see if Eden can help us kill the Creature."

"Well," Leo replied doubtfully, "we can listen to her ideas on how to kill it, not capture it. I don't guarantee I'll go along with what she has to say, but I'll listen."

Harriet nodded and said, "Sounds fair to me."

28

Paula's Sanity was a fast little freighter. It took only two weeks to get to the hypergate, a day to go through, and another week to get to a space station owned by Irwin Gyronetics. It was a relief to finally get off the crowded freighter and get some hotel rooms for themselves.

With great anticipation, they looked forward to eating real food again. Wearing their plastifaces, they decided to go to a nice restaurant for dinner. Walking along the giant promenade of the station, they were suddenly confronted with two-story images of themselves on a 3D holographic billboard.

"Holy galveth!" Tiffany swore.

"Zarking veech!" Leo agreed.

Harriet was mortified to see herself burst into flames on the back of her tigress. Video of Tiffany was next, showing her flying through the air and tossing lightning bolts from her hands. Hugh's dragon appeared, and Leo was shown leaping into the sky. To make matters worse, the sign then displayed video from Earth of them fighting the Creature, surfing down the corridors of the arcology, and disappearing into thin air. Next, it showed still pictures of Harriet, Hugh, Leo, and Tiffany with text that read:

What Are They?
Mutants?
Freaks?
Monsters?
Aliens?
Find out from our panel of experts
tonight at 10 on
Galactic News Network,
the Galaxy's best news source
for over 300 years.

"Freaks!" Harriet hissed. "They're calling us freaks!"

"Sh!" Hugh commanded. "Someone might hear you."

The billboard continued by displaying video of Leo leaping, fighting, and throwing large vehicles as if they were children's toys. A spinning block of text settled itself under his image that said, "The Hunk."

"What's that?" Leo demanded incredulously.

Before anyone could answer, video of Hugh appeared. It was labeled, "Mystery Boy."

Taken aback, Hugh began, "I'm *Mystery Boy*? Couldn't they think of a better name than that?"

Next was video of Harriet flying on her tigress and bursting into flames. Her moniker was, "The Goddess of Fire."

"Well," Harriet murmured demurely, "*That's* a surprise." Her shock and anger of the moment before were forgotten.

Finally, video of Tiffany appeared and received the title, "Mistress of the Sky." In the end, pictures of all four of them were displayed with the name, "The Otherworldly Four."

"Hey!" recoiled Tiffany. "How come *she's* a goddess and *I'm* just a mistress? That's not fair! I should be the *Goddess* of the Sky—or something like that. The Thunder Goddess, maybe. The Goddess of Lightning is good. Who do I talk to to get that changed? I need to find them right now!"

"Tiffany!" hissed Leo. "This isn't a contest. Keep quiet and don't give us away."

"Just ignore it," Foi agreed. "Let's go get dinner."

Scowling, Tiffany followed the others muttering, "It's not fair."

At dinner, they huddled together and made their plans. "Leo helped me set up some dummy corporations," Hugh told them.

Turning to Leo, Harriet asked, "Dummy corporations?"

"Dummy corporations are corporations that don't actually do anything. They just hold assets," Leo explained. "Assets are anything they own, all the money they have, and stuff like that. They hide assets to avoid paying taxes on them. It's a trick corporations have been using for centuries."

Harriet objected, "We don't have any assets. Why do we need dummy corporations?"

Conspiratorially, Leo leaned in, dropped his voice, and said, "Look, we've got some money and we don't want the Alliance cops to find out where it is or where we are when we spend it. Dummy corporations can help us do that. And using dummy corporations will help us get new identities. Not many people outside corporate circles know this, but the Ceti Alpha 12 system allows you to legally buy identities. You just have to know the right people, like I do. I found all this out when I was helping my father with his series of books about business."

"How can that be legal?" Harriet queried.

"There are eight corporations that each own a section of this system. Around here, they're called the Big Eight. They each make their own laws in the sections they own. One of the Big Eight is

Financial Frontiers Interstellar Holdings. They deal in what they call 'special corporate services.' Mostly, they help rich people hide their money, provide protection for them, and sell them legal identities they can use to do their shadier business deals. We'll be using them for our transactions. We can buy anything, including legal identities whenever we need them."

Doubtfully, Harriet asked, "Won't the Creature find us? Foi said it was good with computers."

Leo shook his head and answered definitely, "I don't care how good with computers you are. When you create a set of dummy corporations with Financial Frontiers Interstellar Holdings, no one can untangle the mess of interconnected companies to find out who's really behind them. Alliance Investigators have been trying for centuries."

"Well," Harriet replied, "if it keeps you, Hugh, and Foi from breaking into every computer in the Alliance, I guess it's an improvement."

Foi changed the subject. "I'll find us a ship that will take us back into Alliance space," he said. "The nearest Alliance Star system is the California system. We'll get someone to take us there, and then make it look like we entered legally. After that, all we have to do is book passage back to Earth. If we get a fast ship, we can do the trip in as little as three months."

"That's sure a lot better than the five months it took for us to get out here," Hugh commented.

Nodding his agreement, Foi added, "Tomorrow I'll start looking for a smuggler that can get us to California. It may take a while, so don't worry if you don't hear from me for a few days."

True to his word, Foi was gone the next day when they went for breakfast. Four days later, Foi returned while they were at a restaurant. "Pack your things," he told them. "We leave tonight."

A few hours later, Harriet, Hugh, Leo, and Tiffany found themselves hiding rather tensely inside Foi's ship, which was parked inside the cargo hold of an ancient freighter. They watched on an external camera as Foi talked with the giant, ragged, hairy captain of the smuggling ship. The man's hard life had etched itself into his face, making him appear hundreds of years old. But Harriet could tell that he was probably not more than 50. Scratching his armpit, the man strode toward Foi and eyed him suspiciously.

The tall man growled. "You alone or you movin' passengers?"

"No questions," Foi shot back. "And there's a bomb in my ship that'll go off if anyone scans it. You try to double-cross me and I'll blow the entire ship."

"Listen you little veech," the huge man bellowed as he towered over Foi, "I'll scan whatever I want! Don't you ever threaten me again or I'll carve your little hide to bits." He swiftly bent down and jerked a long knife from his boot.

At the same time, Foi whipped his rifle out from under his coat, shoved it in the man's face, and replied coolly, "Perhaps I need to take my business elsewhere. I'm sure there are other ships that will be more accommodating."

The mountainous man drew back. "You take chances little boy," he hissed.

"So do you. Now have we got a deal or not?"

The man grimaced and then shouted, "Deal! No scans. But I'm gonna lock down this hold. You or anyone else comes out of it, you all die."

Foi holstered his rifle and replied, "Fair enough."

Inside the ship, Harriet realized she was shaking. 'I can't believe the way he can stand up to anyone.' She admired that in Foi.

Foi waited until the freighter captain left and then came back to the zipcraft. "We'll go through the hypergate in about an hour. The transit through hyperspace will be six hours. Then they'll dump us into deep space. We'll use an old smuggling route through the Black Bow Nebula to get into the California System. It'll take us a couple of days."

"A couple of days!" complained Tiffany. "A ship this small doesn't have enough air in it for this many people. What about water and food?"

Foi answered, "I bought us enough food. The water recycler will provide enough water for a two-day trip. And I had an extra air recycler installed while I was getting the QID rifles just in case something like this came up. We won't be comfortable, but we'll get there."

Nobody was happy. Foi returned to the pilot's seat and the others each found somewhere to crash out.

Just as Foi had said, it took them about seven uncomfortable hours to get through hyperspace and make their way to the Black Bow Nebula.

The tiny ship was so stuffed with luggage and people that there wasn't room for all of them to stand up at once. Leo lay on Foi's bunk, while Tiffany stretched out on top of his cryostasis unit. Harriet and Hugh sat on trunks.

Inspired by Hugh's constant studying, Harriet started a course on astronavigation. 'With all of the running around through space we do,' she thought as she read the textbook, 'I might need to be able to pilot a ship someday.'

29

The first day in the absolute blackness of the Black Bow Nebula passed without incident. On the second day, Hugh called out, "Hey guys, I think I found something,"

Harriet sat up on the boxes of food where she had been reclining all day. "What did you find, Hugh?"

"I think I found the Creature again. He's in the history books. I'm sending a link, but the short version is that there was a Russian wizard named Rasputin that was really hard to kill. He told the king and queen of Russia what to do, and they did it. And some of the documents recovered in the late 21st century say he was afraid of a she-demon that lived in the sky. Sound familiar?"

Leo, who had been listening, interjected, "If this Rasputin guy was the Creature, how did he get out of the Medici's urn?"

"Well, I think it was when he was in the Verkhoturye Monastery in Russia. They had an ancient holy relic that was supposed to be from Rome that they called the Guardian of the Medici. Rasputin spent three months there. After that, he became a wandering holy man or wizard or something. He was supposed to have amazing powers. There's even a drawing of the urn that was done in the 1780's."

Harriet put on her dataglasses and followed the link that she received from Hugh. Gazing at the drawing, she asked, "What are these four figures on it? Their top halves are humanoid, but they have legs like crabs."

Hugh replied, "They're the four demons that served Lorenzo de Medici."

Leo asked, "So you think the urn was moved to Russia for some reason?"

"Yeah, I do," Hugh replied. "And I think Rasputin let the Creature out somehow and it took him over. It was rumored that Rasputin was involved with the Germans in starting World War I. So it would all fit. He was doing exactly the same thing then that he's doing now—trying to get humans to fight each other. I wish I knew why."

"But even if we don't know why," Harriet offered, "we know that it fits his pattern." A thought struck her. "Hey, does anybody know what started World War II?"

"I had the same idea," Hugh told her, "so I looked it up. Some weird little German guy named Hitler took over the country and invaded everyone else."

Harriet asked, "Was he a wizard too?"

Shaking his head, Hugh answered, "No. But he was really weird, some say he was insane. I don't think he was the Creature. But, I wonder if he was possessed by a *churei*."

Harriet was reading quickly through articles on World War II. "Hugh," she objected, "it says here that they killed that Hitler guy at the end of the war. He couldn't have had a *churei* in him if they killed him with old-style guns."

"Well maybe he was being controlled in another way. Maybe the Creature did some kind of operation on him like he did to the people on Foi's planet."

Foi broke in, "It's possible. It would fit the Creature's way of doing things. And it might explain why Hitler was out of his mind."

"So does that mean we shouldn't go to the Sistine Chapel?" Leo asked.

Hugh replied, "We could still check there. But I think if this urn is anywhere, it's in the Verkhoturye Monastery in Russia. We should look there first."

Foi interrupted, "We're approaching the edge of the Black Bow Nebula. Hugh, you need to be ready to do your invisibility thing if we're spotted by the Rangers."

Hugh asked, "How are we going to land at the San Bernardino Shipping Station without getting caught?"

"We're not," Foi explained. "The San Bernardino Shipping Station is next to the California hypergate. Later today they're opening a wormhole to the Oregon system. We're going to invisibly slide into the cargo hold of one of the larger ships as it's being loaded. Then we hack into its computer—sorry Harriet, but we have to—and put the zipcraft on its manifest and list ourselves as passengers. We ride that ship to the Oregon system where the Rangers won't be looking for us and then get a transport to Earth."

Though the next few hours were tense, everything went off without a hitch. By the next day, they were aboard a passenger liner called The Ruby and on the first leg of their journey to Earth. As usual, they had to wear their plastifaces whenever they were out of their quarters. But other than that minor inconvenience, they were relieved to be freed from the cramped cabin of the zipcraft.

After taking time to shower and eat, they gathered in Foi's room. He told them, "Because we're running short of money, I jiggered The Ruby's computer—sorry again Harriet—to show that we've already paid for the trip."

"That's stealing!" Harriet objected.

Leo intervened, "I think I can fix it once we get to Earth."

"How?" Harriet demanded hotly.

"If Foi and Hugh can hack into one of my family's company computers, I can transfer money to our dummy corporations."

"More hacking?"

"They're my computers. It's not a crime to break into your own computers, Harriet. The only reason I'm not just logging onto my own computer accounts is that I don't want to be traced. If we hack in, we can get the money secretly. It's not a crime."

"Oh," Harriet said sheepishly. "I'm sorry, Leo. I don't mean to be a pain about this. If we can get some of your money to live on, that would be really good."

"We can," Leo assured her. "And I know just which computer to go after. We have a small startup company that's not doing well. I told my father before school started that we should sell it. If we can break in anywhere, it'll be there. The guys that run the company are a pair of brothers in their twenties. My father put up the money for their company as a favor to their father, who's an old college friend of his. If their company goes under, they'll just be transferred. My father likes them, so he won't fire them. So we won't be stealing, we won't be hurting anybody, and we'll be using money that already belongs to my family."

"Then let's do that," Harriet agreed.

Tiffany broke in, "What's there to do on this ship?"

"Mostly just the AR suites," Foi told her. "The passengers on this ship are mostly the middle class, so they don't have lots of amenities but they have enough AR pods for all the passengers who have coach-class tickets, which is what I chose for us."

"I wonder if they have the winged-horse program we had back at school," Harriet speculated hopefully.

"Speaking of school," Leo mused, "I should probably spend time taking cyberschool classes to catch up on what I've missed."

Hugh agreed with Leo, "Yeah, when we finally get our lives back, I don't want to still be in high school." He paused a moment thoughtfully, "But first," he continued, "I think we deserve a break. Let's play today and start school tomorrow."

The five of them went to an AR suite and looked through the catalog of programs.

"Look!" Harriet exclaimed. "They have the winged-horse program. Anybody want to ride with me?"

"No offense," Leo replied, "But after a couple of days in a zipcraft, I need some time alone. I'm going hypersailing." Harriet was disappointed, but she understood.

"I hear that," Hugh agreed. "I'm going sandskiing in a Mars simulation."

Tiffany sighed, "Well, if I'm on my own, then I'm going shopping in a virtual mall."

Turning to Foi, Harriet asked, "What about you? What are you going to do?"

"Weapons practice," Foi answered simply. He selected the program and got into an AR pod. Leo, Hugh, and Tiffany quickly followed his example. Harriet selected her program, got into an AR pod, and immediately appeared in the familiar green valley. She glanced briefly at her hands and was relieved to see that they were her young hands, not the old hands that she wore with the plastiface.

After some searching, Harriet found a white mare, greeted it, and climbed up on its back. In no time, she and the mare were dancing across the sky and reveling in the pure joy of flying.

A shadow passed over Harriet. Glancing up, she was surprised to see Leo riding on a black stallion. He pointed to a spot by a river in the valley below. Harriet followed him down and dismounted when they landed.

"Hi Leo," she greeted as she walked toward him. "I thought you wanted to be alone."

Drawing near, Leo gathered Harriet in his arms and kissed her. Then he said, "That's what I said in front of everyone else. But I came here to be with you. And I've locked the program, so no one else can enter." He kissed her again.

Harriet's heart raced. She held him tightly. Leo said, "Let's ride together on my horse."

Lifting Harriet easily, Leo set her up on the back of his tall black steed and got up behind her. Reaching around her to take the reins, Leo nudged the stallion forward. Harriet nestled into Leo's arms as they rose above the rolling green vale. Together they wafted across the sky chasing herds of wild, winged horses.

Hours later, Harriet and Leo walked arm in arm along the flowered banks of the river. A family of swans glided by.

'Right now, what do you feel?' Harriet wondered as she gazed at Leo's smiling face. 'When this is over, will we be together forever?'

Seeing her gaze, Leo asked, "What are you thinking?"

Suddenly shy, Harriet stammered, "I ... I was just ... wondering."

"Wondering what?"

"When we were back on Earth, your sister told me that you were engaged to Tiffany. I was wondering ... why you asked me out."

Leo stopped walking and held Harriet close. "Harriet, don't worry about Tiffany. My parents chose her, not me. It was a business decision. I make my own choices. Tiffany is not the girl I'm going to marry. I've told her that lots of times, but she isn't the kind of girl to take no for an answer."

Harriet chuckled, "No, she isn't, is she?"

"She has to face the truth someday," Leo said. "I'm never marrying her. And I asked you out because I wanted to. Isn't that a good enough reason?"

"It is," Harriet cooed warmly as she nestled closer to him. "It's the very best reason."

30

The next three months passed like a dream for Harriet. She took a full load of cyberschool classes. At the rate she was able to learn, finishing her Junior and Senior years of high school took only a month and a half. Harriet immediately started into virtual Space Academy training for the survival skills it offered. She also took courses in piloting vehicles of all types. She learned to drive hovercars, fly small aircraft, and acquired spacecraft piloting skills.

In spite of her busy learning schedule, Harriet and Leo often had time together in the AR suite without the others knowing. They went dancing several times a week, played powertennis, rode the skycats of Herminia, and visited the Singing Caves of Kenogo. Often, they walked together hand in hand at sunset along the marble shores of Lake Enalen under the twin moons of Helabi.

With the fun of learning challenging new skills and the happy times with Leo, Harriet increasingly wished the voyage back to Earth would never end. But all too soon, the ship arrived at Earth. Harriet sat dejectedly in her seat in the space elevator with Leo and Tiffany beside her as it slowly descended toward Moscow, Russia. Foi had Hugh ride down with him in the zipcraft so he could make the QID guns invisible in case they were searched.

It felt strange to be returning to the planet they had fled so long ago. 'I'm just a couple of hours away by suborbital jumpjet from our arcology and Ruth Ann,' she mused as she watched the ground rise to meet the elevator. Then she thought sadly, 'But home is the one place I can't go.'

When they reached the spaceport in Moscow, Foi and Hugh met them at the arrival gate. A roboporter was there with their bags loaded into a hovercart.

"I've put my ship in storage and bought us skytrain tickets to Verkhoturye," Foi informed them. "The train leaves soon, so we need to get to our gate and board as fast as we can." He pointed to the hovercart. The five of them each took a seat behind the robot, which was driving.

"Take us to the skytrain station," ordered Foi. "Platform 88. We need to get there no later than 8:35."

The hovercart shot forward smoothly. Under the robot's guidance, their cart zipped through the spaceport at a breathtaking speed.

Deftly, the robot maneuvered the cart along the route to the skytrain station, which was next to the spaceport. When they arrived, it carried their luggage up to the platform and loaded it on the train into an empty compartment.

Verkhoturye was deep in the Ural Mountains, far from Moscow. The train trip was about three hours. When they arrived, they immediately checked into a hotel.

"This city is one big habitation complex," Tiffany observed. "How are we going to find the monastery? What if it's been torn down?"

Hugh, who was logged onto his autolibrary, told her, "The monastery has religious significance to the people here. It wasn't torn down. The hab complex was built right on top of it. The local tourist information says it's in a big chamber down at ground level."

Their hotel was on level 150, halfway down the hab complex. They found an elevator and rode down to the bottom.

"This is so different from back home," Harriet commented as they exited the elevator. The sun shown over them, warming a peaceful scene of carefully tended lawns and trees. Harriet could even hear real birds singing.

Hugh explained, "We're not outside. The sky is a holographic projection. We're really in a big, huge room on the bottom floor of the hab complex. The monastery is down that path." He pointed to a paved walkway that led through the trees.

Following the path, the five of them soon arrived at the monastery. Hugh was still logged onto the local network. "There are automated tours," he told them. "You walk around the monastery and the spoken information plays on whatever device you're carrying. By the way, the monks in there are all men. No women are allowed inside."

"How rude!" Tiffany exclaimed.

Leo cut her off, "Isn't there a way to talk to an actual human? We need to find out what they know about the Guardian of the Medici, since there's so little about it on the network."

"It says here that the current Abbot," Hugh replied, "who is the head of the monastery, receives visitors at 1:00. That's about an hour from now. Let's go get lunch and come back at 1:00."

At lunch, they discussed their plan. "We want to go inside too," Tiffany asserted. "We didn't come all this way to be kicked out at the last minute. Right, Harriet?"

"Well, yeah. But they don't allow women inside."

Leo interjected, "You could go in if no one could see you." He glanced at Hugh.

Hugh sighed, exasperated. "Just call me Hugh 'Cloaking Device' Benson," he growled.

"What are we going to tell the Abbot?" Foi asked. "We can't just walk in and ask if the Guardian of the Medici is laying around and oh, by the way, can we have it?"

"We'll find out where it is first," Leo instructed. "Then we can worry about how to get it. Hugh, you tell the Abbot that your mother was from the Medici family. Now that you're retired, you're researching your family history. Say that there are family legends about the urn and ask if you can see it."

"Why me?" Hugh asked. "Why not you?"

"Did you forget that when our plastifaces are on, you're supposed to be my father?"

"Oh, right. I'm old."

Hugh asked, "So what are you and Foi doing there with me, then?"

"I'm your son. We're traveling with my mother," Leo pointed to Harriet, "and my wife," he pointed to Tiffany, "and your sister's son, Foi."

Hugh nodded, satisfied with their cover story.

After lunch, they went to the gates of the monastery, with Harriet and Tiffany walking invisibly behind Hugh. At the monastery office, they found the Abbot's secretary, a balding man about 60 years old. He told them, "Why yes, the Abbot enjoys visitors and he's got no one scheduled today. I'll let him know you're here."

The secretary rose and went into the Abbot's office. Leo asked, "Why didn't he just call the Abbot?"

"No phone," Hugh replied. "People go into monasteries for a life dedicated to God without modern conveniences."

"How do you know so much about it?"

"I read the tourist brochure online."

The Abbot's secretary returned and said, "Abbot Daniel will see you now."

They followed the secretary in. Hugh, using the pretext of being old, was careful to walk slowly so that Harriet and Tiffany had time to get through the door before it was closed. Abbot

Daniel smiled from behind his ancient desk. Harriet was surprised when she noticed that it, and the chairs in the office, were made of real wood.

"Welcome, Sirsen Kronkmeyer," Abbot Daniel greeted serenely. "And who are these young men?"

The abbot was speaking in Russian, but Harriet, Hugh, Leo, and Tiffany had learned Russian on the trip to Earth. Leo translated for Foi.

Hugh replied, "This is my son, Henry, and his young cousin, Foi."

"Foi? What an unusual name. He's not American, like you two?"

"No, Abbot Daniel. He's from outside Alliance space. My sister emigrated many years ago beyond the Edge Worlds and out into the Frontier Worlds. When she left, there was no hypergate to the system she and her young husband went to. You had to ride a sleeper ship back then. That's why my nephew is so much younger than my son. His parents were in cryogenic stasis for several years. Now that there's a hypergate, Foi has come back to Earth to complete his education."

'Wow,' Harriet thought, impressed. 'We didn't plan any of that in advance. That's a great story to make up off the top of your head.'

"Ah, the complexities of modern life," the Abbot remarked wistfully. "So what brings you all the way to our monastery?"

Hugh answered, "Now that I'm retired, I'm spending some time researching my family history. I want the younger generation to know who they are and where they came from."

The Abbot smiled. In an unhurried and thoughtful way, he commented, "A very commendable pursuit. We forget the importance of the past and the lives of those who came before us."

"How very true," Hugh agreed.

"But," the Abbot observed, "that still doesn't tell me why you're here. Does your family have some connection to this monastery?"

"Yes, in fact we do. My mother was a Medici, and we have legends that tell of a family relic that was brought here from Rome."

"Ah yes. The Guardian of the Medici. I know it well. History has long been a favorite pursuit of mine even before I came to the monastery. "

"Is it still here? Could we see it?"

"Sadly, it's long gone. The urn was brought here from Rome sometime in the late 1700's, but it was returned to Rome in 2021 as part of an effort to reconcile the Latin Church and the Eastern Church. But if you like, I can show you a drawing of it that was done in the 1780's."

The Abbot rose, and went to one of the many bookcases that lined his office. Harriet had to scurry silently out of the way to keep herself from being bumped into. Extracting a book from a shelf, the Abbot returned to his chair and opened it. Harriet was fascinated; she had never seen an actual paper book before.

"Oh yes," Hugh told the Abbot. "I've seen this picture before. It's on the network."

Nodding, the Abbot agreed, "Yes, along with those stories of the wizard Rasputin."

"What was his connection to the urn?" Hugh asked.

Abbot Daniel hesitated, glancing from Hugh to Leo and Foi. "Well," he said, "I don't often share that type of information. You know, so many people are just after rumors to feed their sensationalistic conspiracy theories. But since this is a family matter for you ..."

The Abbot rose and retrieved another book from the shelves. "This volume," he told them as he opened the large book, "dates back to the time of Rasputin. It's a history of the monastery that's not available on the information grid."

Harriet could see that the cover of the ancient book was real leather. The handwritten text inside was lush and flowery. Laboriously ornate illustrations flowed through the margins. The Abbot turned to a picture near the center of the book.

"Here," Abbot Daniel indicated. "The man Rasputin." He pointed to a drawn figure of a mangy man standing next to a large urn.

"What's he doing?" Hugh asked.

"Tampering with the urn," Abbot Daniel replied. "He was staying here for three months as penance for a petty theft. This story, which was written by the Abbot at the time, says he found out about the urn and tried to steal it. When he did, it is said that he unleashed a demon trapped inside that possessed him to the end of his tormented life."

The Abbot pointed to a squid-like shape in the illustration with tentacle-like arms. "You can see why I keep this information private," the Abbot said. "We who have dedicated our lives to quiet contemplation of the Divine do not need the hordes of the curious that would come here if this information got out. I must ask you to keep it confidential."

"Of course," Hugh agreed quickly. "We don't want to disturb the life that you have here at all." Hugh sighed. "So the artifact is now in Rome?"

"I'm sorry, no," the Abbot replied. "The Guardian of the Medici was stolen from Rome by an agent of Vong Levendakis during World War III. It disappeared when the war ended and has not been seen since. There's not been a single trace of it."

"Vong Levendakis?" Hugh asked, incredulously. "The man who started WWIII? Why did he want it?"

The Abbot shook his head. "No one knows," he answered simply.

A gentle knock sounded at the door.

"Come in please," Abbot Daniel called.

The Abbot's secretary stuck his head into the room. "I'm sorry to disturb you, Abbot. But there's a gentleman here from the city council who says he has an urgent matter to discuss with you."

"Please ask him to wait just a moment," Abbot Daniel replied. Folding the book closed, the Abbot asked, "Well, Sirsen Kronkmeyer, I hope I have been of some service to you today. If you ever want to drop by again, please feel free to do so."

"Yes," Hugh said as he stood. "Thank you for all of this information. And please be assured, we won't discuss this with anyone outside the family."

Leo and Foi followed Hugh out. Harriet and Tiffany slipped quickly through the doorway behind them. They returned to their hotel, removed their plastifaces, and gathered in Foi's room.

"We're going to the Moon," Foi stated without preamble. "That's where Vong Levendakis waged the war from."

Harriet objected, "His base was destroyed. There's nothing left."

"There are rumors," Leo commented, "that the Americans still have secret bunkers full of stuff from his base. It seems possible. After all, it was them that ended the war."

Not to be left out, Hugh demanded, "How do you know? I've never heard rumors like that."

"My family has a place on the Moon," Leo replied. "I've spent enough time there to hear what the locals say about Levendakis. They have lots of stories about him."

Hugh shot back, "That doesn't mean any of them are true."

"We're going to the Moon," Foi repeated.

Immediately angry, Harriet barked, "What do you mean 'we?' You're not in charge of me."

Unruffled, Foi replied calmly, "Fine. You do what you want. Leo, are you coming with me?"

"Yeah," he nodded, "I think it's worth a look. What about you Tiff?"

"I go where you go," Tiffany said gently. Leo smiled at her.

Harriet's hands grew hot, she knew her anger might cause her to burst into flame at any moment, but she didn't care. She glared at Leo. "You agreed we'd listen to Eden's plan for killing the Creature if we didn't find the urn. Now you want to go chasing off to the Moon?"

"I agree," broke in Hugh with uncharacteristic boldness. "We have our QID guns. We can listen to what Eden has to say, and then decide what we want to do. We don't need this stupid vase."

"Urn," Leo corrected.

"Whatever," Hugh retorted. "If it exists, and if it survived World War III, it may not help us at all. From what the legends say, the Spell of the Medici traps the Creature in the urn. It doesn't kill it."

Foi replied, "If we trap the Creature in the urn, we can drop it into space on an orbit that will let it fall into the Sun. No more Creature."

"*If* the urn wasn't destroyed in the war," Harriet shouted, "and *if* we can find it, and *if* we can keep ourselves from being caught by the police, and *if* we can figure out how to use the urn, then it *might* help us. This is just getting too farfetched. I'm contacting Eden." She folded her arms defiantly and glared at Foi and Leo.

Quietly, Foi replied, "You do what you want. I'm going to the Moon to check things out before I give up on finding the urn."

Leo distantly agreed, "Tiffany and I are going, too." His chin jutted upward aloofly.

Harriet continued to glare at them for a moment, and then hissed a quiet, "Fine." She stomped from the room.

After a brief hesitation, Hugh trailed behind her. "Harriet, wait," he called. But Harriet arrowed into a nearby elevator and spat, "Down!" The elevator slid its doors closed and descended.

"How could he be like that to me?" Harriet demanded of the unheeding elevator as she thought about Leo's behavior. 'And of course Tiffany follows along like some clinging vine.' It occurred to her to wonder if Tiffany was the only one who clung to Leo too much.

"What floor please?" the elevator asked, interrupting her thoughts.

Harriet had no idea where she was headed, but then she remembered from the tourist brochures that there was a park along the banks of the river that ran next to the hab complex. "Ground floor," she ordered.

When she left the elevator on the ground floor, Harriet used her autolibrary to guide her to an exit. Outside, she followed a path lined with flowerbeds that led down to the river. Even though the sun was bright, the day was pleasantly cool. Strolling slowly, Harriet let the sparkling flow of the river calm her. She stopped and sat down on a bench close to the water. A gentle breeze ruffled through her hair.

Without knowing why, Harriet grew suddenly uneasy. 'It's almost like there's someone watching me,' she thought. Standing, Harriet glanced around nervously. Hurriedly, she strode back up the path to the habitation complex.

"Harriet."

The familiar voice from behind Harriet made her jump. Turning, she was horrified to see her father emerging from a thicket of small trees.

"You!" Harriet gasped.

"Don't be afraid little Harriet," the Creature said. "You and your friends need to come with me. I'll keep you safe."

Harriet stumbled backwards. The Creature reached out his hand and glared. Harriet felt a growing force wrap around her and pull her toward the Creature. Her feet slid slowly across the ground as she dug in her heels to resist. The force clamped around her crushingly.

At that moment, Harriet realized how foolish she had been. Going off alone without her scanner to warn her or her QID gun to protect her had been a stupid mistake. She knew now it might be her last.

In growing terror and anger, Harriet exploded into flame and blasted an inferno at the Creature. It made no difference; its shield protected it from her flames. Her father's face sneered mockingly.

Harriet's winged tigress appeared next to her and charged the Creature. Her father's voice laughed—until the tigress turned into a white-hot ball of fire and enveloped him completely. It seemed the tigress's fire was too intense for the Creature's shield. He screamed out in pain as he thrashed at the flames that covered him and refused to let go.

Casting a glance behind her as she ran, Harriet saw the Creature gliding through the air. It was coming straight at her.

Struggling to run faster, Harriet pounded up the paved path toward the door.

Suddenly, the tigress reappeared next to Harriet. Grabbing its fur, Harriet heaved herself on the huge cat's back and willed it to a full sprint. Shooting another petrified glance backward, Harriet saw that the tigress wasn't getting away. It was only able to keep the Creature from gaining on them.

"Fly!" Harriet screamed. "Where are your wings? Fly!"

Instantly, the tigress had fiery wings, which it spread wide as it leaped upward. Rising rapidly, the tigress ascended with the Creature close behind. Harriet felt the iron grip of the Creature's will as it reached out with its mind. As it pulled her backwards, she frantically clung to the tigress's thick fur.

A tremendous force push pummeled her, making Harriet scream hideously. Yet she stubbornly clutched the tigress as it tried its best to escape the Creature. The tigress whirled and dove as it tried to avoid repeated blasts of lightning. Another force push hit her, knocking her off the tigress.

As Harriet flaccidly plummeted downward, she felt the Creature drawing her closer to him. Barely conscious, she saw her tigress wheel around and attack the Creature in midair. Harriet could feel the Creature invading her mind. It slowly ripped at her with its cold, searing will. Harriet's tigress roared in pain as Harriet dangled in the sky, held aloft by the Creature's telekinesis.

'The tigress!' she realized, 'It's taking the tigress!'

"NO!" Harriet screamed. "DON'T LEAVE ME!" In her mind, Harriet fought the Creature with every ounce of her will. Understanding that her tigress was a manifestation of her *korei*, Harriet's mind gripped onto the alien life form that lived within her. "YOU CAN'T HAVE HER!" Harriet shrieked at the Creature.

The Creature hit Harriet with another force push, but she clung desperately to consciousness. A blast of energy came out of nowhere and hit the Creature squarely. It roared in pain as its body started to dissolve. The Creature's will released Harriet and she plunged downward.

The last thing Harriet saw before she passed out was Hugh appearing next to her in midair.

Part 4

Even When the Fat Lady Sings

"There are four ways to win a war. First, you can be civilized and find a way to settle it peacefully. Second, you can win by crushing your enemy's will to fight. Third, you can exterminate your enemy completely. And fourth, you can run for your life and live to fight another day." *The Human Race in the Second Age*, Hugh Benson, p. 499.

31

Tilting back in his creaking chair, Hugh put his hands behind his head and pondered as he gazed out over the vast junkyard outside the window of his austere office. Stretching to the horizon, the seemingly endless field of garbage marked the abrupt edge of the city of Incompac. Yellow-brown clouds wafted over the choking, gritty landscape smothering the flat disk of the sun as it drooped lifelessly in the sky.

While Hugh watched, the daily droves of the poor dragged themselves down the road that ran far into the wide zone of refuse. Some pulled carts filled with trash they had gathered in the hopes that they could get some money from recycling. Others carried their repulsive treasures on their backs. The luckier ones were masked in hand-me-down respirators that filtered the air enough to make it breathable. The rest coughed and hacked their way along the road, barely able to get enough oxygen to keep going.

The nearly antique computer on Hugh's desk beeped and flashed a message on its screen to inform him that there was another story about his company on the news. "Display story," he commanded.

"... nearly instant popularity of the new FamilyShip from FamilyShip Offworld, Incorporated has stunned the space travel industry and spawned what some are calling a 'colonization frenzy' among the working classes. People are calling the design a breakthrough in spaceship design and hailing its creator, Benson Leonardo, as a genius."

The image of Benson Leonardo appeared on the screen. Hugh smiled. 'It's a good illusion,' he thought. 'Who would ever think that that old bald guy is really me?'

An image of a scholarly man appeared next on the screen. The words, "Hayden Middleton, Professor of Deepspace Engineering, Yale University," flashed below his face. "These small spacecraft," the Professor told the camera, "are capable of sustaining up to sixteen people for trips as long as five years. They are perfect for a group of four families with two parents and two children each. The unique design of these small ships makes them easy to take apart and use as housing once they have reached the colony worlds. On agricultural worlds, where there is plenty of land, a single

FamilyShip can form the basis of four working farms almost immediately upon arrival."

Hugh turned it off. He'd heard it all before. Because of the special programming he'd added to the obsolete computer, it was able to watch the story and let him know if anything was said about his company. Right now, Hugh had more important things on his mind.

"Sirsen Leonardo," his secretary program interrupted. "Dr. Dickerson is here."

"Let her in and tell her I'll be down by the time the purifier freshens the garage's air."

"Yes, Sirsen Leonardo."

Leaving his office through the rear door, he descended the creaking spiral stairs and strode through the converted warehouse to his private living area. Moving through his quarters, he waited at the inside door of the garage. After a few moments, the air was clean enough for him to enter. The door slid open and Dr. Dickerson emerged from her hovercar.

"Hugh," she greeted warmly. "How's our patient?"

"You're the expert, Doctor. You tell me."

"Well, let's have a look at her first." Dr. Dickerson cast a withering glance at the brown residue that covered her hovercar. "This smog is so awful," she moaned. "I'll be glad when it blows on by. Not that that will be a big improvement."

Dr. Dickerson followed Hugh through the hallway to the medical bay. "The skin grafts are doing well," she told Hugh. "All of the burned skin is replaced and she's got exactly the appearance she had before. Since we did most of the bone and tissue replacements while she was still in cryostasis, we were able to repair many more injuries than usual. Now that she's out of cryostasis, her body is healing better than any human should. It's been three months now and, as I say, her body is well on the way to healing. But her brain patterns . . ."

Hugh stood with Dr. Dickerson next to Harriet's sleeping form. "What about her brain patterns?" he asked.

"They're still . . . sub-normal, even though they're improving. Harriet's body is fine, Hugh. She should be awake. But the experience she had has traumatized her mind. There's not much I can do about that. Harriet will have to find her own way back to consciousness."

"Is there any hope for her?"

"I really don't know, Hugh. But the data I received this morning from her bedside scanners told me she's improving. That's why I came. I want to run some tests."

"I see," Hugh replied. He hesitated. "As always, you'll receive payment promptly."

"Thank you, Hugh."

"And . . . as always, I'm really sorry for . . . I never wanted to do things like this . . . illegal things. But our lives are on the line. I didn't know what else to do. I'm really not this kind of person."

Hugh gazed sadly down at Harriet. "She would know what to do," he told the Doctor. "She and our friends Jeff and Akio always knew the right thing to do. And somehow, they were able to just do it. I mean, yes, they bent the rules every now and then, especially Akio. But still, they always did the right thing. Since the first attack, Harriet nagged us about all the illegal things we were doing. Sometimes it really used to bug me. But she was right, and deep down I knew it. She always tried to find a better way to handle bad situations. Not like me. I try to tell myself I have good reasons for the bad things I do. But wrong is still wrong and right is still right. You know what I mean, Doctor?"

Dr. Dickerson said gently, "Hugh, I realize you're a decent boy. You had to help Harriet. I don't blame you for blackmailing me. I never should have gotten involved in those shady business deals anyway. I was just greedy and that's my own fault."

"I really do promise to erase all the information I have on you when this is over."

"I know you will, Hugh. After nearly a year, I know I can trust you. I'm actually glad you found me and brought me into this. It's been a fascinating case. I've learned quite a bit about the life forms that are inside the two of you. When you give me permission to publish my findings . . ."

"Not until after we kill the Creature," Hugh cautioned.

"Of course," Dr. Dickerson agreed. "But is there a way to breed these *korei* so others can have them as well?"

Hugh shrugged and said, "You tell me."

Dr. Dickerson mirrored Hugh's shrug. Sadly, Hugh left her to perform her tests on Harriet. Casting the illusion of Benson Leonardo around him, Hugh walked out of his quarters and exited the warehouse through a side door. Strolling slowly down an enclosed walkway that connected to the next warehouse, he paused momentarily and gazed at the filthy sky through the clear plastic roof.

"I wish the others were here," Hugh muttered. He sighed and continued on his way.

Entering the neighboring warehouse, Hugh was immediately accosted by the factory's manager, Terrell Nash. "Sirsen Leonardo, I was looking for you," he said. "We just completed the tests on the production line for Factory 3. We'll be ready to open first thing tomorrow."

Hugh smiled. He was glad to have good news. "That's great Terrell. Give everyone my thanks for all their hard work. Have the new workers report to Factory 3 for their first day on the job tomorrow."

"Yes Sir, Sirsen Leonardo," Terrell quipped as he bounded away.

'Terrell really handles the factories well,' Hugh thought. 'Even though he's young, he was the right choice for the job.'

Hugh paused, almost laughing out loud. Terrell was 24, fully seven years older than Hugh. Yet he thought of Terrell as young. 'I guess I'm starting to believe the whole middle-aged man act myself,' he chuckled silently.

Passing through the noise and bustle of Factory 1, Hugh followed another enclosed walkway to the equally frantic Factory 2, passed through it, and went into Factory 3. A few people were milling around inside, apparently relaxing after finishing the tests on all the equipment. When they saw Hugh, they scurried away and tried to look busy. Again, Hugh couldn't help chuckling.

After a brief tour of Factory 3, Hugh returned to his office. Almost immediately, one of his procurement managers wanted to see him. Bursting into his office, the manager, Caleb Spence, blurted out, "Sirsen Leonardo, our scavengers have just come back from the junkyard. They can't find any more thulipropylununbiate alloy in any of the garbage out there. Our supplies will only last a couple of months."

"No problem, Caleb," Hugh assured him. "I've been thinking about that all week. Thulipropylununbiate alloy is literally all around us. Since it breaks down into dust so fast, most of the thulipropylununbiate alloy that was dumped on this planet is now blowing around in the air. I've got a new product here we can sell. It's an air filtration system that pulls thulipropylununbiate alloy, and a bunch of other pollutants, out of the air and reconstitutes them into a solid form. The users of the filter can not only clean the air in their homes and offices, they can sell the residues the filter takes out of the air. I expect that this will solve our thulipropylununbiate alloy problems for years to come."

"Wow, Sirsen Leonardo, that's great. I'll get this into production as fast as I can."

"It needs to be on the market in three weeks, Caleb."

Caleb's eyes widened. But jobs were scarce so Hugh knew that Caleb would have the filter on the market in three weeks no matter what. "Yes Sirsen," Caleb replied shakily. He left Hugh's office.

Hugh turned to his computer and tried to get some work done, but thoughts of Harriet kept him from concentrating. At last he leaned back in his chair and sighed.

"Hugh, we need to talk."

Eden was standing near his worn couch at the opposite end of the room.

"What do you want?" Hugh asked.

"It's time I helped Harriet to heal, Hugh."

"We've talked about this before, Eden. I'm not helping you muck around inside her head."

"Hugh, you've got to trust me. I can help Harriet. I won't be 'mucking around inside her head,' as you put it. I just need you to help me establish a stronger telepathic connection with her so I can help her mind heal itself."

Hugh shouted. "We don't need you! You got us into this in the first place! Get lost!"

Eden disappeared. Hugh's display beeped. It was his secretary program. "Sirsen Leonardo," it said. "Sirsen Gaylord Adkins is here to see you. He says he's an old friend of yours from planet Nason and that it's urgent you see him."

'Nason?' thought Hugh, startled. 'I don't know anyone from Nason called Adkins. And how does anyone know I've been to Nason?'

Hugh stepped quickly to the large safe hidden in the wall behind his desk and opened it. He removed his scanner and QID rifle. Sitting at the desk, Hugh turned the scanner's alarm all the way up and set it in a drawer. He closed the drawer and slid the rifle under the desk where he could grab it easily.

"Show Sirsen Adkins in," Hugh instructed.

The door opened, and a muscular man in his early twenties entered. His sandy hair looked like it had not been combed in a week or two. Spikes of it hung into his eyes. Adkins' harsh appearance immediately put Hugh on edge. He slid his right hand closer to his rifle.

Adkins eyed Hugh warily and opened his long black overcoat, which was made of real leather. He closed the door behind himself and leaned against it, facing Hugh.

'Hmm,' thought Hugh. 'It's no one I recognize. And the scanner would be screaming if it was the Creature. "Tell me who you are," Hugh commanded the stranger. "And tell me why you think I've been to the planet Nason."

Adkins eyed Hugh, then reached into a large pocket in his overcoat and retrieved a hand scanner. Staring at it intently, Adkins stated, "So you aren't the Creature."

Inside, Hugh froze. But he showed no emotion.

"I figured this might be a trap," Adkins explained, looking up from the scanner. He continued, "A company called FamilyShip Offworld, Incorporated. F.O.I. Foi is not exactly a common name. And the president of the company is a fantastic new inventor with Hugh's last name for a first name and my first name for his last name." Adkins opened his coat and revealed a QID rifle. "Either you're Hugh and you've left me a lot of clues so I could find you, or you're someone I need to shoot right now. Which is it?"

Hugh relaxed. Smiling, he greeted, "Hello, Leo. I'm glad you found us." He willed the illusion of Benson Leonardo to dissolve.

Leo visibly calmed down and pulled off his coat. "If you don't mind," he said pulling off his shirt, "I'm going to take off this plastiface. It's not as good as the ones we bought on Venus. It itches like crazy." Leo quickly removed the plastiface and put his shirt back on.

Hugh chided, "It took you long enough to get here."

"I had half the Federal Rangers in the Alliance chasing me all through the Dirasui Sector."

"I saw it on the news. I especially liked it when you made that old bridge float in the air. How did you do that?"

Leo plopped into a chair and answered, "It's a new trick I found I could do. I have power over anything metal. Not just magnetic metals, anything metal. That bridge was old enough that it was made of metal rather than the superstrong plastics they make most things out of these days."

"So you just stood on the bridge and floated away?"

"Yeah. But it was the local cops chasing me. All they had were hovercars. If it had been the Feds, they would have had air cruisers. I never would have gotten away."

"I've seen a lot about you in the news too. A real rags to riches story," Leo said. "The guy who started by building affordable spaceships for colonists in a forgotten warehouse on a backwater planet that was so far into an economic depression that they've spent the last three generations making money by accepting toxic waste from all over the Alliance."

"Well," commented Hugh, "it was the only thing I could think of to make a lot of money."

"Nice company you've built up," Leo complimented. "But you're undercapitalized. You don't have enough money to sustain the growth you're going through."

"Well, you can fix that."

"Me?"

"I need a Chief Financial Officer."

"Me? Work for you?"

"Why not?"

"No reason. It's just funny how life has changed. I started out as the rich kid headed for big things in the world of business. You were the poor kid. Now I'm working for you and you're on your way to becoming the richest man in the Dirasui Sector."

"Oh I think that's exaggerating. Maybe just the richest man here on Interstellar Dynamics," Hugh joked. "But actually, that isn't that hard. This planet has been pretty poor since the company went out of business."

"That's what happens when you live on a company planet," Leo remarked off-handedly. "If the company goes broke, you're high and dry."

A silence fell for a moment. Then Leo asked, "How's Harriet?"

Gravely, Hugh replied, "Better, but still not good. The Creature almost killed her. If you hadn't shot it when you did, it would have succeeded. Eden says it nearly pulled the *korei* right out of Harriet, and it almost burned out her mind in the process."

"You've been in contact with Eden?" Leo asked warily.

"Some, but not very much. I was really mad at her for getting us into this. I guess I still am. She said that the Creature seems to want to be stronger, so he came after us to get our *korei*. He didn't want to just kill us."

"I still wonder how he found us in Russia."

Hugh shook his head. "I have no idea. But it was really unlucky that Harriet happened to be alone outside without her plastiface on and without her rifle."

Nodding, Leo agreed, "Yeah, well only everyone with a window on that side of the habitation complex saw the fight. I wish they'd quit showing the video of it on the news."

Hugh replied, "Well, they really want to find us now. And they know we're here somewhere in the Dirasui Sector 'cause they figured out we all got on ships in the convoy that was coming out here."

"At least I won't have to be Francis Kronkmeyer any more," Leo chuckled mirthlessly.

Hugh looked at Leo intently. Then he asked, "Leo? Do you think you killed it? The Creature I mean."

"No," Leo stated flatly. I missed it when it came out of Harriet's dad. I'm pretty sure it got away and took over another host."

"What about Tiffany and Foi? What happened to them?"

Leo shrugged, "The news said that we all got onto ships in the same convoy, but I never saw Tiff or Foi after you teleported you and me and Harriet away from the Creature. I was hoping they were together. I don't know how well Tiff can do on her own."

Hugh agreed, "I've been putting money into the accounts of the dummy corporations. I wanted you guys to have plenty, in case you needed it. And thanks for showing us how to buy new identities. That came in real handy. I got several identities for me and a couple for Harriet."

Sadly, Leo asked, "Can I see Harriet?"

"Yup. I set up a medical bay in the back part of this warehouse right behind my personal residence. And by the way, I had rooms built in the residence for you and the others in case any of you ever showed up. There's one for Harriet too, but ..." He let his voice trail off.

Leo nodded, understanding. When Hugh stood, Leo followed him out the back door of the office and down to the residence. The doctor appeared to have finished her tests already; she was gone when they entered. Standing by Harriet's bed, Leo murmured, "She looks so peaceful—almost happy. You've taken good care of her, Hugh."

"She's the best friend I ever had."

"Friend? That's all?"

"Yup. That's all."

"You've never wanted more than that?"

"Oh," Hugh replied wistfully, "I had a big crush on her when I was 13 and she was 14. But ..."

"But what?"

"She ... she wasn't over her boyfriend that was lost in the wormhole collapse. At least she wasn't until she met you. And anyway, I figured out that she's not really my type. I'm too introverted. I need a girl who has more in common with me. After a while, I started feeling almost like she was my sister."

"That seems kind of . . . weird."

Hugh shrugged. "It worked for both of us. Neither of us needed anything more than a friend."

Still gazing at Harriet, Leo asked, "When will she wake up?"

Hugh answered. "No one knows."

32

Harry floated on the boogie board as she watched Akio sliding down a five-foot wave. Hooting as he descended, Akio rode to the shallow end of the wave pool where Harry and Jeff waited for him.

"You try," Akio encouraged Jeff.

"I'd rather go eat lunch," Jeff replied.

Harry saw a girl standing by the side of the pool, watching her intently. The girl was old—maybe even 18 or 19. Harry felt like she should know the girl, but she didn't.

"I don't want to know her," Harry muttered to herself. Looking at the girl made her angry. She didn't know why.

"Harriet," the girl called, waving at Harry to come.

"No!" shouted Harry. "Go away! You don't belong here. Go away!"

Two boys appeared next to the girl. One was very handsome. He had short, black hair. The other was smaller and not so good-looking. Harry gazed at him intently as he watched her. "Hugh," she stated, surprised that she knew the shorter boy's name. "You don't belong here either," she groused as she shook her head and turned away.

"Harry," Jeff called as he climbed out of the wave pool. Harry paddled over to him. "Let's go eat lunch." Harry nodded, climbed out of the water, and followed Jeff.

Harry heard Hugh ask the girl, "Why does she look so young?"

Sadly, the girl told him, "She's retreated back to a time when she felt happy and safe. Right now, in her mind, Harriet's only eleven years old."

"Why did that boy call her Harry?" the handsome boy asked.

Hugh replied, "That's what we all called her when we were younger. She didn't want to be called Harriet until she was older."

Harry frowned and hurried away. With Jeff and Akio, she rode an elevator to the floor she lived on. Entering her flat with the boys in tow, Harry was happy to see her mother setting lunch on the table. But it was real food, which puzzled her. "Synthpaste," she commented. "We eat synthpaste."

Jeff and Akio dug in without noticing. The boys each had a mound of food on their plate about three feet high, which they ate in huge gulps. Harry delicately ate her small sandwich. It tasted good. Gazing at her mother and her friends, Harry was happy.

But then the others appeared again.

"The only way she can wake up is if she wants to leave here," the girl said.

Hugh commented, "I don't think she will. She's happy here. She's with everyone she lost."

"Can we talk to her?" the handsome boy asked.

"You can try," the girl answered.

Harry wanted them to leave. But the handsome boy walked up to her, gazed at her kindly and asked, "Harriet, could you come with me? It's really important."

Tears welled up in Harry's eyes. "I don't want to," she wailed. "It hurts to go there. Go away." Turning to her mother, she called, "Mama, make them go away."

The flat's front door opened and Harry's father stepped inside. He looked angry. Harry felt afraid. "Daddy? What's the matter?"

Harry's father glared at her. His head hunched lower on his shoulders, like a large ape. He grew hairier and his eyes got larger and turned yellow. Harry stared, unable to move. Her father grew long fangs and claws.

"Mama!" Harry screamed. Her mother turned around. She gasped and stepped in front of Harry, but Harry's father ate her in one huge gulp. Then he ate Jeff and Akio. Harry shrieked and tried to run away.

Hugh called to her, "Harriet, come with us!"

But Harry grew angry. She stood in front of the father-demon and screamed, "GO AWAY!" Fire bellowed from her mouth and engulfed the father-demon. It fell to the floor and crumbled into a pile of ashes.

"I'm not going to be afraid!" she yelled kicking the ash pile and scattering it everywhere.

Harriet opened her eyes to find herself lying in a bed. Hugh and Leo were standing over her. They were each holding one of her hands. She felt weak and bleary, but she smiled up at them.

"You're awake!" Hugh exclaimed.

"Maybe," she croaked. Both boys smiled.

Leo told her, "I'm glad you're back with us. You had us worried for a while."

Harriet rasped, "Where?"

"We'll talk about that later," Hugh instructed. "We're safe here. Right now, you need to worry about yourself. A doctor is on the way to check you out."

Harriet stammered, "A . . . doctor?"

"Yes," replied Hugh, "but don't worry, she's someone we can trust."

Harriet heard Eden say, "Be careful about who you trust, Hugh."

Pulling a sour face, Hugh turned to Eden and retorted, "You don't have to tell me that. I know enough to be careful."

"I'm sure that's true," Eden agreed. "And I'm glad you finally decided to trust me." Smiling at Harriet, Eden told her, "You'll heal rapidly now Harriet. Get plenty of rest and try to eat some solid food. You'll feel better soon." Eden faded away.

Harriet looked at Hugh and whispered, "Taller."

Hugh smiled. "You're right," he agreed. "I'm taller, finally. I grew six inches while you were asleep. My dad didn't really start growing until college. But I started growing almost right after you were attacked. My dad would be glad ... wherever he is." Hugh's smile faded.

A short time later, Hugh showed a woman into the room and introduced her as Dr. Dickerson. Beaming, Dr. Dickerson chattered, "I'm sooo glad you're awake now dear. There are some tests I've been dying to run on you. I've been studying the *korei* inside you extensively, you know. Hugh has even let me run some tests on him."

Hugh, who was standing behind the doctor, scrunched his face and nodded. Obviously, Hugh wasn't crazy about the doctor's tests.

Dr. Dickerson continued, "I just knew you'd wake up eventually. You, Hugh, and Leo have such an unusually high ability to heal. And your cellular processes are amazing. You know, I'm currently of the opinion that you three might live literally hundreds of years."

"Uh, Doctor," Hugh interrupted. "Maybe you could just check her out right now and leave everything else for later. Harriet still seems like she needs rest."

"Oh, of course," Dr. Dickerson agreed. "I get so excited about the things I'm learning about you three. You're just amazing. Well, you two boys leave the room and I'll give Harriet a quick exam."

Leo and Hugh departed and Dr. Dickerson started poking and prodding Harriet in that annoying way that only doctors can. Half an hour later, she declared Harriet well on the road to recovery.

"Don't try to get out of bed today," the doctor warned Harriet. "You still don't have enough strength. But I'll come by tomorrow and have the boys help you walk around a bit. It'll help the healing process."

Dr. Dickerson said her goodbyes and left. Hugh and Leo reentered the room.

"How do you feel?" Hugh asked without preamble.

"Ugh," Harriet replied simply.

"Dr. Dickerson suggested we give you some oatmeal with some fruit in it."

"Huh?"

"I'm not sure what it is either," Hugh told her, "but I know it's some kind of food. I've ordered some. It should be delivered soon." A doorbell chimed. "Oh, there it is now. I'll go get it and be back." Hugh exited the room.

Leo stood at Harriet's bedside, smiling down at her. "I'm glad you made it, Harriet," he said gently as he took her hand.

"Mess," Harriet rasped, "I . . . must be . . . a complete mess."

"Harriet," Leo beamed, "even when you get rumpled—it only makes you cuter."

Harriet managed a smile and said, "Kiss me." Leo did just that. Beaming softly, Harriet said, "Nap."

Leo nodded and sat in a chair next to her bed. He held her hand tenderly. Contented, Harriet drifted off to sleep.

33

A week passed, with Dr. Dickerson visiting every day to run tests. Harriet quickly grew stronger. She was up and about for a short time every afternoon. After another week, she told Leo and Hugh one evening, "We have to talk."

Leo and Hugh looked up from their dinners in surprise. "Talk about what, Harriet?" Hugh asked.

"About what we're going to do next."

Leo and Hugh glanced cautiously at each other. Then Leo cleared his throat and began, "Well, we've been talking about that, and you see, we still think the urn . . ."

"Forget about the urn," Harriet cut him off. "Going after it was a disaster. We never should have done it. It was probably the fact that we returned to Earth that made it easy for the Creature to find us. We're not doing that again."

Airily, Leo replied, "I don't remember us electing you the leader."

"I don't remember us electing you the leader either, Leo."

"Well, no . . . but . . ."

Harriet gave him a hard stare. "Leo, the Creature wasn't outside that habitation complex by accident. He found us there because we went back to Earth. I admit that going outside without my plastiface was stupid, but do you really think he didn't already know where we were? Think about it. He was watching us. Those plastifaces weren't fooling him. Eventually, he would have attacked us whether or not we were wearing them."

Taken aback, Leo looked to Hugh for support. Diligently averting his gaze, Hugh found something interesting to look at on the other side of the room.

Continuing, Harriet told them, "It's time we ask Eden for help. I'm doing it now." Closing her eyes momentarily, Harriet reached out to Eden in her mind. When she reopened her eyes, the image of Eden was standing near her.

"I'm glad you're doing better Harriet," Eden greeted her gently.

"How do we kill the Creature?" Harriet demanded abruptly. "And I mean kill, not capture, not set it up so you can take over its mind. We're going to kill it dead. How do we do that?"

Eden's eyebrows rose. She paused a moment, apparently considering her reply. Then she asked, "Do you understand that you can't get your lives back if you kill it? Your entire race is in danger. Killing the Creature is only the first step in making everyone you know and love safe. If I help you kill it, will you help me save everyone in both universes?"

Harriet glared at her and replied, "We'll do what we can to help. But you can't expect the fates of two entire universes to be our responsibility alone."

Nodding, Eden agreed, "That's fair. Ok, let's talk about killing the Creature. It's powerful compared to all of you, so you have to be careful."

"No kidding," Hugh muttered.

Ignoring him, Eden continued, "Don't confront him directly. Kill him from a distance."

"How?" Harriet asked.

"He's in a human host, and the host body can only take so much. As you've seen previously, it can be killed. You have to put the Creature into a situation where his host will die and he can't prevent it. You have to kill the host in a place where there are no other people around. That way, he can't take a new host. He won't last more than a few minutes outside of a human."

Harriet pondered Eden's guidance. "Space," she blurted out. "We have to get him into space. It has to be far from an inhabited planet."

Growing excited, Hugh agreed, "That's perfect. We can lure him onto a ship, and then blow it up in deep space. I'll teleport us off the decoy ship and onto another ship that we'll keep nearby. He goes boom. We fly away. The end."

"Unless he can teleport too," Leo countered.

Harriet looked to Eden and asked, "Can he teleport?"

Eden shook her head. "We don't have that ability naturally," she replied. "You remember the two *churei* you killed on the planet Alofi? The Creature was using mind control to bind those *churei* to him in much the same way that your *korei* are bound to you."

"But," Harriet objected, "you said our *korei* like us. We're not forcing them to stay in us."

"You're right," Eden agreed. "Your *korei* are like dogs or cats are in your world. They stay with you because they want to. But the *churei* are intelligent energy beings. They would never voluntarily bind to a *dairei* like the Creature. They have to be forced, and that's what the Creature has done. The Creature can then use their abilities just as if they were his own."

"Just the way we use the abilities of our *korei*," Harriet suggested.

"Exactly," Eden said. "And once a *churei* has been bound to a *dairei*, it's possible for the *dairei* to send the *churei* out to do his bidding while keeping them under his control."

"That's just horrible!" Harriet exclaimed.

"Yes, it is," Eden said. "The Creature is a rogue *dairei* that needs to be brought to justice."

"What kind of justice?" Leo demanded.

"If I could capture him, I'd take him back to our universe to face our laws. But after all that's happened, I can see that that's impossible." Eden said, gravely, "He has to die. There's no other choice. This has to stop."

Leo seemed satisfied by her answer.

Eden continued, "In any case, in answer to your original question, you killed the *churei* that could teleport. It's unlikely he has another one under his control with the same ability. *Dairei* that enslave the *churei* usually try to get as many different abilities as possible. So each *churei* they take control of usually has a set of different abilities."

Hugh asked Eden, "Do you think our plan will work?"

"I think it's probably your best bet for killing the Creature and ending this," she answered.

"Where are we going to get two ships?" Harriet asked Hugh.

"Are you kidding? The company I own *makes* ships," Hugh announced proudly. "But they probably aren't the kind we need. They're too slow and the power plants could never be turned into a bomb. The next planet out in this system is called Decimus. It's a good place to buy ships."

"Do we have enough money?"

"Of course, I've been putting tons of money into the accounts held by our dummy corporations. We've got lots."

Eden cautioned, "Please don't make major decisions in this plan without consulting me. There's lots of help and guidance I can give you." She disappeared.

Thoughtfully, Harriet commented, "For the first time in a long time, I really feel like we've got a good chance of beating the Creature."

"Time," Hugh exclaimed. "That reminds me."

Hopping up from his chair, Hugh went to a cupboard and pulled out a frosted cupcake with a candle in it. He lit the candle, carried the cupcake to Harriet, and said, "I was going to give you this after dinner."

"What's it for?"

"You missed your birthday while you were unconscious. You're 17 now."

"Seventeen? Hugh, it's been two-and-a-half years since the Creature first attacked us. I have to be older than that."

"Nope. You spent about a year and a half in stasis. You're only a year older. The rest of us only spent five months in stasis, so we're two years older. I'm 17, like you. Leo is 19 and Tiffany, wherever she is, is 18."

"So when was my birthday?"

"About a month and a half before you woke up. I just remembered and had this delivered today."

"Thank you Hugh. That was really sweet."

Hugh beamed and suggested, "Make a wish and blow out your candle."

"I think we all know what my wish is," she said gravely.

Hugh and Leo both nodded. "Yeah," Hugh agreed. "We wish the Creature was dead too."

She blew out her candle and ate her cupcake.

34

"The Rangers are closing in on us," Hugh blurted out as he burst into the living room of their quarters in the warehouse. "I was just scanning the news in my office. It said the Feds know that at least two of us are on this planet. They're running background checks on everyone who's landed here since the convoy we rode on arrived in this system."

"Then I think it's time we got out of here," Leo stated. "This star system doesn't get that many people coming in. So that means they may have the resources to do a thorough investigation of everyone that's arrived lately. Our identities won't stand up to that kind of a background check. It costs a lot more to buy identities that will."

Hesitantly, Harriet agreed, "Then I guess you're right. We do need to leave."

"Or ..." Hugh interjected.

"Or what?" Harriet asked.

Hugh grinned wickedly, but the only thing he said was, "I've got to go to my office." He dashed out leaving Harriet and Leo puzzled.

Bounding into his office, Hugh cast the illusion of Benson Leonardo around himself and called up his secretary program on the computer. "Yes, Sirsen Leonardo?" the program asked.

"Ask Caleb Spence to come to my office immediately."

"Yes, Sirsen Leonardo."

A minute or so later, a knock sounded at Hugh's office door. Caleb entered questioningly. "You wanted to see me, Sirsen Leonardo?"

"Yes, Caleb. Please sit down."

Caleb sat in a chair facing Hugh's desk. He shifted himself uneasily.

"Caleb," Hugh began, "you've been doing a great job around here."

"Thank you, Sirsen Leonardo. I feel very lucky to have this job."

"Well this company is lucky to have you. In fact, I think you're so valuable to this company that I'm promoting you."

Caleb brightened, "Promoting me? To what position?"

"Mine."

Shocked, Caleb asked, "Yours, Sirsen?"

"Yes, Caleb. I'm too old to be building a business from scratch. This company is booming, and I'm not getting any younger. It's time to make my exit. I'm going to find some tropical planet to live on somewhere far, far away."

"But . . . but . . ."

"No, Caleb. My mind is made up. Adkins, our new Chief Financial Officer is setting up a buyout of the company for me."

Fear crossed Caleb's face. "Who . . . who's buying the company?"

"You are."

"Not me!" Caleb objected. "I don't have any money."

"Well, not just you. You and all the other employees. Over the next five years, all of you will use the profits from the company to buy me out. I'll leave you the bank account information you need in order to deposit your payments. You personally will own 50% of the company and all the other employees together will own the other 50%. That means they can band together and block your initiatives, so you have to keep them happy."

"But ... I ... we ..."

"You and the rest of the employees will be signing the sale contract first thing tomorrow morning. And by the way, Caleb. I expect that you'll stick to our current plans and double production by the end of next year."

"Sure. Of course. Uh ..."

"I'll be staying on until the end of the month. That's three weeks from today. Then I'm gone. Oh, and Adkins says he's quitting too. It's a family emergency. He needs to leave the planet. So you'll have to start interviewing for a new CFO."

"Yes, Sir. And thank you. Thank you very much."

"Caleb?"

"Yes?"

"You have a family don't you?"

"Yes. I have a wife and a small daughter."

"And where are you living now?"

"We're living with my parents."

"There's a house built into the rear half of this warehouse. First thing next month, you move your wife and daughter into that. You'll find it very roomy."

Caleb was stunned. "Thank you! Thank you Sirsen Leonardo," he effused.

Hugh smiled and said gently, "Now if you'll excuse me, I've got to talk with Adkins and get the contract drawn up."

Hardly able to contain himself, Caleb gushed his thanks to Hugh and left.

35

"This is Alberta Calhoun, live on Galactic News Network. I'm here on the smoggy streets of the city of Incompac on the ailing planet of Interstellar Dynamics in the Felton System in the Dirasui Sector. As you can see," she made a sweeping gesture toward the unending vista of crumbling, orange-brown buildings behind her, "this planet is so heavily polluted that it's dangerous to go outside without a respirator like the one I'm wearing. It's to this decrepit and decaying world that the Federated Alliance Rangers have traced at least two of the Otherworldly Four."

"It's been a little more than a year since Leonardo de Medici, Tiffany Montague, Harriet Brightway, and Hubert Benson escaped from Earth after a spectacular battle in Verkhoturye, Russia that ended with Leonardo de Medici killing Richard Brightway, Harriet's father, in an apparent attempt to keep Brightway from murdering his daughter."

"Since that time, the Rangers have known that all of the Otherworldly Four fled Earth on a convoy of ships that came here to the Dirasui Sector. They've been searching star system by star system and planet by planet until they've positively determined that at least two of the Four are here on this planet."

"Earlier today, Galactic News Network received a tip indicating that all of the Otherworldly Four are here in the city of Incompac, and that they're going to try to make a run for it today. Apparently, they know the Rangers are closing in."

Alberta Calhoun paused as a deep throbbing sounded behind her. A group of police air cruisers zipped by overhead. "As you can see," she continued, "both the local police and the Federated Alliance Rangers are out in force."

A siren sounded in the distance behind her. Alberta Calhoun turned around and peered into the distance through the grungy air. She listened briefly to a radio that was clipped to her ear. "Yes, it seems that the police have spotted something not far from here." She raced to her hovercar, hopped in, and zipped down the street toward a large, open square. Her camerabot glided along behind her, still shooting live video.

Guiding her hovercar into the square, Alberta Calhoun pointed to four figures standing near the middle of the plaza. "There they are!" she shouted excitedly. The camerabot zoomed in. Harriet,

Leo, Hugh, and Tiffany stood frozen in the middle of the plaza. They gaped upward as Ranger air cruisers quickly clustered around them.

"Don't move!" a Ranger's voice boomed over a loudspeaker. "We won't hurt you. Just stay where you are. We know you're carrying weapons. Drop them now."

A large, silver flying saucer shimmered into existence in the sky above the air cruisers. As a hatch opened on its underside, it emitted an intense beam of light that shone down on Harriet, Leo, Hugh, and Tiffany. Suddenly, the four of them were lifted into the air.

"Stop them!" the Ranger commanded into the loudspeaker. Several air cruisers moved to intercept them, but they were levitated too quickly. In an instant, the four of them rose into the flying saucer. The saucer shot skyward and then faded into invisibility.

"There you saw it," Alberta shouted. "The Otherworldly Four made their escape. They've got a ship with some kind of cloaking device! The Rangers appear unable to follow them. We have no idea where they are going, but they've eluded authorities again. Stay tuned to Galactic News Network for further updates. This is Alberta Calhoun reporting."

36

"Those were great illusions Hugh," Harriet praised as she watched the replay of their supposed escape from the planet Interstellar Dynamics.

Hugh beamed proudly, "Thanks. I thought the whole levitating-beam-of-light thing was a nice touch."

"Yeah," Leo agreed. "But did you have to use a flying saucer? That's not just old-fashioned, it's ancient."

"I can only do so many illusions at once," Hugh explained. "I couldn't do a complex-looking ship because I had to make us look really detailed."

"So what do we do now?" Leo asked.

"You and I go to work," Hugh replied, "just like every other day. We'll finish our jobs here in two more weeks. Then we leave quietly."

Harriet sighed, "I guess I'll have to buy another plastiface."

"That wouldn't be a good idea," Leo advised. "The cops will be looking closely at anyone who's dealt in plastifaces in the past."

"You think they'll still be looking for us here?" Harriet queried.

"Don't know," Hugh joined in, "but it's not worth taking a chance. But it's ok. You won't need one as long as you stay near me when we're outside."

"Why?"

"I can cast an illusion around you. It will even fool scanners."

"Are you sure?"

"Of course. I figured it out when we were on the run in Russia. Do you remember when we were on that space station owned by Irwin Gyronetics and we saw that holographic billboard showing video of ourselves?"

"Sure," Harriet said. "I about died when I saw it."

"Well one of the videos showed a dragon illusion that I used to distract the *churei* that came out of Carlene. I realized that cameras can see my illusions, not just people. So I tried it in Russia with the spaceport scanners. That's how I got the two of us onto that convoy that came here."

"So if we have valid identities ..." Harriet began.

"... We can walk right past spaceport scanners and security people without a problem," Hugh finished for her.

Two weeks later, Harriet packed her belongings and joined Hugh and Leo in the entry foyer of their warehouse residence. Leo was already disguised in his plastiface as Gaylord Adkins. Hugh handed an ID to Harriet.

"You're Selena Zamora, age 27," he told her. "You're from the planet Santiago in the Abuan system. I am your mother's cousin. You and I are traveling with Gaylord Adkins, who is the son of my high school buddy, Alphonse Adkins, and your fiancée. Our story is that we're on our way to Decimus to buy some ships and go to the planet Amarnath, which is outside the Alliance in the Behari system. After your wedding, I'm planning on touring the Edge Worlds. You got all that?"

Harriet nodded.

"Good," Hugh said, "then let's get going. A hoverlimo is waiting in the garage. I've already got the air filters cleaning out the air. It should be ok for us to open the door by now."

Leo commented, "I'm surprised you got us a hoverlimo."

"Hey, I'm a successful businessman that's retiring into the good life," Hugh replied. "I even got us first class tickets on the spaceliner. Decimus is the next planet out in this system. It's a fast ship, so it'll only take a few days to get there."

Hugh turned to his luggage and commanded, "Follow." The suitcases and trunks floated into the air and fell into formation near him. Turning to Harriet, Hugh fixed her momentarily with a stare.

"You look good," Leo exclaimed.

Harriet moved to a decorative mirror that hung in the foyer. Gazing back at her was a stunning twenty-seven year old Filipino-Spanish woman with wavy black hair cascading down her back.

"Thank you, Hugh," Harriet said. "It's so nice not to have to look old."

"You're welcome," Hugh called back to her. "Just stay close to me or the illusion will disappear." Hugh cast the illusion of Benson Leonardo around himself. Stepping to the foyer door, he told Leo and Harriet, "You two remember to hold hands a lot when we're traveling. You're engaged; you have to act like it." Harriet could see he was suppressing a smile.

The ride to the spaceport was quick. Harriet was surprised at how easily they got through the security checks, even with the presence of so many Alliance Rangers. 'Hugh's planned things out really well,' she thought.

Knowing that she needed to minimize the burden on Hugh, Harriet spent almost the entire trip in her cabin so that he didn't have to constantly work at hiding her identity with his illusion.

Landing on Decimus, they once again sailed easily through spaceport security. They arrived at their hotel about noon local time and got settled. A short time later, the three of them gathered to go look for ships.

"There are lots of ship dealers in this city," Hugh explained as they strolled down the wide avenue. Shoppers drifted past them as they paused on the sidewalk to talk. "We'll need two ships," Hugh continued, "a big comfortable one for long-haul travel, and a smaller one to keep you-know-who's attention." Hugh glanced quickly around to ensure that no one could overhear.

They grabbed a cab for a short ride to the dealership. "I used my autolibrary to look at their inventory on the grid," Hugh continued as they rode along. "I've already picked out some ships to look at and the dealer knows we're coming."

As soon as they arrived, a stout salesman emerged from the dealership's office. "Sirsen Leonardo?" he asked Hugh as he approached.

"Yes, are you Gillins?"

"Call me Steve. I've got a hovercart here waiting, so if the three of you would like to climb on, we'll go right out and look at the ships you indicated in your message."

The shipyard was large, so it took several minutes for them to arrive at the first ship. As Harriet walked through the first ship with the others, she thought, "What a heap. We can't buy this." When they were outside, Hugh voiced the same thoughts, but a little more politely. They moved on. After trudging through three more ships, they found a nice big one that was in good condition, so they bought it. Steve was beside himself with delight.

"Now we need another, smaller ship for me when I go running around on my own," Hugh told the salesman. Steve beamed again. Hugh slapped his shoulder in the way that older men do. "You're gonna get a good commission this month," Hugh joked.

The salesman's smile only got wider, "Thanks to you, Sirsen Leonardo."

Because they knew it would be blown up, Hugh, Harriet, and Leo were much less picky about the small ship. It just had to be fast. The salesman showed them a zippy sports model that looked rather beat up. But it had a powerful engine and moved fast, so they bought it. Hugh paid the salesman, who told them, "I'll have both of them ready for you at the spaceport first thing tomorrow."

"If I give you an extra two thousand talents," Hugh asked, "could you have them at the spaceport and ready for liftoff by 8:00 tonight?"

"Oh yes, Sirsen Leonardo," Steve effused. "They'll be ready and waiting at eight o'clock."

Hopping a hovercab, they returned to the hotel. Before Hugh could get out of the cab, Harriet grabbed his arm. "We're going shopping," she asserted.

"How come I have to go?"

"Because I can't go anywhere without you."

"Oh, right."

Leo, looking like he got off lucky, slipped out of the cab and hurried into the hotel.

Two hours later, Hugh complained, "I'm really getting a headache. Can't we be done yet?"

"I just have to pay for everything, and then we can go back to the hotel," Harriet told him.

"Let's get dinner before we go back," suggested Hugh. "That will make me feel better." Harriet agreed.

Stopping at a nearby restaurant, they had a quick dinner and headed for the skytrain station to catch a ride back to the hotel. "The ships should be at the spaceport by now," Hugh commented as they waited on the platform.

Hugh's minipod beeped. When he answered it, Harriet could hear Leo's voice shouting from the earpiece, but she couldn't make out what he was saying. She watched as Hugh listened intently. "Holy galveth!" he burst out, and then he paused to listen. "Ok," Hugh continued. "Be careful." He hung up.

"The Creature found Leo," Hugh explained hastily. "He was out getting dinner and it found him. He's on the run now, trying to lead it away. He told us to get our stuff and meet him at the spaceport. We want the Creature to follow the little ship, so we'll get into it and get ready for liftoff. Leo's going to fly the little ship and I can teleport the two of us to the big one. Harriet, you'll have to fly the big ship. I don't know how."

"I don't have a license!" Harriet objected.

"I can get on the grid and buy you one through the same company I used to buy our identities," Hugh responded. "You can have a license by the time Leo gets to the ships. I need to buy one for Leo under the name of Gaylord Adkins. I can't believe I didn't learn to pilot them myself. I owned a company that made ships, for crying out loud! It's too late now, let's go!"

Harriet and Hugh dashed to the hotel, packed frantically, and checked out. The pair hopped a hovercab to the spaceport. Hugh was on his autolibrary as soon as they were in the cab. As they arrived at the spaceport, he said, "I've got pilot's licenses for both you and Leo. But we've got to move fast; the cops know we're here. Leo's been fighting with the Creature. They've damaged several buildings, caused a couple of fires, and collapsed a bridge. The whole downtown area's in a panic."

"We need to get down there and help him!" exclaimed Harriet.

"No," countered Hugh, urgently. "We need to stick to the plan. Leo will make it. We just have to be patient."

"How can you say that? He might get killed."

"The news says that Leo's jumping toward the spaceport now."

"Jumping?"

"Remember, he's super-strong. They say he's jumping a quarter mile with each leap. The local cops are afraid to get near him. He's already trashed two of their cruisers. They're waiting for the Rangers to get here."

The cab was pulling into the spaceport. Time seemed to crawl as the taxi shooshed its way to their ships. The robocabbie couldn't get the bags out fast enough for Harriet. "Move it! Move it!" she urged the beleaguered machine repeatedly as it stowed the bags in the larger ship.

The BOOM of a large explosion sounded not far from the spaceport. Standing outside the small ship, Harriet and Hugh waited grimly. Both of their minipods rang. When they answered, Leo shouted, "I can't make it! Go without me!"

"I'm coming!" Harriet cried. Hanging up, she commanded, "Hugh, get the ships ready."

Harriet's winged tigress appeared in front of her and she bounded onto its back. Leaping upward, the tigress soared into the sky as Harriet guided it in the direction of the explosion. Nearly a mile ahead of her, a hovercar bounced off the side of a tall building as it was tossed into the air. Ricocheting off a communications tower, the car erupted into a ball of flame. The explosion blew off the top of the tower and showered the surrounding area with blue arcs of electricity.

Kicking her tigress's sides, Harriet leaned down close to it. "Faster!" she shouted to it. "Go faster!" The tigress beat its wings frenetically and shot forward.

37

Rapid explosions ripped through the city as Harriet closed in on Leo's location. "There he is!" she shouted out loud.

Leo was standing on the roof of one of the taller buildings. He tore a power transformer the size of a large hovertruck off the top of the office complex and tossed it downward. Seconds later it exploded in a ball of fire sending a shock wave that pitched Harriet and her tigress downward. The winged feline struggled to regain her balance and stop their fall. She fought her way upward again and quickly carried Harriet closer to the battle.

Seeing Leo jump to the ground, Harriet had her tigress circle above the conflict below. Leo was standing a few hundred yards down the street from the Creature on a bare patch of ground where the pavement was torn up. She watched him touch one hand to the ground. A thin metallic shaft about five feet long sprang up from the dirt. Leo grabbed it, stood up, and hefted it at the Creature so fast that Harriet couldn't see it fly.

Moving like a blur, the Creature deftly avoided Leo's metal spear and quickly drew closer. The spear completely embedded itself in the side of a building. As the Creature got closer to Leo, it used telekinesis to grab him right off his feet and bring him flying. The Creature clamped its hand on Leo's throat. Harriet could see a blur forming around Leo's head and hands.

'It's pulling out his *korei*!' Harriet realized, panicking. She knew that Leo would be dead in moments if she didn't do something. 'I can't use my fire,' she fretted. 'I'd hit Leo as well. Wait! I know.'

As she circled lower, Harriet reached out with her mind and telekinetically grabbed the Creature by the throat. It sputtered in surprised and dropped Leo, who crumpled to the ground.

The Creature glared at Harriet and grinned. It rose toward her through the air. Harriet whipped her QID rifle out from under her coat and started blasting the Creature. It reacted by zigzagging to avoid her volleys. As it did, it laughed and shot fire back at Harriet.

Harriet didn't even try to avoid the fire; it didn't hurt her a bit. She let the Creature have another barrage from her rifle. She missed, but then something surprising happened. One of her blasts hit the side of a building not far above the Creature. A chunk of the sheer structure's wall was sent flying by the blast. It hit the

Creature squarely in the head, momentarily stunning it. Blood sprang from a deep gash it its skin.

In a flash, Harriet realized, 'It doesn't have its shield! Or it's not using it for some reason.'

Before the Creature could recover, Harriet shot it again. She hit it in the arm, between the shoulder and the elbow. It bellowed with rage. A metallic spear sailed through the air and skewered the Creature through its injured arm, pinning it to the side of a building. Harriet glanced down to see Leo struggling shakily to his feet. She dove toward him, relieved.

"No Harriet!" Leo shouted, pointing at the Creature. "Kill it quick!"

It was too late. The Creature made an incredibly bright sword-like object appear from nowhere. Grabbing the sword, it cut off its own arm to free itself. As it sailed toward her, a warm yellow glow surrounded it. She could see that it was no longer bleeding. Harriet was shocked as she saw that the arm was already growing back.

"It can heal its host," Harriet blurted out. The Creature grinned predatorily.

Turning her tigress, Harriet struggled to get away. She felt the Creature reaching out telekinetically, trying to grab her. "No!" she screamed and sent a massive force push toward the Creature. The force slammed the Creature against the side of a building, wiping the grin off its face. Another spear zipped through the air and passed completely through the Creature. It grabbed its chest and fell downward.

"Now Harriet! Shoot! It destroyed my gun!"

Anger exploding inside her, Harriet shot repeatedly at the Creature. One of her blasts hit it squarely in the chest. Its human host began to dissolve. The Creature erupted from inside the host and the body fell lifelessly to the ground.

Fear surging through her, Harriet shot at the unprotected Creature as it pulsed and glowed sickly. It ducked through the wall of a nearby building. Knowing that she couldn't follow it, Harriet instead holstered her gun, guided her tigress toward the ground, and landed next to Leo. Leaping off large cat, she wrapped her arms around Leo's neck and kissed him. Leo hugged her tightly, and then released her.

"Be careful," he warned. "It might come back." He kissed her once more, quickly. "Harriet, you were fantastic!" Leo praised. "You saved me. You went up against the Creature all by yourself. Weren't you scared?"

"Terrified. I still am. Let's get to the spaceport."

Before Leo could reply, the side of a nearby building exploded. In the gaping hole stood a man who stared down at them venomously. Harriet's insides froze. "It's taken another host," she said.

Nodding, Leo picked her up, set her on her tigress, and jumped up behind her. "Let's go!" he shouted.

Harriet willed the tigress into movement. Glancing over her shoulder, Harriet saw the Creature grin again and fly toward them. It let loose a blast of fire, searing toward Harriet and Leo. Harriet was completely unaffected, but Leo screamed in agony.

The Creature reached them before they could get away. Hanging in mid-air, it grabbed them each by the throat. Harriet struggled to muster her fire. Blearily, she saw her tigress clawing at the Creature, trying to free her. The Creature cursed angrily and glared at the tigress. It screeched hideously as it dissolved into thin air. Harriet pawed her gun, trying to pull it from its holster. She heard Leo scream.

Suddenly, a blast of lightning hit the Creature, shocking Harriet and Leo as well. Bellowing, the Creature dropped both of them. Harriet heard a volley of blasts from a QID rifle, and then a flurry of wings and blonde hair appeared. Harriet felt her fall slowing as the world around her came slowly into focus.

Looking up, Harriet saw that Tiffany was holding both her and Leo by their arms. Tiffany beat her wings as hard as she could, struggling to get them all safely to the ground. Hearing another blast from a QID rifle, Harriet looked downward. Below them stood Foi, grimacing maniacally as he shot at the Creature.

When they landed, Harriet let herself plop down into a sitting position on the cool pavement. Foi shouted, "Are you alright?" He warily watched the sky. "Do you see the Creature? It dodged and I don't know where it went."

Harriet looked up to see Tiffany kissing Leo. Angrily, she struggled to her feet and erupted into flame. Leo pushed Tiffany away and shouted, "No Harriet! Now's not the time. Just get your tigress back. We need to get out of here."

Struggling to control herself, Harriet made her tigress reappear. It looked thin and weak. With a shriek, Harriet wrapped her arms around its neck and buried her face in its snowy fur.

"Harriet," Foi urged, "we've got to go. The Creature's gone and the cops are coming."

Releasing her tigress, Harriet climbed gently on its back. "Are you alright, girl? Can you fly? Can you take me to the spaceport?"

The tigress nodded and pawed the ground. Trotting forward, it flapped its wings with great effort and took flight. Tiffany followed. Leo made his surfboard appear and Foi jumped on the back. They fled toward the spaceport as police hovercars closed in.

"It's the Feds," Tiffany shouted, "not the local cops. They're Rangers." Harriet's tigress struggled to increase its speed.

"Where did Leo and Foi go?" Harriet asked, realizing that she couldn't see them any more.

"Probably back to the hovercar that Foi stole," Tiffany answered. "Foi's ship is at the spaceport."

"Ours is too," Harriet told her. They flew on in strained silence. Behind them, police sirens closed in.

A blast of fire arced from below, almost hitting them. Harriet looked around in alarm. Below them, she saw the Creature rising upward with a look of hungry anger on its face. Tiffany shot lightning down at it. Harriet threw a ball of fire and drew her gun.

Police air cruisers appeared, surrounding them. "Drop your weapon," a man's voice commanded from one of the cars. Harriet ignored him.

The Creature propelled a column of fire upward. Harriet and Tiffany dodged. Harriet tried to get a clear shot at it, but it zigzagged too quickly. To her surprise, a QID blast erupted from one of the police cruisers. Turning her attention to it, she saw that the vehicle had QID guns mounted on the front and back.

'They've learned from watching our fights,' she thought. 'They've figured out that only QID guns kill the Creature.'

"All three of you stop fighting and land now," the Ranger commanded again. "We know QID weapons will harm you and we're all armed with them. For your own sakes, stop fighting now."

The Creature responded by knocking three of the cruisers out of the sky with a force push. Another three police cars opened fire on it. Avoiding the gunfire from the Rangers, the Creature dropped downward into a cluster of tall buildings. The Rangers followed.

'It's a good thing there aren't many Rangers stationed on this planet,' Harriet thought, 'or there would be some following us as well.' Harriet did her best to fly toward the spaceport as fast as she could.

In just a few minutes, they arrived at the spaceport and descended to the small ship. Leo and Foi were there loading luggage from a hovercar into the small ship.

"Why don't you put that in the other ship?" she demanded as she dropped from her tigress's back and made it disappear. Tiffany landed behind her.

"We've got to make it look like this is the ship we're escaping in," Leo answered.

An explosion erupted not far away.

"The Creature's almost here," Hugh shouted as he emerged from the small ship. "We have to hurry up!"

Once the luggage floated into the little ship, out of sight of anyone who might be watching, Hugh teleported it to the big ship. When he returned, he said, "Ok, now I'll take everyone but Leo."

They gathered together and Hugh teleported them to the control cabin of the big ship. "You'd probably better start the pre-flight checks," he told Harriet. Nodding, Harriet slipped into the pilot's seat and began preparations for takeoff.

Tiffany stood watching her for a moment and then said, "Wow, you've changed."

Surprised, Harriet paused and asked, "What do you mean?"

"When you showed up at school, you looked like you were scared of everyone and everything," Tiffany told her. "But now you take on the Creature by yourself and you're piloting a big ship like it's nothing. You didn't say anything, you just sat down and got to work even though you've never flown a real ship before, just simulations."

"Thank you Tiffany," Harriet said simply. She continued her preflight checks on the ship.

Hugh rematerialized and told them, "I didn't want to risk radio communications. We don't want anyone to know you're on this ship. So I teleported."

"What's up?" Harriet asked.

"I just heard on the radio that the Creature is on his way. I hacked into their secure channel. The Rangers are fighting it out with the Creature, and it's killed about half of them. They've got the spaceport locked down and on alert. The local cops and spaceport security saw us get in the small ship and they're going to try and prevent takeoff. They're just waiting for a Ranger fighter ship to arrive. It has a tractor beam on it. As soon as we try to take off, they're going to pull us in and take us into custody. That's the plan anyway."

Harriet asked, "Are you guys ready for take-off?"

Nodding, Hugh told her, "Yup. Leo's just finishing the preflight checks. We'll lift off now and meet you at the rendezvous point."

"Ok, we'll wait until lockdown ends and then follow you."

Hugh nodded again and moved to the communications console. "I'll get you logged onto all the secure channels the cops are using." His hands briefly flew over the controls.

From the back of the control cabin, Foi said warmly, "Hugh, you are becoming someone I really admire."

Harriet scowled, but said nothing. Hugh got them logged on, waved goodbye, and then disappeared. Seconds later, the small ship took off. Immediately alarms blared around the spaceport and police ships closed in on Hugh and Leo's spacecraft. Harriet, Tiffany, and Foi used their ship's external cameras to watch the chase. The sky was rapidly filling with spacecraft small and large. The small ship weaved and dodged as it made its way upward. Excited chatter from the radio filled the control cabin.

"Tower this is 1-Adam-12 city police patrol. We've just observed the suspect enter a small sportship. We believe he's about to take off."

Foi commented, "That must be the Creature."

"Roger 1-Adam-12. A Ranger fighter group has just arrived. We are dispatching to your location. ETA 50 seconds."

"Negative Tower. The ship is already lifting off in pursuit of the Otherworldy Four. Forwarding the vector now."

"Roger 1-Adam-12. Flight vector received. We have dispatched four Ranger fighters to intercept."

"Roger. 1-Adam-12 out."

"He's taken the bait," Foi said.

"That bait is Leo," Tiffany shot back hotly.

"And Hugh," Harriet added tersely.

Foi just gave them one of his stony stares. Then he said, "I'm going to my ship. As soon as the spaceport's lockdown has ended, we'll leave and I'll dock with you in orbit." He left the control cabin.

Harriet heard shouting from the radio. "I swear it!" a man's voice hollered. "The ship with the Otherworldly Four! It just disappeared! We can't see it anywhere and there's nothing on the scanners. We almost got a tractor lock on them and they disappeared."

"That's not unexpected," a woman replied. "Red Leader, stand by. Control to Gold Leader, what's your status?"

"Still in pursuit," another woman said. "This one doesn't seem to have the tech for invisibility. But each time we get a tractor lock, an unknown force breaks it."

"Roger Gold Leader. You have clearance to fire on that ship. Red Leader, take your group on the vector I'm transmitting now and assist Gold Leader."

"Roger Control. We're on our way."

Harriet heard Gold Leader shout, "Whoa! What's that?"

"Gold Leader, what's your status?" Control asked.

"GOLD GROUP PULL BACK!" Gold Leader screamed in terror. "WATCH OUT! IT'S COMING!"

Silence.

38

Harriet and Tiffany sat listening to the radio in strained anxiety.

"Gold Leader, what's your status?" Control demanded. No answer. "Gold Leader are you there? We're no longer tracking your signal. Gold Leader?" Empty airwaves were the only reply. "Any member of Gold Group?" Control called forlornly.

Silence. Only silence.

"Red Leader, this is Control. You should be approaching Gold Group's last known position. What do you see?"

"Control, this is Red Leader. There's nothing out here but debris. It's in a low orbit, so some of it is starting to fall back into the atmosphere. The entire group is gone. Destroyed. No sign of the suspect ship."

After a pause, Control said, "Acknowledged Red Leader. Hold position. A destroyer group has just arrived in the area. We are dispatching them directly to your location."

Harriet looked warily at Tiffany. "What do you think happened?"

Tiffany shook her head gravely. "I don't know, but it makes me worried. I mean, if that thing can destroy an entire Ranger fighter group, what chance do we have against it?"

That thought worried Harriet as well. Then something occurred to her. "If he has that kind of power," she mused, "why didn't he use it on us?"

Tiffany tilted her head and replied, "I've been wondering that too lately. I don't think he really wanted us dead. I think he just wanted us injured enough so that we couldn't fight back. Think back to the first attack at the concert. He had all those powers, but he shot at us with a plasma pistol. I think he knew a plasma pistol wouldn't kill us like it does regular humans."

"You think he wants us alive? Why?" Harriet asked. But as soon as she said it, realization swept over her. "He wants our *korei*. And if he kills us, our *korei* will die too. So he wants to capture us and rip them out of us,"

Tiffany nodded. "Something's happening to him. He had a shield when he attacked us before, but he doesn't have it now. He's losing powers and he wants ours."

"He's losing powers? Why?"

"I think Eden gave us the answer," Tiffany answered. "We killed two of his *churei*. One of them was the one he used to teleport, remember? I think the one that gave him a shield is dead too. So now he's after us."

"But why? He can probably conquer the whole human race with just the powers he's got."

"There can only be one reason. He's got an enemy to fight. An enemy that's more powerful than him."

Harriet's eyes widened. But then she mused, "Maybe . . . maybe that's good for us. There's an old saying that the enemy of my enemy is my friend. Maybe the Creature's enemy will help us."

"There's another one that says the enemy of my enemy is still my enemy. Just because someone hates the Creature doesn't mean they'll like us."

"I suppose."

"And I wouldn't want contact with any more aliens. Look what it's got us so far."

"True," Harriet agreed, shrugging.

"We probably already know the Creature's enemy," Tiffany conjectured. "Maybe his enemy is Eden. After all, just because they're the same species doesn't mean they're friends."

Harriet considered this and wondered if they should contact Eden and ask her. But her thoughts were interrupted by the control tower releasing the lockdown on the spaceport. Their clearance to take off came through, so Harriet started the engines.

Although she'd practiced with similar ships in AR programs, her heart thumped loudly in her ears as she lifted off. Carefully following the flight plan she submitted, Harriet guided the ship into a standard orbit.

Tiffany manned the scanners. "No sign that anyone's noticed us," she told Harriet. "But there are a lot of Ranger ships in the area. Another destroyer group has just arrived."

"Do you think they'll be a problem for us?" Harriet queried.

"No, but they're scanning all departing ships. Before Foi left, he listed the people on this ship as Selena Zamora, Mia Gillespie, and Owen Shields. Mia Gillespie is the identity I've been using for the last year and Owen Shields is an identity of Foi's. He seems to have a lot of them. The Rangers will scan us before we leave orbit, but Foi will be on board before then."

They waited for an entire orbit, which took about an hour and a half. At last Tiffany reported, "Foi is approaching from aft. He should be docking in just a couple of minutes."

"Good," Harriet sighed, relieved. "I'm laying in a course for the hypergate. Let me know when he docks."

Less than ten minutes later, Foi's shuttle was safely attached to the outside of their ship and Harriet signaled to planetary space traffic control that they were ready to break orbit. "Standby," was the controller's answer.

A Ranger fighter approached and scanned them. Tiffany plugged a small data device into a slot in the communication system. She noticed Harriet's quizzical look. "It's a program that I use a lot," she replied to the unasked question. "It alters the image that the comm system transmits and makes it look like the plastiface I bought a year ago."

The comm system beeped, and Tiffany answered it. "This ship belongs to you?" a Ranger asked without preamble.

"No," she replied. "It belongs to Benson Leonardo, but he's not on board now. He and Gaylord Adkins had business on the Donaldson Shipping Station. We're meeting them there."

"Who are you?"

"I'm Mia Gillespie. I'm traveling with my friend, Selena Zamora, on the way to her wedding. She and Gaylord Adkins are getting married on the planet Amarnath. We also have Gaylord's friend Owen Shields on board."

"That small ship that just went up also belonged to Benson Leonardo," the Ranger said.

"I know," Tiffany replied. "I reported it stolen before we lifted off. We haven't been able to contact Sirsen Leonardo yet to tell him."

The Ranger looked at something off-screen. "You're cleared," he said. The screen went blank.

Harriet checked their course repeatedly for errors. When she finally felt confident in her navigation, she broke orbit and set their course toward the hypergate.

When Foi arrived at the control cabin, he advised Harriet, "You should get some rest. You look tired. It won't be until late tomorrow that we meet up with Leo and Hugh. I'll take the helm."

Harriet heaved a sigh. With all the excitement, she hadn't realized how tired she was. "You're right," she agreed. "It's been a long day." She slid from the pilot's seat and let Foi take over. Exiting the control cabin, she went into the ship's large common room which had a kitchen, entertainment console, and relaxation area. Their luggage sat on the floor in the middle of the room.

"Follow me," she said to her luggage. Obediently, her bags floated into the air and trailed after her as she went down the corridor toward the crew cabins. Entering the cabin she had selected for herself when they first toured the ship, Harriet pointed and told her bags, "Over there by the foot of the bed." Her luggage stacked itself neatly in the spot she indicated.

After changing and getting into bed, Harriet quickly fell asleep. She didn't wake up until nearly noon the next day. When she walked into the common room, Tiffany was watching the news.

"What's up?" Harriet asked.

"They've spotted Leo and Hugh a few times, just like we planned. The Creature's ship disappeared into the Vagula Debris Field. I never knew there were star systems with so much junk in them. Anyway, they can't scan in there because it's so radioactive."

"You think it's headed for the hypergate?"

Tiffany nodded. "Probably. Everyone on the news has figured out that that's where Leo's ship is headed."

"Is Foi still at the helm?"

"Yeah. You'd better go take a turn. He looks like he's getting tired. Too bad I can't fly this thing."

Harriet relieved Foi, who gratefully went off to bed. A short while later, Tiffany brought in some breakfast for Harriet. Surprised, Harriet thanked her.

"It's the only thing I can do to help right now," Tiffany replied.

'I guess I'm not the only one who's changed,' Harriet thought.

Harriet checked their course and then ran some diagnostics on the ship. Everything was working perfectly, so there wasn't much more to do until they entered the Narbet Sulfur Cloud.

Tiffany ran a few scans. "Lots of Ranger ships around," she commented.

Harriet asked, "Tiffany, when we got separated in Russia, how did you survive?"

"I made it onto a ship going to Decimus," she explained. "I was all alone. Foi didn't find me until a few months ago. I got a new plastiface, a new identity, and got a job as a fashion reporter on a 3V channel."

"You were a reporter?" Harriet grasped. "And you were on the 3V every day in front of everyone in the system?"

"Sure," Tiffany shrugged. "No one would ever expect me to do that, so that's what I did. When Foi found me he called it 'hiding in plain sight.' I just figured it was the best way of not looking suspicious."

In awe, Harriet told her, "Actually, I think it was brilliant."

Clearly surprised, Tiffany smiled and said, "Thanks, Harriet."

A thought occurred to Harriet. "Hey, you're Mia Gillespie! I used to watch your show!" she exclaimed.

Tiffany just smiled demurely, fluffed her hair, and replied, "Well, I did have the best ratings in my time slot."

Hours later, Foi entered the control cabin looking rested. Harriet said, "Good timing. We're going into the Narbet Sulfur Cloud right now." She punched up a forward view on the main viewer. An angry mass of red and orange quickly engulfed them.

"Humph," Tiffany commented, "More pollution. Interstellar Dynamics really messed this system up before they went out of business."

The sulfur cloud engulfed the ship. "How long until Leo gets here?" Tiffany wondered out loud.

"And Hugh," Hugh interjected from behind them. "Don't forget Hugh," he continued.

Harriet scolded, "Hugh! You just about gave me a heart attack! When did you teleport on board?"

"Just now. We've been flying along beside you for a couple of hours. Open the shuttle bay doors."

Harriet quickly opened the outside doors on the ship's small shuttle bay. Using the external cameras, she watched the smaller ship ease itself inside. She closed the outside doors and pressurized the bay. Not long after, Leo entered the control cabin. "It's getting a little cozy in here," he said.

After setting the ship on autopilot, Harriet set the alarms up to maximum volume so that the computer could notify them if something went wrong. She followed the others into the common room. Glad to be together again, the five of them shared stories of their time apart. After a while, Harriet warily said, "I think it's time we contacted Eden."

Sour expressions passed across the faces of both Leo and Tiffany. Through gritted teeth, Leo growled, "I suppose so." He called out, "Eden. Are you there?"

Eden appeared and answered, "At last. Where have you all been?"

"Trying to survive," Leo shot back.

Puzzled, Foi asked, "Do you guys actually see this Eden person?"

"Yes," Harriet told him. "Can't you?"

"No."

Eden interjected, "I haven't yet made telepathic contact with your friend. I can see him through your eyes, but he's so closed off that I can't get through to him."

"We have a telepathic connection to her," Harriet explained to Foi. "She can't make a connection with you." Hesitantly, she added, "She says you're too closed off."

"Suits me," Foi said. "I don't want aliens in my head. Just tell me what she says when you're done."

They turned their attention back to Eden. "We'll be at the hypergate to the Shamoro system in a few days," Harriet informed her. "Then we can go to the wormhole at the coordinates you gave us. Are you sure the wormhole is safe?"

"Absolutely," Eden assured her. "Akio and some of his friends passed through it last year."

"What happened to Akio?" Harriet exclaimed.

"I really don't have news on him right now," Eden answered.

"No news?" queried Harriet. "What does that mean? Is he alive?"

"Yes," Eden soothed. "He has many challenges ahead. But for now, he's safe."

Leo broke in, "You say that others used this wormhole?"

"Yes, Leo. Akio and his friends use many of them. The wormhole you'll be taking leads to a junction system. There are many wormholes there."

Hugh was skeptical. "It's impossible for there to be a junction system of naturally-occurring wormholes."

"I didn't say they were natural, Hugh."

"What? You mean they're manmade?"

"Yes."

"How can that be? It's impossible for humans to create a large group of stable wormholes!"

"Not if someone detonates a series of gravitic bombs in a wormhole created by a hypergate," Eden explained.

The four of them fell into shocked silence. Foi eyed them warily. Finally Eden asked, "The other ship you have, can you make it explode?"

Hugh nodded. "If I bypass all the safety features, I can flood the neutron matrix with fusion catalyst and make its fusion plant feed back on itself. It would have been easier if we'd bought something to make a real bomb with."

"The Feds would have found us," Leo countered.

"I guess so," Hugh agreed. "So anyway, we'll have to start the feedback reaction as soon as the Creature boards and keep him on there for at least three minutes."

Leo added, "That shouldn't be hard. We can tear up the manual controls so he can't pilot the ship and we'll just control it remotely. I'll set it on a crash course with something so it kills him even if the reactor doesn't blow."

"Then I think you are as prepared as you can be," Eden praised them. "Contact me again when you arrive in the junction system." Her image disappeared.

The next few days went slowly. Harriet, Leo, and Foi took turns at the helm and used the autopilot as much as they dared. Tiffany and Hugh did most of the cooking and cleaning. The passage to the Shamoro system was uneventful. When they arrived, they immediately made for the Welard asteroid cluster. On the way, Tiffany entered the control cabin and asked, "Do either of you know a doctor named Dickerson?"

"Yeah," answered Hugh as he manned the scanners. "Why?"

"Because she's all over the news," Tiffany replied. She strode to the communications system and put a news broadcast on the main screen. Sure enough, Dr. Dickerson was there talking about her newly-published book.

"So much for waiting until we killed the Creature," Hugh muttered.

"She's telling them everything," Tiffany said. "Her book contains all the data she collected on you two and Leo. And everything she knows about the *korei* and the Creature."

Thoughtfully, Harriet commented, "Maybe this isn't a bad thing."

Surprised, Hugh queried, "Why?"

"Well," Harriet explained, "maybe it's best for everyone to know that there is an alien running around. That way, they'll know the danger. And at least they won't be saying we're aliens or freaks any more. Maybe my sister won't think I'm some kind of monster now. And she'll know what really happened to Dad."

The others were silent for a moment, gazing at her sadly. Then Hugh agreed, "Maybe you're right. You know, I gave Dr. Dickerson the brainwave pattern we use to detect the Creature with our scanners. If they start programming scanners in spaceports to scan for the creature, it'll make it a lot harder for him to move around."

Tiffany softly sighed, "I wonder what my parents think of all this?" She added, "I wonder if my mother even cares?"

They all fell silent. Later that day, Leo and Hugh used the Welard asteroid cluster for cover as they departed in the small ship. Harriet, Foi, and Tiffany went onward to the coordinates that Eden had given them.

Harriet announced, "We're coming up on the wormhole's coordinates."

The wormhole was invisible to the naked eye, but it emitted a pulsating flow of neutrinos and tachyons, which Eden had told them to scan for. Harriet was able to pinpoint its exact location without too much trouble. With more than a little hesitation, she guided the ship through.

The trip through the wormhole took about a day. Emerging in an unnamed star system, they found that it contained only one Earth-sized planet. Its atmosphere was barely breathable and it wasn't far from the wormhole they entered the star system through.

From the images on the scanner, it appeared as if something had crushed nearly everything in the system but the one remaining planet. A thick disk of dust, asteroids, and planetoids spun around the small, blazing sun. There were dozens of wormholes, possibly hundreds, scattered among the rubble. They were easily visible because they made the cloud of dust glow as it passed them.

Avoiding the other wormholes, Harriet found a nearby planetoid with a cavern big enough to hide the ship in. There was nothing to do now but wait.

Back in the Shamoro system, Leo and Hugh let themselves be spotted by Ranger ships several times over the next few days. It wasn't long before the news reported that the Creature's ship was seen in the same area. Finally, they were able to cross paths with it. In full view of the Creature's ship, they made directly for the wormhole.

39

Alarms blared, jerking Harriet awake in the pilot's seat. Scanning quickly, she saw that Leo and Hugh were in the star system. Before the Creature could arrive, she transmitted their location. Then she called out, "Eden! It's time."

Eden appeared next to her. "I'll give you all the help I can," she said reassuringly.

Leo guided the small ship toward the planetoid. Harriet connected to the small ship's computer and accessed one of the external cameras. The Creature's ship spewed from the wormhole. It arrowed rapidly toward the smaller craft, which accelerated as if it were running away. Vectoring in swiftly, the Creature's ship pulled up alongside. An airlock opened and the Creature emerged in a spacesuit. Slamming its hand on a panel on the outside of the small ship, the Creature opened the airlock and went in.

"He's inside," Hugh announced as he and Leo appeared next to them in the control cabin. Harriet connected to an internal camera. It was video only, no sound.

Watching the main viewer intently, they saw the Creature's rage as it pounded on the remnants of the ship's flight control panel. Harriet noticed Leo smile. "Sometimes it's nice to be really, really strong," he gloated. "It makes it easy to tear things apart."

Nodding, Hugh added, "Before Leo smashed everything, I programmed the little ship's computer to lock the airlock doors as soon as the Creature got inside. He won't be able to get out. And the feedback loop has just two minutes and twelve seconds left before the ship blows."

"And did I mention that I set it on a course that will crash it into that planetoid over there?" Leo asked triumphantly.

"What's that?" Foi broke in suddenly.

The Creature was holding an intensely bright, glowing sword.

"Zarking veech!" Leo spat. "Where did he get that?"

"It must be one of his powers," Harriet speculated. "We've seen it before."

"Yes," Eden agreed. A worried look passed over her face. "Something's happening! I'm losing contact!" Then Eden was gone.

Harriet's gaze shot warily to the screen. In a few deft strokes, the Creature cut a gaping hole in the side of the small ship.

Thrown into space by the outward flow of air, it recovered itself and flew at a leisurely pace toward its own ship, which it immediately boarded. The Creature's ship arced away from the small ship. A few seconds later, the tiny craft exploded.

Foi ordered, "Shut everything down! We don't want him to scan for our energy emissions."

"Too late," Harriet gasped. "We're being scanned."

"Get us out of here!" shouted Foi.

Beating her hands on the controls, Harriet made the ship lunge forward. Moments later, it rocketed its way out of the planetoid as the Creature's ship bore down on it. Harriet increased the engines' thrust to maximum, knocking everyone else backward. No one complained.

A deep WHAM echoed through the ship.

"It caught up to us!" yelled Foi as he pulled his rifle from his coat. "Harriet, get us to that planet over there. If there's a fight, we don't want it to happen on board the ship. Tiffany, use the scanners and find out where the Creature is. Everyone else, go get your guns."

"We already have ours," Leo and Hugh said in unison.

Harriet asked Leo, "Wasn't your gun destroyed?"

"I took one from a Ranger that the Creature killed back on Decimus," Leo explained, pulling the sleek rifle from his overcoat.

Foi demanded, "Harriet and Tiffany, where are your guns? I'll get them for you."

"They're both right in the next room," Harriet shot back as her hands flew over the controls.

THUD!

"Tiff? Tell us what's going on!" Foi shouted with his weapon at the ready.

"It's inside!" Tiffany cried. "It just got the shuttle pod bay open. I don't know how."

Leo leaped out of the control cabin and sprinted toward the shuttle pod bay. Foi and Hugh were close behind. Tiffany got on the ship's comm system and gave them a running commentary over the ship's internal speakers.

"I've got a video feed. It's pulled off the control panel next to the inside door of the bay. The door is locked because the bay's depressurized. I can't tell what it's doing. Oh wait." There was a pause. She continued ominously, "The outer doors are closing."

Frantically trying to calculate an entry course to the planet's atmosphere, Harriet heard Leo's voice over the comm system.

"Hugh, get into a spacesuit. You're going to teleport us into that bay and I'm going to shoot the Creature before it can get through."

"You're going to fire a QID gun inside a ship?" demanded Hugh.

"Yes! Now suit up!"

Tiffany broke in, "Never mind the suits. The bay is pressurizing. It'll be safe to enter in three, two, one, now!"

The ship hit the small planet's atmosphere with a violent lunge.

"Harriet?" Leo asked, "Are we going to make it?"

"Yeah," Harriet answered, "but it's going to be a rough ride. We're going in fast. Tiffany, can you get the outer doors of the shuttle pod bay open?"

"No," she answered, panic rising in her voice. "Something's locked me out."

The ship tossed and pitched several times. Drenched in sweat, Harriet locked her attention on the ship's controls. She worked feverishly to slow their descent.

Tiffany shouted, "The Creature's been thrown to the other side of the bay!"

"We're going in," Leo announced.

"No wait!" Harriet yelled. The ship shuddered and lurched. Tiffany was thrown across the room. Harriet, strapped into her seat, was able to stay at the controls. She leveled the ship and accelerated the engines to full power. It felt as if a giant hand was crushing her into the floor. The room began to fade around her.

WHAM!

The ship bounced off the soft sand that covered the surface of the planetoid. Harriet fought for control of both herself and the ship. They bounced again, not so hard. Skidding through the sand, the ship shuddered to a standstill.

"Now!" Leo screamed.

Looking up, Harriet saw that Tiffany had a view of the shuttle pod bay on the main screen. Leo and Hugh were facing the Creature, guns raised.

"Doors Tiff!" Harriet barked. "Open the outer doors!"

Tiffany worked at the controls feverishly. Then she exclaimed jubilantly, "They're opening!"

Looking back to the screen, Harriet was horrified to see that the Creature now had Leo by the throat. Hugh was lying on the floor. Grabbing her gun, Harriet pounded through the ship to the shuttle pod bay. The inner door was already open and Foi was nowhere to be seen.

Harriet bounded into the pod bay. Hugh was painfully pulling himself up off the floor. "They went that way," he rasped as he pointed to the now open outer doors. Harriet's tigress appeared and she leaped on its back. Sprinting outside, she paused to look around.

Leo's gun lay on the ground, cut in half. Foi shot frenziedly at the Creature as it zigzagged through the sky. Each time it dodged, the Creature moved closer to Foi. Leo put his hand on the sand and a shower of metal blades exploded upward toward the Creature. It screeched when a few of them found their mark. A yellow glow passed quickly over the Creature's body. It stopped bleeding and glared at Leo vengefully.

With his hand still on the ground, Leo transmuted the sand into several large boulders. He picked up one and flung it at the Creature, who dodged deftly as Foi let loose another volley from his gun. In rapid succession, Leo threw boulder after boulder as Foi continued to shoot.

Harriet thundered up near Foi and Leo. In her anger and fear, she produced a cascade of dozens of fiery globes that seemed to fall upward and flow over the Creature. It bellowed as several of them seared into it.

Recovering somewhat, the Creature plunged directly at them. Hugh appeared next to Harriet and reached out his hand toward the Creature. Just for a fraction of a second, the Creature paused in midair. Its grimace deepened and darkened.

The momentary pause was just long enough for Foi to hit the Creature in the leg, which started to dissolve. Its bright sword appeared in its hand again. Without even pausing, the Creature cut off its own leg and healed the wound closed before the effect of the QID blast could spread and dissolve its entire body.

The Creature stretched out its grasp toward Leo. Harriet knew it was about to use telekinesis to grab him.

"Look out!" she screamed as Leo dodged to the side.

Another blast from Foi's gun almost hit the Creature. To avoid it, the Creature let itself drop into the sand with a sickening thud. Rocketing into the air again, the Creature flew toward them so fast it was nearly a blur.

Again, Hugh reached out his hand and made the Creature pause in midair for just a fraction of a second. Leo hit it with a boulder. At the same time, Harriet threw a firestorm that engulfed it completely. Foi waited for a clear shot.

The Creature erupted from the top of the firestorm with its spacesuit almost completely burned off and tossed out a torrent of frenzied fire that cascaded downward, hitting Harriet and Leo brutally. Harriet was knocked several yards from her tigress, which bellowed angrily and barreled toward her. It spread its wings over them protectively.

At the same time, Foi and Hugh fired. Both blasts hit the Creature square in the chest. It fled its host. The empty body dropped to the sand unnoticed. For what seemed like an endless moment, Harriet stared up at the repulsive energy creature. Her hand foundered convulsively for her gun, but it lay far across the sand.

The Creature flailed its tentacles toward them. She knew it was seeking a host. 'But we're all immune,' she thought. Searing realization flashed through her mind.

"Watch out!" she screamed in near panic. "FOI, WATCH OUT!"

Both Hugh and Foi were shooting frantically, but the Creature avoided their blasts. It streaked through the air and dove into Foi. Time seemed frozen. For just the tiniest fraction of a second, Harriet saw horror and grief on Foi's face. Then he sneered, raised his weapon and shot at Hugh. Just in time, Hugh teleported away.

"Get in the ship!" ordered Tiffany's voice from the sky. Harriet saw her plummet toward Foi. 'Not Foi,' she told herself. 'Not any more.'

With her telekinesis, Harriet pulled her gun to her and scrambled to Leo. Having taken the brunt of the fire blast, Leo was just coming around after being unconscious for a few moments. He was badly burned, but he could still move. Harriet helped him to his feet.

At the same time, a large humanoid made of loosely coupled boulders stomped toward the Creature. 'Leo's rock man,' Harriet thought as she watched it attack the Creature. Flying upward, the Creature dodged the rock man's attack and escaped its reach. The rock man fell apart. Tiffany created a shower of electrical flashes around the Creature that momentarily blinded and stunned it. Hugh shot at it.

"No, Hugh!" Tiffany commanded. "Get everyone in the ship!"

Leo forced another shower of metal blades to explode from the ground. While the Creature dodged, Hugh appeared next to Leo and Harriet. He teleported them inside the ship. Leo ran for the control cabin.

The comm system was still on. Tiffany's voice bellowed through the ship, "I'm inside! Go!"

Just as Harriet arrived at the control cabin, the ship jerked upward. Harriet stumbled against the force of acceleration and plopped into the chair at the communications system console. She quickly punched up a view of the planet below. The main screen showed the ground falling away rapidly.

Hugh jabbed a finger at the screen. "There!" he yelled. "It's still coming!"

He was right. Harriet could see the Creature, rising from the barren planet's surface. With ponderous horror, she watched it draw slowly closer to the ship.

"It shouldn't be able to live!" Leo screamed. "The atmosphere is already too thin to breathe."

Flashes of yellow danced over the Creature's body.

"It's healing itself continually," Harriet blurted out. "That's how it's staying alive."

"It can't keep that up forever," Hugh opined. "We've got to get away. Faster Leo!"

"The drive's already at maximum!" Leo shot back.

"IT'S CAUGHT UP TO US!" Hugh screamed.

Harriet couldn't see the Creature. "The pod bay doors! Are the pod bay doors closed?" she demanded.

Tiffany's voice came across the comm system. "No! The outer doors are still open. I'm just inside the inner door. I think something's happening in the pod bay."

Immediately, Harriet displayed a view of the pod bay. The Creature was inside. In his hand was the shining sword.

Hugh shouted, "He's going to cut through the inner door! Close the outer doors! Fill the pod bay with air!"

Leo slammed his hand on the control panel, and the outer doors closed. "Pressurizing!" he yelled. Hugh raised his gun, took a large lungful of air, and teleported from the control cabin.

On the screen, Harriet was appalled to see Hugh next to the Creature. His hair danced frenetically in the wind created by the rush of air into the pod bay. Before he could fire, the Creature lopped off the end of his gun with its sword. Hugh disappeared from the pod bay.

"Hugh!" Tiffany said. "Are you alright?"

"Where's Hugh?" Harriet called out.

Tiffany replied, "He's here with me. He's collapsed. I think from lack of air."

Leo grabbed Harriet's gun and bounded out of the control cabin yelling, "Take the helm, Harriet!"

Harriet leaped into the pilot's chair. She could see on the screen that the Creature was doing something to the circuitry in the wall of the pod bay. "I think it's getting in!" she called. "No! IT *IS* IN!

The inner door was open. The Creature bolted for the door, but it was hit with a massive blast of lightning that played havoc with the ship's systems. Tiffany appeared in the door and zapped the Creature again. Grabbing Tiffany and thrusting her back inside, Leo bolted into the pod bay and shot at the Creature. The Creature dodged and the QID blast blew a massive hole in the pod bay doors.

Instantly the emergency systems shut the inner pod bay door.

"LEO!" Tiffany wailed.

On the screens, Harriet saw Leo and the Creature get sucked out into the blackness of space. "NO!" she screamed.

Hugh and Tiffany appeared in the cabin. "Go after him!" he shouted.

"I can't see him!"

"Use the scanners!"

"Tiffany's lightning burned them out! I can't find him!" Tears filled Harriet's eyes and streamed down her face. She gazed at the main screen desperately.

Tiffany pointed to the viewer. "Something's out there!"

It was the Creature. It was flying to its ship, healing itself as it went.

Molten fury coursed through Harriet. She pounded the control panel. Their ship lurched sideways as it swung around and pointed itself straight at the Creature's ship. The Creature was already inside.

"Harriet," Hugh yelled, "what are you doing?"

Without answering, Harriet rammed the Creature's ship. Because it was smaller, it rebounded through the void of space. As it tumbled out of control, it neared a wormhole. Before anyone could react, the Creature's ship fell through the wormhole, which immediately disappeared.

"It must have been unstable," Hugh breathed. "The wormhole was unstable. Who knows when, or even if, it will appear again? Let's get out of here."

"No! I won't leave Leo!"

Quietly, gently, Hugh replied, "Harriet, Leo's dead. There's no sign of his body."

Harriet sat, unmoving.

"Harriet," Hugh urged softly, "you're the only one now who knows how to fly this ship. You have to get us out of here."

For a while, Harriet didn't react. She heard Tiffany's sobs. Finally, she asked, "Where?"

"Huh?"

Distantly, Harriet asked again, "Where . . . are we going?"

Tiffany interrupted. "Home!" she sobbed. "I wanna go home!"

Harriet stared at the viewer. After a pause, she slowly said, "No."

"WHAT!" Tiffany screeched, nearly hysterical.

"We can't go home. This isn't over."

"WHAT DO YOU MEAN? OF COURSE IT'S OVER!"

Soothingly, Hugh interjected, "Of course it's over, Tiffany. Harriet, please set a course for home."

Cold certainty washed over Harriet. She felt strangely detached from the universe around her. She dried her tears and forced herself into calmness.

"Go ahead and go home if you want to," Harriet challenged. "You saw the Creature get into his ship. Do you know where that wormhole goes? I don't. He could be anywhere. He could be back on Earth by now. Are you really sure you want to go there and find out? Are you absolutely sure he'll never come after you? Are you willing to bet your life and the lives of every member of your family? Maybe you don't mind if that thing takes over your dad like ..." Harriet's voice broke. She took a deep breath and continued, "... like it did mine."

Less confrontational now, Tiffany asked, "Well what do you think we should do? We can't live on the run forever. I ... I just can't do this any more."

Sympathetically, Harriet replied, "No. None of us can. We have to go somewhere safe, at least for a while. Somewhere that thing won't think to look for us."

"Like where?" Tiffany demanded.

A faint, weary smile passed across Harriet's face. "Eden told us that our friend Akio is alive and safe. If he can hide, we can. She even said Akio passed through that wormhole over there." Harriet pointed to one of the wormholes outside.

Angrily, Tiffany asked, "You want to take us into a war zone? You call that safe? That is NOT what I call safe!"

Heaving a sigh, Harriet answered, "Tiffany, with that Creature after us, wherever we go is going to become a war zone. We've lost Leo. Our only hope of fighting that thing is to get more help. Eden said she gave gifts to Akio like she did to us. He's the only one who can help us stay alive."

Hugh asked, "You really think so? What about Eden? She can still help us."

"Can she?" Harriet countered. "She disappeared as soon as the Creature entered the system. It has a way of cutting us off from her. We need help we can count on. The only one I can think of is Akio."

"You think we can find a safe place where Akio is?"

"There's only one way to find out," Harriet told him as she laid in a course toward the wormhole. "We've got enough fuel and supplies to keep us going for three months. If we don't find him, we can come back here and use the wormhole to get back to the Shamoro system. After that, I guess we can go anywhere."

Hugh countered, "Just because Akio passed through that wormhole once doesn't mean it leads to where he is. He could be anywhere now."

"There's only one way to find out," Harriet repeated. She powered up the engines and accelerated the ship to full speed.

"I sure hope you're right," Tiffany muttered to Harriet. She left the bridge and plodded toward her cabin. Hugh went to his cabin as well.

"So do I," Harriet muttered to herself. Silently, the ship slipped through the eternal night of space toward the shimmering mouth of the wormhole. In a flash, the ship was completely enveloped by the shining blue tunnel through hyperspace as it left the nameless star system behind.

Alone at the helm, Harriet murmured, "You have to be out there, Akio. You have to be. We won't survive without you." Finally, silently, Harriet let herself cry.

Official Web Site: http://possessorwars.com/

Facebook: https://www.facebook.com/chad.spencer.165

Twitter: https://twitter.com/PossessorWars

To be notified of new releases, please sign up for the author's newsletter at:

http://possessorwars.com/subscribe.html